21

(EXPRESS)

528.99

VORTEX

CATHERINE COULTER

VORTEX

AN FBI THRILLER

WILLIAM MORROW

An Imprint of HarperCollinsPublishers

P.S.™ is a trademark of HarperCollins Publishers.

HarperCollins books may be purchased for educational, business, or sales promotional use. For information, please email the Special Markets Department at SPsales@harpercollins.com.

FIRST EDITION

Designed by Elina Cohen
Front matter art © Shutterstock / S. Gvozd

Library of Congress Cataloging-in-Publication Data has been applied for.

ISBN 978-0-06-300408-5

21 22 23 24 25   LSC   10 9 8 7 6 5 4 3 2 1

TO ANTON

*May your bright editorial light continue
to shine on my head. I am blessed.*

Catherine

ACKNOWLEDGMENTS

My continued thanks to the remarkable Angela Bell, FBI, Office of Public Affairs. You are always there for me with the right answer, the right person to fill me in on exactly what I need to know. Thank you.

To my right and left hand and half my brain, Karen Evans. I cannot envision life without you, so see to it, all right?

To all my amazing associates at Trident Media Group, particularly my agent, Robert Gottlieb, and the unsinkable Nicole Robson. Even in this very bizarre year when a pandemic blasted onto the scene and set the world reeling, no one at William Morrow and HarperCollins dropped the ball. My profound thanks.

VORTEX

I

A full moon cast pale shadows over the two men digging and flinging dirt out of a hole, their movements rhythmic. The moonlight was bright enough they could see the small pebbles in each clump of dirt, see each other's sweaty dirt-streaked face.

Snake stopped digging, swiped the back of his hand over his eyes. "I'm tired. Can we give it a rest a minute?" He eyed his best friend, let the words pour out. "It shouldn't have happened, man. She was a gamer, like us, and when I told her my handle was Snake and yours was Dante, she laughed, told me she loved *World of Warcraft*. Her online handle was CoolGirl34, she told me, and then she leaned up and whispered to me she liked to call herself Aolith the dreamer because the name was so magical. I never even found out her real name. She was fun, Dante, she even joked she hoped she wouldn't fail organic chemistry because she couldn't put down her PS4. She wanted more superhero women who don't look like porn stars. She was alive, laughing, just a while ago—"

Dante kept his voice earnest. "Snake, you need to stop the recriminations and calm yourself, look forward. What's done is done, and yes, I'm as sorry as you are this accident happened, and that's what it was, an accident. Don't forget that. Whatever this girl was or wasn't, whoever she was, it doesn't matter now, we can't let it matter. Like I said, we have to look forward, get this task done and get on with our lives."

"You think it's a task? We're burying her, Dante. And it wasn't a bloody accident!"

So much for trying to comfort the idiot. Dante said, voice hard now, "Aolith wasn't your soul mate. She was only a girl you just met whose time had come."

"Yeah, sure, like we should blame her karma. We made her time come. She might have been my soul mate, who knows? All right, so she told me she had a boyfriend, but he wasn't with her tonight, so maybe it wouldn't have lasted. She is— she was—what, twenty? What kind of relationship lasts when you're twenty?"

Dante punched Snake's arm. "Get hold of yourself. There's nothing we can do about it now. She figured out we'd given her my girl-juice, she was about to scream and give us away. Don't tell me you would have preferred she bring us down? I had to hit her to shut her up. We were lucky to get her out of there without anyone noticing, not that most of those drunk young morons would have paid attention, even if we fired off a shotgun."

"Your fire in the kitchen was crazy risky, but I've got to say, it gave us cover. Still—"

Dante shrugged. "Nothing else to do and it got everybody panicked and running, not paying attention to anything else. So maybe it was overkill, but who cares? We're here and we're safe."

Snake shook his head. "I still can't believe she just died, right there in the car."

"So now we have to make her disappear, forever. They'll start looking for her soon enough, but they won't have a clue. We can't be here all night though, so keep shoveling. It's time you thought about yourself, Snake."

But Snake looked down at his blistering hands, his gloves forgotten back at the frat house. "This shovel we stole is crap, it's got no heft, even for cutting into this soft earth."

"Look, we lucked out even to find shovels and a tarp in that barn without any lights coming on in the house. If you break that crap shovel, Snake, you'll have to use your hands. I'm not doing this all by myself. We're in this together. Don't you ever forget that."

They dug in silence again, shoveling up dirt, throwing it over the side of the grave. Snake stopped. "I think after she'd given us all the sex we wanted and we cut her loose, I would have called her later, gotten together with her, maybe, gamed with her. Who knows? Fact is, you screwed up, let her see you putting something in her drink and you had to kill her."

So Snake wouldn't let it go. Of course Snake blamed him, it was par for the course. Blame on top of his nonstop whining. Dante wanted to hit him so hard his own crap shovel broke, and bury the two of them together. He forced himself to be patient as he said matter-of-factly, "I gave her the same amount I always use. Who knew she'd figure it out? Don't you blame me, not my fault." He paused a moment, studied his friend's face. Time for mending fences, a touch of sympathy. "I'm sorry, Snake, you liked her. Sure, you wanted to spread her out and have at it, but what happened wasn't anybody's fault." He bumped his fist against Snake's shoulder. "Hey, I guess we can only give this one a projected score, right? On spec? Hey, what's this?" Dante leaned down, picked up a shiny piece of metal, raised it. "It looks like a really old belt buckle."

Snake, distracted, studied the buckle. "I'll bet it goes way back, maybe one of the Revolutionary soldier's belts from the camp at Valley Forge. There's writing, maybe a name on the back of the buckle, I can't see well enough to make it out."

"Look, here are some buttons, too." Dante shrugged, slipped the buckle and the two buttons into his jeans pocket.

Snake froze. "Did you hear that? Someone's out there, maybe a hunter, or a couple of kids making out? They'll see us, call the cops."

Dante didn't spare him a look, just kept digging, heaving shovelfuls over the side. He swiped sweat out of his eyes. "Sure—a hunter in a park at midnight. If it's kids making out, believe me, they're not going to be paying any attention to us. Come on, Snake, I know you have bat ears, but there's nothing out there to worry about. We were really careful when we carried her in, there's no one around. But we don't want to be here this close to Godwyn or that freaking fraternity house any longer than we have to be. Another foot should do it. We've got about four feet, yes, another foot should keep the animals from smelling her, digging her up."

Smelling her? Animals digging her up? Snake looked over at Aolith's tarp-covered body, felt bile rise in his throat. She'd been so beautiful, so alive. "Really, I know she'd have gone for me if I'd asked. I don't want to do this anymore, I don't want to troll with you anymore."

Patience, patience. Dante said, "She was pretty drunk so she might have agreed to sex, but she wouldn't have gone for both of us at the same time, not without some help from my girl-juice. Yes, I agree with you, I hate it as much as you do." He shrugged. "It's a real pity, but what's done is done." Like Snake, he looked over at her body. The pity was she hadn't waited to die until he'd enjoyed her. "Anyway, we don't have to think about anything now except finishing this up. After you've thought it over, accept it was a tragic accident, I think you'll change your mind about going trolling again. You have too much fun with the girls."

Dante stopped digging a few minutes later. "Deep enough. No reason to get any dirtier." He threw his shovel out of the hole and Snake followed suit. Dante cupped his hands under Snake's foot, took his weight, and heaved him out of the grave. Snake looked down at his friend, always in charge since they were boys, always deciding what they were going to do and how they were going to do it. Until tonight his girl-juice had worked like magic. They'd always used condoms, cleaned the girl up, and gotten her clothes back on before they left her in her car or her apartment. Did any of the girls they'd had ever even suspect what had happened to them? Who knew? There'd never been any blowback. Snake remembered one of Dante's girlfriends in Boston. They'd shared her over and over that night, and what a rush it had been. What was her name? Biffy, Button, something like that. She'd broken up with Dante not long after that magic night. Had she remembered anything? No one could ask her now. She'd died in a car crash only months after they'd shared her.

Since Dante was bigger, heavier, Snake had to brace himself to pull him out of the grave.

They stood a moment, looking down into the black hole. Dante nodded toward the body. "Let's get her in and covered up. I'll call Alan, tell him we're on our way. We can shower, spend tonight at his pad. Shouldn't take more than a half hour to Philadelphia this time of night."

Snake said, "We're filthy. What do we tell Alan?"

Dante shrugged, gave a laugh. "Not the truth, that's for sure. We'll tell him we had a wild party in the woods and he should see the girls. Don't worry, I'll come up with something perverted enough even for Alan's jaded palate. Can you see him as a US congressman like his dad one of these years? Boggles the mind."

"Well, what about you? That's what your family wants for you, too."

"I haven't made up my mind yet. Not important now, Snake. Let's focus on what we're doing."

Snake looked down at Aolith's body, felt cold grip his guts, and the rising bile again. He whispered, "I wish you hadn't died, Aolith."

Dante's hands fisted, his patience nearly at its end. "Well, she did. She was asking for it, Snake; she came on to you with all the gaming lingo. She did that, not you. Think of it this way: at least she went out happy. She'll be young forever."

Snake stared at his friend, wondering if Dante was dissing Aolith on purpose because he knew Snake liked her. He realized he couldn't talk because he'd start crying.

They lifted the body over the grave and dropped it in. Snake saw a clump of her black hair as he dug his shovel into a mound of dirt and swallowed convulsively.

Aolith the dreamer wouldn't be forever young. She'd be forever dead.

When the grave was flat enough, they spread rocks and branches on top. When Dante was confident everything looked natural, they carried the shovels back to Dante's Jaguar, fit them diagonally in the small trunk, slammed down the lid. Snake watched Dante pull out his cell and call Alan Brandt in Philadelphia, ask him if he'd like to have guests tonight. Snake heard him laugh at something Alan said.

They drove slowly along the narrow dirt road to the Schuylkill River Trail, to turn onto I-76 E to Philadelphia. They made one stop to throw the shovels away.

The night once again became still and silent. An ancient naked-branched oak tree hovered near the grave. A deer came to sniff at the flattened earth, paused, raised her head, and slowly backed away into the forest.

The earth settled, bluebells grew through the branches they'd left, blanketing Aolith's grave in the spring. The oak tree spread its thick green-leafed branches over the grave.

Year after year.

2

Mia, stop!"

When Mia looked over at her friend, she pulled up. "What? You don't want to go to the rave?"

Serena Winters took her friend's shoulders between her hands, shook her. "Of course I want to go, but this moment, I want you to pay attention. Now, listen up. Yes, he's a creep and a loser and a cheat, and you were smart enough to see what he is and kick him out the door. What did you expect from that jock? He probably keeps a scorecard."

Mia sighed, kicked a pebble out of her path. She still felt angry enough to spit. She said, "You did tell me Rod would cheat on me if I didn't put out—and right away. Like buy a girl a hamburger and she owes you sex? Them's the rules? I heard some of these frat boys keep their scorecards posted in the common room."

Serena said matter-of-factly, "Some of the girls in our dorm collect guys, too, keep count, they just don't advertise it as loudly. Look, Mia, it'd have been worse if you'd slept with him, so that's something you don't have to feel mad about."

Mad? After how he'd treated her? Mia wanted to kick him in his crotch until her knee hurt. Then use her other knee.

Mia said, "Doesn't it ever worry you that Tommy Maitland's a jock? And not just any jock, the starting quarterback?"

"Yeah, he is, but Tommy's one of a kind, you know that. Of course I wondered about him at first, but it didn't take me long to realize his head's on straight. Of course he thinks about sex a lot—he has to since he's a guy and it's hardwired—but he isn't out to score all the sex he can get in four years. He wants to be an FBI agent, like his dad, a bigwig in Washington, so Tommy knows he's got to be disciplined, take all his decisions seriously. And he's been raised right, he and his three brothers. Tommy tells me his old man is tougher than any of them. He says the only one tougher is his mom."

Mia looked at her best friend grinning at her from ear to ear, her beautiful hair all twisted up on top of her head, to make her look taller, she said. Serena was a dynamo, full of energy, always ready for almost anything, not to mention she was a knockout with her black hair, white skin, and blue eyes. Black Irish, Serena claimed.

Mia splayed her hands. "All right, I give up. Tommy's a fricking saint, and unlike me, you lucked out."

Serena wiggled her eyebrows, whispered, "I wish he'd come with us tonight to this rave, but his mom had her appendix out yesterday. He and his brothers all zipped back to Washington to hold her hand. They say it's a good sign when a son really loves his mother, right?"

Mia didn't have any brothers, but she supposed that was true. She said, "I've never been to the Delta Rho Phi rave before, but I do know we'll have to be careful. There'll probably be drugs. I heard there'll be guys from other schools there, older guys, too, so be watchful, okay?"

"A bunch of our friends will be there. We'll stick close to them. We'll be fine. But look out for more guys like Rod, they litter the ground."

Mia looked down at her watch. "It's been going on for a while now, so we'll have some catching up to do. Good grief, listen." They were a block away from the Delta Rho Phi house when they heard the music—a heavy metal band playing on the frat house sound system at a gazillion decibels, crashing through the air. Mia would bet the frat house was shaking from the force of it. They heard voices shouting to be heard over the music, and the manic laughter of people well on their way to being drunk, or high on something.

They wove their way through dozens of students from the hallway into the large common room of the seventy-five-year-old Delta Rho Phi fraternity house. It was a huge old colonial that housed a lot of horny boys who studied only when they were shackled to their desks by looming deadlines. A frat house for academics it wasn't.

All the furniture was shoved to the edges of the room, and about forty boys and girls with beers or glasses of gin or the house specialty, the recipe known only to Delta Rho Phi, vodka-laced lemonade, in their hands were gyrating to the deafening music provided by a DJ who looked like he'd been feeling no pain for quite a while already. Mia smelled the lemons as she slipped into the chaos, spotted friends, and accepted a beer. She and Serena stuck close to them for about thirty minutes, but by ten o'clock, most everyone had sailed past drunk from the specialty of the house. The music seemed to get louder and louder, the dancing wilder. At least seventy-five close-packed kids were on the dance floor, going crazy.

Mia was drunk, maybe not as drunk as most of the others, but she was getting there, laughing, dancing in place with whatever student was getting close, slurping up a delicious deadly drink the frat boys called a Crazy Mary. The boy next to her was glassy-eyed he was so drunk, and even that made her laugh. She'd kissed off two frat guys she'd seen on campus because she could tell they were jerks like Rod only out to score. She admitted to herself it'd be nice to meet a guy who wasn't as drunk as the rest, but good luck with that.

Serena was talking with a guy she'd met, a bit older, probably a grad student. He was another gamer, Serena told her as she hugged Mia on their way back from the bathroom. He was smart and funny, and "how lucky is that?" she said.

The one time Mia paid any attention to them, Serena's gamer guy had his back to her. He was gesticulating wildly, slicing down with some imaginary sword, probably demonstrating his winning move in some computer game, and Serena was nodding and laughing along with him. Mia supposed he looked nice enough. Someone grabbed her arm, whirled her around to dance, and after that she never stopped dancing. With friends, with strangers, with anyone who wanted to. She danced until her legs ached, but she didn't care. She drank, she laughed, she forgot about Rod the Loser. Then she nearly fell and realized she'd fall on her face if she didn't stop. She slipped to the side, looking for Serena, but didn't see her. A guy's arm came around Mia, moved to her breasts, and without thought, she threw the rest of her drink in his face. He laughed like a hyena as he tried to use her arm to wipe off his face.

She was wondering if she should try to find Serena and head back to the dorm when she heard a scream from across the room, then heard someone shout FIRE! For a moment, she didn't understand. She was drunk, yes, very drunk, but the yells and screams got through to her vodka-soaked brain, and suddenly everyone was shoving toward the front doors. Smoke was gushing out of the kitchen into the common room, getting thicker. Mia automatically pulled her shirt over her nose, looked frantically around for Serena. Where was she? They'd danced together not more than a half an hour ago. Or was it longer? Mia couldn't remember, her brain wasn't on reality time. She'd been laughing at a joke she couldn't remember.

Mia yelled, "Serena!" but she didn't see Serena. She was being pushed forward toward the front of the frat house in the middle of a stampede. She stumbled, and an arm grabbed her and half dragged her outside, out of the chaos. She was dizzy, the world upside down or maybe sideways, and her stomach revolted. She leaned over and threw up into a bush until she was light-headed. She clutched her stomach, closed her eyes, and let herself fall over onto her side. She heard sirens, heard students shouting, felt the fear heavy in the very air around her. She staggered to her feet and leaned against an oak tree, coughing, trying to get her head on straight. She saw firefighters pour off fire trucks, train their hoses on the frat house. She saw cop cars, from the town and from campus security, heard more shouts, a high-pitched scream. It was like a fantastical movie. She saw Judy Harkins, one of her study partners, stumble by and Mia caught her. "Judy, have you seen Serena?"

"Serena?" Judy was so drunk she crumpled to the ground, pulling Mia back down with her.

An older cop came by, pulled them to their feet, and herded them back toward their dorm. Mia said over and over, "Please, Officer, I have to go back. I have to find Serena, she might still be in there. I have to—"

The cop said in a father's voice, "We'll get in there as soon as we can and find her, don't worry. The best thing you can do to help us is get yourselves to bed. It might be smart not to do anything like this again, you think?"

There were no casualties from the frat fire, but the cops couldn't find Serena. No one could find Serena. She was simply gone.

3

Balad Military Hospital
Balad, Iraq
Near the Tigris River

PRESENT, SEVEN YEARS LATER

Her name was Olivia and she was alive. She could feel her chest rhythmically lift and fall, the quiet pull of her own breath. She didn't know where she was, but it didn't seem important. She felt cradled in a thick heavy thick fog that seemed to breathe with her. She knew there was something beyond the fog; she heard disembodied voices speaking above her, and her name. She saw jumbled images, some blurred, some stark, faces flashing by, set and hard, and movement, so much movement. She didn't resist them, she wanted to absorb each of them, so she let them settle in and roll like a home movie on a scratchy old projector.

She was with her team in Sumar, Iran, a city devastated in an Iraqi chemical attack many years before, desolate still. The few people she saw looked at them with apathy, even though the team was heavily armed. There were four of them, all wearing dark brown fatigues and caps, assault rifles strapped across their backs, magazines X'ed across their chests like banditos, grenades, Semtex, and timers strapped to their waists. She saw three canteens of water hanging from her belt, a sat phone snug in her breast pocket. She knew there were satellites overhead, watching them, always watching.

The film rolled on, jerky, starting and stalling, and there was no sound, only harsh images of a bleak plateau with the Zagros Mountains beyond, overwhelming with their stark, jagged outcrops of rocks spearing into the sky. Her teammates were talking but she couldn't hear them, couldn't remember what they'd said.

She wanted to see the film through, understand all those images, and wondered if she could be in charge, become the narrator. So she whispered into the fog, "We're trotting along in a single file at a steady brisk pace, but it's so hot it's hard to breathe. Soon all of us are panting, pausing often to drink. I feel sweat running down my back, sticky and hot, feel my body protesting the steady climb over the endless jagged rocks and scattered boulders, loose underfoot, ready to twist or break an ankle. I try to avoid thick ugly brambles with their sharp thorns to rake to the bone, raise my hand to warn the others to be careful. At least if anyone's looking for us, it will be hard to pick us out from our surroundings, we blend so well. I wonder how it can still be so hot when it should be dark in an hour.

"I hear a noise. It's my sat phone beeping and I raise my hand. Everyone stops, and I see them bending over, breathing deep, drinking water like camels. The static is fierce, but I hear our station chief saying Hashem, the man we're here to take out with us, is on the run, Iranian soldiers in pursuit. I wonder how they could know he was here, be on him so fast, but I know if he can only get to us, we might still get him back to Sumar and to the Iraqi border under the cover of night."

The film stalled, she felt her head swimming, but she needed to go on.

"I must find a high rock to see exactly how close Hashem is to us, how close the soldiers are to him. I know they want to kill him, and so does he. I hear the *whomp whomp* of helicopters in the distance. My heart jumps. They could kill us all in a second if they see us. At least there's only one track through the Zagros Mountains large enough for vehicles of any kind, and Hashem is well north of it.

"I climb up a jagged mess of boulders, slip into a narrow crevice, and raise my binoculars. All I see is bleak and hostile land, full of impossible cliffs and narrow passages and plunging drops into rock-strewn gullies. I see Hashem. He's dressed like a herdsman, his robe flapping as he runs, highlighted by the setting sun behind me. I don't think he'll make it.

"There's a beep again—my sat phone. All I hear is ABORT. I pretend there's static and flip off the phone. We all realize there's been a breach, the Iranian soldiers know we're here, but we agree we're not going to let Hashem be taken. We run all out, we're only fifty yards away, but it's tough going. The soldiers see us and fire, their bullets kicking up dirt and rocks all around us. We dive for cover and fire back, trying to keep the soldiers pinned back to give Hashem a chance to get to us.

Bullets ricochet off the rocks around us, and the noise of the automatic weapons is deafening. It's hard to breathe the dust is so thick.

"Hashem is close, he's nearly to us when he's hit and he falls. Mike's closest. He runs to him, throws him over his shoulder while the three of us cover them, changing magazines and firing again and again, kicking up air full of dirt and flying shards of rock. Mike runs back through a narrow gully toward the plateau, and we follow, firing as we run. I run to Mike and try to help stanch the horrible wound in Hashem's chest. I wonder why he wasn't shot in the back since he was running away from them. I suppose he must have turned to see how far back they were, and a soldier nailed him. He's heaving, blood bubbling out of his mouth, but he's desperately trying to talk, and Mike and I both lean closer. But I know it's no good. I hear Andi yelling at me and I have to leave Mike and scramble up to higher ground to join them, and we take cover behind a mess of boulders until we can see the first of the soldiers follow us into the narrow gully single file. We fire and several fall. They can't reach us that way. They back off.

"I mold Semtex, flatten it into a crevice of a rock, set a three-minute timer, and let it roll down into the gully. I see Mike running with Hashem over his shoulder, and I see Higgs and Andi, their faces smeared with dirt, their eyes hard and clear, and we run all out after Mike. Bullets slam into a boulder next to me, close, too close. I feel a rock chip strike my arm, and I stumble. I hear the explosion—hear screams and shouts and I know the Semtex has done its job. Andi helps me up and we keep running, bent nearly double. The helicopter sounds closer, but it's getting dark, and I'm afraid they might have trouble seeing us. Mike yells our man is dead but he's not going to leave him and Higgs yells, 'RPG!'

"I see the grenade coming, hear Mike's shout, and then there's white, so much white it's blinding and I can't see anything else, can't hear anything. There's only noise, like a film feed slapping a projector wheel that keeps whirling."

Olivia didn't realize her heart rate and blood pressure were spiking, didn't realize her monitors and medical staff were making that noise, close to her, very close.

4

One Lincoln Plaza
New York, New York

MONDAY, LATE AFTERNOON, MID-MARCH

Mia Briscoe's heart still leaped with pleasure when she looked out her eighteenth-floor living room window to the stretch of Central Park below, even after seeing it daily for three years. It didn't matter the leafless trees hunkered down, brown and forlorn against blasts of arctic air. To Mia, the park looked magnificent, no matter the season. It was this view that had sold her on her junior one-bedroom apartment—thank you, Mom, Dad, for helping with the down payment. She saw a good dozen serious runners, their heads down, putting in their miles though it was thirty degrees, with snow threatening. To Mia, thirty degrees meant keeping her sweats and warm socks on, with a space heater next to her desk.

She smiled, realized she'd never been more hopeful about her future, and happy in her present. Well, she'd be happier

still when Travis got back from his two-month stint oversee-
ing the construction of international headquarters for Lohman
Pierce in Zurich. As one of the lead structural architects, it
was his responsibility to ensure everything that was done met
Swiss code requirements, and that meant his staying in Zurich
on-site six days a week. They were down to eighteen days
until he came home, both of them counting. If the project
didn't run over, Travis had promised skiing, or even better,
Bermuda, to stretch out on the beach when he returned. He'd
found a gym in Zurich to unwind in after the long hours on
the job site, a good thing since if he didn't work out regularly,
he tended to lose weight. She smiled, remembering when
she'd met her perfect mate on the second floor of Blooming-
dale's, shopping for his mother's birthday. She'd helped him
pick out a sexy teddy, loaded with lace, which, Travis had told
her, would have his mom drooling. From Bloomies, they'd had
coffee, which had led to movies, dinners, and the recognition
they were meant for each other. Both sets of parents were on
board, which was good. And so here they were, six months
later.

She sighed. Even if Travis got back on time, that lovely trip
probably wasn't going to happen now, but for the best of reasons. Milo, her boss at the *Guardian*, had assigned her that very
day to cover a newcomer, Alexander Talbot Harrington, in his
run for mayor. It would be her first dive as a reporter into the
political deep end of a campaign that was already heating up.
She'd spent much of her day researching Harrington, and despite the three very proper names, which in his case really did
mean pots of old money, she was finding him interesting. He

was the scion of the wealthy Boston Harringtons, multigenerational owners of the First Street Corporation, an international banking firm touting roots that went back to the National Bank, founded in 1792. Yes, old, old money and clout, political and otherwise. He'd headed up the New York branch of the family business for the past five-plus years, but when he declared his candidacy for office, he handed the reins to his operational VP for the duration of his campaign, and beyond, if he won. Tonight was to be his biggest fundraiser, and Milo had gotten Mia invited.

Her cell belted out "Bad Henry" by Thorny. It was Travis.

It burst right out of her. "Travis, have I got some news for you!"

He laughed. "Let me guess. I know you're not pregnant unless you've kicked me to the curb and found someone else. I know you weren't fired or your folks would have called me, and best of all, come Tuesday, we'll be down to seventeen days and counting. And wonder of wonders, it looks like everything's on schedule, which means, of course, the American on-site architect is really amazing at his job, able to corral all the wild hares, otherwise known as contractors and their minions. Well, for the most part."

Mia laughed, too. "Okay, tell me how you're doing with the Taj Mahal. Really, it's all on schedule? And what do you mean, most part?"

She heard him sigh. "So far. I speak French and my German doesn't totally suck, but when the head contractor, Gottfried Himmler, wants something I don't want to approve, he speaks fast to try to trip me up."

"No need to flatten him, maybe just take him behind the porta potty and explain how things are done in the US if someone doesn't cooperate."

"Haven't yet, but I do speak back to him in English, lots of idioms, just as fast. We've got this stalemate going."

"So no whips or chains required?"

"It was close once, but I appealed to his perfectionist side."

"Is it as cold there as it is here?"

"Colder, maybe. It's snowing a blizzard here in Zurich and all I can think about is you in a bikini on the beach in Bermuda. Now tell me this news that nearly has you dancing around."

"I'm going to be covering Alex Harrington in his race for New York City mayor."

"Harrington—never heard of him."

"I hadn't either. He's a newcomer, young for politics, only thirty-four. He's got old Boston wealth behind him. He went to Bennington Prep and Harvard and then became the director of his family's New York branch office of the First Street Corporation. Evidently, he's been active politically, working his way up to this. He's got the physical side covered, he's tall, good-looking, charming, and evidently not stupid. I have a feeling I won't be seeing him stumble over his feet or say something tactless."

"With that pedigree and deep pockets, he could maybe have a chance since the mayor's termed out, but I wouldn't bet on it; he's got some stiff competition. So what exactly will you be doing?"

"I'm heading to his big fundraiser tonight to meet him, set

up a time for an interview. Then I'll grill him to his toes, find out all his secrets."

Travis laughed. "If he's a good politician, good luck with that. Imagine, a Bostonian running for New York City mayor. That's pretty crazy, Mia. I mean, the Red Sox or the Yankees? How's he going to straddle that one? Or even if he's a New Yorker? How long has he lived in the city?"

"Hmm, maybe six years, around that. After I've researched him, I'll know the month and day he moved here."

"Well, Hillary Clinton managed to snag a New York Senate seat when her home was Arkansas. But then again, she had powerful backing and overflowing coffers. More power to him, if he can pull it off."

Mia chewed on her lip. "Travis, the thing is, I don't know if I'm going to be free to go to Bermuda in seventeen days. We'll see." She stared down at her watch. "Oops, gotta go, Travis. I've got to put on my little black dress and go out into the frozen tundra. I love you and I fully expect you to avoid all those pretty *fräuleins*."

He said, "At least I can dream about lying on the beach with you, rubbing sunscreen all over you. I wonder if you can go topless in Bermuda."

She laughed. "Pervert. It's so cold here it makes me shiver to even think about a bikini."

After she disconnected, Mia changed into her dress, pulled her hair back from her face, twisted it up into a thick chignon, added a touch of mascara and lipstick, and decided it was as good as it would get. She pulled on her stiletto-heeled black boots and stylish black wool coat her mom and dad had given her for Christmas, and took one final look in the mirror. She grinned at her reflection. "Yeah, baby, you're the reporter for a great metropolitan newspaper."

She called downstairs so a taxi would be waiting to take her to the Harrington fundraiser at the plush Cabot Hotel.

5

MIA

The Cabot Hotel on East Seventy-Fifth was one of the special few New York hotels Travis admired. He thought the art deco style, lovingly restored, still made its discreet statement—*we cater only to the wealthy and provide anything-they-want service.*

Mia was politely asked her name, checked off on a list, and joined a group of invitees in the massive red, white, and blue–garlanded ballroom with matching red, white, and blue balloons hugging the high ceiling, a clever touch. What a relief the American flag wasn't black and vomit brown. She saw a free bar meant to lighten fingers reaching for checkbooks, tables of clever finger foods including tiny tacos that immediately made her hungry, and an eight-piece band playing mellow background music. Everything was set for Alex Talbot Harrington to present himself.

Mia estimated five hundred guests were roaming around the huge ballroom, dressed to kill, most drinking, all in fine spirits. Liquor flowed, and Mia wondered what the final bar tab would be. It boggled her mind.

She figured Harrington, with his family's support and re-
puted bottomless pockets, didn't much need tonight's contri-
butions, capped as they were, for the campaign. He needed
these fundraisers for the exposure, the publicity, the opportunity to meet the movers and the shakers, people he was
smart enough to know he needed badly as a newcomer.

She worked the room, seeking out people's impressions of
Alex Talbot Harrington, came across a couple of social media
hounds she'd locked horns with a couple of months before and
would like to gullet.

The music stopped, conversation died out, and Cory Hughes,
Harrington's campaign manager, stepped to the microphone
and introduced the candidate. Alexander Talbot Harrington
stepped onto the stage to loud applause. He had to raise the
microphone because he was tall, and wasn't that lucky for him.
Mia set her iPhone to record so she could focus on him. He was
good-looking in person, with fine chiseled features and a square
jaw, all the physical endowments a successful politician could
need. He smiled and began speaking. She was struck by his
lovely, distinctive voice, with only a trace of the Boston Brahmin accent, and wondered how long he'd worked at blending
it with New York–speak. He came across a bit like another J.
F. Kennedy, but easier on a New Yorker's ear. His speech itself
was smooth enough, self-deprecating at the right places. He
obviously had good writers. He acknowledged he was young, an
outsider to New York City government, and apologized, with
a smile, for being from Boston, and he just about managed to
turn those New York negatives into positives. He focused not on
partisanship, but on solutions for the city's festering problems,

left unsolved for too long by the current administration. He said little of real substance, and Mia wasn't surprised when the few specific positions he took were greeted with applause since the room was filled with like-minded people. After ten minutes, he grinned at the room and stepped back to thunderous applause.

The band blasted out "Happy Days Are Here Again." Someone touched her arm, and she turned to see Miles Lombardy, Mr. Harrington's senior staffer. He was a fair young man no older than thirty, an up-and-coming political wunderkind. Mia thought he looked like a wise owl, with his big round glasses and goatee. He introduced himself, smiled, and said, "Mr. Harrington was pleased to hear you'll be the chief correspondent for the *Guardian* covering his election for mayor. I'm confident you'll feel quite supportive when you learn more about him." He sounded slick as streambed rock, even smoother than Harrington.

She gave him a fat smile. "Don't you mean his *run for* mayor? You do know it's in my contract to be as objective as I can be, right?"

Mr. Lombardy returned her smile, showing perfect straight teeth. "One naturally prefers optimism, Ms. Briscoe. Whatever you need, please contact me, or Mr. Harrington's campaign manager, Cory Hughes." He gave her his card. "Mr. Harrington would like to meet you. Please wait here."

Mia accepted another glass of soda water with lime and ice. She never drank alcohol, not since that long-ago night that had devastated so many lives, hers included. As she waited for the candidate to come to her, she wondered if it was her blog or the articles she would write about him in the *Guardian* he thought more valuable to him. Probably both. Her three-year-old political blog, *Voices in the Middle*, had garnered over three hundred thousand readers to date and was growing daily. Her scope was usually national, not local, and her readers a pretty fair sampling of the country as a whole.

"Ms. Briscoe?"

Mia turned to see Mr. Lombardy, and beside him, the candidate. "Alex, this is Ms. Mia Briscoe of the *Guardian*." Miles stepped back and nearly bowed as if Harrington were royalty.

She took in Mr. Alexander Talbot Harrington up close and personal. She had to admit he presented the complete package. He smiled down at her, not all that far since she was five feet nine in her stocking feet. With her three-inch stilettos, she looked him almost straight in the eye. She felt the force of his complete focus on her. *Potent* was the first word that popped to mind. Natural or learned? It didn't matter, she had no doubt it would serve him well.

He took her hand, held it in a firm grip, and said in an intimate deep voice, "It's a pleasure to finally meet you, Ms. Briscoe. Thank you for coming tonight. I've followed you in the *Guardian*, of course, but your blog—I've got to say I admire your ability to present both sides of a question without prejudgment or bias for either side. No matter how divisive the question you pose, you always find ideas to bring the disparate sides together. That's exactly what I hope to do in my campaign, and as mayor. As you know, holding on to solutions that make sense can be very hard to do."

She wondered who'd done the research on her blog and given him a rundown. She was impressed.

Mia said with a smile, "Sometimes I have to hang on to sensible ideas by my fingertips because few who sit in the center say much; it's always the two extremes who shout out their views, dominate the news. They never shut up. But I do say that in my blog, don't I? Is that where you read it?"

He managed to wince and smile back at her at the same time. "Since it's what I believe, too, does it matter? I know I'll be experiencing much the same. But all those folks in the middle? Aren't they our real strength?"

Mia responded to his smile, even knowing it was highly practiced, part of his shtick.

He leaned forward. "Do you get a lot of hate mail from the extremes?"

She had to laugh. "More than I can count. Either I'm an idiot and deserve to be hit with a hammer or I'm a mealymouthed wuss and why can't I take a stand?"

"Do you ever hear from the voices in the middle?"

"Oh yes. Usually they tell me I'm not entirely stupid."

He grinned, lightly laid his hand on her arm. "I hope to meet with you again soon, talk all this over with you. Unfortunately, right now I have a lot of people to meet." And he was gone, working the room like a pro.

Mia taxied back to her building from the fundraiser, exhausted and freezing, since the heater in the taxi had been on strike. As she shivered, she recorded some impressions so she wouldn't forget them. Alex Harrington had been fluent, engaging, and careful to keep his actual stands on the more divisive questions unspoken. Still, all in all, his self-assurance was impressive. He managed to present himself as trustworthy, with a goodly dose of charm and charisma to boot. She wasn't surprised he'd met with her personally, it had only been politic. She'd seen him assessing her carefully with his dark eyes, well aware that what she wrote about him in her articles and in her blog mattered.

Now it was time for her to start her in-depth research, time to dig in, find out if he had any skeletons, if he was for real or only another ambitious politician out for himself and for power. She'd even find out the brand of socks he wore. Mia didn't think using personal details was unfair, or cynical. It was her job to find out what was real about him and what wasn't, whether he could be the right person for the job, if there was such a thing.

When Mia was back in warm sweats and thick socks, she bulleted out what she already knew about Alex Harrington and began rhythmically tapping her finger on her laptop as she organized her thoughts, a longtime habit. Still stuff to accomplish before she slept or thought about Travis rubbing sunscreen on her back. Of course she'd give Harrington attention in her next blog since he'd announced he was running for mayor of New York City.

She got up, made a cup of tea to shake off her fatigue, paced her living room while she planned out what she'd write, then returned to her laptop. She looked at a photo of Harrington taken recently at a society party—he looked every bit as charming as he'd been this evening, in command of himself, totally comfortable in his surroundings. She never doubted he'd say all the right things, both to her and to voters. He simply had that look. She thought, then typed, "It's not important what a politician says during a campaign, what promises he or she makes, it's what they actually do when elected." *So let's see how you've actually behaved in your life, Alex, outside the political arena. I'm going to look at your roots.* Milo always said to look at the family first if you want to find out who a candidate really is.

Mia left her laptop and walked into her small kitchen to make another cup of tea. As she waited for the water to boil, she looked at the Christmas card from Serena's parents she'd kept on the counter. She felt the familiar stab of remembered pain, the horrific grief Serena's family had felt. Their not knowing, their tiny flame of hope that she was still alive somewhere. Somewhere. There was no rhyme or reason for them to hope, but it didn't matter, probably never would.

Serena had been gone for seven years now, ever since the fire at the frat house. Everyone except her family accepted she had to be dead, even Tommy Maitland, Serena's boyfriend at the time. Mia and Tommy spoke often, emailed several times a month. He was an FBI agent, for two years now, assigned to the Washington Field Office. She remembered his father, Assistant Director James Maitland, had sent the Philadelphia Field Office to assist with the search for Serena, starting at the scene, and with interviews. They'd found nothing to lead them to her, no clue, only that the fire had been set. When Tommy had graduated from Quantico, the first thing he did was repeat everything that had already been done, with the same result. It had led nowhere.

Mia closed down her laptop for the night when she realized it was two A.M. and her eyes were burning.

6

32 Willard Avenue
McLean, Virginia

MONDAY EVENING

Olivia was bone-tired. She'd been released from Walter Reed a week before and still, she felt drained so quickly. She wouldn't be cleared to go back to work until the headaches from her concussion stopped. At least she wasn't still in the hospital. Tonight, she and Andi Creamer had shared pizza at Benny's Pies, close enough to Olivia's house to be an easy drive for her. Andi, with her spiked black hair and hazel eyes, was as tough as her field boots. She was also one of the smartest operatives Olivia had ever worked with, decisive and hard to beat hand to hand. You wanted her to have your back. They'd been good friends since they'd trained at the CIA Farm together five years before. They spoke of Tim Higgs, who'd been wounded in the leg during the Iran mission and was in Maine visiting his parents. They spoke of Hashem Jahandar, the Iranian undercover

32

operative who'd died, and toasted him. His name would soon grace the Wall of Stars at Langley. And they wondered how it was possible Iranian military knew where they'd be. They didn't have to say it out loud; they knew they were lucky they wouldn't have their own stars on the wall next to his.

Of course they spoke of Mike, where he might be, why he hadn't reported in to Langley to debrief with Mr. Grace, and what had happened to him. Olivia knew something had happened and it scared her to her toes. She wished she could have flown back to the States with him—as least she'd have been close by—but they had wanted to keep her in Balad for another couple of days before flying her back to Walter Reed Hospital. And he'd simply disappeared. Langley's greatest concern, it seemed to Olivia, wasn't for Mike's safety, but for the missing flash drive Hashem had pressed into his hand before he died. Oh yes, Langley was trying to find him, as were all his friends, but they wanted the flash drive first and foremost. Olivia herself had called his cell dozens of times, pestered Mr. Grace with questions, but he told her she was on leave for a reason, to rest and not to worry. They would find Mike Kingman. But she was scared for him, and angry because she'd heard there were suspicions about Mike at Langley. Were they idiots? Mike would never do anything to hurt the agency or the United States. She was frustrated and hated her body for holding her back, and all she could do was worry and be afraid for him. It all hovered over her like a black cloud.

Olivia drove slowly back toward home, cursing the constant fatigue pulling at her. She turned on loud rock to keep herself alert. She couldn't help it, she turned and drove to Mike's condo in Western Heights, not far from her own house. She'd been told to drive only when absolutely necessary. She was to rest, let her body heal, but she had to knock on Mike's front door, peer in the windows. No sign of him.

She remembered Mike being there when she was half conscious in the hospital in Balad, the soft cadence of his voice, the warmth of his hand when he'd held hers, the feel of his mouth when he'd kissed her forehead, her lips, but she couldn't remember his words, or if he'd even spoken to her. Before she was flown back to Walter Reed, one of her nurses told her she really liked her visitor and gave a little shudder. "Tall, dark, and delicious," she'd said. Without a doubt that was Mike.

Olivia rested her forehead against the steering wheel at a red light. Over and over, she thought, *Where are you, Mike? Why won't you call me? If you're not all right, I'll kick your butt.*

She remembered another firefight two years ago in a small ISIS-held town three hundred miles north of Damascus; she and Mike, on another mission, had ended up in the middle of the fighting, when again, they'd nearly died. They'd briefly become lovers then, to reaffirm being alive, she supposed. He'd been part of her life for three years, sometimes sharing her missions, sometimes her bed. But he'd slowly become more, she realized now. He'd become important, vital. Olivia hated being afraid, hated being helpless, hated not knowing.

She turned toward home. Her head began to throb, thankfully not as bad as the day before. She hated taking the pills the doctors had given her; they made her brain feel too fuzzy. As she left her MINI Cooper in her driveway, she heard Helmut barking madly behind the front door as she walked up the flagstone steps she'd laid herself six months before. He recognized her car, her footsteps.

She forgot her headache when she unlocked the door and eighty-five pounds of golden retriever jumped in her arms, licking her everywhere he could reach. She was glad he hadn't knocked her on her butt with his love because she was still weak and it was close. She hugged him, whispered against his soft coat, "Yes, yes, Mama's home. I was only gone for an hour, not back from Iraq again. You're my beautiful boy, and I swear, tomorrow morning you and I will go to the dog park and I'll throw your mangy ball until one of us collapses, and that would be me. Yes, okay, and I'll get you a new chew rope." She'd worried Helmut wouldn't want to leave her friend Julia, who'd kept him while she'd been away. But when he'd seen Olivia, his joy was boundless.

Olivia slowly stood up and looked around her small entry hall into the living room through a graceful arch to her right. She'd fallen in love with the arches that framed every room, and several of the windows as well. The clincher was the big fenced backyard for Helmut. She signed her life away for this perfect little house tucked into a mess of oak trees next to Clifford Park. Three years ago now. Both she and Helmut were very happy with her purchase.

She wanted nothing more than to collapse into her bed. Still, she made her rounds out of longtime habit, checking the window locks in each of the rooms as she pulled down the shades, closed the draperies.

With Helmut at her heels, she walked back to her second mortgage—her marvel of a kitchen—opened the refrigerator and pulled out a bottle of mineral water. She drank deeply to the sound of Helmut's tail thumping like a metronome on the kitchen pavers.

She smiled. He loved sparkling water too. She poured the rest of the water into his bowl and watched him lap it up. "There you go, my man."

Thirty minutes later, Olivia was in bed with Helmut sprawled on his back at the foot of it. She knew by morning, he'd be sleeping beside her, his head on the pillow next to hers, sometimes with the covers pulled to his neck. How he managed that, she didn't know. She'd emailed photos of him snoring on his back to her family and friends. She remembered Mike laughing his head off. He'd met Helmut, thrown a football for him, roughhoused with him. Olivia sighed, forced herself to turn it off. She had to get well, and that meant long stretches of rest.

Olivia was sleeping deeply when she was jerked awake by a low growl from Helmut against her cheek. She laid her palm on his neck, whispered, "What is it? What did you hear?" She'd seen several foxes racing through the trees by the park at night. But Helmut was trained and he was smart. It didn't matter that she lived in a quiet neighborhood, she wasn't going to ignore his warning. It had been drilled into her at the Farm, when she'd first joined the CIA, to be cautious, to always double-check. Olivia slipped out of bed, pulled on her wool robe and sneakers, picked up her Glock from beside her cell phone on the bedside table, and walked slowly to the living room,

Helmut as silent as a ghost at her heels, as he'd been trained. She went down on her knees and gently lifted the bottom edge of the drapery with the muzzle of her Glock, looked outside. It was dark, no moon or stars to give her any light. She scanned the trees out toward the park. Helmut's tail thumped on the floor. Time passed. She was turning to pet him when she saw a quick flash of light, gone in an instant, as if a palm had quickly covered a flashlight. Her brain went to red alert. She was immediately operational. Someone was out there, and that was all she needed to know. She eased down the drapery, moved away from the window, Helmut beside her.

She dressed quickly in sweats and boots, shrugged on a thick dark overcoat, pulled a black watch cap out of her coat pocket and covered her hair. She realized she was shaking from the damnable weakness and cursed her body. Didn't matter, she'd gut it out, find out who was out there. Olivia went down on her knees and looked into Helmut's eyes. "You've done your job. This isn't practice. Stay, sit quietly until I tell you to come." He immediately sat on his haunches, but he didn't look happy. She gave him a quick squeeze and moved as quickly as her body allowed through the kitchen, threw the dead bolt, and eased out the back door.

Olivia walked quietly around the side of the house, her Glock at the ready. There was only a slight wind, barely stirring the stark branches of the red oak trees, but it was icy cold, hovering toward freezing.

She stopped at the front corner of her house, eased down on her knees, looked toward where she'd spotted the flash of light.

She quieted her breathing and eased herself into the night

sounds around her, listening for anything that didn't belong. And she heard it, a man's voice speaking a few words of English in a near whisper before he switched to Farsi. She strained to make out his words, but couldn't.

Another man whispered back in English, but again his words were muffled, indistinct. Then she heard them moving toward the house.

Olivia's blood pumped hot and wild but her brain was calm, focused. She went down flat on her belly so there was no chance they'd see her. She smiled. *Come to Mama, boys.*

When the two dark shadows reached the front door, they tried to avoid the porch light but she saw both were dressed in black, their faces covered, and both carried guns with suppressors. Olivia slowly rose and shouted, "Drop your weapons. You know who I am, and you know I will shoot you."

The taller man dropped to his knees and fired until his magazine was empty, but she was already belly-flat against the ground again and the shots went well above her. She fired twice, watched him fall beside the front steps. The other man was backing up fast, firing, then he turned and ran back into the trees. She fired after him, but she didn't hit him.

7

Georgetown
Washington, D.C.

MONDAY EVENING

Sherlock looked over at Sean, sprawled on his stomach on the living room rug, looking through the first book of the Magic Tree House series, a gift from his grandparents in San Francisco. "Mama, Papa, it's not really a tree house, it's a time machine!"

Savich and Sherlock were sitting side by side on the sofa, enjoying the soft rustling of the flames in the fireplace when Sean shouted, "Dinosaurs!" Savich imagined time travel would be all his son would talk about with his friends in school tomorrow. Savich leaned down and ruffled his son's dark hair, the same shade as his. No head of red curls like his mother's, he'd tell her, and sometimes she punched him for it.

Sherlock tucked her feet beneath her and leaned into Dillon, her curly hair tickling his nose. She tilted her head up, kissed his chin. "This is so nice, Dillon, like another dessert after the tiramisu." She nipped his chin again and he closed his arms around her and pulled her to his chest. Though Sean was time-traveling back to the era of the *Tyrannosaurus rex*, Savich kept his voice low; Sean had bat ears and endless curiosity. "It's going to be even more frigid in New York than here, so dress warm."

She settled in, sighed. "I can't imagine it being any colder. What a March. You know I couldn't say no, and Kelly wouldn't ask me to come up if she weren't in a jam, although what she thinks I can do baffles me."

He raised a dark brow. "Baffles you? Why?"

"It's not like there aren't dozens of really smart agents in Manhattan. Why me?"

He kissed her nose. "I'm not going to feed your ego. I expect you to go to New York and prove how brilliant you are." Fact was Savich didn't want her to leave, even for only a couple of days, but he knew she couldn't turn down a fellow agent in the New York Field Office who'd been in the trenches with her, as Kelly Giusti had. "At least you're helicoptering to New York, not fighting your way through the crowds at Dulles."

"Thanks for the vote of confidence and the pressure. I think Mr. Maitland pulled some strings to get me the helicopter and all because he set up an interview with the *Guardian* while I'm there, revisiting the JFK terrorist incident again."

"He knows you'll make the FBI look good and so you deserve the helicopter." She smiled, turned her face to rest against his, and her hair tickled his nose. He found himself inhaling her scent, a light rose, sweet, inviting, and it made him want to cart her off upstairs, but Sean was now dealing with baby dinosaurs, naming them aloud, telling them what to do, and so

Savich said, "So Kelly's the lead in investigating a triple murder they think might be the work of an unusual serial? That sounds interesting, right up your alley."

Sherlock shot Sean another look, heard him speaking to Cletus, a baby dinosaur, but still she kept her voice low. "She wants my fresh eyes on the crime scene—the kitchen in a spiffy home in Brickson, New York. She said the triple murder was made to look like a robbery, but they realized almost immediately it didn't add up. It seems the murdered husband's ex-girlfriend also had two former husbands, and both of them ended up dead soon after they left her. Both deaths were suspicious, one obviously a murder, but the proof wasn't there so she skated. Both Kelly, her team, and local Homicide think the woman could have killed all of them."

Savich never liked it when they worked apart, but he sucked it up. "Don't get a big head, but no one is better than you at reconstructing a crime scene, sweetheart. If there's something there, you'll see it."

Sherlock rested her face against his heart, smiled as she leaned up to kiss him. His heartbeat kicked up again, hers as well. She whispered against his neck, "Let's get Sean to bed with his time machine and snuggle in under mounds of blankets, maybe discuss how to warm me up for my trip."

8

CAU—Criminal Apprehension Unit
Hoover Building
Interview Room

TUESDAY MORNING

Savich knew two things about CIA agent Olivia Hildebrandt, besides her name, from Detective Ben Raven in his early morning call. She'd been in Walter Reed Hospital until a short time ago recovering from wounds she'd suffered on a recent mission, and she was nearly killed by two men the night before, one of them Iranian. She looked exhausted, her face as pale as her white shirt, the dash of lipstick on her mouth not much help. Her thick chestnut hair was pulled back from her thin face in a fat French braid. She had expressive eyes, a deep blue, nearly navy, but the shadows beneath them were dark enough to hide in. Savich believed he saw strength in her eyes and hoped he was right.

He smiled at her from the doorway of the interview room. "Good morning, Agent Hildebrandt, Detective Raven, and you must be Mr. Grace."

Grace stood, offered his hand. "Yes, I'm Carlton Grace, Agent Hildebrandt's chief—in popular parlance, her handler. I direct and coordinate her assignments. A pleasure to meet you in person, Agent Savich. I've heard of you, naturally. I'm only sorry it's under such trying circumstances."

Savich shook Grace's hand, a slender hand with short buffed nails, but his grip was firm. He was a slight man with narrow shoulders, no taller than five feet eight, a long straight nose, a square jaw. He was comfortable to look at, his clothes sort of wrinkled, a guy you wouldn't give a second look if he walked by on the street. Ben had warned Savich that CIA Operations Officer Grace had only grudgingly agreed the incident at Hildebrandt's house was FBI purview, and he'd been even more reluctant to bring Olivia Hildebrandt and his own superior, Mr. Fulton Lodner, the CIA director of intelligence, to the Hoover Building, as if the FBI harbored a den of thieves. Lodner was late, perhaps to make an entrance? Savich had held firm, he wanted the CIA on his turf. Ben had said about Carlton Grace, "My take is Grace is reasonable enough, very worried about his agent, but he'll follow his chain of command and they'll fight tooth and nail to keep you from getting any information they want to keep classified, no matter how needful such information would be to you. My advice? Keep your boot on their necks or they'll chop off your foot."

Carlton Grace said, "Agent Savich, as you already know, this is Agent Hildebrandt."

Savich gently took Hildebrandt's hand. "I'm Special Agent Savich. No, don't get up."

Olivia nodded. "Agent Savich." *He knows I'm on the edge, and he's being careful with me.* He was being kind and she hated it, hated that she looked as pathetic as she felt. She forced herself to straighten, to sit tall when all she really wanted to do was lean forward into the uncomfortable chair, put her face on the table. "Agent Savich. I've heard of your wife, Agent Sherlock, and her heroism. I was in Germany at the time, but it was all over the news."

Savich felt the jolt of pride he always felt when someone spoke of Sherlock. He nodded, pointed to the coffeepot and cups. "Thank you both for coming. Help yourselves to coffee." He paused a moment. "Agent Hildebrandt, you need some orange juice. All right?"

Her eyes brightened, she nodded, and he excused himself. He was back quickly and handed her a large glass of orange juice. "Our unit secretary, Shirley, keeps juice in a small fridge near her desk for mornings like this."

Olivia drank down the whole glass, closed her eyes a moment, then smiled at Savich. "Thank you." She turned to Mr. Grace. "Sir, keeping juice around at Langley might be a good idea."

Savich looked down at his watch, waited until Grace set his coffee cup down. "While we're waiting for Mr. Lodner, why don't you go over what happened to you, Agent Hildebrandt. I know very little. Please walk me through it."

A bit of a smile appeared, disappeared. "You mean last night."

She had a lovely smooth voice, with a hint of southern, maybe Georgia origins.

"Yes. I'm sure there's much more, but tell me about last night for a start."

Olivia told him about her nightly routine, Helmut's waking

her, and seeing a brief flash of light. Her voice was emotionless, her recounting clear, no digressions. "I was hunkered down beside the front of my house when I heard the two men whispering. One of the men spoke Farsi, the other English, but they spoke very quietly and I couldn't make out their words. When they approached my front door, they were illuminated under my porch light; I saw they were both wearing black, and black masks. I yelled for them to drop their weapons. The taller man was fast, he got off seven rounds before I shot him. The second man was backing up and firing, then he turned and ran. I missed him."

Ben Raven smiled. She sounded pissed.

Savich said, "It makes sense these two men were pros. Why do you think the first man missed you?"

"I was lying on my stomach so both men shot well above me."

Savich said, "Well done. Did you search the man you shot?"

Olivia said, "I waited until I heard a car start up half a block away, called 911 and Mr. Grace. Then, yes, I searched him. Nothing in his pockets, not even change or a matchbook, a motel key, not a thing. He had a suppressor on his weapon. It was a Smith & Wesson 9 mm semiautomatic and it was on the ground beside him. I checked the magazine, saw I was wrong, he'd fired off eight rounds before I shot him, not seven. Given his features, I'd say he was Iranian, the one who was speaking Farsi."

Savich said, "Can you describe the other man?"

"As I said, they both wore black masks, but when he fired at me, I saw his wrist—he was light-skinned, probably Caucasian. He wasn't tall, but he moved well, looked fit from what I could see. That's all I can tell you."

"Do you have any idea why those two men were there to kill you?"

Carlton Grace's fingers began to tap on the tabletop, but he said nothing.

If it was a signal to keep quiet, Olivia ignored it. "It seems likely they were there because of my last mission."

"You were in Iran?"

Grace said, his voice firm as a judge, "We'll leave off discussing anything concerning that mission until Mr. Lodner arrives."

Savich nodded, said easily, "Tell me why you were in Walter Reed Hospital."

"An RPG—rocket-propelled grenade—landed near me and the blast knocked me out. I woke up in Balad Military Hospital in Iraq." She stopped cold when there was a knock on the interview room door and Agent Davis Sullivan stuck his head in.

"Savich, a Mr. Fulton Lodner is here from the CIA."

Savich saw Olivia stiffen, but she said nothing, stared down at her clasped hands. He expected Carlton Grace would look relieved, like the cavalry had arrived, but instead he looked stoic, as if he knew there was going to be blood spilled.

After stiff introductions, Fulton Lodner sat beside Grace, clasped his hands in front of him on the table, and stared at Savich. He did not look happy, shook his head at the offer of coffee. He sat squarely in his fifties, his light hair thinning, mostly gray, and worn short. He looked like he didn't compromise often, or wanted to. He was on the tall side, fairly fit, his slight paunch well disguised in a dark blue conservative suit. Savich saw calm intelligence in his eyes, felt Lodner sizing him up as well, imagined Lodner would rather shoot him than have to be in the same room with him and pretend to cooperate. He nodded to Grace, gave Olivia a stingy smile. He said in a calm, stiff voice, "Olivia, I trust you are recovered from your disturbance last night?"

That's what that was? A fricking disturbance? Olivia nodded. "Yes, sir. I'm fine."

Lodner continued in a sharp impatient voice to Savich, "I was unable to be here earlier because I wanted to discuss this unusual situation with CIA Director Hendricks. Agent Savich, you know as well as I do that any investigation you conduct into this situation is unlikely to bear fruit. We have resources in place, we know the players. It is very doubtful you'll be able to find the identity of the foreign national Agent Hildebrandt was forced to kill last night. There is even less chance you will find the second shooter. In short, you face failure, which makes it more obvious that the only intelligent solution is for the CIA to continue working on this case ourselves, even without domestic police power, while keeping you informed, naturally."

9

OLIVIA

So it was gloves off right out of the gate. Lodner's whopping lie to keep him informed if he took over the case made Savich want to smile. Time for his boot on Lodner's neck. Savich sat back in his chair, crossed his arms. "Mr. Lodner, as you very well know, it's our responsibility, in our charter, not yours, to investigate domestic violence that violates federal law whether it involves a mail clerk in the post office or a CIA agent. Since you were perfectly clear, let me return the favor. If you do not cooperate with me today, provide me all the information I need to proceed, our own director will be told. Let me assure you, he will not take this lightly."

Lodner's voice became frigid. "You fail to realize how serious the diplomatic damage would be if Agent Hildebrandt's mission becomes public. You have no understanding of the possible consequences or retaliation, nor should you, because your charter hasn't equipped you to. There are lives at stake as well, lives that are our responsibility, not yours."

"All the more reason for you to tell me what I need to know.

There will be no leaks from the FBI. Now, can we stop the pissing contest? Tell me about the mission to Iran that resulted in the serious injury of Agent Hildebrandt and the subsequent attempt on her life last night."

Lodner's fist hit the tabletop. "There is no definitive proof the attempted shooting last night has anything to do with Iran."

Olivia's eyebrow shot up. She opened her mouth, closed it.

Lodner ground his teeth, turned to Olivia. "Agent Hildebrandt, what did you tell him about Iran?"

"Nothing, sir. Only that one of the men last night was probably Iranian. I heard him speak Farsi."

Grace said quietly, "I believe, sir, you should tell Agent Savich about our mission to Iran."

Lodner looked back at Savich. "Very well. I am prepared to give you an overview of the mission, but certainly not the classified details."

"You may begin with the broad strokes, Mr. Lodner, then we'll see."

"What I will tell you is sensitive enough. Therefore, I ask that you, Detective Raven, leave now. What I will say is for Agent Savich's ears only."

Savich nodded to Ben. He rose, grinned. "Thank you for the show then, gentlemen. What I've already heard will be a cherished memory." He turned dead serious. "Agent Hildebrandt, you can trust Agent Savich to keep you safe and find out how and why this happened." He turned and quietly closed the door behind him. Savich thought he heard whistling.

Lodner's lips were seamed as he stared at the door. He turned back to Savich. "I will remind you, Agent Savich, you will be held accountable for any leak of this information. Do you understand?" At Savich's patient nod, he continued. "Very well. We had an undercover operative embedded at Iranian military headquarters. He was in Tehran for thirteen months when he discovered he'd been identified and was about to be arrested. He contacted Mr. Grace, who arranged for Agent Hildebrandt and her team to pick him up near the Iraqi border." He paused. "It came as a shock to us to find him actually running from the Iranian military. We do not as yet know how the government found out so quickly where he was headed.

"Our operative was killed but the information he was carrying on a flash drive was saved. There was sustained gunfire and the team was hit by an RPG that rendered Agent Hildebrandt unconscious. She was airlifted to Balad Military Hospital, then flown back later to the States for evaluation at Walter Reed.

"The details of the mission, the name of our undercover operative, how we embedded him, the critical information we hoped to obtain from the flash drive one of the team members managed to bring out—that is all highly classified. That's as much information as I can give you."

"Where is the flash drive?"

Lodner shook his head. "We don't as yet have it."

"Why don't you have it?"

"That is classified, Agent Savich."

Savich looked thoughtful. "I see. So the attack on Agent Hildebrandt last night could be an attempt to find the flash drive?"

Mr. Lodner said again, this time his teeth gritted, "That is classified, Agent Savich."

Savich said easily, "It appears that flash drive, with the

critical information on it your operative was bringing out, may well be the key, indeed the reason for the attack on Agent Hildebrandt. Who has the flash drive?"

Lodner said, annoyance radiating off him in waves, "Very well, our operative was scheduled to arrive at Langley to debrief with Mr. Grace and give him the flash drive, but he did not. We don't know where he is or why he hasn't come in. We are searching for him.

"Until we have verified information to the contrary, we will assume the attack on Agent Hildebrandt last night was a retaliatory action against the team we sent to exfiltrate our undercover operative in Iran."

Carlton Grace frowned. "But, Fulton, that would be entirely new, something they've never attempted before. Also, who would possibly even know the names of the agents involved? As far as I can see, there's simply no other obvious connection between Olivia's mission to Iran and the attack on her last night, no obvious cause and effect." He nodded to Savich. "I agree with Agent Savich. It has to be the flash drive."

Lodner smacked his fist on the conference table. "How the devil did anyone know the names of the agents involved in the exfiltration?"

Mr. Grace said simply, "They bought the names from someone who knew."

"I refuse to believe that, Carlton. No more about this; it is highly classified and absolutely none of the FBI's business."

Savich thought he could work with Carlton Grace, but Fulton Lodner wouldn't give him the time of day, unless by a direct order. He was too angry at being forced to hand over the reins to the FBI, resentful at even having to waste his time here at the Hoover Building, the FBI bastion. Savich was considering how to ask Lodner about the obvious conclusion that there was a mole in the CIA, when Olivia said clearly, "Mr. Lodner, what about Mike Kingman? He's the team member, Agent Savich, who retrieved the flash drive and saved my life. He and the flash drive are both missing. Have you learned anything about Mike, Mr. Lodner?"

Lodner drew a deep breath, sent her a death stare. "The whereabouts of a CIA operative is hardly a conversation to be held here, Agent Hildebrandt."

Olivia was past caring about her future with the CIA. She looked at Mr. Grace, then at Mr. Lodner. "Maybe the FBI can help find Mike, sir. And the flash drive."

Lodner looked ready to burst into flame.

Grace jumped into the breach. "Olivia, you look tired, you need to rest. We should continue this later. We'll take you back to the safe house."

Lodner nodded. "Yes, Agent Hildebrandt, we'll protect you. Agent Savich, you may call me if you have further questions. I will give you what information I am allowed to share."

Before she could say anything, Grace stood, looked down at her. "Are you ready, Olivia?"

Olivia was used to doing whatever he said, to carrying out whatever order her chief gave her. She'd trusted Carlton Grace forever, he'd always had her back, her team's back, always had their best interests at heart. He put his agents above the mission. He'd even protected her from Lodner and the higher-ups for ignoring the "abort" order trying to save Hashem, though they all knew she'd put everyone at risk and could have caused an international incident.

But there was Mike; she knew something very bad had happened to him. She looked at Savich. "Can you find out who that man was I had to kill?"

"Yes," he said, "I believe I can."

"Can you find Mike?"

"Yes, I can."

Lodner snorted. "That's absurd, you're grandstanding. The men who attacked Olivia won't be found in your databases. And if we can't find our agent, you won't, either, especially if he doesn't want to be found. Good day to you, Agent Savich."

After this stiff, emotionless speech, there was a moment of stark silence. Olivia looked again at Savich. He winked at her. It was so unexpected from this tough-faced man who looked like he could derail a train, she nearly spurted out a laugh. Savich said calmly, "Mr. Lodner, Mr. Grace, thank you for your assistance. Olivia will call you, Mr. Grace, so you can tell her where the safe house is. For now, though, I need to speak to her further. Good day, gentlemen."

It was easy to see neither Lodner nor Grace wanted to leave Olivia with him, but Savich merely looked at them and said nothing until both Grace and Lodner left the interview room, each with one last look at Olivia.

Olivia said, "I am so screwed."

10

OLIVIA

Savich laughed. "Chin up, Agent Hildebrandt, it'll all work out, you'll see." He took her hand. "You've been through a lot and you don't know me. I know you're tired, running on reserves, and you're scared for your teammate, Mike Kingman. But we need to talk. We'll stop whenever you say, all right?"

Olivia nodded. She'd felt like a Ping-Pong ball bounced between Lodner and Agent Savich. But now, since she was with Savich, she'd say he'd won. At least there were no bodies on the floor. He was a handsome man, tough as nails, as she'd observed, but what impressed her the most was how he'd so smoothly taken down Lodner, and that was enough for now. "I could tell Lodner is starting to believe Mike never intended to bring in the flash drive, that he stole it and will sell it. That's just plain crazy. Mike is sometimes a pain in the butt, a stubborn macho idiot, but he's a man you'd trust with your life, a man to admire, loyal to his bones. Do you really believe you can find Mike? Find out why he went under with the flash drive?"

So this Agent Mike Kingman was important to Olivia, no, he was much more to her. Savich saw the desperate hope in her eyes and said without hesitation, "Yes." It rather shocked him. Was he the macho idiot now? Did he think he was invincible, think he was so bloody smart he could resolve this mess?

Olivia searched his face. A small smile appeared. "All right then."

So be it. Now he had to deliver. Savich rose, offered her his hand. "I think you'd be more comfortable, though, in my own conference room in the Criminal Apprehension Unit. It's nearby. But first I'll make sure we won't have to talk things over with your CIA superiors again."

He pressed a couple of buttons on his cell phone. "Ruth? Please go to the door and make sure our two CIA guests are well gone."

A moment later, Ruth came back on. "They're standing in front of the elevators; the taller man seems angry, seems like he's berating the other one. The doors are opening, and they're on. Doors close, now they're gone."

"Thank you, Ruth. CIA Agent Olivia Hildebrandt and I will be right with you." He rose, stepped back, and motioned Olivia to join him. They walked into a large room full of workstations separated by short partitions and shelves. She heard voices, the sound of typing, saw an older woman with violent red hair give her a little wave. Shirley Needleham, the unit secretary and the keeper of the orange juice? She smiled, waved back. At the back of the room, a large glass window showed another office, this one with a view of the park outside, probably Savich's. A man stood up, smiled at her.

Savich said, "Olivia, this is Agent Davis Sullivan. Davis, Olivia Hildebrandt, CIA." He was a good-looking man, obviously surprised she was CIA. He smiled. "Don't worry, you're safe in here from the FBI gestapo."

Olivia laughed. "And I have your big boss to protect me."

Davis said, "None better."

Savich introduced her to three other agents in the area before he led her into the glass-windowed conference room. Savich paused a moment when Shirley came into the conference room after them with tea and a plate of cookies. He thanked her, said to Olivia, "Shirley is famous for her sugar cookies, they're made with Splenda, actually." He poured Olivia a cup of tea, offered her a cookie.

So this big man bothered about cookies. Olivia felt more of her uncertainty fade away. She drank the tea, nibbled on the cookie, swallowed, took a deep breath. The blanket of fatigue lifted a bit.

"As I said, Olivia, we don't know each other yet, but we have two common goals—finding Mike Kingman and the flash drive, and bringing down whoever is behind this. Well, that's three actually, but I imagine we'll find out soon enough they're each a part of the whole. By the way, you can call me Dillon."

"The most important to me is finding Mike. Alive." She hated it but felt tears burn her eyes. "Your agents, they all seem nice."

Good, she was trying to keep herself together. Savich said, "They're the best. Now, before we break off today, you'll give me all of Mike's usual haunts, even those you've already checked yourself. Names of relatives who live in the area, their haunts, you know the drill. I gather you know Mike well?"

"Yes," she said, then added, "Okay, truth is, I know him more than just well. We've worked together at times for the past several years, in most of the hot spots on the globe, primarily the Middle East and Northern Africa, since both of us speak Farsi and Arabic. He's smart, Dillon, and besides being a macho idiot, he has great intuition. I've often been afraid for him, because when there's obvious danger, he runs toward it, not away, and he never second-guesses himself. He risked his life to save me in Iran, to try to save Hashem, the operative we were sent to bring out."

Savich saw the tears on her cheek. "You're more than teammates."

She blinked at that, started to shake her head, realized it was true. "Yes, I suppose we are. Our assignments have separated us for periods of time, so we've been on and off, I guess you'd say. But I've trusted him with my life many times." She paused and another tear trailed down her cheek. She brushed it away angrily. "I'm sorry to be so weak, but Mike is very important to me."

"Have you seen him at all since your injury?"

"Yes, he came to see me, in Balad, but I was too confused to speak to him. It's possible he wanted to warn me, tell me he'd discovered something was off, but he couldn't. I was dead to the world."

"Why do you think he disappeared?"

"I have no doubt something bad happened or he would be here, ready and eager to fight. I think he went under to protect himself, protect the flash drive, maybe even me and the rest of the team." She stared at him, swallowed again. "I won't accept that they've found him, killed him to get the flash drive even though the logical part of me, the experienced part, keeps trying to convince me he has to be dead. The people who want that flash drive will stop at nothing."

"Which means what's on it provides evidence of malfeasance."

"I shouldn't be telling you anything classified, but—" She shrugged. "Hashem was embedded in the Iranian military. I'm guessing he found out who was selling missiles and guidance systems to Iran. And whoever it is will stop at nothing to get it back." Olivia looked down at her clasped hands that were close to shaking. *Firm up, Hildebrandt.* "If he's alive, no, no, he is alive, but why hasn't he called me? I'm well enough to kill a man, I'm certainly well enough to help him. So I'll give you a list of where I've looked, who I've asked. How can you possibly find him when I can't?"

Savich said, "Like your Mr. Lodner, I have resources, Olivia, resources he doesn't have. Trust me. Maybe after Mike visited you in the hospital, he decided he needed to figure some things out on his own, and he believed staying out of sight would keep you safe. You say he's smart, he's experienced. Your mission was compromised, and you all were almost killed. It's possible your satellite communications were intercepted or that there's an internal data breach at the CIA, or even a mole."

She was nodding. "Yes, everyone at the CIA, including the director, is aware of those possibilities, and taking steps. I'm just afraid they'll look no further than Mike."

Savich sat back, smiled at her, and said, "He sounds too tough to let anyone get him."

He saw color bloom on her face, and there, again, that desperate hope in her eyes. "Yes, you're right about that. He's one of five sons, and both of his parents are Marines. He told me surviving his brothers is how he learned his survival skills, that, and the street fighting in all the countries he's lived in. He speaks street Farsi, Arabic, and some Italian from a Neapolitan grandmother."

Savich nodded. He'd find out everything about Mike Kingman, including his high school prom date. "Olivia, I think Mike will contact you now, if he can, because whoever is behind this tried to either take you or kill you. He won't want to leave you in the dark any longer, it's too dangerous."

"But I don't know anything!—not even where he is."

He took her hands, strong hands, calloused, short buffed nails. "It's obvious someone believes you do. And that's why the two men came to your house last night, to take you because they believe you know where Mike is."

She sighed. "I've told you what I think is on the flash drive, but of course I shouldn't have. Don't rat me out. Everything at the CIA is held close to the vest, need to know only, which is important for national security."

"What about your two other team members, Olivia? Are they being protected now?"

"As far as I know, they aren't, not yet. I had dinner last night with Andrea—Andi—Creamer. Both she and Tim Higgs were debriefed, then put on R&R. Tim was wounded in Iran, but now he's in Maine visiting his family, so he's safe."

"When you were debriefed, what did you tell them about the wounded operative, Hashem, and Mike before the RPG hit?"

"I told them the truth. I still have gaps in my memory. All I can remember is Hashem gave Mike the flash drive, and maybe they spoke because I remember Mike leaning close to him, and yes, I was close by trying to help stanch the chest wound, but if I knew what was said I can't remember."

There was so much more to talk about, but Savich could see Olivia was flagging. "I think it's time for you to call Mr. Grace for the safe house address. It'll be your home until this is over. After you've rested, text me the list of places you've looked for Mike. Here's my private number. Make it one of your emergency numbers." Savich rose. He watched her take a final bite of cookie, slowly rise. She didn't move for a moment until she'd steadied. She turned to him and managed to smile. "This is what they call a real SNAFU in the army, right?"

"Looks that way now, but you know what? In the end, in my experience, I bet it will turn out to be straightforward." He escorted her to the elevator, waited with her. When she got on, he smiled, said, "Olivia, when this is all over, you'll come to my house for pizza, meet my wife and son, Sean."

II

Henri Delos gently replaced the elegant receiver into its art deco cradle. He preferred it to his soulless cell phone that wanted to be everything, telling him when to exercise, when to brush his teeth. The antique phone had been his grandfather's, a savvy old pirate who'd founded the Armament Météore at the start of the First World War. He'd sold weaponry and armaments to any country willing to pay his price, except to Germany, of course, because he was, after all, a French patriot. Henri's father hadn't appreciated either the phone or his own father and was fast running the company into the ground when he'd keeled over dead from a heart attack. Finally, Henri took over. Henri had expanded into aeronautics and aerospace and, like his grandfather, sold to anyone he could, except the Chinese, who stole the technology from other countries and had the brains and hands to build as many weapons as they wished. His major clients of late were in the Middle East, on all sides, an endlessly profitable place with its bone-deep hatreds and tankers of oil to finance never-ending attacks. Of course, many of his sales were off the books, the profits funneled back into his own pockets. He thought of the lovely little cliffside getaway near Portofino both his wife and his mistress enjoyed. Better in Italy, and not France, no reason to take chances. He'd learned early that dealing with the bureaucrats in the Direction Générale des Finances Publiques required a bit of stealth and subterfuge. As for the Sûreté Nationale, he knew the players, knew whose pockets required a few euros to look the other way, how to skate smoothly through their loopholes. All in all, everything had been working very well in his world. Until now.

He looked over at a painting of his father, done only six months before his death. Tufts of white hair stood up from his bone-white skull and Henri saw a familiar hint of a snarl in his compressed lips. His father had been a vicious drunk, a bad combination for a wife and son but now he was gone, forever. Henri thought of his mother living in luxury with her handmaiden divorced daughter, his older sister, to see to her every whim. When his mother spoke of her husband, it was with near reverence. He'd prefer to believe her myriad medications had altered her memory.

Henri did have to admit the old man had done one thing right. He'd been active in establishing the Organisation for Joint Armament Co-operation, or OCCAR, which had positioned his company, Armament Météore, as one of the actual authors of its export restrictions and their loopholes. Henri himself was a very vocal presence in the European Defence Agency, the EDA, which gave his company a position with far-reaching influence and respect.

Except with the cursed Americans, who bulled their way around Europe, threatening companies with their sanctions, telling them who they could and couldn't do business with, interfering with their sovereign rights as French citizens to follow their own laws, see to their own interests. Americans sought the role of the world's peacekeeper, depending on who was in power any given year, but Henri thought them imperialists, like their cousins the now toothless English had been throughout history. What choice did they leave him but to find ways around them? Off the books, of course—disguised shipments through third countries, payments in cash through small regional banks, even using the ancient Persian system of havaleh and its regional brokers to make sure his payments moved across borders secure and out of sight, as they had since the eighth century. No traces of anything to piss the Americans off, all under their radar.

He sighed. All was going so well, until the unexpected cock-up by the Iranian military, and loss of the flash drive that could end with the American CIA tracing it all back to him. It would mean prison and the destruction of his company, and he wasn't about to let that happen. He'd railed at the Iranian general who'd sent the soldiers after the CIA agent, and he, naturally, had blamed the captain for disobeying orders. And now the flash drive had disappeared as well as one of the CIA agents. Henri had sent his own man to the US to take care of the matter, and he'd failed. Claude Dumont, the idiot, had left a dead man behind, and not just any dead man. Razhan Hasid was an Iranian security agent they'd insisted be involved. Well, that hadn't worked out as they'd hoped, had it? Henri had no doubt the American CIA would identify Hasid soon, what with all the new computer technology the Americans had. He rubbed his fist into his palm. Dumont's incompetence was unacceptable, and anyone who worked for him knew it. He hated failure.

In fourteen years he'd had to use mortal discipline only three times. Perhaps now he'd have to make it four if there was any chance the Americans could trace Claude back to him. But how could they? He might give Claude one more chance.

Henri drummed his fingers on his ebony desktop, thinking through the blunders that shouldn't have happened. For the first time, he felt a tingling of fear. He got hold of himself; he could deal with this.

He rose, walked to the window of his sixth-floor office to stare beyond the thriving city of his birth to the hills beyond, toward his family vineyard. His vineyard now, since he'd saved it from bankruptcy along with the company from his father's excesses and stupidity.

At a knock on the door, he called out, *"Entrez."*

His own personal assistant, Trevor Cavandish, minced into his office, a frown on his face. A dapper little man, maybe five and a half feet in lifts, he was dressed in his habitual too-tight Savile Row suit, a frown on his face. He was older than Henri, at least sixty, and he dyed his hair black as midnight, reminding Henri of a manager for a second-rate cabaret on the Left Bank. Still, he was useful, had the brain of a chess master who saw twelve moves ahead.

"Oui, Trevor? *Qu'est-ce qui se passe?"*

Trevor knew his boss spoke French only to remind him a Frenchman ruled his life—Henri spoke only minimal French—as a point of pride. Because Trevor was very well compensated, he let it go. His status-conscious boss didn't know Trevor had been born in Liverpool to two very common parents named Smythe, though he claimed Mayfair in London. He said smoothly, in his carefully learned Oxford Brit, "You are aware the CIA agent, Olivia Hildebrandt, killed Hasid at her house last night."

"Of course I know. Claude called me, whining."

"Yes, well, he will arrive within the hour. He wishes to explain what happened to you personally, which, I imagine, will find no favor."

Henri said, "You of all people know I despise failure. He knows quite well what this could mean. It's a fine kettle of fish, isn't that what you English say? I've decided to send René to straighten things out."

"René will not be happy. He enjoys his current mistress in Cannes."

René had always been a vicious creature who wallowed in death and mayhem. "I hope he doesn't hurt her since he takes after the old man." Henri shrugged. "He will do as he's told." René was many things, but he understood necessity and financial recompense. He would clean up the mess Claude left in the United States. "I will deal with our clients."

Trevor knew Henri preferred leaving any killing he needed done to his vicious younger brother. Trevor hoped René would never be sent to visit him.

"We must move quickly. Get René on the phone, Trevor."

12

Mia's Apartment
One Lincoln Plaza
New York City

TUESDAY MORNING

Mia didn't have to show herself at the *Guardian* until the afternoon, so after happily chowing down her latest favorite breakfast, a cup of tea and an English muffin loaded with peanut
butter, she sat at her ancient desk in her sweats and wrote notes
about her impressions of the players she'd met at the fundraiser. She'd finished her second cup of tea when her boss,
Milo, called, and said right out of the gate, "I didn't want to
wait. Tell me about the fundraiser."

She grinned into her cell. "Well, hello to you, too, Milo,"
and she told him about the Cabot Hotel, the ballroom with a
gazillion red, white, and blue balloons, open bar, everything
first class down to the bite-sized tacos . . .

When she finished, Milo said, "Harrington's campaign

manager, Cory Hughes, costs big bucks, but I think he's a good choice, smart, an excellent debater. He could even bring my mother-in-law around, so watch out for him.

"Now, you don't have a lot of hours to spend researching the Harrington family, so I asked our intern Kali to put together a landing page for you with some of what you'll need to know and some photos." He gave her the link. "I've met the Harrington family so I can add some things Kali wouldn't know. First off, there's Harrington senior, Theodore Talbot Harrington. Theo's quite a character, decided years ago he was too ugly, too short, and too honest to be a politician, and besides, he sweats too much under lights. But I'm sure he's very pleased to be backing his son. He's been one of the powers behind the throne in Boston politics for over thirty years now. A politician wants a big lift, thinks the right way, and maybe Theo will put some bucks in his coffer and good words with other movers and shakers."

Mia scrolled to his picture. Ugly was right. He was squat, heavy, even his arms seemed too short. He wasn't smiling, but she saw intelligence in his dark eyes. She imagined he was a formidable opponent. Mia said, "He looks ruthless."

"Yeah, both in politics and in business."

"I hope he has a great personality."

Milo grunted. "Not particularly, but he's got the gift of the gods—the gift for making money. He still rules as chairman and CEO of the First Street Corporation in Boston with all its real estate and manufacturing assets.

"Now, take a look at his wife, Brianne Gregory Harrington, Alex's mother. Lucky for Alex, she gave him his handsome face and his height. She's a social powerhouse in her own right, on the boards of a number of charities, sponsors up-and-coming artists. She's a poster girl for good breeding and old money."

Mia admired her wonderful bone structure, and her smile, charming but aloof. And her great posture. There was a picture of the three of them together, with Theodore Harrington looking like a poorly carved quarry stone between two statues of fine marble. "She looks like a princess. I wonder why she married Theo? For his money?"

"Nah, it would make sense if that was the reason, but she's from a rich family, no need to marry for more. In fact it's said her daddy considered Theo no better than a low-class dockworker. Word is it's a love match. Go figure. They had two children, Alex, now thirty-four, nearly thirty-five, and a younger sister, Liliana, thirty-one. Bless her heart, she looks more like daddy, but in her case it wasn't a drawback. She's done well, married to a physician, has three young children, and lives in Newport. Actually I've met her. She's homely, true, but she's sincerely nice, Mia, she's kind. And she's as smart as her daddy.

"I don't know if you met Kent Harper last night, but he's going to be a player in this campaign, whether officially or not. He's Harrington's oldest friend, also from Boston, also old money. Look at the photo Kali found of the two of them in their freshman year at Harvard drinking beer at the local hangout. They're having a great time, both big gamers, both wearing gaming T-shirts. They've been friends since they were kids.

"And next there's Pamela Raines Barrett, Harrington's fiancée of three months. They'll be bringing her front and center into the campaign when the time comes. They're to be married in a big August society shindig on Nantucket, where the

Harringtons have a summer home. You can see she's a looker, has a pretty smile, but my buddy at the *Globe* who's been around her says Pamela's got a solid underlayer of mean, doesn't give a crap about anyone who's not in her own social class. She's thirty-one, married and divorced early, no children, and lucky enough for that not to matter because she was born into a solid Boston Brahmin family with scads of old money. She's doubtless known Harrington most of her life since they're in the same social group. Oh yes, she's an interior designer with ready-made access to monied clients, and she's making something of a splash for herself in Boston.

"Get a good taste of what to expect, Briscoe, she's an important piece. You'll want to interview her when you go to Boston tomorrow.

"Oh yes, and here's a photo of Juliet Ash Calley, too. She was Harrington's fiancée for a while, some two years ago. Maybe you've heard of her, she's—"

"You mean Juliet Ash Calley, the concert pianist?"

"That's her. Never heard her play myself, but she's performed at Lincoln Center and Carnegie. She's a knockout in the photo, lovely warm eyes, maybe a bit on the shy side? People like her, praise her. Who knows why she's out of Harrington's life now, but it'd be interesting to see what she'd have to say about him. So give her a call, set up an interview. Kali checked. She's at home in Boston.

"I'm out of time, gotta go, the FBI is calling back." He laughed. "I knew they'd jump at the Agent Sherlock fluff piece I dangled in front of their noses. Be here by one o'clock."

"FBI? Agent Sherlock? What piece?" But Milo was gone.

* * *

Mia was reading about Harrington's years at Bennington Prep when her cell buzzed again, and she jumped. Milo again? More dirt to dish about the Boston players? But then she smiled. It was Gail Ricci, one of her friends from Godwyn, calling her from Rome, where she'd lived for the past six years with her Italian husband, Francesco Ricci, and her daughter, Lucia. Gail had told Mia she'd be grateful to her parents forever for giving her the Italian trip for her graduation present. She and Mia still kept in touch, with emails and an occasional phone call.

"Gail! Goodness, what a treat. What's going on? Everything's good, right?"

Gail laughed. "Everything is good in Ricci-land. Mia, I know it's your workday, but I found something and I need to talk to you. Do you have time?"

"Sure, for you I've always got time."

"Actually, Lucia was playing in my dresser drawer and she found my ancient Apple 5 cell phone, the one I had at Godwyn. Long story short, I was looking through the gazillion stored photos on it and there are a couple of shots from that frat rave on the night Serena disappeared. I actually forgot I took them, but remember, we were all drunk as skunks. The photos aren't great, there's some motion, some blurriness, but I want you to see them. Emailing now."

The rave? The night Serena disappeared? Mia froze, couldn't breathe. She whispered, "Do you see her, Gail? Do you see who took her?"

"I don't know, but maybe you can see something."

Mia brought up the photos. The first one showed a roomful

70

of college kids, laughing, talking, dancing, most of them drinking, even on the dance floor. She made herself out, standing beside—yes, it was Norton Canberry, now a professor at MIT. He was probably trying to explain vector analysis or some such thing to her and she was laughing her head off.

"The second photo," Gail said, "Serena's photo—it's blurry because I probably just raised my cell and snapped it."

Serena, Mia's best friend for three years at Godwyn. She looked wildly happy and wildly drunk. Mia felt a horrible punch of loss, of rage. She managed to get hold of herself, swallowed her tears, and concentrated on the man standing next to Serena. A profile, but she could see he was gesticulating with his hands. "Gail, do you recognize the man talking to Serena?"

"No. Remember, Mia, there were lots of grad students who crashed the rave, hoping to find an undergraduate hookup, or at least get laid. This guy could even be from another college. The Godwyn Delta Rho Phi raves were legendary." She paused. "You told me Godwyn canceled every rave on campus after Serena disappeared. Mia, do you know someone who could work some magic on these photos? Help identify all those people, especially that man with Serena?"

Mia's heart was pounding. Finally, after all these years, seven years to be exact. Maybe now, just maybe. "Yes, I do. His name is Dirk Melcher, the *Guardian*'s photographer. He's a pro's pro, has a gift, really, and if anyone can sharpen up these pictures digitally he can. Now, the guy she's talking to, I can tell he's not that much taller than Serena, which makes him maybe five foot ten, eleven. And look, Gail. Do you see the other man standing off to the side? We see only his profile. He's wearing jeans, a black tee. He's much taller, at least six foot two. Look closely, Gail. Isn't he reaching his hand out toward those drinks on the table? And he's got a bracelet on his wrist."

Gail said, "I don't know him, either. You think he might be roofieing Serena's drink?"

"Maybe. Gail, look at the bracelet."

"Okay, he's wearing what looks like a chunky silver chain on his left wrist. I never knew any Godwyn boys who wore a bracelet like that."

"Me either. Even blurry, you can recognize lots of people, right? Even if you've forgotten their names? But this guy talking to Serena, and the other one standing off to the side—Gail, I don't think they belong there. One of these guys might have drugged her, took her, maybe even set the fire to get her out."

"Lots of maybes, Mia. Don't jump the gun. Maybe this Dirk Melcher can sharpen the photo enough so we can identify them. Then maybe the police can contact them, speak to them."

Mia magnified the photo of Serena, sharpened the edges with her cell phone photo app. "Okay, the shorter guy has light hair, nearly blond. He's slender, nothing really distinctive about him that I can see. He's waving his arms, maybe slashing down like he has a sword? Like he's acting out a character in a video game? And look, Serena is laughing, pretending she's getting sliced through. I remember Serena told me, when we were coming back from the bathroom, about a guy she met, but I never saw him. She said he was a gamer, like she was. *World of Warcraft*, that was Serena's favorite. Her handle was Aolith." Mia swallowed. "Serena thought Aolith was a magical name.

"Wait, Gail—look closely at the guy with the chunky

bracelet. Do you see a sort of notch in his earlobe, like he was wearing an earring and it was ripped off? Or maybe it's a shadow, can you tell?"

"Okay, maybe, but I can't be sure. Look, we have only the two photos I shot at one point in the evening. Early? Late? I don't remember. There were so many of us packed into the frat house, and we were all over the place, including the upstairs bedrooms." Gail paused a moment. "Mia, I wondered if I should even send you the photos, but I knew I had to. You loved her so much."

"Thank you, Gail. I'm so glad you did. Now I have to do what I can with them. After Dirk works his magic, I'll email them back to you, see if they ring any bells." As she spoke, she was staring at the notch in the larger man's earlobe and the chunky silver bracelet on his wrist. "Give Lucia a big kiss for finding your old cell phone."

"Mia, wait! I'll admit I was hesitant to send them to you because I worried what you'd do, that it could be dangerous. I know you, and I want you to promise me you won't go playing Lois Lane and haring off after these two men by yourself. Please promise me after this Dirk cleans them up, you'll give the photos to the police."

"And tell them what, exactly, Gail?" Mia said. "Serena was murdered, Gail, probably raped. You know as well as I do that's what happened. I owe her whatever I can do, and right now I can do more than the police can. I promise I'll be careful, and I'll give the police whatever I find." That wasn't the promise Gail wanted to hear, but it was the best Mia could do.

She ended their call and dialed Dirk Melcher at the *Guardian*, caught him just before he was off to a crime scene in SoHo with a reporter. She offered to make him her famous meatloaf if he'd sharpen two old photos for her. Dirk had told her once he'd kill for her meatloaf, and so the deal was quickly sealed. She emailed him the photos. She got to her feet, stretched, stared again at them, then got herself a fresh cup of tea and went back to Kali's landing page, but it was hard to concentrate. Mia got up and walked to the large window overlooking Central Park. Not many people out, too cold, the wind whipping the naked tree branches. For the first time in seven years, she felt a leap of hope. The two young men in the photos, they were seven years older now, in their thirties. Were the bastards still out there somewhere roofieing and killing women? Was Serena just one of many? Did they even remember her? No matter if they'd stopped, they were still monsters, still deserved to be in prison for the rest of their lives.

The police and the FBI had both done their interviews, looked into date rapes, deaths, and disappearances at other universities at about the same time. They'd had no luck.

But that was then.

13

The Guardian
1185 Houston Street

TUESDAY, EARLY AFTERNOON

The Guardian was an old grande dame of a building, mellow redbrick, built in the thirties by Alfred Lowell to an impressive fourteen stories. The newspaper, still owned by the Lowell family, sprawled over most of the top five floors.

Mia stepped into the noisy newsroom, one floor below where the bigwigs hung out. She was so used to the chaos she barely heard the clacking keyboards, people talking to one another and on their cells, a senior editor chewing out a reporter inside one of the glass offices lining the room about something involving a lame-ass tagline as she walked to her cubicle. She saw a soda can go flying toward Janine, who deftly caught it. Janine was the *Guardian*'s woman-about-town writer, known as the Scooper by her colleagues. She saluted, popped the top, and drank.

Dirk Melcher waved to Mia. She gazed fondly at him; he was supertalented and always ready to help, always ready with a joke. He was thin as a stick and movie-star handsome, but even at twenty-four, he hadn't picked up yet when a woman was into him. He wore Lady Gaga T-shirts in the summer, primarily those with her singing her heart out, and thick Madonna hoodies from January to the end of April, primarily with Madonna with very few clothes on.

"Hey, Briscoe!" Dirk handed Mia two eight-by-ten prints. "Best I can do, Mia. I tried everything, even swallowed my pride and called my buddy Thor, master of all things pixel. Thor has access to some NSA software he has no business having, but even then, because of the limited resolution, the camera motion, and the compression, neither of us could get the two guys' profiles any clearer, sorry."

Mia took the photos from him, cursed under her breath. She'd hoped, prayed, but she still didn't think she could identify these men if they were standing right in front of her, waving in her face. At least now she could see the taller man's outstretched hand more clearly, a large hand with a smattering of dark hair, reaching toward a drink on a side table. The heavy silver link chain around his left wrist was clear enough. She looked more closely. Wait, was he reaching for one of the glasses, or was his hand right above it? She couldn't tell, but why wouldn't he reach for a drink that was closer? Would any glass do? No, Serena was close by. The glass had to be hers, had to be.

She saw the healed tear in his left earlobe, the notch more obvious with Dirk's enhancements. She leaned down, gave him a big hug, kissed his cheek, knew he'd pulled out all the stops, and so she said, "You're my hero. What you've done is amazing, beyond what I expected." She lifted a foil-covered pan out of her messenger bag. "Your meatloaf, my man. Defrosted, ready to pop in your oven at 350 for thirty minutes. Mashed potatoes suggested as a pleasing accompaniment." No need to tell him it had been in her freezer for three weeks. "Really, Dirk, thank you. You're a genius. And thank Thor."

He grabbed the meatloaf, breathed it in through the foil. "Smells like ambrosia, then again"—he gave her a wicked grin to break hearts, if only he knew—"I'm a god, so I deserve it." He cocked a dark brow at her. "God or not, I'm the one who made out on this deal. And no, I'm not about to let Thor in on my payoff." He cocked his head, studied her face a moment. "What is this all about, Mia? Why these photos? They're old, blurry, I mean, look at the technology, maybe eight years out of date. Who are these guys and why are they so important to you?"

Mia kissed his thin cheek again, breathed in the sandalwood soap he used. "I promise to tell you when I know. Enjoy the meatloaf. Maybe add a stick or two of broccoli, adds nice color." She would have given him another hug, but he was clutching the meatloaf to his chest like a baby.

She walked over to Kali Knight, their intern studying journalism at Columbia, and, for the moment, Milo's gofer. Mia always wanted to cuddle her, she was so small and shy, her blue eyes huge behind her large black-framed glasses. She was the baby in the newsroom, the youngest on staff at only twenty, but she was already their social media guy's right hand. Benny was all of twenty-six and nabbed Kali whenever Milo gave her a free ten minutes. She'd done an excellent job in a very short time researching Harrington's life and the Harrington family in Boston. She was as good at online research as any of them, but she had at least five more years of technology tucked under her arm, which made her faster.

Kali was bent over something at her desk. Mia lightly touched her shoulder. Kali looked up and smiled.

"Thank you, Kali, the Harrington landing page was perfect. You saved me hours of research."

"No problem, Mia. I enjoyed it. The Harringtons, the facts about the family, the jazzy photos, it's all amazing. And a summer place on Nantucket. They live in a different world. My dad would hate them."

"Maybe my dad would, too." Mia made her way to her desk, put her messenger bag in a drawer, and sat down in her squeaky chair. She laid the two photos on the desk and studied them, traced her finger over their profiles. Truth be told, she couldn't be sure if the blond guy gesticulating to Serena had anything at all to do with Mr. Notched Ear with his thick silver chain-link bracelet. *Who are you? Gail didn't recognize you, I don't recognize you. You crashed the rave, didn't you? You're both older, too, I think, and you know each other. I'll bet my new dolphin earrings you do. You were there together to pick out a girl and roofie her, weren't you? You've done that before? Of course you have. I bet you two have a plan in place that works for you. You know the steps to follow, what to do and when to do it. Find a girl both of you like, shouldn't take you long. I don't think you wanted to kill Serena, why would you? But this time something went wrong, didn't it? Is that why you set the fire in the kitchen, so you could get her out of there? You know what, you bastards? I'm going to figure out who you are, you'll see.*

"What'd you say, Briscoe? Stop garbling your words, speak up, I didn't hear you."

Mia jumped, craned her head around to see her boss, everyone's boss, Milo Burns, standing beside her desk, arms crossed over his chest. As usual, Milo looked like he'd slept in his trademark khakis and golf shirt—Augusta green today—always short-sleeved, even in this early spring that had dumped truckloads of arctic air on the East Coast, no end in sight. He told everyone he was born bald as an egg, a lie of course; everyone knew he religiously shaved his head. Mia both respected him and liked him because he thrived on off-the-wall ideas, some of them his own, some of them amazingly clever, but he never stinted on praise when one of the staff came up with a winner. And he was a natural debater, could take the other side of any question and have you nodding in agreement before you caught yourself. He lived in the Village with his new wife, a bright young tax attorney from Hong Kong, named Kiki, about Mia's age. Milo called her Lotus Blossom. She was small, delicate, and firmly in control of her husband. Seeing her holding Milo's big paw for the first time had made Mia shake her head at what life dished up. Milo loved Chinese food, a good thing since Kiki was a gourmet cook of all things Chinese, her steamed pork buns to die for. He'd brought his own birthday cake to the press room, claimed it was chocolate filled with chunks of crispy fortune cookies, with Hunan icing. No one wanted much to try it when he offered, a smirk on his face.

He picked up the photos, frowned. "What are these photos?

Quality's crap, we can't use them, whoever they are. Who are they?"

Mia gently removed the photos from her boss's hand.

"It's something I'm checking into in my spare time, no worries, Milo. They're not work related."

He gave her the stink eye. "You still have spare time with the deadline I gave you? It's for your blog, isn't it? Lucky for you it's so popular and brings readership to the *Guardian*. I expect your first five-thousand-word background piece to run in this Sunday's edition. No flu, no colds, just work."

Milo picked up one of the photos again, studied it more closely. He cocked his head. "Hmm. You know, this one guy looks familiar, even though it's only his profile. Who is he?"

It was on the tip of her tongue to tell him what she suspected, but no, it was way too soon. "That's what I don't know, Milo. If I find out who he is, and what he is, I'll tell you."

He stared at her a moment, ran his hand over his bald head. "So you're after him about something. Whatever. Come into my office, Briscoe, the yahoos are too noisy out here. I want to hear more about your plans for Harrington. Tell me what you're planning to do in Boston, who you're going to see. You're leaving tomorrow, right?"

Mia followed her boss into his large glass-windowed office and settled back into what everyone on staff called the electric chair. "To spare you some time, Milo, my plan is to interview everyone from Kali's landing page I can get to in Boston, and Harrington's campaign staff here in New York, of course. I hope to talk with the man himself today. And I'd like to make time when up in Boston to head over to Harvard, talk to his professors. I'm thinking about calling his coach at Bennington Prep in Connecticut. Alex Harrington was really into lacrosse, helped win a championship for Bennington Prep. Coaches often remember more about their kids than anyone else." *Like bad habits, suspected bad behavior, drugs, who knew?*

Milo said, "Never played lacrosse, a snooty private school game, my dad always said, not nearly as tough as football." Milo called up one of Kali's photos, angled his laptop so both of them could see it. "There he is, good-looking kid. What, about seventeen, eighteen? You can tell he's going to grow up to be a chick magnet."

She pointed. "The kid next to him is his BFF we talked about, name's Kent Harper."

"Yeah, as I told you, he runs his family's New York branch in New York, Harper Strategic Services, huge in insurance. I'm thinking he's a string to pull too. Maybe you can worm a secret or two out of him." He studied his photo again. "Kent definitely has the look of the wingman, like Robin to Batman."

Mia studied the photo again, slowly nodded. "Thank you, Milo, you just might be right."

Milo frowned at her, sat back in his big tufted black chair. "So if you don't have any more to say, get out of here and find out everything Harrington's done since he was sucking his thumb and finger-painting the walls of his nursery. I don't pay you to sit there grinning at me."

14

Sherlock called Dillon while waiting for Special Agent Kelly Giusti of the New York Field Office to pick her up from the Thirty-Fourth Street helicopter pad in her new white Fiat she called Baby. "I'm here at the helipad. Kelly's not here yet, probably caught in traffic so I have a few minutes. How's Sean? What's happening on the Southern Front?"

She heard him pause, knew something was going on, waited. He said, "Sean is fine. Actually, I have something interesting involving a CIA operative and the CIA brass. And yes, I won the first round. The operative, Olivia's her name, is up to her neck in trouble. I'll know more when we speak tonight. Is it as frigid in New York as here?"

"More so, I'll bet, given the cold air whooshing down the long canyons between the tall buildings. I'm bundled to my eyebrows, don't worry."

"I can't imagine Brickson, New York, is a hotbed of crime, but New York certainly is. You be careful, all right? And call me when you figure out what happened or if you need any help on my end."

She grinned into her cell. "Of course I'll be careful and I'll keep you posted. Here's Kelly. Brickson's roughly an hour east, depending on traffic, so she can give me all the details. Miss me. Talk to you later. Make sure Sean brushes his teeth."

Savich laughed and disconnected.

"Hey, Sherlock! Bless you for coming."

After Sherlock stowed her go-bag in Baby's back seat and quickly climbed in, Kelly fired her up, turned the heat on high. "You ready? Baby loves to let it rip, but since this is business, I'll keep her law-abiding. There won't be much traffic, since it's freezing and only crazy people are out today. And cops. And we don't need that embarrassment. Listen to that wind, it's howling louder than a chorus of witches."

Once they were out of the worst of Manhattan traffic, of which there wasn't much, Kelly turned, gave Sherlock a smile. "Thank you again for coming. My SAC, Mr. Zachery—well, of course you know him. He sends his thanks, said to tell Savich hello for him. He, ah, wanted me to tell you you weren't to feel pressured to find answers to solve this mess."

Sherlock groaned. "Thanks loads."

Kelly turned, grinned at her. "All right, that was a whopper. We're all praying you'll see something everyone missed." She gave Sherlock a fat smile, then grew serious. "We're driving directly to the crime scene in Brickson. You know the basics, but let me give you all the details so you'll know what to expect. As you know, we weren't involved in this triple murder until four weeks ago. It happened at the house of a Dr. Douglas Madison. He, his wife, Ellen, and a neighbor, a Mr. Stanley La Shea, were shot to death. The local police thought it was a home invasion or a robbery gone bad at first—their jewelry, rings, and wallets were missing, but it didn't quite add up. They found out Dr. Madison had recently broken off an affair with a local real estate agent, Angela Storin. The same Ms. Storin had reported her Walther PPK stolen two weeks before the murders, and it turns out the bullets were the same caliber as the crime scene bullets, which doesn't prove anything, but still. We've checked the few traffic cams, surveyed the neighbors, but nothing.

"The Madison house is large, like most of the houses in that neighborhood, the lots big and filled with mature trees. Easy to sneak around, and like I said, we interviewed everyone in a three-block radius of the house. We checked Storin's cell phone location records, but we haven't been able to put her near the crime scene.

"Storin claims she was at home by herself, but I'm as sure as I can be she murdered all of them—Dr. Madison, his wife, and the neighbor. Storin's been married twice, and both her previous husbands are both dead, probably murdered.

"Her first husband, Martin Orloff, divorced her six years ago and remarried, died in a hang glider accident while on vacation in Rio with his new wife. It was obvious someone had cut partly through the flight controls, but no one was ever arrested. Angela Storin's passport records show she was in Brazil at the time, but again, not enough. That case is still open too.

"Her second husband, Philip Storin, was shot to death in

his car three years ago, about a year after he divorced her and moved to Alabama. From Ms. Storin's credit card records, they were able to show she was in Alabama at that time, too. She'd attended a real estate conference in Huntsville and that was the reason she was even in Alabama. Unfortunately, she had an excellent alibi, a seminar with a dozen other real estate agents. I know in my gut she did it, but I can't figure out how, no one can. The case is still open.

"When the local Brickson police discovered all this, they called the FBI in New York City to investigate her as a possible Serial. I've worked the case solid for a week now, turning over every rock I can find. I hate to admit it, Sherlock, but I've hit a wall; I can't see my way through to nailing Angela Storin. And I know she's guilty. I've interviewed her, of course, not that she said much; her lawyer did the talking. She simply repeated she was innocent, but she barely kept the smirk behind her eyes. But I saw that smirk, that gleam of 'I'm smarter than you,' and she knew I knew, but—" Kelly shrugged. "She did it on purpose, all the while acting like this brave little soldier being tortured by the gestapo. I've studied people like her, Sherlock, as have you. Other than the placid façade she never dropped, I still saw the arrogance. And I could see there's something off about her, something missing, you could say. The lead police detective I spoke to believed that, too, said when he spoke to her she was 'scary calm,' utterly emotionless, and expressed surprise he even called her, much less actually came to see her, to question her. *Her?* And that's why he was pleased to turn it over to us.

"She has flummoxed everyone, Sherlock; even the lead

detective in Brickson admitted it. He told me he was relieved to hand over the case to the FBI and that I was made the lead."

Sherlock said, "So she admitted the affair. Did she admit Dr. Madison had broken it off?"

"She didn't deny it, she couldn't, but added that that sort of affair always fizzles out, no harm no foul, both parties unhurt. But according to Madison's sister, he said he'd slept with her for about six weeks, but got his act together, realized he loved his wife, and told Storin it was over. When asked about this, Storin said his sister hates her, and we can't believe anything she says about her or their affair.

"You've seen her photo. Storin's a plain, frumpy forty-year-old woman who wears low baize pumps, suits in dull colors with no particular style, no makeup, hair that hangs limp. The thing is, behind that plain and proper person she presents to the world, she's what I said—she's arrogant, thinks she's smarter than me, than everyone.

"She's recognized as the best upper-end real estate agent in the area. The locals no longer wonder why she presents herself as a dowd, they just shake their heads, call it her shtick."

Kelly banged her fist on the steering wheel and apologized to the Fiat. "It really threw me when I first met this prim, plain woman who badly needed a makeover. And all I could think was, how did you land two husbands and a lover? You must be great in bed." Kelly spurted out a laugh.

Sherlock repeated slowly, "You sensed something was off with her, Kelly, sensed there was a lot more going on with her than she showed to the world. That's a powerful feeling, and it can be the best clue we've got. What interests me is you told me Storin has traveled from New York to Washington dozens of times in the past three years. Planes, trains, automobiles. But you said you didn't know where she goes, or why."

Kelly said, "We do know she took Dr. Madison with her five or six times when they were together, so everyone's thinking it has to be some kind of convenient hideaway where they wouldn't be recognized. Of course we examined Dr. Madison's records, Storin's as well, but we don't know where they stayed. Washington, Maryland, Virginia? We don't know. We're stuck, Sherlock. We have only a bone-deep knowledge she's guilty of multiple murders. We have no witnesses, no gun, nothing I can grab on to, nothing to shake it out of her, and believe me, I've tried. Her lawyer, Abel Clooney, is a powerhouse, articulate, and he protects Storin, treats her like she's Mother Teresa. Makes you want to kick his capped teeth off. You'll meet him."

Sherlock laughed. "He's expensive, I gather?"

"Costs the moon. She's the top in her field, lots of substantial commissions from the properties she sells, so she can afford him. I can't dispute it, she does have a very healthy bank account."

Kelly fell silent as she passed a slower SUV.

Sherlock watched Kelly tap her gloved fingers on Baby's steering wheel. She said, "I wonder why she murdered the wife and the neighbor? Why didn't she kill only Dr. Madison?"

"Differing ideas about that," Kelly said. "My opinion is Storin hated the wife, decided she was the only stumbling block to true love and had to be removed. Or she believed Dr. Madison betrayed her—that fits with her murdering her two ex-husbands—and the wife was bonus points. Or she wanted to murder them both. You'll look, tell me what you think. But it's obvious Mrs. Madison was shot first.

"Bottom line, I can't let her get away with murdering three people, five counting the ex-husbands. I know who she is, Sherlock, what she is, and that's a psychopath, a stone-cold killer."

Kelly signaled, steered the Fiat around an eighteen-wheeler, earning a honk from the driver and a thumbs-up.

Sherlock thought about this. "Angela Storin owned a Walther PPK, had a license?"

"Correct. She claims the Walther was stolen two weeks before the murders. She called the local cops to report it. She claims she'd only shot it once, that her second husband gave it to her, registered it, showed her how to use it, but she says she hates guns, never used it. She also claims she put it in a cardboard box in her garage, simply forgot about it." Kelly turned on her blinker and took the Brickson exit. "Brickson is one of Manhattan's bedroom communities, mostly middle-class, a mixed community, but the doctor's neighborhood, in the north end, is the primo spot to live."

A few blocks off the highway, Kelly turned right onto Hickory Street. The lots grew larger, as did the houses. Most were older, established, their yards filled with trees hunkered down in the frigid winter wind.

The Madison house was at least a hundred years old, with a deep wraparound porch. It sat in the middle of a heavily forested lot, looked for all the world like a precious old queen from a bygone era. The closest neighbors were a hundred feet away through swells of maple and oak trees, a good cover for someone not wanting to be seen. It was obvious no one had been taking care of the yard. Potted hanging plants were dead, the grass overgrown.

Sherlock wanted to be alone in the house so Kelly handed her the keys and stayed in the car, heater on high, working on her tablet. Even bundled up to her eyebrows, Sherlock was shivering as she removed the yellow crime scene tape and stepped into the empty house. She stood silent a moment in the bare oak entry hall. There was a faint smell of chemicals from the CSI team.

She imagined the house had been welcoming when it was filled with life and light and central heating, but now it felt abandoned, as if even the spirits had moved on. It was all shadows and emptiness and stale air. And very cold.

15

SHERLOCK

Sherlock left the lights off as she walked through the down-stairs—a living room, dining room, family room added on in the back of the house, and Dr. Madison's study, all dignified burgundy leather with an art deco vibe. She saw labeled and numbered bloody shoe prints, black now, smeared into one another, as if the supposed robbers were confused about where to go, or wanted to seem so. She backtracked along the bloody prints to the kitchen where three people had died. Unlike the rest of the house, the kitchen was newly remodeled, starkly modern. She'd seen photos of Mrs. Madison, both alive and dead. She'd been a comfortably plump older woman, rolling out dough for an apple pie at the counter, maybe hoping the crust would turn out flaky enough, when she turned at a sound, a voice perhaps, and Storin shot her in the face. Or had she? Had they argued before Storin shot her? Erased her face, erased her?

Sherlock saw Mrs. Madison had hit the counter as she fell, and the flour spewed upward. She bounced back and crashed to the ocher tiles, on her back, her face covered with bloody flour. She looked down to see gobs of flour still mixed with dried blood on the tiles where the wife had lain. A bowl of rotten apple slices still stood on the counter next to the blood-spattered pie dough. It looked obscene.

The frigid air still carried the taint of copper from all the blood, not surprising given the murders had happened only four weeks before, but the chemical smell that overlay it was heavier. How long would it take for those smells to sink into the walls and the floor, into the very bones of the house? Who would ever want to live here again? But of course, the horrific crime would either fade away or gain more gruesome proportions in the years to come.

Sherlock looked down at the chalk outlines of the three bodies, Mrs. Madison on her back, arms flung away from the body, Dr. Madison's and Mr. La Shea's bodies twisted because they'd hit either the center island or the stove when they'd fallen, both on their sides.

All that was left of three human beings were their white chalk outlines and the bloody flour. There wasn't much near the two men. Sherlock knew Mrs. Madison was murdered before Dr. Madison had come home. Had Storin known Mrs. Madison was alone in the house?

Sherlock backed up and stood quietly in the doorway studying the kitchen. Who was first to die of the men and why? Happenstance? A picture of what had happened didn't come together for her. She knew only that the conclusion reached by the ME and the Brickson detectives and Kelly didn't work for her. She walked out of the kitchen, then walked back in, looked with fresh eyes, and she noticed a kitchen chair was pulled away from the small kitchen nook table, its three brothers still tucked in. All right, the chair could have been moved by the crime scene techs, but she knew they wouldn't do that, no reason to. She then started to see it, nearly clear in her mind. Storin had turned the chair to face the body of Mrs. Madison, and the kitchen doorway, to wait for Dr. Madison to come in. Of course she'd planned all along to kill him as well.

Sherlock smiled as the pieces began to slot themselves together. Yes, Storin pulled out the chair after she killed Mrs. Madison, sat down, and waited. How long had she sat near where Mrs. Madison's body lay on its back, face destroyed, blood all around her head? Kelly had described Storin as emotionless, a psychopath, and that's what she'd have to be. She'd accepted Dr. Madison wasn't coming back to her and it enraged her, sent her over the edge, set her to planning the murder of both him and his wife. Otherwise why wait for him in the kitchen with his dead wife? To make a point. She wondered again if the two women had spoken before Storin shot her. Had Mrs. Madison told her he'd confessed the affair to her and sworn he'd never go back to Storin? When Storin had faced her, had Mrs. Madison insulted her, called her a slut? Is that when Storin shot her? Did Storin even feel a moment of regret? No, Sherlock didn't think so. If anything, Storin had felt justified and excited for the betraying bastard to come home. Soon he would learn what she was made of, that no one screwed around with her, just as those other two bastards had learned their lessons. *What were you feeling when you sat there, Angela? Excited when you heard Dr. Madison call out to his wife because you were about to kill another man who'd left you, betrayed you? Were you eager to see his shock when he saw his dead cow of a wife? Did you preen, laugh, imagine that when he saw her and then saw you he would know he was a dead man? Did he yell at you? Plead for his life, swear he hadn't meant to break it off with you? He loved you and no one else?*

If he'd said anything, it hadn't been enough. She'd killed him and his unfortunate neighbor. And she'd thought sorry, no apple pie for anyone.

Sherlock walked carefully around the chalk outlines and sat down in the chair where Storin had waited. Did she know exactly when Dr. Madison was coming home? It turned out not to be long. The ME had said the killings were no longer than thirty minutes apart.

Thirty minutes sitting in that chair. After she shot Dr. Madison in his forehead, did Mr. La Shea hear the shot, come running in? Or had he been standing with Dr. Madison? And she'd shot Madison, then him. No, that didn't feel right. She didn't think La Shea was in the kitchen when Storin shot Dr. Madison.

Odd how Storin shot Mrs. Madison in the face rather than the forehead. Why? Because she was pissed off to lose? So many questions that would never be answered.

Sherlock knew the ballistics showed Storin had to have been standing when she shot the men, so Sherlock stood up. The investigating team believed Storin had approached Madison with her gun, the supposedly stolen Walther PPK, held in front of her, tracking through Mrs. Madison's blood, and shot him up close. And when La Shea had run in, she fired again, both men shot in the center of the forehead. Steady, steady hand. The team thought she'd already taken Mrs. Madison's jewelry, including her wedding ring, and emptied her jewelry case upstairs, and then she took the men's wallets and their watches to make it all look like a robbery. Then she ran from the kitchen out through the side door, mixing up the bloody footprints, took off her shoes, and left the house. The side door, the team believed, because Storin wouldn't take the chance of going through the front door and being seen. She'd dumped her shoes, her clothes, in case there was blood splatter, and of course the Walther.

The ME determined she'd shot the two men from no more than four or five feet away, any closer and there'd have been gunpowder residue. But that wasn't right. Sherlock looked back at the chair. It stood at least twelve feet from the chalk outlines showing where the men's bodies had fallen. Sherlock sat again in the chair, willed the scene to come clear. Storin heard Madison, and she stood up. But she hadn't moved toward Madison. The jumble of bloody footprints came later.

You stood up and shot them, Angela, which means you're a very fine shot. Twelve feet away and you shot both men in the forehead. With a handgun. You're beyond good, you're excellent.

Sherlock dialed Kelly. "You told me Storin denied she'd shot the Walther, right?"

"Only one time, she said. She claimed she barely knew how it worked, said she only noticed it was gone when she went looking for some papers in her garage safe. Why?"

"I'll tell you in a minute," and Sherlock hung up. She stood, looked down again at the chair. *I'll bet you like to shoot, it gives*

*you a rush. I'm an excellent shot but I doubt I could have made
two such perfect kill shots from twelve feet away, all hopped up on
adrenaline and rage like you were.*

Sherlock walked out of the house, locked the front door,
reattached the crime scene tape, and walked quickly back to
Kelly's Fiat. She got in and quickly closed the door. Thankfully,
the heater was going full blast. She said, "Verify for me, Kelly.
How far away from the victims did the ME say the kill shots
were fired?"

"Mrs. Madison, really close. The two men maybe four to five
feet."

Sherlock said, "Kelly, Storin pulled out a chair from the
kitchen nook table after she shot Mrs. Madison and she sat
there, waited for Dr. Madison to come home. When he and
Mr. La Shea came into the kitchen, she simply stood up
and shot them both. She shot them from twelve feet away, I
counted it off."

Kelly stared at her. "The chair—no one noticed. Twelve
feet? Are you sure?"

"It's what makes the most sense to me. Twelve feet. Everyone assumed that with such perfect kill shots, she had to be
close, within five feet, but she wasn't. Kelly, could you fire two
fast rounds into two foreheads from twelve feet?"

Kelly said slowly, "Maybe, but I'm really good. If I was hyped
up, in a real firefight, with people juking around, it'd be iffy."

"It means she's a shooter, maybe even competed. Shooting
is something she does often, so she needs a gun range to practice. I can't imagine she'd pick one that far away from Brickson.
Let's find it."

Kelly threw herself at Sherlock, hugged her tight. "Would you marry me?"

"What about Cal and Dillon?"

"I'm sure we can find them other duties at which they'll excel."

16

New York City

TUESDAY AFTERNOON

Mia stepped out of the Guardian Building into a splattering cold rain that could freeze your bones and couldn't believe it when a taxi actually pulled over. She stepped quickly into amazing warmth. The driver addressed her in pure Brooklyn. "I hope you're going more than two blocks, lady."

"I am indeed," Mia said and settled herself. "Eighty West Forty-Ninth, at Sixth Avenue."

He fed the taxi into the sluggish traffic, looked in the rearview. "I've taken three or four people there in the last couple of days—it's that guy Harrington's campaign headquarters, right?"

She'd lucked out. A native New Yorker, a nearly extinct breed in New York City. His driver's ID said he was Vincent Toledo. He looked to be in his midfifties with sharp dark eyes and ears sticking straight out from a nearly bald head. He had a flattened nose, probably broken more than once. "Yes, that's

97

right. And what do you think of Harrington? Will you vote for him for mayor?"

He gave her another look in the rearview. "Nah, fellow's just a calf, can't know his butt from his elbow, too young to know any of the players who make this town run right. I know he's swimming in dough, his mama and daddy bankrolling him. No, give me Paulie O'Connor, he's my guy, Brooklyn born and raised, our borough president since the Bloomberg days. He knows all the players, all the right people, he knows how to get things done. Remember the garbage strike last month? He put a word in the mayor's ear and got that shut down like that." And Vincent snapped his fingers. "Paulie knows whose palm to grease, knows whose back to scratch. I'll tell you, the mayor knows what he's got in Paulie, listens to him all the time. But, if not Paulie, then maybe they should change the law; it'd be okay if the mayor stayed in."

"Unfortunately, the mayor is termed out. No changing that law."

"I know, I know, but I can wish, can't I? Bums me out. But Harrington? No way. With him, we'd have garbage up to our armpits."

Pure gold. Mia opened her tablet as fast as she could and kept him talking. By the time the taxi pulled to a stop at the curb in front of Harrington's campaign headquarters, it had stopped raining. Mia gave him a big tip. "Pleasure to meet you, Mr. Toledo. Thanks for your opinions. I'll be sure to include them in the article I'm writing."

"You might win a fancy award if you do. Nobody could disagree with me, unless they're idiots."

She stood a moment, staring after his cab, barely moving

in the heavy traffic. She wondered if Harrington knew Paulie O'Connor. She looked up at the Walcott Building, five years old, all steel and glass. Even in the dull winter light, the acres of glass sparkled. Did his family own the building? She wouldn't be surprised. She glanced down at her watch. Five minutes until her scheduled interview with Harrington.

Mia took the escalator to the second floor and stepped into a long open room that would soon be Harrington's official campaign headquarters. It was filled with people on a mission, some carrying chairs, printers, boxes of supplies, setting up workstations. Mia barely missed running into a plump older woman carrying an armful of large cardboard posters with Harrington's handsome face, his mouth beaming out a smile, a pithy quote underneath, on their way to being plastered throughout the city. The woman only nodded and sailed by her. She spotted Cory Hughes, Harrington's campaign manager, looking as dapper and smooth as he had last night, only today he was in his shirtsleeves, eyeing his watch. She knew he'd been around the political block many times, for both parties, a politico to his heels. Milo had told her Hughes didn't believe much in political philosophies, what he loved was the game and winning the game. His last success was running Governor Siever's campaign. Milo thought Alex Harrington had a good chance of winning with Cory driving the bus.

Hughes spotted her, jogged over, a big smile on his face. "Good morning, Mia, good to see you again. You're right on time, but then you always are, I'm told. Alex is up to his eyeballs today with interviews but I know he particularly wanted to meet with you."

A line she'd expected, but that was okay, it was one of the

rules of the game—make the candidate seem as busy and important as the president but with just enough time for one special journalist.

She gave him a grin and followed him past cheek-to-jowl desks, tangles of electrical cords, computer monitors, and signs everywhere, propped against the desks, against every wall. Many of the volunteers, most under twenty-five, had their cells pressed against their ears or were stuffing envelopes, making huge stacks of them. She could easily tell the volunteers from the paid staff because only the volunteers bothered watching her, wondering who she was and if she was important. The old hands who drew a check recognized her as a reporter and didn't pay her any attention. She saw Miles Lombardy, Harrington's senior staffer she'd met at the fundraiser last night, leaning over someone at a desk, speaking quietly. He looked up, gave her a small wave, but didn't come over.

Cory Hughes ushered her into a glass-walled office to see Alex Harrington sitting behind a banged-up rented desk, with several rented chairs as derelict as the desk in front of it. Obviously a man of the people. He'd taken off his Armani jacket and rolled up his sleeves, the poster boy for the busy candidate hard at work. He ended his cell phone call when he saw her and rose.

He gave her a big smile. "Thanks, Cory, for bringing Mia back." When Hughes had removed himself, closing the door behind him, the noise level fell magically to a low distinct rumble. He said, "Thank you for coming. Cory has assured me he trusts you to be unbiased. As I told you last night, I've been impressed with your blog *Voices in the Middle*. I think you'll find echoes of some of your thoughts in my own campaign, and in my agenda for the city. It's very brave of you, isn't it, given the current no-holds-barred political climate? Too many of us have reduced politics to defending our own tribe, our own turf, rather than nurturing what unites us, and working to make the city a better place to live. Bloodying each other isn't going to get us there."

Harrington had quoted practically verbatim from her blog, which meant he'd done his homework before she'd arrived. He was being smart, careful, stacking the deck in his favor as best he could. Mia nodded, smiled at him as he came around his desk, pulled out a chair for her. She stepped forward and shook his outstretched hand, a strong hand, with a firm grip. Had he practiced it? She looked down and froze, her breath caught in her throat. On his left wrist was a thick silver link bracelet. Automatically, she looked at his left earlobe. Of course there was no sign of a tear. *Stop it—don't be an idiot, lots of men wear bracelets like that, they're popular, manly. Get a fricking grip.*

Harrington said in his pleasing baritone that had carried, she remembered, to the very back of the large ballroom, "Please call me Alex. Come, sit down, let's talk. May I call you Mia?"

He'd already called her Mia, but of course she nodded, sat, and opened her tablet. A staffer knocked and came in, bearing coffee, tea, and cookies. She said as she set the plate down on the desk, "I rescued these yummy Scottish shortbreads before the hordes could ravage them. I love your blog, Ms. Briscoe." She was out the door before Mia could even say thank you.

"That's my campaign secretary and guard dog, Mrs. Millicent.

Her last name is never used. Her sister's been my secretary at First Street Corp. for as long as I've been New York director."

Mia took a shortbread to be polite, but since it wasn't chocolate it didn't really count as a treat. She accepted a cup of black coffee.

Alex Harrington sat back down, steepled his long fingers, and cocked his head.

Mia said, "My taxi driver thinks you're too young, too green to know your butt from your elbow and your daddy and mommy are bankrolling you. And what does a Bostonian know about what New Yorkers want and need?" She smiled, paused a second. "Are you ready to deal with opinions like this?"

To her surprise, Harrington threw back his head and laughed, a rich laugh. Sincere? Mia waited, the smile still firm on her mouth, and watched him.

He stopped laughing and straightened, suddenly serious. "I consider myself a New Yorker. I've lived here seven years now, it's my home. As I'm sure you know, I've been in charge of the New York office of the First Street Corporation for six of those years, which means my elbow and my butt have done a lot of living in New York, and believe me, I've learned a lot. Am I green? Well, if your taxi driver means am I buddies with all the movers and players in the political game here in New York, I'm not, but that has its benefits, too, and I'll be saying so in my campaign. When I'm elected you can be sure I'll meet them fast enough because they will come to me, and I'll be the one who decides what I'll give them, if what they want is in the interest of keeping New York the greatest city in the world. That's what a good manager does, Mia, in politics or in business; I'm a very good manager with years of practical hands-on experience, and I have the vision and drive to make New York flourish under my hand."

She typed in *canned, fluent, a dollop of humor, well spoken.*

Her attention was caught again by the chunky silver chain-link bracelet. Why not? She pointed. "Tell me about the bracelet, Alex. Does it have any special meaning to you? Is it a gift from a friend? A lover? Have you had it long?"

He cocked his head to one side, his smile as firmly on his mouth as Mia's was on hers. He raised his hand and studied the bracelet. "My first bracelet was a gift from my uncle Xavier on my thirteenth birthday. He said, and I quote, 'A real man does and wears whatever he wants.' He told me never to forget that as long as I live."

"Uncle Xavier?"

"My father's second cousin, not really my uncle. My family thinks he's a nasty old man because he thumbs his nose at all their rules, still likes his cocaine, and spends much of his time cruising the Back Bay, carefree, his own man. Ah, but when I was thirteen, he was my idol." He laughed, shrugged.

Was that the truth? Or was Xavier a bit of exaggerated family lore to show her how human he was? "You said the original bracelet. Have there been others?"

"Why all the interest in the bracelet, Mia?"

"Human interest, Mr. Harrington—Alex. It's something personal about you, a proven draw, just like your story about your uncle Xavier. If people can connect to you as an individual, as a real person, not just a politician who wants their vote, well, you get the idea. That's what my first piece will be about—your background, your family, your personal anecdotes, and talk about a draw, Uncle Xavier."

"Fair enough. Actually, it's the third silver link bracelet I've had. My mom bought me this incarnation last Christmas when the second one broke."

She typed *three*, nothing more, and sat forward, her eyes sparkling with interest. "How did you break the first and second bracelets? Anything fun?"

He laughed again. "I broke the first one when I was playing lacrosse at Harvard. I was heading to score and one of the Yalies whacked me on the bracelet. Probably saved my wrist from getting broken, a lot of pain time in a cast, but the bracelet was toast. The second time was only a couple of years ago, when I fell off a mountain bike, and no, I learned my lesson. No more mountain bikes."

Mia said easily, "I saw a photo of you holding up a championship trophy for the Bennington Prep lacrosse team."

His eyes lit up with remembered pleasure.

"And your friend Kent Harper is standing next to you; you have your arm around his shoulders."

He nodded. "Kent and I have been close friends since we were boys. Like me, Kent manages his family's branch office here in New York. I imagine you'll be speaking to him." He cocked his head again, a longtime habit, she supposed. It made him look friendly, approachable.

"Oh yes. I'm hoping he'll have some clever stories about you."

"I'll have to tell him to be very selective."

Mia smiled, said without pause, "Tell me about your stand

on guns, Alex. Your party is in favor of a gun ban. What is your position?"

"I'm not a hunter, but some of my friends take off for Canada to hunker down in blinds while other friends enjoy competitive shooting. Why should I want to deny them an activity they enjoy? But assault rifles, now that's another matter entirely. Gun violence in schools, it sickens me. So, even though I'm not in favor of a complete gun ban, I am committed to banning all weapons that could kill people."

She nodded, made notes. "Let's talk about education. What do you think of charter schools?"

He sat forward, his hands clasped. "I believe some charter schools can fill a need, but I also believe caution is mandatory in terms of how the schools are structured, their educational approaches, their philosophies, their underpinnings. We don't want a Hogwarts school here in New York City."

Mia obligingly smiled since she saw he expected it. She wrote down, *Charter schools—waffles well.* So what did he really think?

She asked about unions and their influence in the lives of everyday New Yorkers and was treated to his political "tribe's" honored position, that is, unions must continue to flourish to protect New York citizens and the rights of the worker. And taxes. "Ah, taxes, the bane of all our existence, from rich man, to poor man, to Indian chief."

Again, she gave him an expected perfunctory smile.

He leaned forward, his eyes on her face, sincerity ringing in his voice. "Regardless of who we are, how much money we earn, we must all contribute fairly to the city coffers. Our great city must function at a high level, to keep not only our citizens safe, but our thousands of yearly visitors. Of course we must also keep our social programs properly funded, and this means evaluating need and impact." He continued in this vein and Mia kept looking at the bracelet on his wrist. He used his hands a lot. He was articulate and sometimes amusing, but still, she could have written what he said without speaking to him. She could have also written what the termed-out incumbent would say without speaking to him. Political tribes repeated their stands like mantras.

When Alex glanced down at his watch, gave a rueful shake of the head, Mia rose. "Thank you for the enlightening interview. As I said, in my first article I'm planning a background piece to start off as an introduction to a series on your campaign. What we spoke about today, that will be in my second article. I'll be heading up to Boston to speak with some of your family there, friends, college connections. Perhaps you could give them a heads-up for me? Tell them I don't bite?"

Mia wished she didn't have to ask him to pave the way, it gave those she was going to speak to time to carefully plan what to say. She'd much rather catch them off-guard. But Milo had insisted.

"Certainly. Unfortunately my parents are on a cruise at the moment, but there are people in Boston who can tell you everything you need to know for a background article better than I can." He gave a rueful smile. "I can only hope they'll be kind. I'll have Mrs. Millicent text you a list of people to see."

Mia said smoothly, "Thank you. Of course I won't have time to speak to all the names on your list." She wondered if any of the names on his official list would cross with the people she wanted to speak to.

She was shown out of his office by the big kahuna himself. He smiled at her and touched her elbow at the door.

During her torturously slow taxi ride to Kent Harper's Madison Avenue address, Mia pulled out Dirk's print of one of the photographs from the Godwyn frat rave. She stared at the chunky silver bracelet on the man's wrist as he reached out his hand toward Serena's glass, well, maybe toward Serena's glass. Maybe. What could she do with these photos by herself? She could look up college friends she remembered were at the rave, and then what? Why would anyone remember more than she did after seven long years? But maybe, just maybe, someone would remember something they'd seen and wondered about. All she could do was try.

17

MIA

Mia's taxi tucked in behind a long black stretch limo in front of the Harper Building at 320 Madison Avenue. She paid the driver, still on his cell, and stood on the sidewalk, people flowing around her, staring up at another tower of glass and steel. Unlike the Walcott Building, this structure looked more like a monument to the future, or the late-twentieth-century's vision of the future. About fifty stories with a steeple on top, it speared into the sky, like the Transamerica Pyramid in San Francisco.

Kent Harper had been a major player in Alex Harrington's life, his closest friend he'd said. Was Kent still his confidant? Like Harrington, he was also the director of his family's firm, Harper Strategic Services, in New York and that meant still more money, more connections for Harrington to draw on. But how involved was he now in his best friend's political campaign? Could Mia catch him off-guard, get him to open up about the Alex Harrington he knew? It was doubtful. Politicians' close friends, especially those used to protecting power of their own, rarely went off-script. Mia hadn't called ahead, but she'd bet her sneakers Kent Harper wouldn't be taken by surprise she was here to see him and had already prepared for her. Fingers crossed he'd see her, she took the express elevator directly to the forty-fifth floor to the Harper Strategic Services executive offices. She stepped onto a large black-and-white marbled floor shined to a high gloss, with art deco sofas and chairs in groupings next to the large windows, their draperies drawn against the dismal weather. Across the expanse an older woman sat behind a dark mahogany desk. Both she and her desk looked uncluttered, sleek and intimidating. Unlike Alex Harrington's Mrs. Millicent, she didn't look the type to waste her time baking cookies; she looked like a dragon guarding the gates, the head of the neighborhood watch.

Mia smiled at her, all warm bonhomie. "Hello, my name is Mia Briscoe. I'm a journalist with the *Guardian*. I don't have an appointment, but I've just come from an interview with Alex Harrington and he really wanted me to meet his best friend, Mr. Harper. Is he free to give me a few minutes?"

Mrs. Irene Wallaby eyed the pretty young woman with the long streaked blond hair loose and shiny around her face, a loose curl here and there, and silently complimented her hairdresser. She noted her face was dominated by intriguing blue-green eyes, high cheekbones, and a lovely mouth that looked like she'd just added a bit more rose lipstick in the women's room. She was tall, which made the slouchy black Hugo Boss jacket, black pants, white shirt, and black stiletto boots look very stylish. Add the lovely smile, not to mention the deferential tone of voice, and Irene decided she would let her into the inner sanctum. She said easily, "I believe you may be in luck, Ms. Briscoe. Mr. Harper just concluded a meeting, probably taking a Mountain Dew break until the next one, which, in fact, never seem to stop." She picked up the phone, turned, and spoke quietly. She turned back, smiling. "He's pleased you're here, Ms. Briscoe, and agrees to see you." She looked down at her iWatch. "You'll have ten minutes."

"That's perfect. Thank you, Ms. Wallaby." When Mrs. Wallaby stood up, she reminded Mia of her own mother, a high school counselor, always well dressed and utterly self-assured. She walked Mia down a gray-carpeted corridor with closed doors on each side and a series of enlarged photos of New York City in the nineteen twenties. Mia wished she had time to browse, but Mrs. Wallaby tapped on a set of beautifully carved ebony double doors, opened them, and stepped aside. Mia walked past her and stopped in her tracks. It wasn't the large office with glass windows and the city spread out below that made her suck in her breath, because Kent Harper was the big boss, after all, it was the incredible display of gaming paraphernalia and posters of game characters that covered the white walls. Because of Serena, Mia recognized the large poster of the tough, patch-over-his-eye warrior from *Metal Gear*. She didn't remember what his name was, or who the other characters on the walls were, but they were all iconic game heroes. Between the posters, gaming artifacts—swords, knives, and elaborate helmets—were beautifully displayed on specially-made shelves.

She saw only one warrior woman, with huge breasts, legs encased in bright red thigh-high boots, a skimpy black crotch-hugging sort of bikini, a vicious curved sword gripped in her hand. Mia remembered how that sort of blatant sexism had burned Serena.

She looked at Harper again, who only now turned from the window to face her. So this man, Alex Harrington's best friend, was a gamer? Her mind flew to the photos in her purse. Did he look like the man who'd been talking with Serena? His hair was more blond than brown, and his build was roughly the same, but there was no way to say. *You're being crazy. Focus, woman. You're here to talk about Alex Harrington.*

She saw something in his left hand. He was squeezing a yellow tennis ball in and out. A stress reliever?

Mia studied him. Her first thought was that Kent Harper didn't have the look of a man who sat in the big office. Where was the Italian suit, the hair perfectly cut, the tie shrieking power? There was no attempt to impress. He wore black wool slacks, a white shirt, open at the neck. He was wearing the requisite Italian loafers at least, but his black wool jacket looked like it had been flung toward the coat-tree behind his quite beautiful art deco ebony desk, and barely managed to hook it. His blue eyes were full of curiosity as he looked at her. He had a laid-back vibe in a young college professor sort of way, his aviator glasses completing the image. But she didn't think he could be all that laid-back, not squeezing the yellow tennis ball.

He nodded to Mrs. Wallaby, and she left, no offer of coffee, no offer of shortbread. On the other hand, Mr. Harper wasn't running for office and Mia was a walk-in.

"Ms. Briscoe," he said and smiled at her showing nice straight white teeth. He discreetly slipped the yellow ball into his pocket, stepped forward, shook her hand. "Please sit down. May I take your coat?"

"No, I'm fine, thank you."

"Alex just called, said you and he had enjoyed a short conversation. He told me you'd probably be dropping by and to make room for you." He laughed. "You didn't waste any time. I told him you'd have to buy insurance from me if you wanted a scoop about the skeletons in his closet."

Mia changed her mind. She'd been expecting a longtime sidekick, Harrington's Robin. But she didn't think he was a Robin; he looked clever, his own man. She smiled back at him as she sat down in the chair he held out for her. She waited until he returned to his big chair behind his desk and said, "If you have any skeletons to offer, Mr. Harper, I'll be happy to buy flood insurance, always a hazard for my eighteenth-floor apartment."

He gave her a quick smile, nodded. "Call me Kent, please. May I call you Mia?"

"Of course."

He said on a sigh, "Let me thank you for breaking up a day crammed with boring meetings. Can you imagine what that's like in the insurance business? I guess I shouldn't disparage the industry that makes me and my family a very nice living, but I tell you, Mia, meeting with Harper's senior accountant, brilliant as he can be, is a trial; there's not a single funny bone in Merkel's body. He doesn't even look at me, stares at my walls and makes me want a drink. Maybe he wants a drink too." A self-deprecating smile, inviting her to join in, and she did.

"You and I have never met, but as I said, Alex told me last night after his fundraiser that you write an excellent political blog, which, alas, I haven't had a chance to look at yet. I assume you came to talk about Alex?"

Mia pointed to the displays on his walls. "This is an awesome display. You're a big gamer, obviously, or were. Is Mr. Harrington a gamer, too?"

If he'd been standing, he might have bounced on his feet. His eyes lit up like a hundred-watt bulb. "Oh yes, at least at Bennington Prep, Alex and I gamed together more than studied, or so our parents thought. We cut back in college, of course, didn't have much time for it. I'm still more of a fan than Alex is; I play to relieve stress, when I need it."

And you squeeze the yellow tennis ball. Mia suddenly heard Serena's voice—*Aolith the dreamer, she's magic. I can see her floating through a green forest, birds fluttering around her, singing to her. And she's a survivor.* What had Serena called that name, Aolith? Her handle, yes, that was it. She said, "Do you have a favorite game, an online handle, I believe it's called?"

"Sure, all gamers do. I go by Snake, short for Solid Snake." He pointed at the large center poster on the wall opposite. "That's why Snake there dominates the stage."

Mia studied the poster. "Talk about domination, with that sword he looks ready for destruction, right? And he really needs a shave."

He was silent a moment, and Mia wanted to kick herself. Then she saw him decide not to be offended. He laughed, stroked his hand over his smooth face. "Good point. It's part of his trademark."

"Your collection is awesome, Kent." Serena had tried to hook Mia on gaming, but it never took. Why was she asking him about gaming anyway? All right, the truth was she couldn't help herself. She said with regret, "Alas, I was never introduced to gaming, even online."

Another wrong thing to say. Mia saw him frown slightly, look down at a piece of paper on his desk. She'd lost his interest again. She sat forward and focused on his face, became the eager student. "I was always interested, but there was no one in my circle to teach me. They're called gaming consoles, right? Like PlayStation 5, Xbox? Is that a console on your shelf there?"

He perked right up, leaned forward, the enthusiastic master ready to instruct the ignorant but willing student. "Oh yeah, it's a classic, my first PlayStation."

"Do your friends call you Snake?"

He shook his head. "Snake, like you said, is a handle and isn't used outside of gaming. Well, almost never," he added. "Alex and I sometimes called each other by our handles when we were growing up. He was Dante—" He pointed to the poster next to Snake, not quite as large. "Dante is an avatar in *DMC*—"

Mia cocked her head and he snapped out, his voice impatient, "*DMC*, the game *Devil May Cry*."

She studied the outrageous character on the poster, a swashbuckler with longish gray or blond hair, wearing a billowing red velvet coat over tight black leather that showed off a ripped body. He held an elaborate sword above his head, ready to lop off a head. He looked sexy and hard and determined. Is that how Alex Harrington saw himself?

"And you and Alex played games like *World of Warcraft* online, with other players?"

"Sure, that's what gamers do, mostly."

"Did you or Mr. Harrington ever wear those outfits when you were kids? Red velvet coats and such? Pretend you were them?"

"Sure, kids and teens do, mostly for Halloween and dress-up parties. But you shouldn't think gaming is any part of Alex's life now. We play together rarely now to amuse ourselves. We both have more important things to think about, Alex in particular. And, well, so do I, really."

"Does that make you sad?"

He gave her a flash of a smile. "Sometimes, I admit it. My youth, great days."

"How about Alex?"

"I'd say Alex is completely focused on becoming the next great mayor of New York City."

"Of course." He was leading her back to talk about Alex, but she didn't want to let it go just yet. She sat forward, her eyes sparkling, and waved her hand at the other posters. "And who are they?"

"That's Nero next to Dante, then Trish, Vergil, all iconic characters. And that's Garrosh Hellscream, Deathwing the Destroyer, Uther Lightbringer—they're all from *World of Warcraft*." He made a sweeping gesture. "All of them are avatars or icons, or portraits or emblems—shorthand for the players' characters."

"And your own avatar, Snake, how does he fight? Does he have a superpower?"

"It's all hand to hand for Snake, no superpower." Kent got to his feet, grinning like a maniac, mimed having a sword in a tight grip above his head and swung it down, cleaving the air.

Mia froze. It was a snapshot, a single moment locked in time, and she saw the man with Serena that night—bringing down a sword and Serena staggering back, pretending he's killed her, laughing. He was that man.

She didn't know how she did it, but she applauded. "Talk about a death blow. You blow me away."

To her relief, the phone buzzed on his desk. He stared at it, sighed, picked it up, slowly repeated, "Mr. Merkel's waiting outside? Now?"

He looked at Mia, shrugged.

She let disappointment fill her voice. "Oh, I'm so sorry, we got so caught up in your display"—she swept out her hands—"I've let what little time we had slip away."

He laughed, raised a finger, spoke quietly into his phone, and hung up. "We can take a few more minutes. I'd like to clear up any questionable impression I may have given you about Alex. As I told you, gaming is something he and I did together when we were young, and now we play only on rare occasions. Adulthood comes to all of us. Both of us have had adult responsibilities for many years now, people who depend on us."

He sat forward, clasped his hands, and tried to look dead serious, even with the gaming icons staring down at them. "Alex is tremendously talented, a born leader. And he's a man of principle, a man you can trust. I firmly believe he's the mayor New York needs now, if he can get himself elected."

The phone on his desk buzzed again. He sighed, rose. "I wish we had more time, but alas, duty calls." He came around his desk, shook her hand, held it a moment longer than was customary. "It was a pleasure meeting you, Mia. If you make an appointment next time, Irene can clear a block of time for you. I'll convince you Alex is the man New York needs as mayor. Ah, maybe you'd like to have a drink with me sometime? I could teach you more about gaming."

She smiled at him. "Yes, I'd like that."

18

New York City

TUESDAY AFTERNOON

When Mia stepped into the newsroom, the first person she saw was Judy Larrson, an assistant editor, who was married to a gamer husband she threatened to divorce twice a month. Should she ask to speak to Judy's husband? Maybe, and she could study online, ask around. Gamers were thick on the ground everywhere, weren't they? Kids, teens, adults of all ages—and Serena. Next time she spoke with Kent Harper, she could know enough to engage him.

She made her way to her desk, sat down, shoved her messenger bag in a drawer, and wondered: Why did she want to engage Kent Harper? *Because I'm nuts, that's why. Because I saw him slash down his gaming sword like that man did that night at the rave with Serena.* Even after seven years, Mia would swear his movements looked exactly the same, fluid, fast, practiced, the warrior. She remembered how excited Serena had been that night; she was having so much fun. *He's a gamer, Mia. How lucky is that? He knows everything.*

And Alex Harrington wore a chunky silver link bracelet, like the man in the photo. She shook her head. It simply couldn't be. Harrington was running for mayor of New York City, and both he and Kent Harper ran the New York branches of their families' companies, both successful, upstanding citizens. And best friends, partners in everything? Had her imagination gone off the rails? All coincidence, that's what it was, what it had to be. *You don't believe that for a single fricking second.*

No, she couldn't, she wouldn't just shake off what she'd seen with her own eyes. Even the possibility that both Kent Harper and Alex Harrington really were the men at the frat rave at Godwyn that night seven years ago made her question her own sanity. But she was a reporter, a good one, so she wasn't about to allow herself to leap headfirst to a conclusion based on how a man handled a gaming sword and another man wore a bracelet. She could hardly tell anyone at the *Guardian* about it, least of all Milo. He'd think she'd lost it. What she had to do was—

"Hey, Mia, you having a meltdown? You haven't moved in forty-one seconds, I timed it."

She jerked, managed a laugh at Benny Tate, their social media and website guru, young, of course, and always coming up with crazy new app ideas that were oddly intriguing, the latest, *Alone in the Serengeti: A Beginners Guide.* "Nah, just thinking about how you'd make a great date, Benny."

"Har har," but his eyes lit up as he shot a sideways look at Kali Knight.

"Yes! Yes!"

Both Mia and Benny turned to see Millie Jones waving her arms and doing a happy dance by her desk.

Mia said, "What's going on with Millie? Did she win the lottery?"

Dirk looked up from the photos he was working on, called out, "This is her second spontaneous eruption. We're going to start calling her Krakatoa. A couple of minutes ago, she burst out with "The Sound of Music" and fist-bumped herself. Gotta admit, she's got some moves."

"So she did win the lottery?"

Dirk raised his iPhone, snapped a photo of Millie tap-dancing. "Nope. Milo got a call from a 'friendly' who works at One Federal Plaza and told him that the FBI agent who took down the terrorist at JFK—Special Agent Sherlock—will be in town for a couple of days about an overlapping case, or whatever, who knows? Milo got through to an FBI bigwig in Washington to see if one of our reporters could meet with her. He sold it by saying what an awesome job the FBI agent did saving the world—you know, the sort of crap he thought the FBI would latch on to. Of course they did, they can always use positive publicity. And of course a nice article with a photo of Agent Sherlock might sell some issues of the *Guardian*, too. I think Milo assigned Millie to do the article because she dated an FBI agent last year. Didn't end well, but she probably knows more about them than any of the rest of us."

Mia felt a stab of envy. She remembered, like most Americans, what Special Agent Sherlock had done. Sherlock—what an amazing name. She said, "If Agent Sherlock ran for mayor,

I think she might even get herself elected. Voters would know she'd clean up the streets, keep crime down."

To everyone's surprise, Kali the intern said, "I saw a photo of her husband, he's an FBI agent, too, Agent Dillon Savich. He's extremely hot. They've got a little kid, too. I wonder how it all works."

Benny gave Kali a long assessing look, slowly smiled, and nodded. *Good, maybe he'd ask her out.*

Milo, the boss, came striding out of his office, waving his big hands. "Cut out the dancing, Jones, and sit your butt down. I can see you from my office. You look like a spastic kangaroo. Time to hunker down, get your questions together for Agent Sherlock so I can review them. There you are, Briscoe. Did you interview Alex Harrington?"

All the voices died, as did Millie's dance, but not her indignant, "Kangaroo?"

Milo gave her the stink eye when she executed a rather cute last little skip before sitting down. They hadn't been all that loud and Milo's door had been closed, but everyone knew their boss had Spock ears. Mia said, "Yes, I had an initial interview with Harrington already, Milo, and his best buddy, Kent Harper, too. You know he runs the New York office of his family business—"

"Yes, yes, Harper Strategic Services, in the Harper Building on Madison, ugly modern piece of crap, full of itself. Okay, good. Then you're all set to get up to Boston tonight?"

She grinned at him. "Yep, I'm all set, no worries. However, Harrington's parents are off on a cruise somewhere, won't be back for another month or so, so I'll have to wait on them, but he did text me a list of people he'd like me to see. As if he expects me to talk only to the suck-ups he's cherry-picked for me. Fat chance."

Milo grunted. "All right, I trust your judgment, at least in this." He raised his voice. "Jones, I want you in my office about that Sherlock interview in"—he looked down at his watch—"two hours, no longer. Move, people, it ain't happy hour yet."

When the newsroom recovered, Mia hunkered over her desk and called Tommy Maitland at the Washington Field Office. *Seven years*, she thought, and wondered if Serena hadn't gone missing, if what he and Serena had shared their senior year would have become permanent. She and Tommy rarely spoke of Serena now, but she was there, always, a ghost hovering over them. Serena had bound them together for life. Mia liked Tommy, occasionally wished he were her brother, admired his brain, and knew it was time to bring him in, but too soon to bring him all the way in. She needed his help finding proof.

After two rings, "Mia? Good grief, woman, we haven't spoken in far too long. What's going on?"

"Well, I'm working my butt off, but that's not why I called. Tommy, it's about Serena."

A beat of thick silence, then, "Serena? What about her?"

"I don't know if you remember Gail Ricci, but she found some photos on her old iPhone from that night at the rave. Our photographer here at the *Guardian* enhanced them. They're still not very clear, but I'm sending them to you."

When Tommy had the photos, he said only, "Two blurry guys, and you don't know who they are? What do they have to do with Serena? Talk to me, Mia."

"No, I didn't recognize them, either, and neither did Gail. I wanted you to see them. They were at the rave, Tommy. I was thinking maybe facial recognition? Compare them to photos you already have that the police might have collected from cell phones that night? Ask the police chief to show them to some of the students who were interviewed?"

"Yes, of course, I can do all of that, but what makes you think they could be the guys to take Serena? And that's what you think, isn't it, Mia?" She hadn't heard such excitement in his voice since he'd told her he'd been accepted into the FBI.

"Yes, I'm sure leaning that way." Mia pointed out the earlobe tear, the bracelet, told him about the gamer. "And look, Tommy, couldn't he be ready to put something in Serena's drink?"

"If it is her drink."

"It is, it has to be."

He paused a moment. "Mia, tell me who you think these two men are. Where did you spot them? You're going on a torn earlobe and a bracelet? A gamer?"

"Yes. Tommy, I don't want to tell you yet. I don't want to prejudice you or the sheriff."

Tommy had learned over the years how stubborn Mia could be. "All right. But don't you go showing these photos around, all right? If you have come across the two men who took Serena, you know they'd do anything to keep from being exposed. They wouldn't hesitate to kill you. You know that, right? Come on, Briscoe, I don't hear you nodding." He sighed deeply. "You're not going to leave it to me, are you? You're going into full reporter mode."

She said, "Tommy, be realistic. It's nowhere near a sure thing that these photos show the same two men. And yes, I'll be careful, just in case. Please don't worry. You'll keep me posted, all right?"

"Only if you promise you'll tell me what you're doing on your end."

"Sure, of course, we'll see. Now, before you head off to arrest some crooks, tell me, how are your folks?"

When she punched off her cell, Mia felt a blast of guilt. No, she'd been right, it was too soon to tell him about Harrington and Harper when she had no real proof. She couldn't ask Tommy and the FBI to investigate a candidate for mayor based on a hunch, it wouldn't be fair. She had to learn more first and she fully intended to. Sins of omission, she thought, weren't really sins if there was good reason for them. That was her reasoning and she was sticking to it.

19

23 Swan Court
CIA Safe House
Washington, D.C.

TUESDAY NIGHT

Whomp, whomp, whomp—the helicopter blades were vicious loud, the vibrations scoring through her head. Olivia felt hands on her, felt a needle slide into her wrist, but oddly, she didn't feel any pain, but she knew it was there, waiting. She heard voices speaking quietly above her, but they were only meaningless sounds. Then she heard Mike's voice, low and harsh, close to her face, she'd recognize it anywhere. He sounded upset. Were those his fingers stroking her cheek? Was she afraid she'd die? She wished she could understand what he was saying, but even so close she felt his warm breath on her face, she couldn't understand. She wanted desperately to reassure him, to tell him everything would be all right, but she couldn't. She could only lie there, huddled deep inside herself, and wait.

Olivia jerked with a start at the sound of her cell phone buzzing. Her heart was beating so fast, it took a moment for the images to fade, longer to realize she'd been dreaming about her half-conscious helicopter ride to Balad Military Hospital. As she fumbled for her cell, Helmut licked her face, gave a gentle woof. "Hello?"

"Olivia, it's Andi."

She was instantly awake. "Andi, what's going on? Are you okay? No, Helmut, it's Andi, go back to sleep."

"Give Mr. Gorgeous a hug for me. Olivia, I was worried about you. Why haven't you called me? I had to hear about what happened to you last night from Mr. Grace."

Olivia looked over at her iWatch. It was a little past ten, not late at all. "I'm sorry, I should have called, but the truth is I hardly got any sleep last night and I was exhausted. I'm really okay, Andi, I'm fine." She knew Andi was afraid for her, so Olivia tried to lighten it up a bit. "I looked at myself in the mirror and knew I needed more beauty sleep so I went to bed early after eating take-out Chinese with Agent Gaylin, my babysitter. You know him, don't you?"

She heard Andi take a deep breath, smooth out. "Sure, he's an old warhorse, tough as my desert boots, and always needs to shave."

"That's Gay. Found out tonight he loves Szechwan beef. Since I'm trusting him with my life, I'm glad he's as tough as he looks."

"Olivia, Mr. Grace only gave me the bare bones of what happened to you. He told me to leave my house, go to a hotel, and make sure I wasn't followed, and, of course, to keep him informed. I asked him about Higgs and he said Higgs went off to Canada on his motorcycle, as if it isn't cold enough for him in Maine.

"Tell me exactly what happened, Olivia. Mr. Grace said two men came to your house and you had to shoot one of them. I couldn't pry anything else out of him. You promise you weren't hurt?"

"No, I'm fine. If you strip all the bark away, yes, that's about exactly what happened. The one I killed, he was speaking Farsi. No ID on him, so no one knows who he was."

"Mr. Grace didn't bother to mention that, either. Of course they're searching high and low for Mike, but again, Mr. Grace made it clear he didn't want us involved. I sometimes wish they didn't keep everything so compartmentalized, feed us little cubes of knowledge to keep us begging for more. I know, it's CIA, no way that's going to change."

"You're right about that. Did Mr. Grace tell you about our meeting with the FBI?"

"What? You were all at the FBI? You're kidding me. No, wait, of course they'd be involved with a shooting on American soil. Okay, walk me through it."

"Well, Mr. Grace and I were escorted to the third floor of the Hoover Building into an interview room, you know the kind, a long scarred table, uncomfortable chairs, plain white walls, and we met with Special Agent Savich, who's in charge of the investigation. Mr. Lodner made a late entrance and he was obviously pissed at having to come to the enemy encampment. They were both tight-lipped, but Agent Savich got most everything he wanted out of Mr. Lodner, even got them both to leave so we could talk privately. He seems very smart, and I think I might even trust him. He promised he's going to find out who the man I shot last night was, and that he's going to find Mike. Of course he agrees all this is connected to our mission, and that flash drive Hashem gave Mike that disappeared with him."

Andi heaved out a breath. "Makes sense, obviously. This Agent Savich sounds interesting. I've never heard of anyone having his way with Lodner, Mr. Stiff Lip himself. But, Olivia, I don't see how this FBI agent, however smart he is, could possibly find Mike when we can't even identify a foreign agent."

"You might think I'm crazy, but I think he will."

"Of course I wish him well, finding Mike and that flash drive. I remember Higgs asked Mike on our flight to Balad if Hashem told him what was on the flash drive before he died, but Mike only shook his head and didn't say anything. I'll tell you, Olivia, the way it's looking now, you can hardly say the mission was a success—Hashem died, you were hurt, Mike's missing, and no flash drive. And now you were almost killed again. There's got to be lots of stuff going on we don't know about, Olivia, bad stuff."

Andi drew a deep breath. "I don't know if you remember, but I tried to get over to help Mike when Hashem was shot, but Higgs shouted to me. He needed cover. I remember you were close to them. Did you hear Hashem tell Mike anything when he gave him the flash drive, something that could help us?"

Olivia said, "I remember he spoke to Mike before he died,

but if I heard what Hashem said to him, it didn't register, or that RPG blew it out of my brain. The doctors don't know if I'll ever be able to fill in all the blanks from that day.

"Andi, tell me again you're tucked away where no one can find you."

"Yes, I am, and I was ordered not to tell anyone, even you. If things get dicey, I'll call you if I want to come over, all right?"

"I'd still prefer we were together. We could protect each other." Olivia heard the tension, the fear, in Andi's voice and made her own voice light. "Like we did those insane two days outside of Kirkuk, remember? Holding off a dozen insurgents? We had tea at the Baba Gurgur Hotel that day after the army showed up."

"Insane is right. That was a time, wasn't it?"

"Yeah, good times. I remember we were sitting behind this mud wall when you told me about the lawyer you nearly married until you realized he bored you brainless, and it was after that you joined the CIA."

Andi laughed. "Let's say I didn't want to disappoint my parents, so I let him cancel the wedding."

"How did you manage that?"

Andi laughed again. "I went joyriding on his teenage brother's motorcycle, nearly killed myself, and came out laughing, and he was well and truly shocked, called me crazy. My mom told me he married a paralegal. He has two kids and lives in the New Jersey burbs."

Olivia chuckled. It felt good, but it lasted only until Andi threw a bucket of cold water. "Listen, Olivia, we have to consider someone at Langley could have been involved in the attempt on your life, maybe Mr. Grace, maybe Mr. Lodner, maybe someone we don't even know. And we have to face up to it, Mike could be dead. The possibilities are so endless, I'm nearly ready to believe Putin's turned Christian."

Olivia said without hesitation, "No. I'd know if Mike were dead." She believed her words, but Olivia wished she could take them back. It was too raw, too personal.

Andi said matter-of-factly, "I know you and Mike have been involved the past several years. When the RPG hit close to you, you were slammed back against a boulder, unconscious, maybe dead, and Mike went nuts, cursed a blue streak. He was a wild man, throwing rocks off you, pulling you over his shoulder and running back toward the plateau. It was insane, the gunfire, the RPGs landing around us. He yelled to us to carry out Hashem. And we did." She paused a moment. "I think that was the closest either of us has come to getting blown up. We were lucky, Olivia. We could all have been killed. Yeah, I'd say Mike really cares about you, as much as you care about him."

Mike already knows I'm crazy. The thought brought a fleeting smile, and then Olivia thought of what Mike had done and swallowed hard. "Thanks for telling me that, Andi. I still think we can find him, and so does Agent Savich. Check with me every day, and whenever you like, I'll clear your joining us here at the safe house. Please come if you don't feel safe where you are."

"Sure I will, but as I said, I'm well hidden. And unless Mr. Grace orders me to come in, I'd rather be out here than in a safe house. I have some sources and plan to use them. Hey, don't worry, I'm CIA, I know how to take care of myself."

Olivia tapped end on her cell, saw it was nearly eleven o'clock. Too late to call Dillon Savich. She snuggled against Helmut, pressing her face against his soft fur.

20

**Agent Kelly Giusti and Agent Cal McLain's apartment
New York City**

WEDNESDAY MORNING

Sherlock perked up when Greeny's "Give Me a Wet One" blasted out of her cell. "It's Dillon," she murmured to Kelly and Cal. She took a quick bite of Cal's awesome strawberry crepe and excused herself from the breakfast table. She walked into the hallway with its bright prints of the Italian Riviera against a soft yellow wall. "It's great to hear your voice. Tell me everything is peaceful, Sean ate his French toast, and Graciella took him to school?"

Savich laughed. "Yes, to all of the above, only I wasn't paying attention and accidentally poured Cheerios and milk in Astro's bowl. He couldn't scarf it up fast enough. He's sleeping off his Cheerios high, snoring like a freight train. How are Cal and Kelly?"

"Both of them are fine. Kelly says even though Cal is a

pain in the butt, he's a good boss. She doesn't let him forget he wouldn't have gotten the promotion if he hadn't been assigned to be my bodyguard during those insane days before we brought down that terrorist on the steps of the Lincoln Monument. You caught us at the end of breakfast, only a few more bites of a strawberry crepe left. I wonder if Cal could teach you how to make those crepes. A little flavor of France to go with your amazing Italian? Oh yes, they're planning on a June wedding."

"I would never horn in on another man's territory. Would you believe Cal called me and I told him how to make crepes. Sounds like he did them right." After she snorted out a laugh, Savich continued. "Congratulations to them and to you for figuring out what happened. Have you had any luck finding the gun range Storin's been using?"

"No, and I don't know why. Kelly and I called most of the gun ranges within a three-hour drive of Brickson yesterday, texted them Storin's photo, in case she used a fake name, asked the owners to show it around, but no luck. Today, we'll be trying southern Connecticut.

"I'll tell you, Dillon, after watching Kelly's two interviews with Storin, I agree with her. Storin's a card-carrying psychopath. She's smart, very articulate, but like Kelly said, there's something very off about her." Sherlock sighed. "I'm tired of hearing myself talk about her. What's happening at your end? How are you managing the CIA? And the operative?"

There was only a slight pause, but she knew something was going on but he didn't want to tell her about it, didn't want to split her focus; maybe it was dangerous and he didn't want to worry her. "Come on, Dillon, spill it. I can multitask. What's going on? Is it that bad?"

He laughed. "Never miss a thing, do you? All right, two men tried to kill the CIA operative, Olivia Hildebrandt, at her home Monday night, that or kidnap her. Her golden retriever, Helmut, woke her up. She killed one of the two men, the other escaped. There's more, of course, but this really is top secret, and our cells aren't secure. Since the man she killed is a foreign national, the FBI is in charge. We're talking international intrigue here. And no, I shouldn't tell you any more."

Sherlock wanted to know every single detail, but she knew he'd shut off the spigot for now. She said, "I wish I could be there with you. You be careful, you hear me?"

"Don't worry." Because he wanted to distract her, he said, "When do you have your interview at the *Guardian*?"

"I spoke on the phone to the reporter, told her I'd stop by when I have time. Tell Mr. Maitland not to worry. She's gung ho, so it will be a positive piece, as advertised.

"Dillon, I gave MAX a kiss before I left, told him I was counting on him finding out where Storin is always traveling to in Washington. Has he found anything at all? Maybe some kind of property?"

She could practically see his smile over the phone at the image of Sherlock kissing his laptop.

"Come on, spill it. What, Dillon?"

"MAX has come through like gangbusters. You're going to like this."

21

Beacon Hill
Boston, Massachusetts

WEDNESDAY MORNING

On her cab ride from the Constitution Inn to Boston's Beacon Hill's famed Louisburg Square, Mia read a comment to her blog from a reader who wrote that reducing the time to appeal the death penalty to three years before the fatal injection would certainly reduce the murder rate. He didn't understand why everyone didn't realize this. Idiots, all who didn't agree. Mia grinned, posted her reply thanking the reader, and sat back. She was content to let the readers take over, which they always did. In Milo's opinion, her lack of making pronouncements was why her blog was so popular.

She opened Kali's landing page and studied a photo of the woman she was about to interview, Pamela Raines Barrett, Alex Harrington's fiancée. She was standing beside her desk in her office, her arms crossed over her Armani jacket, looking elegantly thin. Her fine-boned face, while not beautiful, was compelling. Mia scrolled to the Facebook page of Belinda Raines Barrett, Pamela's younger sister, only nineteen, obviously a latecomer to the family. Bless her gregarious teenage heart, she'd posted a good dozen photos of Alex Harrington. Only one of them was of Alex with her big sister Pamela, but there were at least a dozen recent photos of herself with him, at dances, sailing, at a clambake in Nantucket. Was there infatuation in her pretty brown eyes when they focused on Alex? And she had posted some photos of Alex and Kent together, golfing, swimming, sailing. Whatever Alex did, the young Belinda seemed to want a picture of it. One photo showed Alex and Kent gaming, both absorbed, unaware anyone was taking their picture.

Mia closed down Kali's landing site and wondered if Kali liked meatloaf.

Her taxi pulled up in front of a town house set in a long row of town houses, all of them much the same, red brick with white trim, all very old. Even in the tail end of winter, on a frigid overcast Wednesday, the neighborhood looked locked in time, a revered row of monuments announcing to the world the social standing of the occupants. For the Bostonian elite, Louisburg Square was the address. Mia paid her Roxbury driver who'd entertained her with nonstop commentary on the fate of the Red Sox this upcoming season.

Pamela had asked to meet Mia here rather than at her office on Newbury Street, and of course Mia knew why. Ms. Pamela wanted to impress her, intimidate her, make her understand she was dealing with power—and she'd best tread carefully, respectfully. Fine by Mia; she'd always wanted to see the inside of one of these testaments to old Boston wealth and, naturally, good breeding.

She was met at the front door not by a butler or a maid, but by Pamela Raines Barrett herself. Alex Harrington had obviously called his fiancée, told her this was an important interview, and Pam didn't want to appear a snob. She looked very stylish in another black Armani suit, a white-as-snow turtleneck sweater under the jacket, three-inch Louboutin heels on her narrow feet. Her dark hair was loose, worn around her shoulders, lovely really, pulled back from her face by two golden barrettes.

Mia knew Pam was examining her thoroughly as well, all in a split second, a skill all women seemed to share. Then she smiled, a lovely welcoming smile, showing perfect white teeth.

"Ms. Briscoe? I'm Pamela Barrett. Please come in."

They shook hands and Mia stepped into a rather small entrance hall displaying an antique table with gorgeous winter mums in a blue colonial vase, an equally old mirror above it, and a single ladder-back chair. For those waiting for an audience? Pamela laid Mia's coat and scarf neatly on the chair and showed her into a living room that made Mia catch her breath, as it was meant to. The walls were painted a vivid dark red, the intricate moldings a stark white. The room wasn't large, but neither was it overloaded with antiques. It was sparsely furnished, minimalist even, reflecting Pamela's decorating style. Artful splashes of color brightened the room, making it warm and welcoming. Mia wondered how deep the town house went, with how many livable floors. She would like to see the kitchen and bathrooms. She wondered how many times they'd been redesigned and updated, certainly a few since the town house was built back in the time of the Colonial Ark, or thereabouts.

"Your home is lovely."

"Thank you. My grandmother deeded this house to me because she knew I'd tend it, keep it fresh and loved." Pam waved a graceful hand, her seven-carat engagement ring shimmering even in the soft light. "Please sit down. You like your coffee black, I know." She poured, without waiting for an answer, from a silver Georgian pot Paul Revere himself might have fashioned, into impossibly fragile-looking porcelain cups Queen Charlotte herself might have used more than two centuries before.

Mia merely raised an eyebrow.

Pamela laughed. "Alex told me you like your coffee straight. He's very observant. He was pleased you wanted to come to Boston to meet with me but he did warn me you'd probably try to pry all sorts of secrets about him out of me." She laughed again as she passed Mia her coffee. "Of course I've read your blogs, Ms. Briscoe. I find you—" She paused.

"Too far to the left? Too far to the right? Too conventional?"

Pamela smiled, waved Mia's words away. "No, I think you're courageous, actually. You take on some topics most people avoid, topics that reflect how polarized the country's become, and you offer compromises you obviously know won't please either side. That's brave."

"Believe it or not," Mia said, sipping her sinfully rich coffee, "there are many more people in the center than you might think. It's only they never say much, and that's a pity. I try to give them a forum where they can be comfortable saying what they think. It's a pity more centrists don't take part; it's usually those to the far left or the far right to chime in with their opinions they believe are solid gold."

"Alex agrees with you about that," Pam said smoothly, an excellent segue. Again, Mia was impressed.

"He wants to remind New Yorkers they have common goals—the city's welfare, its education and job opportunities, and finding the golden compromise between public safety and personal freedom."

Mia nodded, pretended to type silently on her iPad.

Canned, but Pam spoke fluently. "Tell me, Ms. Barrett, how did you and Alex meet?"

"Please, call me Pamela, and I'll call you Mia, is that all right?"

"Certainly."

"How we met—now there's a story. I was six years old, Alex was eight, I think, and we both wanted to play quarterback on the same team in a neighborhood pickup football game. I recall he picked me up and threw me like a football at his friend Kent, who dropped me. I sprained my wrist. Things didn't improve between us for a very long time." She laughed.

"That's a good one. Readers will like that story. It shows, too, that Kent and Alex have been friends since childhood. They're still close. I assume you forgave his throwing you when you were six?"

"Yes, I did, but not until we were teenagers. I even forgave

Kent for dropping me. He's smart, fun, and a better gamer than Alex, although Alex hates to admit it, claims before he got out of practice because he has to work so hard, he could beat Kent with only one good eye." She grinned, shook her head. "As you know, they went to school together from Bennington Prep through Harvard. I respect what Kent's doing, expanding his family's legacy. He's as committed as Alex to what he does. As I'm sure you've seen for yourself, Alex is an outstanding leader, always thoughtful in his decisions, always praises his staff for a job well done, freely gives credit when it's due. His people are loyal to him for that, they respect him."

"I suppose your families vacationed together? Perhaps at the Harrington cottage on Nantucket?"

"Oh yes. I have wonderful memories of those warm summers, swimming, sunning, clamming. For the kids, it was magical, only of course, kids take the magic for granted."

"And the memories become even more magical when we're older and looking back, right?"

"Yes, that's it exactly."

Mia said without pause, "I understand Alex was engaged to the concert pianist Juliet Ash Calley two years ago? I assume they decided they weren't suited, or was it your coming onto the scene that made Alex realize he'd made a mistake?"

She watched a myriad of emotions flash across Pamela's face—anger, distaste, and a final dash of triumph. All there, if you were looking closely, which Mia was.

Clever, amusing Pamela was gone. With infinite pity in her voice, she said, "I feel very sorry for Juliet, despite her talent. Have you heard her perform?"

"I haven't seen her in person, no, but I've listened to her CDs. She's extraordinary, very talented."

A perfectly timed pause, then, "I agree with you. I've heard her many times as well and seen her perform here in Boston. Of course there's pressure performing in front of an audience but she does well in that setting. But the fact is, in keeping with her being an artist of sorts, Juliet's always been rather sensitive, delicate, if you know what I mean. She and Alex agreed their engagement was a mistake once she fully understood Alex's ambitions to be in the public eye, to be a politician. He was quite forceful about it and poor Juliet knew she would have been lost in that kind of life, that world." She gave Mia a discreet smile. "Then Alex and I were thrown together again as adults, and we clicked."

But you still dislike Juliet, don't you, even though you're the one he's going to marry.

Mia only smiled. "Delicate? Could you tell me what you mean?"

Pamela quickly retrenched, gave Mia a rueful smile. "As I said, artists are known for their delicacy, aren't they? Their sensitivity? Everyone in our group knows Juliet has always avoided any sort of confrontation whenever possible, unlike Alex, of course, who relishes competition, going head-to-head with anyone on any topic, any physical activity. You should see him and Kent go at it, at whatever they do." Pamela shrugged. "No, poor Juliet would never have been comfortable being center stage, and that's exactly where Alex belongs. It was obvious to everyone, almost from the beginning, that they weren't a good match."

"You mean she wouldn't be comfortable on the political center stage?"

"That's right. Performing before an audience, by yourself, why, it's entirely different, don't you think? No one to disagree with you, no one to tell you you're foolish, no one to tell you to shut up."

"You're right. It doesn't sound like a good match. You mentioned she was a part of your group? So you and she and Alex grew up together?"

Pamela was comfortable again on familiar ground, where Mia wanted her, for the moment. She said, "I'm sure you understand, Mia, that certain families share long histories. Alex, Kent, Juliet, and I, along with a score of others, were thrown together as children and grew up together. It was normal for us, it was our accepted milieu, if you will."

Mia chuckled. "Sounds a bit like inbreeding." Before Pamela could decide whether to be insulted, Mia said, "Did you attend any of Alex's lacrosse games at Bennington Prep or at Harvard?"

"No, I attended school in England, with Juliet actually, but of course I know about the championships they won. I believe I already mentioned Alex was and still is an amazing athlete."

Mia quickly called up a photo she'd transferred onto her iPad that showed Alex holding up a trophy, turned it for Pamela to see. "He looks triumphant, doesn't he?"

"Oh yes. I remember he wrote me how proud he was, but he gave all the credit to his teammates. That's Alex."

That's a lie, Pam, but smoothly done. Mia suddenly looked

more closely at the photograph. "Oh goodness, his earlobe—
it looks like his earlobe's been ripped. Maybe playing lacrosse?"

Pam looked closely, frowned. "I don't see anything."

"I guess I'm mistaken, but I understand lacrosse is a very
physical game, always the possibility of injury."

"I suppose so. Boys were always getting injured, but nothing
serious I can remember."

Mia didn't pause. "Do Alex and Kent still game a lot?"

Pamela blinked, gave an elegant shrug. "They don't play all
that much as adults, they're far too busy with business responsibilities. And now, of course, Alex is running for mayor of
New York. But I don't mind them playing now and then since it
seems to relax Alex. It's probably healthy for him."

"Me? I might be jealous. You really don't mind?"

"Of course not. I've teased him about it, but Alex just
laughs since he's also a great one for jokes and teasing himself.
And did you know Alex coached Little League in Roxbury?"

"How very giving of him. I imagine your family is excited
about your becoming the first lady of New York City?"

"My parents always counsel never to count your chickens,
but of course it's their fondest wish that I be at Alex's side
when he wins the election."

"And your interior design business? As you know, the may-
or's wife has many obligations."

"I know, and I accept that my business might suffer with my
move to New York. But still, I will find time to work, and my
family has many friends with apartments in the city."

Mia listened to Pamela talk about her family and friends, all powerful, all connected. When she knew she'd hit a wall with Pamela, Mia smiled, thanked her, and put away her iPad.

When she stepped into the bitter wind, she knew Pamela was prepared to do whatever it took to get Alex Harrington elected mayor of New York City. She wondered which of them wanted it more.

Mia couldn't wait to meet Juliet Ash Calley, the ex-fiancée too delicate to handle a powerhouse like Alex Harrington.

22

Beacon Hill

WEDNESDAY, EARLY AFTERNOON

Mia pulled her bright red wool coat close, worked her hands into her snug leather gloves, smashed her red knit cap over her head, and walked into the stiff wind the quarter mile from Pamela Raines Barrett's digs to Juliet Ash Calley's family home. Kali had found out Juliet wasn't currently living in her small cottage near the Harvard campus; she'd moved back to her family home to tend to her ill mother. Milo had been enthusiastic about Mia seeing Juliet, the former fiancée. He'd given her his shark smile, waggled his thick salt-and-pepper eyebrows, and said out of the blue, "She's yet another person with three names. If your family is worth a billion dollars, it's an unwritten law you have three names or you get booted out of the club. Don't even think about using that bit, Briscoe. I think she'll see you. She's used to reporters interviewing her about her piano playing. I remember Jim Perry of the *Boston*

Globe interviewed Juliet Calley for us, wrote a piece about her performance when he heard her play Ravel in Boston. Said it nearly made him weep."

Mia lowered her head when a gust of frigid air hit her full in the face. Still, lots of people were out and about, with places to go; nothing could keep them inside, just like New Yorkers.

She stopped in front of a stately early-nineteenth-century mansion, mellow gray stone rising above iron gates covered with acres of ivy. She double-checked the address, pressed the button beside the gate, identified herself to the unknown man whose deep disembodied voice was loud and clear. The gate slowly swung inward. She walked into a wonderland along an old meandering flagstone path through an elaborate garden, hibernating now, ah, but come spring, it would be glorious. There were only hushed sounds of traffic, but nothing else, outside the iron gate. Mia heard yew bushes whispering in the wind, heard the arms of tree branches moaning as the wind swayed them back and forth. The house rose three stories, with ten chimney stacks—she had to count them, couldn't stop herself. The ivy didn't grow wild up the sides of the house; it was perfectly trimmed around the large windows and the large dark gray front door.

Mia banged the antique lion's head, heard skipping footsteps coming downstairs. The large door opened and Juliet Ash Calley herself appeared. An older man dressed in a beautiful black suit materialized behind her. She turned to him. "I'll see to Ms. Briscoe, Weldon, thank you."

A butler. Well, of course.

Weldon nodded his iron-gray head and melted away.

Juliet Ash Calley held out a competent hand with long tapered fingers, short buffed nails, and shook Mia's gloved one. "I'm Juliet Calley and you're Mia Briscoe, right?"

Mia gave her a warm smile, difficult because her face was so cold.

"Come in, come in, quickly, before you're frozen to the bone."

Mia stepped inside and Juliet quickly closed the front door, flipped the dead bolt, and turned, shivered. "I think Admiral Perry would be at home here today. Mother's sleeping, so your timing is perfect. I admit I was surprised to hear a reporter wanted to speak to me, and not about music but about Alex Harrington. I haven't been part of his life for over two years now. Let me take your coat."

Juliet hung Mia's winter gear on an old-fashioned coat-tree, and said, "Come into the living room and we can hunker down in front of the fire Weldon always lights for me when I practice."

Mia followed Juliet Ash Calley out of the dim entrance hall and into a large living room filled with extraordinary light even on this grim March day. Old and gracious was Mia's impression of the large rectangular room, all its English antiques looking settled and comfortable, everything in the room a part of the whole. A twelve-foot ceiling made the room seem even more spacious. The walls were painted a soft cream, and pale-blue-patterned wallpaper framed the front bow windows. But the focal point was the shiny black eleven-foot Steinway grand piano. Mia said, "I've listened to some of your recordings. I remember sitting back, closing my eyes, and letting your amazing Scarlatti melt away every bit of stress. I got right back to work, whistling." Mia pointed at the beautiful instrument. "You grew up with this Steinway?"

"Yes. It was originally my grandmother's. She was an amazing musician, but she didn't wish to pursue a career. Now the piano is mine."

"And your mom?"

"My mom had lessons, but she always said they didn't take and my grandmother nodded, sadly. I've always found talent genes to be very unpredictable. Believe me, I'm grateful they came together for me."

Mia waved her hand around the living room. "There's such peace in this room. Do you think you'll live here someday?"

Juliet blinked, cocked her head. "I haven't thought about it. It's my parents' house. My grandparents gave it to them when they moved to Florida ten years ago. Honestly, I can't imagine my folks ever being gone. As to this house, it has their stamp on it. For me, it's a bit too opulent." She waved Mia to a red velvet Victorian love seat with graceful scrolled arms. Juliet poured a cup of tea from a whimsical teapot and placed a cup in front of Mia. "Oolong. I hope you like it. It's my early afternoon treat."

Mia thanked her, took a sip, and nearly swooned. Hot and pungent, just what she needed. "Thank you. It's delicious."

Juliet nodded and sat across from Mia, the light from the bow windows full on her face.

For the first time, Mia really looked at Juliet Ash Calley. She was riveted. Of course she'd seen her photos, but the woman in person was . . . Mia, the wordsmith, could only come up with—drop-dead gorgeous. Juliet was blessed with skin like porcelain, eyes so pale a blue they were almost silver, and absurdly long lashes, even darker than her hair. She was several years older than Mia, not as model thin as Pamela; that is, no bones were showing. She looked fit and strong in dark blue sweats, the jacket open to a white silk cami, soft black ballet slippers on her feet. Her dark brown hair was pulled back into a thick ponytail and fastened with a pink poof ball, an oddly charming effect. Mia said without hesitation, "Forgive me for staring, but you are the most beautiful woman I've ever seen in my life. Mr. Harrington must have thought he'd died and gone to heaven when he laid eyes on you."

Juliet blinked, reared back in her chair. "What? Oh, well, thank you, but I strongly doubt that was Alex's reaction when he first saw me. I was about six years old, missing a front tooth, wore tight braids, and pink tights on my skinny legs."

Mia said, smiling, "I like the visual."

Juliet said, "Of course I googled you, Ms. Briscoe. I realized I'd read some of your *Guardian* articles that appeared in the *Boston Globe*. I came away thinking you're bright and a good writer. You're not about doing political hatchet jobs or pushing an agenda, and that's refreshing in these contentious times. That's why I was fine with seeing you.

"I don't suppose you'd like to talk about my mother's big charity bash for breast cancer research next Friday?" she continued, a twinkle in her eyes. "Or perhaps my father's most recent trade talks with Indonesia?" She laughed, then sighed. "I know you want to talk to me about Alex Harrington and his run for mayor of New York City. But I really have little that's interesting or pertinent to say to you or your readers about him. In short, I'm old news, two-year-old old news to be exact."

Mia kept her voice smooth, matter-of-fact. "Still, you were part of the fabric of his life, you knew him very well indeed, Ms. Calley. You were slated to marry him."

Mia saw a flash of distress on her beautiful face before she slowly nodded. "Well, yes, of course. Very well, Ms. Briscoe, but please realize whatever I might say about Alex wouldn't be of much interest to the voters of New York City. I don't know much of anything about his politics, or what he advocates."

Mia didn't say it, but she didn't care at all what this woman thought of Alex Harrington's politics; she wanted to know why their engagement had been called off. She'd bet her prized Indian Head nickel Juliet was the one who'd called a halt. The question was why. Mia didn't take her tablet out; she simply leaned forward and looked directly at Juliet. "I accept that voters wouldn't be much interested in your opinions of Mr. Harrington's political stands. I'd guess you probably don't care what he thinks about much of anything these days. I would find it odd if you did."

A forced smile from Juliet. "Yes, you're quite right about that. Actually, I rarely give him a thought."

She wasn't a good liar, and this lie perched on the end of her perfect nose. Mia said, "I met Mr. Harrington at a fundraiser and interviewed him for a series of articles I've been assigned to write for the *Guardian*. I spoke to him yesterday. He was charming, which I suppose he'll have to be to get many votes. He's good-looking, tall, well built, seems to relate well to both men and women. In short, he's got everything it takes to be a successful politician. So far as I know he's been an athlete and an avid gamer, that he runs the New York branch of his family's business. He seems like a man who'd appeal to would-be voters, at least to those voters not too far on the left or the right. What I'd like to know, Ms. Calley, is what you think of him as a person. Is he as admirable as he seems to be? Trustworthy? Knowing him as you do, would you vote for him?"

Hardly a pause, then Juliet said, her voice flat, "I imagine many people would say yes to that list and yes to voting for him."

But you wouldn't. Mia gave her a crooked grin. "Forgive me, I fear I've made him sound like a perfect pet dog."

"I really can't add to what you said, Ms. Briscoe." Then the words burst out of her mouth. "Except if Alex were a dog, he'd be a vicious hunter."

The words hung naked between them. Juliet opened her mouth, closed it. *That's right*, Mia thought, *saying any more would only make it worse.* Mia said, "Could you tell me what you mean, exactly?"

Juliet shook her head, tried for a disarming smile, but she couldn't pull it off. She said finally, "What I meant was, when Alex is set on a course of action, absolutely nothing will stop him. He'll be a dogged opponent, forgive the pun, do anything he sees necessary to get what he wants, as the other candidates for mayor of New York City will soon discover."

It was a nice save, as far as it went. "I imagine those qualities might make for a strong candidate for mayor, but not so attractive in a husband?"

"Yes, those qualities did have something to do with our breaking up, yes."

Mia waited, but Juliet said nothing more. All right, she'd move along for the moment. "What do you think of Mr. Harrington's current fiancée, Pamela Raines Barrett?"

Juliet said without hesitation, "For as long as I can remember, Pammie's family has been front and center on the political stage, ever since her uncle, Wilson Carlson Barrett, was governor. Even her mother, Marilyn, was an elected judge. I would say without reservation Pamela and Alex are perfect for each other."

Mia wasn't deaf to what she'd left unspoken. She throttled back. "I understand you and Ms. Barrett were once very good friends and you were sent to England together for school. Tell me about it." She pulled out her tablet, sat poised.

Juliet eased, Mia saw it. "Yes, when we were sixteen Pammie and I were sent to England, near Bath, to a posh girls' school. We are very different people, but as teenagers together in a foreign country, we did well together, we had each other's backs. I don't know why Pammie's parents agreed to England—it was always cold and rained incessantly—but my parents wanted me to study with a famous piano teacher.

"I remember the day I began to understand Pammie—no, she's Pamela now—and why I think she's perfect for Alex. We were visiting Westminster Abbey on a day trip. She didn't want to move away from Queen Victoria's tomb. She told me even though she couldn't be a queen and reign over a country until she died, and the chances of her becoming president were slim to none, she'd decided to make do with being First Lady. I believed her. I still do."

She paused a moment. "She and I never viewed the world in the same way. As I said, we did well together away from home, only the two of us, but when we came home things changed; we became adults and more or less went our separate ways. I threw myself into becoming a concert pianist and Pamela tried many things, but it was always the local political scene that drew her, and, of course, interior design. Her first husband, Andrew Schlosser, was a very nice man who ran for governor and lost in the primary. She divorced him shortly after that."

"Because he couldn't give her what she wanted?"

"I don't know. I did ask her once what issues she believed in politically. She didn't give me an answer, only said most of it was nonsense, male and female posturing, and the only important thing for most politicians was power, not the issues they talked about, that saying what voters wanted to hear was the only way to get elected and gain power. She dated a number of politicians, but she cut them all loose. It got to be a joke in our group, like, who's Pamela auditioning now?"

Mia said, "I wonder if it burned her when her best teenage girlfriend hooked the big prize—Alex Harrington?"

Juliet said quickly, too quickly, "I never thought about it that way, and I don't want to know. Honestly? I wish her the best of luck."

Mia said, "And now she might become first lady of New York City."

"She might. And for Pamela, New York is a lovely stepping-stone. She wants to be First Lady of the United States." Juliet actually smiled.

"There's many a long mile from Mr. Harrington being mayor of New York City to being the president of the United States."

"That's certainly true, but I don't doubt for a minute Pammie will relish every step to Washington."

Mia set down her tablet. "Off the record. May I ask how you and Mr. Harrington got together?"

"When I attended Juilliard, I lived with another musician, a violinist, but that didn't work out, and I moved back to Boston. The same old group was still here, hanging out together, at parties, movies, dinners. It was a comfortable routine, always there for me after I practiced or performed, always a welcome break."

"And then Alex?"

"Yes, and then Alex. It started at a clambake in Nantucket."

"He was with several women over the years, but never married."

"Yes, that's right."

"Just like Kent Harper never did?"

Juliet flinched—Mia saw it—then she slowly nodded. "Yes, very much like Kent."

"And the two of you didn't realize you weren't suited until only three weeks before the wedding?"

Mia saw Juliet was used to this question. She eased, gave an elegant shrug, trotted out her canned response. "Like many women, I suppose I was all wrapped up in the excitement. It was a whirlwind time, so much to be done even with a wedding planner, who, I might add, would have made an excellent Nazi general. My parents were ecstatic, his parents were ecstatic, all our friends approved. We finally realized we'd simply dived into the deep end, both of us ignoring our real feelings, not thinking objectively." She looked down at her tightly folded hands, and the words spurted out of her mouth. "And there was Kent."

23

Mia saw a flash of revulsion. And fear? "Kent Harper had something to do with your wedding being called off?"

Juliet shrugged, but Mia saw her fingers digging into her pant legs. "Let's just say Kent is Kent. And if you're with Alex, Kent is a part of the package."

Mia said, "I had a boyfriend once whose best friend was always hanging around. It came to feel like I was dating both of them. Is that how it was with you?"

"Well, yes, I suppose so."

"Did Kent have something to do with your breaking your engagement with Alex?"

"I've told you, the decision was mutual, Ms. Briscoe, and we do deserve some privacy, don't you think?"

Mia looked down at her tablet, as if she were checking her notes, looked up. "I understand Mr. Harrington and Mr. Harper have always been like brothers, from their earliest years. Gaming was and still is one of their major pastimes?"

"Gaming, yes, and most anything else they could do together.

Alex and Kent both played lacrosse at Bennington Prep and then, of course, at Harvard. But you're right, gaming was their staple growing up. They've cut back now that they have to be responsible adults, particularly Alex and the political path he wants to take. From what I hear, they're both doing well. I imagine they're still very close."

"You mentioned Alex played lacrosse. Do you remember if he was ever injured?"

"No, I don't remember. And I wasn't even here. I was in England until I was eighteen and then I was off to Juilliard."

"Pamela told me this morning she believed you were too delicate to deal with Mr. Harrington on equal footing, that you wouldn't have been able to deal with all the demands that would be expected of you as the wife of an ambitious politician. She hinted Mr. Harrington was really the one who wanted to break off the engagement."

Juliet chose her words carefully. "Pamela knows I never had any desire to oversee and direct other people's lives. Of course I hope to move people in my concerts, but that's only for their pleasure, nothing more. As for Alex wanting more than I to break off the engagement—well, who knows? Perhaps Pamela saw something I didn't. It really doesn't matter now, does it?"

"Ms. Calley, let me be honest. You seem to me to be a strong woman who's making every bit of use of her talent. I'd hardly call you delicate. I don't think calling off your engagement was mutual or had anything to do with your being unable to deal with Mr. Harrington's personality or with being the wife of a politician. I think it was your own decision."

"You think I'm strong? That . . . that is very kind of you to say, but you only just met me." She looked away briefly, then back at Mia. "It's appropriate the two of them marry, they match up perfectly. And Pamela was smart enough to recognize Alex as the man she's been looking for. I do wonder why she said I was delicate. She's never said that to me."

"Come now, that's easy. She's jealous of you and perhaps even more to the point, she wants to protect him. If it were known you were the one who dumped him, there'd be endless speculation and questions, like, did he cheat on you? Pamela doesn't want anyone to doubt his honor, his trustworthiness. Be honest with me, you broke off the engagement and not because you didn't suit, no, you broke it off because of something else entirely."

Juliet jumped to her feet. "As I told you, Ms. Briscoe, I don't wish to share that experience with your readers. If that's all you wish to know, I should go see to my mother."

Mia slowly rose. "Ms. Calley, I have no intention of writing about what happened between you. You're the only person who's been really close to Alex who suddenly cut him out of your life. I wasn't sure whether to show something to you, but now I will. And I hope you'll tell me the truth."

Mia pulled the two photos out of her bag. "Please look at these photos, Ms. Calley. Do you recognize Kent Harper or Alex Harrington? You must remember how they looked seven years ago."

Slowly, as if reaching to touch a snake, Juliet took the photos. She walked slowly to the window and held them up to the light. Mia watched her, stayed silent. Juliet went tight as a rubber band, but she didn't turn. She said over her shoulder, her voice not quite steady, "Where were these photos taken?"

"Seven years ago at a fraternity rave on my campus, God-wyn University in Pennsylvania. My best friend is the girl in that photo. She disappeared after that party. We all think she was roofied, and I think those two men were responsible. Of course we have to accept she's dead. Her name was Serena and she was my best friend. She was also a big gamer, like Kent. I imag-ine he used that to get her trust. I think he and Alex drove all the way from Boston to that fraternity rave at Godwyn because they knew there'd be lots of prey and they wouldn't be recog-nized. So many students there, graduate students as well, so they wouldn't stick out, they'd fit right in. The hand reaching toward Serena's glass—look at it, Juliet—that's Alex's hand, isn't it? After they roofied her, they set a fire in the kitchen because something went wrong and they had to get her out of there without anyone noticing."

"No! That would mean they killed her—no!"

It was now or never. Mia stared Juliet right in the eye.

"You broke off the engagement because you realized some-thing wasn't right, with Alex, or with Kent, right? Did you overhear something they said about women, about sex, did you see something that frightened you, disgusted you? You didn't know what to do so you did the only thing you could do—you broke off the engagement. You let everyone believe it was mu-tual because you didn't want to cause a scandal. Did you ever even tell Pamela why you broke it off?"

Mia studied Juliet's white face, added quietly, "We never found Serena, of course, because they buried her after they'd killed her. I wonder when they started that fine sport. As teen-agers at Bennington Prep? Probably, and they got away with it. They were smart enough and rich enough to travel as far as they needed to. I wonder if any other girls they roofied have died?"

Juliet Ash Calley stood motionless, her back to the bow window in the opulent living room that screamed old money, excellent manners, and good breeding. Her hands were fisted at her sides, and she was staring into space to a point beyond Mia's left shoulder.

Mia said quietly, "No, it wasn't overhearing them speak about women and sex. It was more, wasn't it? It was personal. They roofied you, too, didn't they? Alex Harrington, your own fiancé, and his best friend, Kent? The man you thought loved you, raped you along with his best friend? Is that why you broke it off, Juliet?"

A shudder went through her body. Then she squared her shoulders, looked Mia in the eye. "You can never write about this."

"Of course not. Please, tell me, help me."

Juliet still looked uncertain, perhaps afraid. She drew in a shuddering breath. "Very well." Again, she paused and Mia could tell the memory still slammed her with incalculable pain. "All right, I woke up one morning and I felt hungover, from the wine I'd drunk the night before, I thought. I wanted to blame the alcohol for the soreness, too, the hazy memories I had after drinking it. Then I began to remember and I clearly saw both Alex and Kent in my bedroom with me, not here, in my bedroom at my cottage. Both of them. At first I simply couldn't accept it. Both Alex and Kent in my bedroom? How could that be? But then I remembered hearing them talk and laugh, and I saw them over me and now they were talking about what each

of them wanted to do, and what order would be most fun—"
Her voice fell off a cliff.

Juliet swallowed. "Regardless, you can't write that, Ms.
Briscoe, there's no proof. There was never any proof and there
never will be."

Mia said, "You've lived with this for two years."

"Yes, every single day for two years."

Mia said nothing, watched Juliet pace the length of an exquisite antique Tabriz carpet.

"Did you accuse him, Juliet? Or was it you couldn't hide
your rage, so Alex guessed you knew anyway? I bet that gave
both Kent and Alex a few sleepless nights."

Juliet jerked around. "I did tell Alex, in this very room. Do
you know he never missed a beat? He tried to hug me, but I
stepped back. He tried to soothe me, he told me I'd had a bad
dream, that what I believed I remembered was ridiculous. We
were going to be married. He loved me, but I knew him well
enough to know he was lying, and he knew me well enough to
know I knew it. He flushed, and his eyes darkened, and I realized he could hurt me. I was glad I met him here, my parents
upstairs, and I wasn't alone with him. I told him I never wanted
to see him again, threw my engagement ring back at him. He
told me I was a fool and he left. Since that day I haven't spoken to either Alex or Kent."

Mia studied Juliet's face. "But time passed and when you
said nothing to anyone else, Alex realized you wouldn't be a
threat to him. He knew if you did accuse him and Kent, he
could tell a very different story—that he was the one who
broke it off, and that your story was revenge. They've left

you alone only because they were certain you couldn't hurt them."

Juliet said finally, "The photos—I could testify the photos look like Alex and Kent, but I can't really be sure. Any accusations I could make now would only cause a hideous scandal. I love my mother and my father very much and I would never put them through that, nor would I ever want them to think they'd somehow failed to protect me. And my father, I think he would kill Alex."

Juliet straightened, looked down at her watch, her voice now brisk. "My mother will awaken soon. Good-bye, Ms. Briscoe. I-I'm sorry about your friend."

"Serena's mother and father are very sorry, too, Ms. Calley."

Juliet's face froze, then she slowly shook her head. "I'm sorry about them, too," she said.

Mia took out a card, laid it on the lovely Victorian coffee table. "We both know now Alex Harrington and Kent Harper are serial rapists, obviously with no qualms, no scruples, seeing as Alex was perfectly willing to roofie you and share you with Kent. And they've killed someone, a twenty-year-old girl so smart, so bright, she lit up a room when she walked into it. She died that night they decided to have their fun. I doubt either of them worried much about it. Do they even remember that night? I doubt it. They don't deserve your silence, even to protect your family. Call me, Juliet. We can help each other make this right."

24

Olivia said hello to Shirley Needleham, the CAU gatekeeper and unit secretary. Shirley gave her a big smile. "Hey, CIA, you're back. Hey, people, CIA in the house."

She smiled at Agent Davis Sullivan, who gave her a little wave and said, "We'll have to speak to security, can't have you interlopers running loose in our house."

"I couldn't stay away, Sullivan. Shirley gave me an amazing cookie yesterday. I'm back for more."

Savich walked out of his office, smiled to see Olivia now speaking to Agent Lucy McKnight and looking at photos of her little boy, Eric, making all the right noises.

Lucy also introduced Agent Ruth Noble to Olivia and the women shook hands. Ruth called out, "I can take her if she causes any trouble, Davis, don't worry your handsome little head."

There were laughs and snorts from Ollie and Griffin.

Savich called out, "Olivia, get your cookie from Shirley and come into the conference room."

Savich closed the door, gestured Olivia to a seat. She sat next to him, a big cookie made with Splenda in her hand. "I didn't come alone. Agent Gaylin, my shadow, is waiting outside, didn't want to come into the Hoover Building, said he didn't want to take a chance of being shanghaied."

Savich laughed. "Tell me how you're feeling, Olivia."

She grinned at him. "Honestly? A bit on edge, even with Gay as my second coat. Andi Creamer—one of my teammates—called me last night, and no, she didn't tell me where she's staying, a big no-no. Mr. Grace told her to stay out of sight and keep her whereabouts to herself."

"You have no idea where Creamer is staying?"

"They told her not to say, even to me. She promised if she gets into trouble or feels unsafe, she'll come to the safe house."

Even though Savich already knew most everything that could be known about Agent Andi Creamer, he wanted Olivia's take. He said, "That's smart. Tell me about Andi."

"She and I trained together at the Farm, so I've known her for a long time. We've been on maybe a dozen missions together, had each other's backs, but to be honest, she's something of a loner, prefers to depend only on herself. Her father abandoned her and her mother and so she grew up very fast, she told me, learned early how to take charge, so it's like her not to want to come stay with me. She likes to be in control if she can, but she's worried about what's going on, and about Mike, of course."

"So how does that mesh with her being a team member?"

"I don't mean she doesn't function well on a team, she does. What's critical on a mission is that every team member trusts every other, and we do." Olivia paused, took another nibble of her cookie, gave him a lopsided grin. "I guess you could say we all love to push the boundaries some, but we know we need each other to survive."

Savich liked Olivia Hildebrandt. She was tough, she was smart and incisive, she had a sense of humor, not easy with the nail-biting career she'd chosen. "All right. What about the fourth team member, Higgs."

She took a bite out of the cookie, hummed it was so good. "I haven't been able to get ahold of Tim; he doesn't answer his cell. Andi told me Grace told her Higgs was headed to Canada on his motorcycle. I think he's really smart to get out of Dodge." She shrugged. "Mr. Grace probably told him to leave, too."

"So you don't think Higgs is in any danger?"

"Not now, he isn't. No one could find him. Higgs is a master at staying off the grid."

"All right. Tell me about Mike Kingman. We're alone, there's no one to tell you what not to say. I want you to tell me why you think he hasn't called you or the CIA."

"I don't know, unless he can't. Look, I know you think someone in the chain of command might have betrayed our mission, and you think it might have been Mike, and that's why he disappeared with the flash drive. I'm sure some people in the CIA are thinking that as well. That flash drive Hashem Jahandar brought out could have named names that could bring down some powerful people. I don't know who these people are, but I am positive Mike wouldn't be part of that, he wouldn't."

"All right, I'll accept that, but Mike has that flash drive, and he's missing. If you're right, the information on that flash drive is worth killing to keep hidden. It could be anything from details of Iranian military capabilities and plans, their weapons development, illicit trade, and as you said, the names of those involved. An Iranian national was part of the team that attacked you. Maybe they hoped you could lead them to Mike, or they thought you might know too much. Do you know of any particular friend who might have helped Mike stay out of sight in or around Washington? Anyone who owns property?"

Olivia shook her head. "There's his condo, of course, but I don't know about any of the properties his friends might own. I've sent you a list of everyone I've called, most in the CIA, some not, but they said they don't know where he is and they haven't heard from him." She'd laid her half-eaten cookie on a napkin beside her, sat forward toward him, her hands clasped. "Please tell me you've found something."

Savich said, "The name of the man you killed Monday night is Razhan, an Iranian security agent who did wet work for them. He's worked globally for fifteen years. The fact you shot him and not vice versa is amazing."

Olivia chewed that over. "If you could find him, then the CIA found him too." She paused. "But why wouldn't they tell me?"

"Actually, I called Mr. Lodner, gave him Razhan's name. He

wasn't happy, said of course he knew of Razhan and was on the point of calling me and giving me the information. Then he wanted to know how I'd found out so quickly."

"You embarrassed him." She grinned, quickly quashed it. "I wish I could have heard you. I imagine Mr. Lodner never believed you'd find diddly-squat. How did you find out it was this Razhan?"

Savich glanced down at MAX beside him, smiled. "I have my ways. Now, Razhan entered the US alone on Sunday, using an excellently forged French passport. We're working on where he stayed and who he met here in Washington."

Olivia said slowly, "A French passport. I wonder why French?"

He nodded. "Common enough not to be noticed. But there could very well be a connection."

"I've never heard of him, but I think it's luck that saved me."

"Don't be ridiculous. You saved yourself."

She cocked her head at him. "All right, going belly-to-the-ground was a reflex I guess you'd call it, the result of really good training. You said the team who attacked me at my home didn't necessarily mean to kill me."

Savich said, "On the surface it seems so, but whoever was behind it could have believed you know what's on that flash drive, or where Mike is. As I said, it's more likely they were there to take you, find out what you know, maybe lead them to Mike. I can see no reason for them to bring in an assassin to kill you if there were no reason."

"Yes, yes, of course you're right."

Savich leaned forward and took her hands in his. "Olivia, you say you don't know anything, but there are blank spots in your memory about what happened in Iran after the RPG knocked you sideways, isn't that right?"

She nodded. "The doctors said my head injury was serious, that it might take a long time for me to remember everything that happened that day. Maybe I never will."

He said, "I know a psychiatrist, Dr. Emanuel Hicks. Would you like to see if he can help you find out if you heard what that dying agent told Mike Kingman?"

"You mean hypnosis?"

"Yes. Dr. Hicks is the best I know. You can trust him completely. I've worked with him for years."

"I've never been hypnotized before. Maybe I wouldn't go under."

Savich looked down at his Mickey Mouse watch, then up at her again. "Let Dr. Hicks worry about that. To be honest, I already called him, told him a little bit about you. He said since you were CIA, you might be more comfortable coming to his home rather than to Quantico. Shall we go see him?"

25

Dr. Emanuel Hicks's home
McAlister, Virginia

WEDNESDAY MORNING

Savich pulled the Porsche into Dr. Hicks's driveway. Olivia said, "Gay wasn't happy I was going with you, alone, without him to protect me."

"He'll get over it. Come lunchtime, Ruth—you met her, Agent Noble—is going to take him to the cafeteria. He can see up close how well the cooks do Mexican food."

Olivia laughed. "Gay only eats hot dogs and pizza."

"He's in luck with the pizza, too, particularly pepperoni, my wife's favorite."

He and Olivia stepped out of the Porsche and into bitter cold and a vicious wind that whipped the tree branches. They hurried, heads down, to the covered front porch, relieved when Dr. Emanuel Hicks immediately opened the solid oak front door of his beloved colonial. He waved them in and quickly closed the door.

Dr. Hicks shook Savich's hand, inquired after Sherlock, then turned to Olivia. "You're my first visitor from the CIA." He studied her face. "Do you know, I was picturing an Amazon from how Agent Savich described you."

Amazon? Olivia liked the sound of that, made her think of Wonder Woman. "Where could I get a chariot and a breast-plate?"

Savich laughed. "Dr. Hicks, this is Agent Olivia Hilde-brandt."

He took Olivia's hand in his, held it, and smiled down at her, not that far down because she was tall, a lovely young woman, her thick French braid showcasing her strong face with its high cheekbones and dark, nearly navy blue eyes. He said, "Your hair, my Mary has nearly the same, so many shades. She calls the color chestnut. Do come in. Agent Savich asked me to see you here because he didn't think you'd be comfortable in a nest of FBI students at the academy in Quantico."

He gave her a smile impossible to resist and Olivia smiled back. She studied him a moment. He was a tall man, skinny as a sapling, with beautiful, gentle, kind eyes. "On our drive here, Dillon said you impersonate Elvis, that you always play to a full house." She grinned. "He also told me you have to belt a pillow around your middle."

"That I do. My wife, Mary, always tries to fatten me up, but it's no go."

"Do you play 'Heartbreak Hotel'? My grandmother says once upon a time she danced the night away to that song."

"Oh yes, but my specialty is 'Blue Suede Shoes.' Now, Mary left some tea and scones out for us. Let's go back to my study."

They followed Dr. Hicks into a long high-ceilinged room with French windows at the back, giving onto a walled-in garden. Olivia imagined it would be beautiful when spring arrived, ivy and roses twining up the mellow red brick. It was a masculine room, obviously Dr. Hicks's study, all soothing earth colors and three walls of floor-to-ceiling books. A fire burned in an old blackened fireplace. It was cozy and welcoming, the morning sunlight pouring in an added bonus.

Dr. Hicks waved her to a worn burgundy leather sofa. "Do sit down. May I call you Olivia?"

She nodded and sank into the soft leather, imagined a great many rear ends had settled there over the years. Dr. Hicks sat across from her in a high-backed leather chair, a matching footstool at its side, Savich on a love seat to his left. Dr. Hicks picked up a Georgian teapot. "Jasmine tea. My wife swears it makes her mellow. And a blueberry scone, if you would like."

Olivia accepted a cup of tea, sat back, waited for him to hand Dillon a cup. She said, "Dillon told me you're the very best, but, well, being hypnotized, I can't imagine it really. To be honest, I've always wondered if hypnosis was fake, sort of like mediums calling in spirits, but Dillon assures me you're legitimate." She paused. "I'm willing to try anything to remember. Dillon believes you can help me."

Dr. Hicks smiled. "Yes, I believe I can. Now, Olivia, I understand you've been through a great deal in the past couple of weeks. Agent Savich filled me in on much of it. He told me you suffered a head injury on a mission to Iran and can't remember facts that could be critical to a current situation. I'm sure your doctors have told you after a bad concussion, it's not a surprise you aren't able to remember everything that happened near the time of your injury. It's called post-traumatic amnesia.

"Agent Savich told me our main purpose is to find out if you can remember what a dying operative said to one of your team members, Mike, about a flash drive."

"Yes, Mike has the flash drive but we can't find him. He's missing. I was close by, I do remember that, but I can't remember if the undercover operative—Hashem was his name—if he said anything at all that could help us."

"So our purpose is to find out if you heard what the dying operative told Mike."

"Yes. Try as I might, I can't remember anything."

Dr. Hicks smiled at her. "Don't worry about it. That's my job. Let's begin. Olivia, I want you to remember a place you visited that made you happy."

Olivia thought a moment, smiled. "Three years ago, Mike and I were coming back from a vacation to Maui and stopped to visit a friend who owned a vineyard in Napa. I'll never forget Mike and I were sitting under an oak tree, looking out over the vineyard, the summer sun shining through the branches, hot on our faces, soaking deep. He was holding my hand, playing with a silly fake ruby ring he'd bought me on Maui. We could smell the ripening grapes, the air was still, soft. We both fell asleep. It was a perfect day—" Her voice caught and she swallowed.

Dr. Hicks said, "I understand. It's a lovely memory. Now, Olivia, please close your eyes. Picture the vineyard spread out in front of you. Smell the grapes, feel Mike holding your hand.

You feel the sun's warmth on your face. You're with Mike, you're happy, content, not a care in the world. Everything is perfect in that moment."

Her lashes fluttered, a small smile bloomed on her face. It was so clear, all of it. Mike was running a finger over the back of her hand, slowly, lightly, slowly turning the ring this way and that. How could she ever forget? She heard a bee buzzing around her, and a beautiful yellow bird she didn't recognize landed on a lower branch of a nearby willow. Odd, she could hear and feel her own breathing, how it had slowed even more. Was that Mike's breathing she heard, too, or was it Dr. Hicks?

Dr. Hicks studied her painfully young face, knew a warrior was behind that face. He pulled a shiny gold round watch on a chain from his jacket pocket and held it up. "Open your eyes now and look at this very old watch."

Olivia opened her eyes, blinked. "You really want me to look at a watch?"

Dr. Hicks smiled at her sarcasm. "Of course, a swinging watch sounds hackneyed. It's nothing more than something to look at, really, but this watch belonged to my grandfather, it's an old friend of mine. Look at the watch now, Olivia, nothing else. Listen to my voice and look at the watch moving, empty out all the questions from your mind, all the worries, let them float away from you until there's only my voice. You're safe with me, never forget that."

Olivia kept her eyes on the shining gold watch as it swung gently back and forth, the hot sun warming her face and the buzzing bee slowly fading, and there was only the gentle swaying of the watch and Dr. Hicks's voice. She slipped away.

Dr. Hicks leaned toward her, his voice quiet, calm. "You are perfectly safe, Olivia. Nothing can hurt you. Do you understand?"

"Yes, I understand."

"I want us to go back together to that day when you and your team went into Iran. Where are we?"

"We've crossed the plateau and we're hiking in the Zagros Mountains. We're going to meet Hashem there and escort him to the border into Iraq."

"Do you see Hashem?"

"Yes, through my binoculars I see him running all out from Iranian soldiers. The soldiers are firing at him. I see him stumble, but he gets up, keeps running. I want to protect him, but all we can do is cover him from our position on high ground, and now the soldiers see us and fire at us, too. He's so close, I can see he's heaving for breath, and then he's hit and he stumbles to his knees. Mike is closest and he runs and picks Hashem up while we cover them, and Mike carries him behind a boulder. I run over to them." She stiffened, shook her head, back and forth.

Dr. Hicks took her hand. "You're safe here with us, Olivia, with me and Agent Savich. Nothing can hurt you. These are memories. They feel real, but they won't hurt you. Don't forget that." Dr. Hicks nodded to Savich.

Savich said, "Olivia, I know you want to help Hashem, and you're close to him and to Mike. Is Mike bending over him?"

"Yes, he's pulled him onto his side, trying to stop the bleeding from his chest. I yell at Higgs and Andi to cover us. Andi wants to come over, but she can't, she's got to help Higgs."

"But you're there, next to Hashem?"

"Yes, both Mike and I are. I'm tearing off my sleeve so Mike can press it against the wound in Hashem's chest. There's so much dirt and shards from the rocks flying, and the noise, it's deafening."

"Can you hear what Hashem is saying to Mike?"

Olivia gasped, her head jerked back. Dr. Hicks squeezed her hand. She calmed.

"Hashem is whispering, 'They betrayed me, they betrayed us.'

"I'm on my knees. I lean in closer. I hear him wheezing for breath, see blood bubbling on his mouth. He knows he's dying, his breath is failing, but he's hanging on, desperately. He's looking directly at Mike, manages to pull him closer, presses something into Mike's hand. 'The guard knew where I was headed, came out of nowhere. Someone told them. Langley? The field office? Take this flash drive to Washington, deliver it only to someone you trust completely.' Hashem's choking on his own blood, shivering violently, but then he manages to whisper, 'Missile guidance components—not Chinese or Russian, they're French. You have to stop them.' He pulls his hand from Mike's and leaves the flash drive in Mike's hand, tries to close his fist over it. His blood is on it. He whispers, 'Tell my wife I love her.' He seizes and then he's gone, just gone, and for an instant I can't believe he's dead, don't want to accept it. Then I hear Andi yelling to me for more ammo, and I jump up and run to her and Higgs, lay down more fire, but Mike stays with Hashem.

"Higgs yells, 'RPG!' Then there's nothing." Olivia jerked her head, heaving. Savich squeezed her hands, felt her slowly calm.

He looked over at Dr. Hicks, who whispered, "And yet she survived. Amazing."

Savich nodded. "She was told Mike carried her out, and Andi and Higgs brought out Hashem's body." He leaned close to her again. "Olivia, did Mike visit you in the military hospital in Balad?"

"Balad? Yes, a nurse told me he did."

"Remember Balad, Olivia. You're sedated, you're confused, but do you hear Mike talking to you? Do you remember what he said?"

She shook her head back and forth. "His voice, I love his voice, all deep and scratchy. He smoked until he got smart and quit, when he was twenty-two, he told me. Yes, he's with me, close. I can feel his breath on my check, and he's kissing me, smoothing my hair."

Olivia was quiet, frowning. "He's saying he has to leave me, he won't see me again until I get back home. He wishes I could come with him because there's no one he can trust, except me. Then he kisses me again. I don't want him to go, but I can only lie there."

"And you haven't heard from him since that day in Balad?"

She slowly shook her head, swallowed. "I'm so afraid for him. They'll want to kill him, they'll want him dead."

Savich wanted to tell her Mike wasn't going to die on his watch, but he remained silent, nodded to Dr. Hicks. "Olivia, on the count of three you're going to wake up. You'll feel refreshed and relaxed, and you'll remember everything you told us."

Olivia opened her eyes, blinked several times, and smiled. "So it's about some kind of missile technology, and it's French."

Savich smiled at her. "Yes, that's what Hashem told you and Mike. You did it, Olivia."

Olivia looked at Dr. Hicks and said with wonder in her voice, "I remembered everything, all of it. Thank you, Dr. Hicks. Will you give me tickets to your next Elvis performance?"

26

Bennington Prep
Glenbridge, Connecticut

WEDNESDAY AFTERNOON

Mia canceled her afternoon plane reservation to La Guardia, rented a bright blue Audi after she left Juliet, and drove two and a half hours from Boston down I-95 to Bennington Prep, a half hour north of New Haven. She didn't expect Bennington to look as glorious as the pictures she'd seen, all taken in the fall to show off the incredible autumn leaves. Now, toward the tail end of winter, the campus looked starker, all the plants and trees hunkered down in survival mode. It was still a marvel in person. *Stately* was the word that suited it perfectly. Bennington was known to be everything a parent could possibly want for their child, the incredible campus itself, the quality education, and the all-important "snoot" factor. If you went to Bennington Prep, enough said. It was part of the pedigree for politics, for Wall Street, for making it big in whatever you wanted to do.

She drove slowly, admiring the classical-style redbrick buildings, the open vistas. Students weren't strolling to their classes, they were rushing, it was that cold, the wind sharp as a knife. She drove slowly by thick stands of maple trees, their branches swaying in the wind in a silent winter dance, and parked her Audi in a visitor's space in front of a state-of-the-art athletic complex. She looked beyond toward a football field surrounded by high bleachers that doubled as their lacrosse field, she guessed.

Is this the beautiful place where you and Kent got started, Alex?

Mia pulled on all her winter gear, braced herself, and walked toward the main athletic building where she'd managed to snag an appointment with one of the two lacrosse coaches at Bennington who'd been there long enough to have coached Alex Harrington and Kent Harper.

She had to get through a department secretary and a student trainee before she was shown to Mr. Hodge Wiliker's small office that looked toward the tennis courts. He was a big man, well into his fifties, still trim and fit, his black-framed glasses pushed up on his bald head. He beamed at her, greeted her enthusiastically, pumped her hand. Mia imagined he rarely got to take center stage at Bennington Prep, and now he was meeting a reporter who was interested in writing about him and about lacrosse because he'd coached Alex Harrington sixteen years before.

Mia knew the drill. She complimented him on the lacrosse trophies she'd seen on display when she'd walked into the building, admired his family in the photos on his desk. She let him assist her to remove her coat, turned down the offer of a cup of coffee, and settled in. "I was looking at the students and wondering if I'd ever been that young."

He laughed. "You're still a young sprout. Imagine what I feel at my age."

She smiled, leaned forward. "As I told you on the phone, Coach Wiliker, I'm writing a background article on the New York City mayoral candidate Alex Harrington. You were his coach during his years here at Bennington. You may remember you also coached his best friend, Kent Harper, also from Boston?"

Wiliker beamed out a smile. "Yep. They were some of our best years at Bennington Prep, championship years, because of them, especially Alex. I knew that boy would go places. I'm pleased he's running for mayor of the Big Apple. Now, Ms. Briscoe, what exactly would you like to know about Alex?"

"May I record this, sir? I want to be sure I'm completely accurate." At his nod, she set up her iPhone. "I hoped you could tell me your impressions of him—his habits, his strengths, his friendships, that sort of thing. Whatever comes to mind about him and Kent, in your own words. I know it's been a long time, but it seems you have fond memories of both of them. I'll ask questions if I need more."

He nodded, leaned toward her, clasped his big hands on top of his desk. "I remember Kent and Alex were the greatest of friends, smart boys from the best families. Both were into those computer games at the time, every spare minute— you know boys—but both were really popular, with the boys and the girls." A wink. "Alex wanted something, he'd go after it."

"And Kent?"

"Kent was the more thoughtful of the two, maybe more careful, but Alex threw himself into an activity, his goal always to win. Kent might dip in a toe first, if you get my meaning. I guess I'd say Kent was more the junior partner of the friendship, but again, it was a long time ago, and boys become men and change. I remember Alex was a superb athlete and was one of the most competitive students I'd ever met. I do remember in lacrosse he always took charge, never quit out there on the field; only winning was good enough for him. Of course that rubbed off on his teammates, and that's why we won those championships. As I recall, both Alex and Kent were looked up to by their teammates for their skill, their desire to win. But maybe it'd be fair to say Kent wasn't as much in-your-face." He cleared his throat. "I didn't mean that exactly as it came out. Alex was—is—as I've said, a natural leader, that's all I meant."

"Of course. Now, Alex was the captain of the lacrosse team in both his junior and senior years, right?"

"Yes, well, he was named captain his junior year only because the senior-year captain, Jordan Jeffers, was injured in an automobile accident and couldn't play." Wiliker shook his head. "An awful thing, I remember it clearly, a hit-and-run, left the boy on the side of the road. He might have died if a jogger hadn't found him. Broken arm, broken leg, internal injuries, poor kid. It's a miracle he survived."

Your work, Alex? Because he had something you wanted? Mia jotted down Jeffers's name.

"Do you remember if Jordan and Alex were friends?"

"Of course they were. I remember Alex and Jordan's younger sister were chummy for a while—sorry, can't remember her name, been too long."

"Don't worry about it. Your memory is amazing, Coach. So after the Jeffers boy was injured, Alex became the captain?"

Coach nodded. "I remember how hard he worked out with the trainers in the weight room to improve his strength and endurance, encouraged his teammates to do the same. That and his never-say-die leadership, that's why we won those championships."

Mia asked, "Any other girlfriends you knew of, Coach? For Alex and Kent?"

Wiliker tapped the side of his head. "Girlfriends—sorry, it's impossible to remember the kids' romances from sixteen years ago. I only remember Jordan's sister because of the accident. There were probably other girls, sure, since both Alex and Kent were popular. I do remember the boys were always as close as fleas, did everything together."

Mia said, "And that would include dating, no doubt?"

"Well, probably, but kids even then seemed to prefer going out together in packs. That's one thing that hasn't changed."

Mia had done some research on missing girls from prep schools, and had hit pay dirt. She said, "Do you remember Teresa Jacobs? She disappeared in her senior year?"

Wiliker scratched his bald head, dislodged his glasses, grabbed them, and slid them back up his forehead. "Of course, now you say her name. She was in that same class, I think. It was quite a hullabaloo; there were rumors, never substantiated, that she was doing drugs and ran away, common enough, but not here, not at Bennington. The local Glenbridge police weren't ever able to turn anything up or I'd know about it. It was a sad thing, scared all the kids and parents."

Mia said, "Do you happen to remember if Alex knew her? If the police spoke to him?"

Wiliker looked surprised, but said easily, "Well, the police spoke to everyone, me included, even the nutritionist, Ms. Busbee. No one knew anything. Of course Alex knew her, she was the captain of the girls' lacrosse team, another reason she wouldn't touch drugs. She was an athlete. Her parents—imagine not knowing what happened to your child? Living your whole life without knowing? I remember after Teresa disappeared I kept my own kids really close."

"Ah, and did Teresa and Alex date?"

Coach shook his head. "I don't remember. It was sixteen years ago—" He tapped his head. "Old brain."

Mia pulled the two photos Dirk had enhanced out of her messenger bag, placed them on Wiliker's desk. "Do you recognize either of these men?"

Wiliker pulled down his black-framed glasses and studied the two photos. He said, "These are older, aren't they?"

"Yes, seven years old."

She saw he wanted to be helpful, but he finally shook his head. "I'm sorry, Ms. Briscoe, but it's hard to make out their features since they're not facing the camera, only bits of their profiles, and they're a bit blurry. I can't imagine why these particular photos are important to this article you're writing about Alex Harrington."

Mia held her breath, pointed. "Bear with me. Do you see

the notch in this man's ear? Like he was hurt, maybe playing sports?"

Coach brought the photo close. Slowly, he nodded. "I see it, looks like an injury that healed years ago. I've seen several like that when a boy gets hit on the ear with a lacrosse stick."

"Do you remember if Alex Harrington was ever injured? An injury like this?"

"As a matter of fact, I do. It was back in his junior year before the captain, Jordan, was hurt. He accidentally hit Alex with a lacrosse stick. The reason I remember his injury so well is because I was the one who took him to our nurse."

"Tell me, what is Jordan Jeffers doing now?"

"Why do you want to know about Jordan Jeffers?"

"Again, Coach, just being thorough."

"Jordan never played lacrosse again but he did graduate, probably went to some Ivy League college, no doubt, which is what the great majority of Bennington students do. I heard he's fine now, lives in Montpelier, runs his family's chain of restaurants." He paused a moment, pointed to the photo. "You think this man is Alex? Why do you care? Why would anyone care?"

Mia shrugged. "Just a bit of interest, that's all. Since you knew him very well for four years I thought I'd ask."

"It could be Alex, but Ms. Briscoe, you should show this to Alex, not me." He straightened in his chair, suddenly stiff, his eyes narrowed. "Wait. Why did you show me that photo? Why does it matter if Alex Harrington tore his earlobe? Surely an injury that minor can't be important to your article."

Mia gave him a fat smile. "A friend of his showed me the photo, name of Benny Holmes, said he'd been to a great party with Alex, celebrating something, he couldn't remember, someone took this photo and he'd kept it. Before I used it, I wanted to be sure it was really Alex."

Wiliker was getting suspicious. She couldn't blame him, she'd gotten too heavy-handed. But she'd gotten what she wanted. Time to pack up her tent and go home. Mia tucked her tablet back in her messenger bag, slipped her cell into her coat pocket, and rose. She quickly pulled on her coat. "I won't take any more of your time. Thank you, Coach Wiliker, you've added depth, some fine details I'll be able to use in my article. When I see Alex, I'll tell him I spoke with you, tell him how fondly you remember him."

That bit of praise unbent him enough to shake her hand.

Mia was back on the road and headed to New York City a few minutes later. Now she could keep her promise to Pilar Kaplan, the administrative assistant she'd spoken to at Harvard when she had stopped there to talk to Alex's professors. No need to give her name out to anyone as a witness. Pilar had been quite sure it was Alex in the picture, claimed she recognized his old bracelet, said he never took it off. Now Mia knew Alex Harrington's earlobe had been torn by a lacrosse stick when he was sixteen.

You didn't get it fixed until much later, right, Alex? Why? Was it when you took charge of your family's business in New York? She could find the doctor who repaired his earlobe if he denied it, and Tommy Maitland could get the police report on Teresa Jacobs, the girl who went missing at Bennington, just as Serena did at the Delta Rho Phi rave.

27

Safe House

WEDNESDAY EVENING

Chas Gaylin sat at the banged-up table in the ancient kitchen that looked older than he was, drinking coffee. He eyed Olivia as she paced up and down the small kitchen, then stood at the counter staring at a box of lasagna pasta as if she were trying to figure out what to do with it, then started pacing again.

Gay had come back on duty at the safe house an hour before and would stay with Olivia until eight o'clock in the morning, when Sue Ling Smith would relieve him again. He said easily, "I wish you'd stop pacing, makes me nervous, and don't look out the window, keep the curtain closed. Sue Ling told me that FBI agent set you to calling everyone you and Mike ever met to ask if they'd seen Mike. Sounds like a waste of time, you ask me, busywork to keep you off the street. Seems to me it's making you a little crazy. You want to tell me about seeing the shrink with Agent Savich?"

"No," she said and tossed him an apple, then took one for herself and bit in.

"Thanks for the apple," Gay said, polished it on his sleeve, pointed to the pasta. "So we're having lasagna for dinner?"

"Lasagna? Hmm. Maybe. Did you eat a taco with Ruth in the FBI cafeteria? Any belly pains from FBI food poisoning?"

"Gut's fine. For a taco, it tasted okay. I like Ruth. She's sharp, a real go-getter. Do you know she has a stepson who's a big-deal baseball pitcher? He's going to Virginia Tech on a scholarship? She told me he brought in the regional championship. So did you make the calls Agent Savich told you to do? I don't suppose you found out anything?"

She gave him a crooked grin. "Well, one of Mike's soccer team buddies told me he'd spotted Mike coming out of Sunny's Bar in Tyson's Corner a couple of days ago."

"Idiot. Mike wouldn't be caught dead in Sunny's, it's basketball on all the TVs, not soccer."

"Agreed. I think he told me that because he's divorced now and wanted to ask me out on a date. I think you're right, Agent Savich was only trying to give me something to do. He couldn't have expected any of those people would tell me anything new. Gay, you're still checking in at Langley, and I know you've got your own sources. Does anyone have any more of an idea where Mike could be?"

Gay shook his head. "You know I'd tell you if I knew anything." He eyed her a minute. She'd stopped her pacing, poured herself a glass of water, but she still looked like she wanted to bust out of her skin. Of course she was scared for Mike, for herself, but there was something else.

Gay said, "You gonna tell me what it's like being hypnotized? Did that shrink fill in any of the blanks for you?"

Olivia felt a surge of guilt. She wanted to tell him she'd remembered what Hashem had said, but Dillon had asked her to keep it to herself because both Hashem and the mission had been betrayed and they didn't know who on the food chain was responsible. She said, "I couldn't really imagine going under, I mean, he had this swinging gold watch, and how silly was that? But I did. There was nothing to it really. I just sort of faded out of the picture." She paused a second, then asked, "I heard your daughter is having a baby. Congratulations."

So it was need-to-know and he wasn't in the loop. Gay said, "Yeah, thanks, wife's so excited she's already bought out one of those baby stores. She's over with Delia right now, the two of them are wondering what color to paint the frigging nursery. I told her to flip a coin."

Olivia laughed. "At least she didn't shoot you, so that's good."

Helmut knew that word and barked, waved his tail nonstop, like a metronome.

"About the lasagna, I was planning on making my mother's recipe, but I forgot the fresh tomatoes. Helmut, yes, yes, I know you're starving. I've got your dinner." She poured his food into his bowl, petted his head, and watched him dig in like it was his last meal.

"He's a great dog, Olivia. How old is he?"

"Two years. When I'm out of the country, Linda in Eastern Affairs or my friend Julia takes him in."

Gay said, "You know, we can't eat lasagna without tomatoes, so how about we have pizza instead? I'll go for pepperoni and artichoke." He looked at her like a kid on Christmas morning.

Olivia's stomach growled. "Okay, sounds good to me, but no artichokes for me, I'm pepperoni with onion and black olive."

Gay paused a moment. "Like Mike."

When he called in their order to Pizza Nirvana, double pepperoni and artichokes for him, he sounded positively buoyant. He punched off his cell. "Thirty minutes, then I'll go pick it up, won't have it delivered for obvious reasons."

"Obvious?"

"You already forget the bad guys came to your house Monday night?"

"Of course not, but we're in a safe house, for goodness' sake. No one knows we're here, unless you and Helmut sold me out."

He shook his head. "When I get back, I'll tell you a story about a hoagie delivery boy with a Beretta under his hoodie, happened about five years ago."

She snorted. "You're making it up. Come on, Gay, you called it in, I'll do the pickup."

"Nope, forget it. You're going to stay behind locked doors."

"Come on, Gay, Pizza Nirvana's only half a mile away, lots of traffic all the way, lots of people. I'll be in and out in a flash. No worries." She pulled her car keys out of her jeans pocket, tossed them in the air, caught them again, leaned down to rub Helmut's ears. "I really need to get out, breathe some of this crisp air."

"It's thirty degrees out, a bit beyond crisp."

"Gay, really, I'm going nuts. I'll leave Helmut to protect you. He saved my bacon Monday night." She went down on her knees, took Helmut's head between her hands, looked into his beautiful eyes. "You will stay here and guard Gay. I'll bring you one of those cheese sticks you like." She looked up at Gay. "You could give Helmut a short walk, but not too long, he hates the cold."

Gay took a final bite of his apple, banked the core into the wastebasket, and clapped his hands. Helmut trotted over to him, butted his golden head against his hands. "My old dog, Gamble, died a couple of years ago. Helmut here makes me wonder if I should get another mutt." He remembered there was a basketball game on tonight between his beloved Wizards and the Bucks. He sighed, looked at his watch. "Okay, you fetch the pizzas and I'll walk Helmut, give both of us some exercise. You got your Glock?"

"Of course."

He walked with her to the front hall. "I know in my head you're right, no one can know you're here, but—you be careful anyway, Hildebrandt. Oh yeah, when you get back you can tell me what you were doing on the Web for hours."

That brought her to a stop. "How did you know?"

"It's not a big house. I walked behind you, you never heard me. I'm a ghost."

Olivia sighed. She couldn't tell him, so she lied clean. "Only thing interesting I found was a nest of drug dealers out of Rwanda who supply the Middle East."

"Sure, Hildebrandt, like I'll believe that."

She patted his hand. "Don't worry about me, Gay. And you stay, Helmut. Guard Gay." Olivia bundled up against the cold and bitter wind, wondered how winter could still be so dug in in the middle of March.

Gay watched her run to her car, climb in, and lock the doors before he closed the front door again.

Olivia turned the heater on full blast and settled in until it began to warm. Of course Gay knew she was cutting him out. She couldn't tell him she was researching French arms dealers, studying their glossy web pages, and then, frustrated, anything she could find on the dark Web. Why had she picked Rwanda of all places? She wondered what Dillon Savich was doing.

She backed slowly out of the narrow driveway, looked over all the cars parked in the pleasant middle-class neighborhood, didn't see anything suspicious. Everyone was inside, eating dinner, staying warm. She headed out.

Olivia turned onto Wilton Avenue and into traffic, and again, checked her rearview. She saw no one following.

She pulled into the Willow Springs strip mall. Not many people about except the few inside the pizza place. She parked, dashed into the awesome warmth, heard her stomach growl at the divine smells. She breathed them in, gave her name, chatted with the counter girl while she waited, a perky eighteen-year-old, if that, and paid. She walked out carrying two pizza boxes and cheese sticks for Helmut, and again, she paused, looked all around her. She saw a young couple hurrying toward the Mexican restaurant, another man hurrying to his car. Nothing suspicious.

She slid into her RAV4, turned on the heat, and got ready to back out. A man's voice, with a French accent, came from behind her.

"You did not think we could get to you, did you?" Olivia felt the cold muzzle of a pistol at the base of her skull.

"How did you find me?" Was that her voice, so calm and steady?

A moment of silence, then the man said, "Reach for your weapon, slowly, and give it to me." He dug the muzzle into her neck. "Do it, now. If you try anything stupid, believe me, you will regret it." He held out his right hand.

Actions and consequences sped through her mind. She realized she didn't have a chance, not now. She passed him her Glock. "How?"

He said close to her ear, "Nice red Porsche the federal cop drives. Easy to follow."

28

She heard Agent Cliff's voice from the Farm, telling her to blank out fear, to focus on what would come next. Gay would worry soon something had happened, try to call her. Then he'd come looking, maybe track her phone, but he'd be too late. And this man had no reason to let her live once he had what he wanted from her. Whatever would happen was all up to her.

"Drive out of this hideous place and turn right on Wilton Avenue."

Olivia drove slowly out of the Willow Springs strip mall, turned right.

"Where are we going?"

"It is not your problem. Drive slow, but not too slow. Go straight until I tell you."

"Where are you from in France?"

He laughed, a scratchy, Gauloises laugh.

"You like the accent? Most American women do, it makes them think of sex and sweaty sheets."

"Or of smokers' breath, heavy on the garlic."

She heard an angry hiss, felt the muzzle dig in, and she flinched.

"*Ferme ta gueule!* Keep your mouth shut, bitch. No, stop, do not go through that yellow light."

Olivia stopped as the light turned, watched the crossing cars stream through the intersection, homeward bound. She wanted to ask him which French arms dealer he worked for, but she had to pretend she knew as little about the flash drive as she could. "What do you want?"

"You know very well what I want. You are going to take me to Mike Kingman or you are going to summon him to us. You are lovers, of course you know where he is. You will tell me now or I will have to persuade you."

"I don't know where he is, no one does. Don't you mean what your employer wants? You know, the man who tells you what to do, the man who gives you orders? Who do you work for?"

The muzzle dug in again. She said, "Listen to me, whoever you are, if I knew where Mike is, if the CIA knew where he is, I wouldn't be in a CIA safe house, hidden from you people. Of course you know all about Monday night, about those two men who came to my house. One of them was called Razhan, an Iranian security agent who's been killing people for fifteen years for his masters. But you're French. Who's your master?"

Olivia felt his gloved hand reach around her neck and squeeze, hard enough that she jerked and the RAV swerved. He cursed, dropped his hand. She looked at him in her rearview. He was wearing sunglasses, a hat and scarf. She wouldn't know him if she walked past him on the street, but she'd never forget his voice. She grinned at him. "You know Kingman is gone, disappeared. Everyone's thinking he stole whatever it is your boss wants and plans to sell it to the highest bidder. Chances are he'll try to sell it to your boss, so why threaten me when your boss can buy whatever it is from him? What's a few million euros, petty cash to him, right?"

She heard contempt in his voice. "You give me an excellent joke. You are saying this agent is a traitor? This man you have sex with?"

Olivia shrugged. "Sex is only sex, isn't that what you French say? Enough people believe Kingman's a traitor. He'd be a fool to tell me, tell anyone, where he is. Hey, maybe he's already contacted your boss."

The muzzle against her neck relaxed a tiny bit.

Was he thinking through this new development? Would his boss be willing to pay Kingman for the flash drive rather than have him kill both agents? It would be much cleaner.

Olivia said, "Besides, do you think I haven't already tried to call Mike? Do you think he's stupid enough to have his cell phone on? It would be traced and he'd be found—caught—and this something you want would be in CIA hands. I'll bet you he's smashed his phone, bought a burner that can't be traced to him. Seems to me he's calling the shots, and you people are blundering around trying to take me when I have no idea what's going on or where he is. If I did, I'd tell my superior and he'd find him, arrest him."

"Even if part of what you say is true, you may be in this with him."

She gave him a quick look again in the rearview. "But you should call your boss, ask him what he wants you to do, right?"

A snort. "I do not need to speak to anyone until you tell me everything you know. Shut up, keep driving straight. We are leaving this ugly city."

They were already several blocks down Wilton, and traffic was thinning out. They'd end up in Maryland unless they turned at some isolated place he had ready for her and Mike. Olivia said, "Your boss wants this something Mike Kingman has. Why don't you tell me what it is?"

"Stop your ridiculous lies. You already know, you are playing the games with me. Be quiet and keep driving. I will tuck you away if I have to, make sure Kingman hears I have you. Then he will come to me, or I will wring your neck like the chicken." He was leaning forward now, his breath on her cheek. "Turn right on Krager. It is what you call a shortcut."

There was a red light coming up ahead, and a busy intersection. A chance. Olivia readied herself, studied the cars. She saw a big black Ford F350 driving fast toward the light on Krager, saw the driver was yelling at the person in the passenger seat, not paying much attention. She slowed a bit as if she was going to turn then suddenly floored it into the intersection. She saw a brief flash of the truck driver's terrified face, felt the muzzle of the gun fall away, heard the man cursing in French as they slammed into the rear driver's side of the truck. She was ready when the airbags exploded, but the Frenchman was leaning forward, thrown sideways. She pushed back hard against the airbag, reached down, and pulled her small Walther PP2 from its ankle holster. She flattened herself under the airbag and fired through the front seat, heard him yell in pain; she kept firing until the magazine was empty.

"Bitch! I could kill you now, but you are going to pay first."

He didn't fire back, so she knew he didn't want to take the chance he'd kill her. He shoved the door open and ran. Olivia jerked up, pulled herself free of the collapsed airbag, and saw him—a tall man in a long dark winter coat, his face hidden by a thick black scarf wrapped around his neck, clutching his shoulder. Her Walther was empty. She looked in the back seat, saw her Glock, grabbed it. Horns were blasting, people yelling, and the driver of the truck she'd hit jumped out and stared dazedly at the RAV smashed into the rear of his truck and the woman running with a gun after a fleeing man.

Olivia yelled "Federal agent!" and didn't slow. The man was running flat out, shoving people out of his way, but she was gaining on him. He was only half a block ahead of her when he turned off Krager onto Baker Street, then ducked into an alley connecting Baker and Mansford. He was fast even holding his hand against his shoulder. When she came through the alley onto Mansford, she couldn't believe it, he'd already jumped into a taxi. Too dangerous to shoot at him or the tires. She memorized the license plate, stood for a moment, hands on her thighs, panting. Then she pulled out her cell. She didn't call Gay, she called Dillon.

When Savich jumped out of his Porsche twenty minutes later, Olivia was sitting on the sidewalk, her RAV's engine still sending up small plumes of black smoke. Two police cruisers and a fire truck were blocking off traffic, an ambulance standing by with nothing to do. Chas Gaylin sat beside her, three METRO officers hovering nearby.

She jumped to her feet. "Please tell me you got him."

"METRO's all over the taxi. You shot him in the shoulder, so we've alerted the hospitals and clinics in the area. Are you all right?"

She smiled. "Yes, yes, I'm fine. Dillon, I couldn't see him through the front seat, the airbag was collapsed on me, so I just kept shooting until my Walther ran out of ammo. Luckily he decided he shouldn't kill me, so he gave it up and ran." She reached down, pulled the PP2 out of its holster. "I love this little pistol, it probably saved my life."

Savich smiled. "My wife always wears her ankle pistol as well. You did very well, Olivia."

Gay rose, introduced himself, and shook Savich's hand. "If it's all right with you, I've been told to take Olivia to another safe house." He stared at Olivia, shook his head. "This shouldn't have ever happened. I was an idiot to let you talk me into getting the fricking pizzas. Believe me, Mr. Grace isn't happy with me. I've got a big dressing-down coming and I deserve it. I'll probably be reassigned."

Olivia said, "Gay, I'll speak to him, explain it wasn't your fault, that I insisted since it was only a short drive." She glanced over at the intersection. "My poor RAV, it really came through for me, gave itself up. Now I'll have to get another one. Hey, maybe the pizza's still okay, just needs to be heated up—"

Savich nodded. "Yes, to all those things. First, though, I'd like you both to come with me to the Hoover. Agent Hildebrandt, I'm going to make sure you're never lost to me again."

29

New York City

WEDNESDAY EVENING

Two hours later, Mia walked into her condo, shed all her winter gear, turned up the heat to roast. What a day, since six A.M. this morning to Boston, then to Connecticut, then back home. She wasn't exhausted, though; she was revved. She looked around her small living room and realized she hadn't cleaned before she'd left. It showed. She picked up a sweater draped over a living room chair, dropped it on the blue comforter on her bed, decided it was enough, and walked back to her table, spread all her work out, and googled Jordan Jeffers, the captain of the lacrosse team who'd accidentally hit Alex's earlobe with his lacrosse stick before a hit-and-run driver ran him down. She had a few minutes before changing to meet Miles Lombardy, Alex Harrington's senior staffer.

Of course she got caught up in the tragic story of Jordan Jeffers. When Mia looked at her watch, she jumped out of her chair, knew she had to hurry. She thought about Miles as she changed, fair complexioned and only a couple of years older than she was. He was known as a political whiz. She remembered he looked like a wise owl in round glasses and neatly trimmed goatee. They both knew the rules: he wanted to find out what she was going to do and she wanted to find out what he knew about Alex. She hoped her wits would win out.

Mia wound her long blue-and-green woolen scarf around her neck, buttoned her coat to her chin, pulled her watch cap down to her eyebrows, and found her Uber waiting for her. At least she wasn't walking from the *Guardian*, head down into a tonsil-freezing glacial wind. The streets weren't congested. The only New Yorkers outside were those leaving work, rushing toward the subway.

She directed her Uber driver to the Confluence, one of the current downtown in-spots only two blocks up from the *Guardian*, on a small side street. Her Uber pulled up to the restaurant with five minutes to spare. Even though it was frigid outside, it was warm inside and the bar bulged with happy hour New Yorkers. The Confluence sported a huge old mahogany bar trucked from a 1920s speakeasy in Chicago. Its specialty was mango-chutney pizza, served up by a waitstaff of mostly flamboyant would-be actors and dancers.

Mia was impressed when she spotted Miles at a booth near the back and wondered how he'd managed to snag that primo spot. She smiled at his wave, thought again he had the air of a wise owl. She wove her way through the happy crowd, everyone forced to speak louder to be heard over the pounding jungle-beat music. Mia had no doubt Miles's phone call as she was leaving Coach Wiliker's office to meet him that evening was an assignment from Alex Harrington. Miles was to charm her, pass on some of Alex's talking points, pump her on what she'd found out in Boston and whether she'd do right by candidate Harrington in her upcoming feature on him. Mia smiled at Miles. This would be fun.

"Mr. Lombardy, good evening." She began unwinding the scarf around her neck. "Isn't this a great place? A bit on the noisy side, but who cares? The pizzas are incredible, and the waitstaff will give you a little performance if you ask them. If the music's not playing too loud, they'll sing, maybe mime from a show. *Cats* is always popular, singing and dancing."

"That sounds like fun. There's a place in L.A. where all the wannabe actors do the same thing." He slid out of the booth and helped her off with her coat.

"Thank you. I heard this was your first year in New York," she said. "How are you surviving our winter?"

He smiled, stuck out his hand, shook hers. "I'm from L.A. where it's always warm, the sun always shines. You do have to worry about skin cancer from too much sun. I do love the energy of New York, the feel of excitement in the air, but I've got to be truthful, I hate the weather."

"That answers my question."

"This place is a find. I haven't been here before. I've enjoyed a few places in the Village, but never made it here. Do you think our waiter would dance a Gene Kelly number?"

"I doubt it tonight. Looks like they're too busy running their feet off to dance and that music is blasting anyway. Please, call me Mia."

"Mia. And I'm Miles." Mia slid in, laid her coat beside her.

A waiter wove his way through the standing patrons to their booth. Miles said, "A beer, please, whatever pale ale's on tap. How about you, Mia?"

She started to nod, then ordered the house white. She leaned forward and raised her voice so he could hear her. "So what's going on, Miles? Has Alex—Mr. Harrington asked me to call him that—decided to drop out of the race? Get married now in Tahiti? What?"

He laughed, a nice full-bodied laugh that fogged up his glasses. He took them off, wiped them on a napkin, slid them back on. "Mr. Harrington asked me to check in with you, and I was glad for the opportunity. We met only briefly at the fundraiser, didn't get a chance to talk when you were at campaign headquarters yesterday. I have quite a bit I'd like you to be aware of for your article—Mr. Harrington's hopes, his campaign, his plans. He also wanted me to ask you whether your trip to Boston went well, what your impressions were."

Mia nearly smiled. Right out of the gate, down to business, no pretending over a social drink, and that was a pleasant surprise. She said on a grin, "He could have sent me an email."

"I prefer a more personal approach. How else can I be sure you understand what's really important to him—his program for minority schools, gun control?"

She saw then he looked tired. "A lot of late-night strategy sessions with Mr. Hughes and Alex?"

He gave her a singularly sweet smile. "Sure, and it'll only get more intense as the election heats up. I'm used to that, but what I'm not used to is this cold. When will it warm up around here?"

Their waiter magically reappeared through the packed-in crowd, a small tray held up high, and expertly set their beer and wine in front of them. "Might warm up in April, sir, if we're lucky. Sorry I can't stay. Holler when you'd like more." He disappeared again, weaving his way through bodies, too graceful not to be a dancer.

"Here's hoping for April," Mia said, and she clicked her wineglass to Miles's beer.

Time to bait the bear. "I had a nice conversation with Pamela Barrett, Alex's fiancée, and of course with his professors at Harvard he'd picked out for me to talk to." She sipped her wine. "Turns out Boston was very informative, particularly my interview with Juliet Ash Calley, Alex's former fiancée."

Miles showed no hesitation, no sign of alarm. "I never met Ms. Calley but Cory told me she's the most beautiful woman he's ever seen. I looked her up, and I agree, she could give all the L.A. girls a run for their money. I read she's a concert pianist, though I've never heard her play."

"She's mainly classical, and immensely talented. Cory's right, I've never seen a more beautiful woman."

"I'm a jazz man, myself. New Orleans."

"Do give her a listen, Miles, she's incredible. Let me add, what's really refreshing is that her beauty doesn't seem to matter to her at all."

Miles took a drink of his beer, wiped a bit of foam off his mouth with the back of his hand. "I was told she's really sensitive, arty, if you know what I mean, so it was a good thing they didn't marry."

"I wonder if Alex was afraid she'd upstage him, take the limelight, get all the publicity?"

"No, that's not Mr. Harrington—music, politics, they're two entirely different kinds of fame. Seems to me it just wasn't a good fit." He paused a hair. "What did she tell you?"

Worried now, are you, Miles? Which meant that Alex was worried. Mia cocked her head at him. "I understand why you could be concerned Ms. Calley might have bad-mouthed him to me."

"I have no reason to suppose Mr. Harrington would be worried. In fact, he thought you might see her. Understandably, he wouldn't want to be blindsided. I mean, he is running for a high office. You're known as an excellent interviewer, Mia, so who knows what she might say to you, out of bitterness, perhaps, or something else—"

"You mean like revenge?"

Miles shrugged. "Who knows? Anything could be possible since Mr. Harrington was the one who broke off their engagement—" Miles's voice died. He looked down at his USC ring as if it were his consigliere. Evidently the ring didn't have any wise counsel because Miles took another quick swig of his beer and carefully set the mug on a napkin.

"Is that what Alex told you, Miles? He was the one who broke off the engagement?"

"Well, no, I'm surmising, since he told me she's quite shy, introverted, not at ease with people. Even a concert pianist, if she's socially awkward, wouldn't be comfortable as a politician's wife." Miles shrugged.

Mia said, "Otherwise what woman in her right mind wouldn't want to be Alex's wife? Have I filled in the blanks correctly, Miles?"

30

No, I didn't mean that, exactly." Miles sighed. "But yes, Mr. Harrington is an impressive man." Mia sensed a canned recording snapping on when Miles added quickly, "Mr. Harrington really cares about New York, Mia, he wants to make it better. Just take his budget for minority schools—"

She raised her hand to turn off the spigot. "Before you go on, Miles, let me set the record straight. Ms. Calley broke off their engagement, not Alex. Tell me this—did Alex already know I'd spoken with Juliet Calley?"

Miles grew very still. Nothing showed on his face, but his glasses started to fog up. Mia took another sip of her chardonnay. She felt sorry for him, but she wasn't about to help him out of his lovely deep hole. He'd been sent to worm information out of her, and he should have known he'd be the sacrificial goat if things didn't go well.

He cleaned his glasses once again, slid them back on. "He did, yes. I believe Ms. Barrett mentioned to him you might."

Mia said, "I wonder how Ms. Barrett guessed? As I recall I

didn't mention my visiting Ms. Calley." She smiled. "Oh well, I suppose word travels fast in their circle." Mia wasn't about to throw Juliet under the bus, and so she said easily, "Don't make yourself crazy, Miles. Ms. Calley didn't accuse Alex of kidnapping babies or running down people he didn't like with his Jaguar." Mia wondered if Miles would quote that line to Alex, and whether Alex would know she meant Jordan Jeffers. She wondered if Alex even remembered Jordan Jeffers.

Miles said, "Alex doesn't drive a Jag, he drives an F150."

Mia lightly tapped the heel of her hand to her forehead. "How could I have doubted that for an instant? Of course he drives an American truck. Does he haul away old furniture for his mom?"

Miles tried for a laugh, nearly made it. "You're joking. You know some political opponents will do almost anything, say almost anything, if they catch a scent their opponents might have a weakness. And who wouldn't be worried about an ex-fiancée? Mr. Harrington's current fiancée, Ms. Barrett, she'll make quite an impressive first lady of New York City, don't you think?"

Mia took another sip of her chardonnay, slightly woody, as she liked it. "Oh yes, Pammie would surely make a fine first lady of the manor. She's confident, smart, and after speaking with her, I think she'd do anything to help him win this election. Pammie and Alex Harrington make a fine team."

The sarcasm hit him in the face, but he ignored it. "Good, I knew she'd impress you, she impresses everyone. She and Alex have agreed not to refer to her as Pammie, by the way. It's too casual, not fitting for a first lady of New York City. Could you please not refer to her by her nickname in anything you write?"

Mia stared at him. "What? Mr. Harrington is worried about his future wife's nickname? Voters would drop away if they heard it? Me? I think Pammie sounds all sorts of cuddly and fun and ready for a pillow fight. Pamela, on the other hand, sounds a bit stuffy, standoffish, makes her sound full of herself, don't you agree?"

Miles Lombardy blinked owl eyes behind his black-framed glasses. "You know, Mia, what I think really doesn't matter to anyone. What did you learn about Mr. Harrington from his former professors at Harvard?"

"Since Mr. Harrington sent me a list of names, I assume he fully expected the three professors to praise his eyebrows, so why do you ask?"

"I'm covering all the bases. You talked to some of the departmental staff, too, right?"

So Alex had heard she'd spoken with the departmental secretaries, a student's best friends, if the student had a brain. How? Had one of them called him? She nodded, smiling. "Of course. Any good reporter would." Mia looked at him squarely. "Listen, Miles, there's no need to worry about Ms. Calley, for now. She was very neutral about Alex and his fitness to be the mayor of New York." She saw relief flood his face, and then she added the spur, "All of you will find out exactly what everyone I spoke with said about Alex when you read my article."

He downed the rest of his beer in one draft and stared at her, mute.

Mia's cell buzzed a text from Travis. ICICLE COLD HERE IN

ZURICH. DRINKS WITH BIG HONCHO OF LOHMAN PIERCE. HE WASN'T
PISSED ABOUT ANYTHING, JUST WANTED TO TOUCH BASE. ALL GOOD.
LOVE YOU, MISS YOU LIKE CRAZY, TRAVIS.

A hammer of guilt slammed her head. The last couple of days
had been so hectic, she'd forgotten to call Travis. She looked at
her watch, realized it was getting late. She was surprised he was
still awake. She was surprised she was still awake, too, given
the hours she'd put in today. She slipped her cell back into her
messenger bag, grabbed her coat, and scooted out of the booth.
As she wound her scarf around her neck, she looked down at
Miles. He didn't look happy. She raised her voice to make sure
he could hear her. "However this turns out, you've got a bright
career ahead of you. Remember that. Good evening and thank
you for the wine."

Mia didn't leave the blessed warmth of the restaurant until
she was wrapped to her eyebrows. She pulled on her gloves as
she stepped outside into the middle of a crowd, all of them
looking for a taxi. She hadn't called an Uber, hadn't thought
of it. She called now, was told it would be twenty minutes. She
watched as taxis pulled up to take in people in front of her.
She huddled in her coat, wrapped her arms around herself. No,
this was ridiculous, she wasn't going to wait for an Uber. She'd
hike to the subway station on West Fourth near Washington
Square, only three blocks up if she took a shortcut. If she hurried, she could call Travis from the station, and if the trains
were running smoothly, she'd be home in under half an hour.

She made her way to Sullivan Street and headed toward
Washington Square. The businesses in the neighborhood were
closed for the day, the only light coming from the streetlights

and from apartment windows. Mia walked fast, head down against the wind. She saw an occasional taxi, but of course they were already occupied. She paused next to a dark building, the NYU School of Law, when she saw two men on the corner passing something to each other, probably a drug deal. She walked to the other side of the street and kept trudging.

She heard a car engine, her first thought that it might be a taxi. She half turned, an arm raised to flag it down, but it wasn't a taxi, it was a large dark sedan and it was coming fast, too fast. It swerved suddenly and drove straight toward her. Her heart jumped and a hoarse scream burst out of her mouth.

31

Headlights hit her full in the face, blinding her, and Mia stumbled back, tripped on the curb. She went down and rolled behind two garbage cans as the sedan jumped the curb and plowed into them. The cans bounced over her, the lids went flying, sending bags of garbage raining down. She covered her head with her arms, kept scrambling backward on her elbows. She heard the car engine revving, then the blessed sound of a man's shout. He was running toward her, yelling, waving his arms at the car.

It seemed like forever the sedan didn't move, until the driver slammed into reverse, dragging one of the toppled garbage cans with him, and roared away up the empty street. The man was panting when he came down on his knees beside her. "Are you okay?"

It was one of the two men she'd seen on the corner. Mia caught her breath, forced herself to breathe deeply until she stopped shaking. But she couldn't stop her heart kettle-drumming or the nausea rising in her throat. She swallowed convulsively. She wouldn't vomit, she wouldn't. *Okay, better.* "Thanks for chasing him off." How could that be her voice, all calm and together? When he helped her sit up, she kept hold of his arm. "I'm glad those garbage cans were full, and the bags didn't burst open. If they'd burst, can you imagine what could have come flying out? And on me? This is the wool coat my parents gave me for Christmas." She sucked in a breath. "Sorry, I'm babbling. If you hadn't been nearby I-I don't know what would have happened. Really, thank you."

Mia saw her rescuer's face for the first time under a street-light. He was dressed head to foot in leather with a heavy black leather coat, black leather gloves, and chunky black boots. He didn't even look to be voting age yet. He stared down the street, shook his head. "You're welcome. The moron was drunk, or maybe high on something, hallucinating, maybe. I've seen it before. He saw you, thought you were the devil or something. Do you want me to call an ambulance? 911?"

Mia did a mental check of her body parts, moved her arms, her legs. "No, I'm okay. You really think he didn't just lose control?"

"Can't say, but I doubt it. There's nearly a full moon, and that's when the wackos come out of their caves. Good thing your coat's so heavy, or you'd be all scratched up, or worse. My name's Lex—my friends call me Lex Luthor, you know, like Superman's nemesis."

"Sure, I always rooted for Lex as a kid. Didn't seem fair Superman had all those powers." She blinked. Where had that come from? She shut up. Her brain was tripping with adrenaline.

Lex helped her stand up. Thankfully, her legs held her. "Thank you," she said again and shook his gloved hand. "I'm Mia Briscoe. I don't suppose you saw his plates, or at least the make? Those headlights pretty much blinded me."

"Not really. I was more concerned about whether you were all right."

"Not much point in calling the police, then, I guess. By the time they get here, he could be well on his way into New Jersey. I know I wouldn't hang around. Where's your motorcycle?"

"Motorcycle? You won't catch me on one of those death traps, not in the city. I was just walking back to my apartment, met up with a friend. Oh, I get you, you mean all this hard-rock leather? I wear it for Roz, my girlfriend, she really gets off on black leather. The more I wear, the luckier I get. I don't get hassled as much in bars, either. You headed to the subway?"

At her nod, he said, "I'll walk with you, might as well make sure no more morons are out in the neighborhood. You sure you're okay?"

No, I want to throw up. But she made herself nod again. Mia took another step, weaved, stopped. "Lex, I think I'd better call an Uber. I don't think I'll take a chance with the subway, I might fall on the tracks." She paused a moment, shook her head. "I've never thought of myself as a weak-kneed wuss before. It's humiliating."

Lex waved away her words. "Forget it, you're entitled. I'll stay with you until they come. It'll all make a great story for Roz. Hey, I'm glad those garbage bags didn't burst open too."

He patted her shoulder, and they sat side by side on the curb to wait for the Uber.

When a gray Lexus pulled up beside them six minutes later, Mia gave Lex her card. "If you're interested in an internship or maybe a job at the *Guardian*, give me a call."

Lex stared at the card a moment, gave her a big smile. "Roz'll like this, too."

Mia confirmed her address with the Uber driver and settled in, leaned her head back against the seat, and closed her eyes. Low-level nausea still hovered, too close. She took deep, even breaths and the nausea eased enough for her to text Travis. NEARLY HIT BY A DRUNK DRIVER. FEELING SHAKY, BUT EVERYTHING'S FINE. DON'T WORRY, TALK TOMORROW?

Thirty-five minutes later, Mia stood naked in front of her bathroom mirror, staring at bright purple bruises on her arms, her shoulders, her chest. She looked over her shoulder, saw her back looked like a multicolor flag and the bruise on her butt something like Australia. If she hadn't been wearing her thick coat, what would she look like now? Would she even have gotten up? She took three aspirin, looked in the mirror again at the pale face staring back at her. She looked like oatmeal. *It was a drunk idiot or a druggie. Wrong place wrong time. It's New York, get over it. It's no big deal since I'm not dead.*

She pulled a warm flannel nightgown over her head and eased her aching body into bed, pulled the covers to her chin. No more nausea, thank goodness. Mia lay there not moving, waiting for the aspirin to kick in, the only light her bedside lamp. She couldn't stop reliving the shock of the headlights, tripping over the curb, those wonderful garbage cans, pushing desperately backward to get away from the car. It was when she pictured how the car had come at her that it hit her—What if Lex was wrong? What if the driver wasn't crazy drunk or drugged out? What if he was trying to hit her on purpose?

Oh, shut up. Lex was right. Full moon, too much booze or drugs. But once she thought it, she couldn't let it go. Had Alex Harrington tried to kill her? Was it because of what she'd found out, what she might prove? Someone she'd spoken to had called him, Miles Lombardy had confirmed that. It made sense he'd found out about the photos, that she knew about his ear. Maybe she'd been followed. Alex could have known exactly where she was since she was with his chief staffer. Could it mean Juliet was in danger, too?

Mia sat up, pulled her cell out of the charger, and dialed Tommy Maitland.

He picked up on the second ring, surprise in his voice. "Mia, isn't it late for you to be calling?" At her silence, his voice changed to what she called his FBI voice, lower, more controlled. "Something's happened, hasn't it? Are you all right?"

"Yes, I'm all right." She rushed through her evening of drinks with Miles Lombardy, her walk to the subway, the sedan coming out of nowhere toward her, her rescue by Lex Luthor, yes, that was his name. "I'm making myself crazy, Tommy. I mean, Lex was probably right, wasn't he? A crazy drunk? Or a hallucinating druggie?"

Though Tommy was silent, Mia could nearly hear him thinking. He said finally, "Sure, it's possible, but . . . is there something you haven't told me?"

She let out a breath. "There's a whole lot that's happened in the last couple of days. Even if the car tonight hadn't nearly hit me, I still would have called. Are you sitting down?" She started with what she'd seen at the rave, her suspicions after she spoke with Kent Harper, still the gamer with his sword, about Juliet Calley and Alex Harrington's lacrosse coach at Bennington Prep confirming his earlobe was torn by a lacrosse stick. "I know it all sounds circumstantial, Tommy, but here's the thing—once Juliet Calley admitted Alex, her fiancé, and Kent, had roofied and raped her, together, I have no doubt they killed Serena."

Mia closed her eyes. She knew how deeply he felt the pain of Serena's loss, felt his rage at knowing Serena had been murdered and no one had ever paid. She couldn't imagine what he was feeling. "I'm sorry, Tommy. I shouldn't have just blurted it out. I know this is a fist to the gut."

"No, no, it's okay, just a huge surprise. What's going on, Mia?"

"Listen, Tommy, until tonight I thought Alex Harrington didn't have any idea I suspect him, or at least of what, exactly. And now a car has tried to run me down. Again, Tommy, I'm sorry. I didn't mean to hurt you."

He said finally, his voice calm, "It's been seven years, Mia, and now when I think of Serena, I try to remember how much we meant to each other, how much fun we had together, how much we enjoyed each other, but it's become blurred with the passing years, just warm vague memories. I can't even see her face clearly anymore. I still speak to her parents some-times and it throws me back, of course. It's still very hard for them. It's a giant hole in their lives. For me, it's been mixed with anger that I haven't been able to find anything. Then Gail's daughter finding the photos, Gail sending them to you, and now what you've discovered, Mia, it's hard to take in, but thank you.

"And to think we're talking about a candidate for mayor of New York City." He paused. "Mia, listen, Harrington could have easily found out you attended Godwyn University and the years you were a student. He could suspect you were at the rave. You met him recently. Could he be afraid you recognized him?"

"We never met, Tommy. We never even got close at the rave. But I suppose it's possible. But why would he care enough to try to kill me? Why would a man in Harrington's position try to kill someone who had nothing she could prove?"

"Think of where he finds himself. He finds out about the photos Gail took that night, the photos you've been showing around, the questions about his torn earlobe. That would spook him, scare him. Of course he wouldn't expect you to print anything without more proof, but even a rumor of what you think he did would derail his campaign in a magic second. Worse, if you could prove any of it. So tell me, do you really believe the driver of the sedan who tried to run you down was some anonymous drunk or addict?"

"I want to, Tommy, I really want to, but . . . no."

Tommy was silent a moment. "You're sure you're only bruised, no concussion?"

"I'm bruised all over. I look really funny actually, but I'm downing aspirin, and it's not too bad now."

"I can't come up, Mia, I'm too close to finishing up a case here in Washington. But I know someone who can help you, someone who can protect you until I get there. And she's in New York this very minute."

32

New Safe House
Washington, D.C.

WEDNESDAY NIGHT

Olivia hummed as she slathered on body cream, brushed her teeth, checked out her bruises from the airbag. Not too bad, she'd been lucky. She'd certainly had worse. She smiled at herself in the mirror and chanted, "Mike is alive, Mike is alive." She'd have shouted it out if Gay wasn't watching TV in the living room. She did a little skip and gave the mirror a high five.

No sooner had she stretched out beside Helmut on her new bed, this one hard as nails, than it hit her. What about Andi? Why hadn't she called? Had the Frenchman gone after her? She dialed her number with shaking fingers. "Andi? Olivia. Tell me you're safe."

"Of course I'm safe. I was actually about to call you, but you beat me to it. Mr. Grace told me what happened to you today, while you were picking up pizza for you and Gay. I imagine

Gay's in big trouble, letting you go out alone like that. Where's your brain? What were you thinking?"

And Olivia heard herself say, "It was only a short distance from the safe house, really, and I checked, no one was following me." She paused. "All right, yes, I was an idiot, I'll never do something like that again."

"All right, enough penance. You saved yourself, kicked big butt. But you didn't kill him."

"No, not through want of trying. But I did wound him. I hope he's really hurting."

Andi laughed, then her voice hitched. "I was so worried. Mr. Grace told me to hold off calling you, said you'd be too busy for a while. You really are okay, aren't you, Olivia?"

"Only some bruises, I promise."

"That's twice now, Olivia, they've tried to kill you."

"Andi, they didn't want to kill me, they wanted to take me, force me to lead them to Mike. And you know what that means? Mike's alive! Andi, he's alive and they don't know where he is. I've been repeating that to myself over and over and I'm only now beginning to believe it."

"You're right, now that's a load off. My own minder, Agent Cox, was going on about Mike being a traitor, but I kept telling him that made no sense at all, it was stupid, just plain crazy, if you knew Mike. I wonder what happened? Why he went to ground? As far as I know he hasn't even checked in with Mr. Grace. He has to have a good reason. Any ideas?"

Olivia knew Mike had the flash drive, was probably trying to decrypt it, but how would he without the encryption key? If there was a way, he'd find it. Was he researching French weapons manufacturers, as she had? She said to Andi, "I think Mike is trying to figure some things out, just like we are." She sounded really lame to her own ears, but luckily Andi didn't question her.

Andi said, "Olivia, did the man who attacked you today tell you anything? Was he Iranian too?"

Olivia saw Dillon holding her hands, saying, *There's no way that man followed my Porsche. Trust me, I would have seen him. He lied because someone right here in the CIA at Langley told him where to find you. We have no idea who or how high up, so keep whatever you can close to your vest. Don't volunteer any information to anyone.* Still, she wished she could tell Andi everything because she was one of the team, as worried about Mike as Olivia was.

"Andi, I'm under orders not to tell anyone anything and I hate it, but that has to include you. But the most important thing I learned is that Mike's alive and they don't know where he is."

She heard Andi sigh. "All right. I'll tell Higgs when he checks in with me again. He's in Halifax, being a tourist. He told me he can't think of anything he could do to help if he came back. He's worried about us, Olivia. Well, he's really worried about Mike, too, but since no one knows where he is, Higgs thinks you and I should join him. I'll tell you, I'm tempted. But then I think what about Mike? We can't leave him in the wind. I guess we just have to wait. I hate it."

"Believe me, I do too."

"You and I, Olivia, we've been thrown in with nasty hostiles before, but what's happening now isn't a head-on something we can even understand, and I'll say it again—I hate it, hate feeling helpless. It's crazy, Olivia, and I'm scared, for you, for me, for Mike."

"I'm scared, too, Andi."

"My minder, Agent Cox, told me they arranged a new safe house for you and Gay. How about I try to talk him into letting me come to you?"

"See what Agent Cox says and I'll speak to Gay. It isn't the Ritz; it's like the first one, a clean, nondescript house in a non-descript neighborhood, ancient plumbing, mother's old attic furniture. At least there's a big-ass TV and a comfy easy chair for Gay. Let me know what Cox says, Andi, I'd love to have you here with me." Olivia yawned. "I'm sorry, but it's been quite a day. My body is telling me to shut down. At least the pizza was good, heated up nice and crisp."

Andi laughed. "You always find the rainbow, Olivia, always. Let's see if we would be allowed to hook up, stay together. I'm so relieved to talk to you, to find out Mike's all right. I'm proud of you."

"Come on, Andi, you're Wonder Woman. You'd have done the same, and you know it." She heard Andi laugh again, and it felt really good. They both rang off.

Olivia set her cell back in its charger, pulled the covers over both her and Helmut, whose head was on the pillow next to her, and lay back. He didn't stir. She heard Gay's basketball game playing on the TV in the living room. Mr. Grace had reamed him for letting her out of the safe house by herself, but Gay hadn't been angry with her, more philosophical, said next time he'd follow her even to the bathroom, and happily ate his warmed-up pepperoni and artichoke pizza. At least Lodner had let Gay stay with her.

She ran her hand lightly over Helmut's head, rubbed his ears. "Do you think Mike can decrypt that flash drive? I wonder if Dillon could."

Helmut raised his head to lick her hand. "Andi's right, I did good shooting that Frenchman, but that shoulder wound might not be much at all."

He licked her cheek and she hugged him. "I know, you think I can do no wrong. But I can." She settled back and reviewed every word the Frenchman had said, everything she'd done, until she fell asleep.

Olivia's cell pounded the drums from Koothra's "Night in the Jungle." Helmut had moved down to the foot of the bed, taking part of the blanket with him. He raised his head. "It's okay, boy." She answered. "Olivia."

"It's me, Mike."

33

Her breath whooshed out, her heart pounded as loud as the jungle drums. "Mike, I've been so worried, so scared for you. I didn't even know you were alive until today. You swear you're all right? Can I come get you?"

He actually laughed. "Slow down, sweetheart, slow down. I'm okay. Let me be worried about you. They've come after you again, it was on the police band. Believe me, I didn't expect them to. I thought I was protecting you by staying away. I was going to come to your house to get you after the first attack, but I found out you were okay, and they'd put you in a safe house. No way I could do better than that." Mike paused, and his voice sounded tired. "And then today happened. I'm so sorry, Olivia; I was wrong to believe you were safe."

"Come off it, Mike, if you blame yourself, you're an idiot and I'll have to hurt you when I see you again. I promise, I'm safe. Where are you?"

"I'm not going to tell you because you'll want to join me,

and believe me, that isn't a good idea. I'm calling from a burner phone. Babe, these people aren't fooling around. I'd no sooner gotten off the plane at Dulles and headed over to pick up my backpack when I realized I was being followed. I wasn't armed, of course. I slipped out of the terminal through an employee exit and jumped behind a pile of luggage on one of those motorized carts. I saw them run out after me, but they didn't find me.

"Here's the deal. How did they know which flight I'd be on? Only the CIA knew I had the flash drive on me, so someone told them, just like someone knew about Hashem, and our mission, and that someone wanted me dead, the drive destroyed. I had to protect that flash drive, protect myself, and you were still in the hospital, sweetheart. No way was I going to involve you, even trying to set up a meet could be dangerous. I didn't want to take any chances, not with you. What about Higgs and Andi? Are they all right?"

Olivia wanted to cry and scream at the same time, but her voice came out calm. "Andi finally got herself a minder after what happened to me today, and Higgs is in Halifax. Mike, you swear you're all right?"

She could see him smiling his crooked smile that always charmed her and disarmed her at the same time. "Aren't I always? You've told me several times I'm like a cat. I figure I've still got a half-dozen lives left. Olivia, you just got out of Walter Reed and now you rammed your RAV into a truck. Are you even over your concussion? Tell me you're not injured, and don't try to lie to me."

"Mike, it was the only thing I could think to do, and it

worked, only I lost him when I ran after him. And yes, I was lucky. I've got a couple of bruises, that's all."

He cursed. "I probably shouldn't believe you. Wait, you're saying you went after him?"

"Yes, of course. But he was lucky, too, this taxi was sitting right there, and he hopped in and was gone or I might have gotten him. All I know for sure is he's French and he's determined."

She could hear him chewing that over. Finally, he said, "I've been scared out of my mind for you ever since that RPG went off. I see no reason not to continue being scared," and he cursed again.

Olivia smiled, realized both of them kept saying they were scared for each other. "Okay, I am still reeling a bit, but I'm in bed right now. Helmut just moved up to see who I'm talking to. Helmut, say hello to Mike." Helmut licked her cell. Olivia said, "Did you hear his tongue?"

"Hi, Helmut. You keep him with you, Olivia." He paused. "We're quite a pair, aren't we? But this situation, it's more insane than even we're used to."

"That's what Andi said. But Mike—"

"No, let me finish. Since we're still running blind, I'm not going to come in yet. Not until I know more."

"Mike, I know something about what you've been looking for. I was hypnotized and remembered what Hashem told you. A French armament company selling parts for guidance systems to Iran, isn't that right?"

"So you heard him. I wondered. And the man who tried to take you is French so that leaves no doubt. Before you ask, yes, I've spent a whole lot of time researching them all, public filings, shipment manifests, product inventories. Haven't found anything yet to point in a specific direction, but I was able to contact an old friend of mine at the NSA, and she's giving me time on their mainframe when she can, no questions asked. I've been working on trying to decrypt the flash drive. It could tell us everything we need to know, maybe even help us trace their communications with whoever they have in their pocket. But it's a long shot, Olivia, even with the mainframe, because without the key, the possibilities are endless."

"Listen, Mike, you don't have to do this on your own. The FBI is involved now. I'm working with Special Agent Dillon Savich. Yes, yes, I know it's only been a day, but he's smart and I think, no, I know, we can trust him. He could make sure the drive gets to the right people. He could help us find out who's behind this."

Mike was silent a moment. "He's FBI, Olivia."

She laughed. "It's not a hotbed of terrorists, Mike, only a different fiefdom."

"I don't know him and you said you only met him yesterday. You didn't trust me for a good six months."

"No, it was longer than six months. Remember that actress?" She chuckled. "Listen to me. Agent Savich isn't putting the moves on me like you were. Do you know his wife is Agent Sherlock, the one who stopped that terrorist at JFK?"

"Okay, how about I trust her."

Olivia talked over him. "Dillon's the one who took me to an FBI doctor this morning, the hypnotist, and like I said, I remembered everything Hashem told you. Savich's sources are good enough he found out who the Iranian was I shot at my house Monday night. He was the one who told Mr. Lodner."

Mike said, "That must have burned Lodner's butt."

"I hope so. Have you heard of Razhan?"

Mike sucked in his breath. He said very slowly, "You're telling me Razhan was one of the men at your house? And you killed him?"

"Yes. Why?"

"Didn't this FBI guy tell you Razhan's a known assassin? I don't know how many kills he's registered over the years. I don't even know what he looked like. I'm wondering if he could have been one of the guys at the airport." He paused. "And you were the one to finally bring him down. Remind me never to piss you off."

"You're always pissing me off. Yep, I did bring him down, just like I shot that jerk Frenchman in the shoulder today."

He laughed, sobered immediately. "Tell me again no injuries, and don't try to lie to me."

"Well, the bruise on my rear end looks a bit like a continent, you know, green for land and blue for water, a dash of purple for the sky. Yes, when we're together again, you can check it out."

"You're trying to make me crazy. Stop it. You're in another safe house, right? Gay is still with you?"

"Yes, but Mike, listen to me. Agent Savich can help us. Tell me where you are, and we can both come to you."

Mike grinned into the phone. She was always a bulldog. "Sorry, sweetheart, but I promise to think about calling this Dillon Savich. But for now I've got more to do and I want to be sure you stay protected until this is over. And when it is, you and I can go hang out together on a beach in Aruba and I'll rub sunscreen all over your gorgeous back. I wonder if we can get married in Aruba?"

"*What? What?*"

But he'd ended the call.

34

Mia's Apartment
New York City

THURSDAY MORNING

Mia put her feet on the floor and stood up before she real-ized all was not well. Who knew the result of rolling around in garbage cans to avoid a car trying to run her down would be every inch of her body aching and throbbing and screaming in protest? Even her feet hurt. After three aspirin and a very hot shower, she forced herself to look in the bathroom mirror. A laugh spurted out of her mouth. She looked like a bunch of sugar-high kids had finger-painted all over her. She gingerly rubbed on bruise cream, whatever good that did, blow-dried her hair, and eased into loose sweats. She heard the doorbell ring as she managed to bend over to pull on thick white socks.

She knew who was there, but when she opened the door, all she could do was stare at the tall, slim woman dressed in a black leather jacket, white shirt, black pants, and black boots standing at her door. Her hair was amazing, a red nimbus around her fine-boned face. With her light blue eyes, she looked like a fairy princess. Mia would have told her so, but she didn't want to sound like a groupie.

"Good morning," the princess said in a pleasant voice. "I'm Special Agent Sherlock. And you're Tommy's Mia. He told me you were too pretty for your own good."

Tommy's Mia? Tommy thought she was pretty? Given the face she'd seen in her bathroom mirror minutes ago, *pretty* was an awesome stretch. Mia laughed. "If Tommy could see me now, he'd pull out his Glock and put me out of my misery." She stuck out her hand. "At least I'm ambulatory, and believe me, that's a big relief. Sorry I look like crap. When the aspirin kick in, I won't look better, but I'll feel better."

Sherlock only lightly touched her fingers to hers. "Nothing broken though, right?"

"Thankfully no, all my bones are where they should be. But I ache in places I didn't even know I had."

"I've been there. You don't look like crap, you look like you've been on a bender." She smiled. "In three or four days, you'll feel back to fighting strength. I remember aspirin was my lifeline."

Mia grinned. "I wouldn't be surprised if my energy hasn't flown south for the rest of the winter." She paused a moment, couldn't hold it in. "I've written about you, of course, but to see you here, in my apartment—I'm sorry, I'm keeping you standing here in the doorway. Please come in. You're very kind to come, Agent Sherlock."

"Please just call me Sherlock and I'll call you Mia. It'll save time."

"That'd be great. Can I hang up your jacket?"

"That's okay," Sherlock said as she stuffed her gloves into her leather jacket pocket. "I know it's early, but Tommy is very concerned, well, no, he's scared for you, upset he couldn't be here right away, and that's why he asked me to be here to keep you safe." Sherlock paused a moment, looked at Mia Briscoe, said slowly, "I have to say I was very concerned. I've never seen Tommy scared. He's usually unflappable, like his dad, and his mom, too."

Mia swallowed at the sudden memory of Serena saying, *Mia, his mom is awesome. She'd fit under my armpit, but she runs the show, all four giant-size sons and her giant husband.* Then she'd waggled her eyebrows, whispered, *Maybe she can teach me how if Tommy and I decide to—well, we're both young, and who knows?*

Mia brought herself back, swallowed tears. "I don't know Tommy's parents well myself, only met them at Serena's memorial, ah, but Tommy's incredible. We've stayed close, emailing and calling. I was thrilled for him when he graduated from the FBI Academy. I remember he told me his dad was over the moon, kept pumping his hand and bear-hugging him."

Sherlock said, "Tommy's dad, Mr. Maitland, is my husband's boss. We are very fond of him and his family."

Mia ushered Sherlock into her living room, waved her to Mia's own favorite chair, and stood over her, still aching all over. She felt clumsy and pathetic next to this amazing woman. "Ah, I was just going to make coffee. Would you like some? And maybe an English muffin slathered thick with chunky peanut butter?"

Sherlock could see Mia was hurting and said matter-of-factly,

"Why don't you take me to your kitchen. You will sit down and tell me where everything is and I'll make us both breakfast. When was your last dose of aspirin?"

Mia wished she didn't feel like the remains of a lousy meal. She wished she could fold herself up and sleep. "Three aspirin, about fifteen minutes ago."

"Good, they should kick in soon. I won't burn the muffins, I promise. Come along before you fall over." Sherlock nodded toward the living room window. "This is an incredible view you have. When you have friends over do they ignore you and simply stare out the window down on Central Park?"

"Usually. All I have to do is put a glass of wine in their hands and let them look to their heart's content. The view is gorgeous, but prepare yourself for a very small kitchen. At least it's open so you can see the view while you cook." Mia stopped in her kitchen doorway. She was supposed to sit down and let Sherlock feed her?

Sherlock walked straight to a kitchen chair and pulled it out. "Down you go, right there. Your kitchen's nice and bright. I have a half dozen of those little herb pots you have lined up on the window ledge in my own kitchen. You're right about the view. Central Park in all its winter glory, which makes me shiver just looking. You have a coffee maker I recognize, so, no problem. Everything else is in the fridge?"

Six minutes later, Mia sipped delicious coffee, closed her eyes, and whispered, "Thank you. You even heated the cream. It's wonderful."

"My mother-in-law taught me that. You're welcome. Here's your muffin, lots of peanut butter. The protein should perk you up."

While they ate, they spoke of the frigid New York weather and the murder case Sherlock had come to New York to consult about. Sherlock gave her a few of the details. At the mention of a creative murdering psychopath who happened to be a real estate agent as well as a gun expert, Mia was leaning forward, her aches and pains forgotten. She wanted a name, only a name, but knew she wouldn't get it. Sherlock only smiled at her, shook her head. "I'm hopeful we'll close the case today. Then I'm sure you'll hear about it."

Mia watched Sherlock take their plates to the sink, pour two more cups of coffee, add the lovely hot cream, and sit down again.

Sherlock said, "Tommy's already spoken to the current police chief in Creighton, sent him clear photos of Harrington and Harper back when they were twenty-seven, the age they'd have been at the rave at Godwyn. He'll show them to his old list of witnesses, but it's unlikely the photos will jog any memories. He's tracked down the cars registered to them at the time—a Jaguar and a BMW, and their license plates. That might help put them at or near Godwyn that night, if we're lucky. Tommy can't check credit card records yet that could help put them coming or going from Godwyn that night seven years ago. Those aren't in the public domain and we don't have enough yet to get a warrant, especially on a candidate for mayor of New York City or a bigwig businessman. And since it's unlikely Harrington and Harper started and ended their roofieing spree with Serena at Godwyn, Tommy's going to check nearby colleges for unsolved rapes or disappearances. That kind of luck would be a lot to ask for though.

"Now, about last night. The NYPD will review the CCTV

feeds, send a forensics team to West Third. The sedan struck some garbage cans, and there could be traces of paint or maybe a piece of broken headlight. They'll spot the car, but it's not likely they'll see the driver well enough to make an ID."

"Maybe the license plate?"

"We'll hope."

"Sherlock, do you honestly think Alex Harrington, now a candidate for mayor of New York City, would be crazy enough to try to run me down himself? Even Kent Harper, he's the head of his family's company here . . . it's crazy."

Sherlock said matter-of-factly, "No, I can't see either of those two being directly involved. Since the attack happened so quickly after you got back to New York, they probably already had someone on their payroll or available to them. I doubt checking their phone records would help turn up anything valuable. I can't imagine either of these gentlemen would be stupid enough to leave a record on their cell phones, or at campaign headquarters. But the records might tell us who tipped them off, from Boston or from Bennington Prep. Of course, it's academic, no way to get a search warrant.

"Mia, if you're right about this, about what those men have done, about their being responsible for what happened last night, you're very lucky to be alive."

Mia said, "I know, believe me, I've had a few bad moments thinking about that. I said I couldn't see either of them involved directly. I take that back. Not Kent Harper, but Alex Harrington would. He's got guts and he would view me as an obstacle like any other, to be overcome, or obliterated as the case may be."

Sherlock studied the myriad emotions racing over Mia's face—frustration, sadness, maybe a dollop of hope? She said, "I wasn't in the FBI yet when your friend Serena Winters disappeared from the frat rave, but I heard about it later from my husband. He told me Tommy was wrecked over it, that it influenced his decision to join the FBI, like his dad. Tommy went on the warpath, determined to find out who killed her, but when there were absolutely no leads, and as time passed, as it always does, her case went cold, and even Tommy realized there was nothing more he could do. But no one who loved her forgot about her, least of all Tommy.

"Now, you think you've found the men who roofied her, killed her." Sherlock sat back. "You've given Tommy hope again he'll find out what happened to her, hope he thought was dead. He told me about everything, going back to the rave when Serena met that guy who was a gamer, about the two photos, the bracelet, the notch on Alex Harrington's earlobe. And Kent Harper being a gamer too. Tommy's retention is amazing so I'm confident I have all those facts.

"What I want you to tell me are your firsthand impressions of the people you spoke with in Boston, and at Bennington Prep."

Mia said, "It's hard to believe I met these people only yesterday, not twenty-four hours ago. Okay, first I went to Louisburg Square and met Pamela Raines Barrett, Alex Harrington's fiancée. She's pretty, polished to a high shine, shows off Armani very well. She knows her own worth and values herself highly. She's arrogant and tried to hide it for the most part since I was there to interview her about her fiancé. She tried to make nice, but her belief in her own superiority shimmered off her.

235

"She's smart, Sherlock, and I think she'd be as ruthless as she needed to be to get what she wants. And she wants Alex to be mayor as much as he does, maybe more. It's her first big step toward the top of the power food chain, where she knows she belongs. So she really wasn't of much help. But one thing struck me between the eyes. She's still jealous of Harrington's ex-fiancée, Juliet Ash Calley. She told me calling off the wedding was Alex's idea, but it wasn't. It was Juliet who called it off.

"I'm sure she doesn't know about Juliet being roofied and raped by Alex Harrington and Kent Harper, or anything else. Yes, I imagine Tommy mentioned that to you. Even though it sounds unbelievable, it's true. He not only roofied and raped his own fiancée, he also invited his friend Kent Harper to join the fun. And I wondered—if Pamela knew, would she be willing to cover it up to get what she wanted? I don't think so, but I could be wrong."

Sherlock cocked an eyebrow at her. "Let me guess. You really didn't like her."

35

Mia looked down at a ragged fingernail, doubtless from banging against a garbage can last night. "I made Pamela sound like the wicked witch. She really didn't come across like that. She was polite, solicitous, well-spoken, gushed about Harrington, only to be expected. Maybe, too, I think I was predisposed to dislike her, my fault." Mia sighed. "She's focused, Sherlock, committed to being the first lady of New York City, then, who knows? The United States? Oh yes, no doubt in my mind. And bottom line, what's wrong with that?

"Moving forward. I walked to Juliet's parents' house after I left the freeze queen. Juliet was there taking care of her ill mom. Juliet's a concert pianist."

"Yes, I know, I've heard her in concert at the Kennedy Center. An incredible talent and a jaw-dropper."

"Yes, she's awesomely beautiful. I liked her very much. She seemed sensible, she cares about other people, particularly her parents, and as you said, she's immensely talented. She doesn't trade on her beauty, either; she ignores it as best I could tell.

It's amazing, really, how she's managed to move forward after those two roofied and raped her. Imagine, your own fiancé, the man you believed loved you, rapes you. He's a monster, Sherlock."

"No argument from me," Sherlock said.

"I was thinking Alex had already decided Juliet wasn't suited to be his wife now that he wanted to be a politician, was already planning to break it off. Or not, I can't be sure either way. If so, like I said, I can see him thinking why not have his BFF Kent enjoy her, too? I also believe Alex never thought she'd remember, but she did."

Sherlock sat back and marveled. "You actually pried the roofie and rape out of Juliet Ash Calley, a stranger you only just met? You're beyond good, Mia. Okay, Alex must have suspected she remembered when she broke off the engagement."

"Well, he knew for sure because Juliet confronted him; of course, he played it off, said she had a bad dream. That's when she broke off the engagement. I imagine he was really worried, though, until he realized he and Kent would be safe, that Juliet would keep her mouth shut. She didn't go to the police, nor did she ever tell a soul. She's very protective of her parents. She still doesn't want to deal with any of it, didn't want to hear any questions about it at first. She didn't even contradict Pamela telling me that breaking off the engagement was Alex's idea, until I pushed her about it. I doubt even her parents know she was the one who ended it, and not the why, that's for sure. I think she shoved her rage at what they did to her down deep, but it's there, festering, and it's costing her, even after two years.

"You wondered why she told me, a perfect stranger, and a

reporter to boot? I really worked on her, Sherlock. She was shocked when I told her about Serena. It was kind of manipulative but it still wasn't enough to make her come right out and admit what they'd done to her and agree to come forward. I asked her if she's thought about warning Pamela about what Alex and Kent really are. You should have seen the guilty look on her face. She hadn't said anything to Pamela, because she knew it would get back to Alex and what would he do to her? I felt really sorry for her and impatient, too. How could she let these two go on with what was their fun sport?

"Maybe it's different now for her, now she knows they're responsible for killing someone. I don't know. I told her I was going to make sure they paid, left her my card."

Sherlock met Mia's eyes, slowly nodded. "It's a lot to ask of her since she can't prove anything, and it would impact her life, her family, and her career. But if anyone can bring her forward, it would be you, Mia, you and Tommy; you both loved Serena so much, it would make it very real for her. Now, tell me about Coach Wiliker at Bennington Prep."

Mia ran through the interview. "It's obvious to me now I didn't handle him well. He was probably the one who called Alex, told him about the strange questions I asked. Maybe, too, Pamela got suspicious, or someone thought it was odd I spent so much time speaking with the departmental secretaries at Harvard. It also occurred to me Alex could have asked his senior staffer, Miles Lombardy, to have drinks with me last night so the candidate would know exactly where I'd be."

Sherlock said, "It was a spur-of-the-moment plan, but it might have worked if not for Lex."

"If Lex weren't so much younger, I'd have asked him to marry me."

Sherlock grinned at her, took another drink of her coffee, set down the Minnie Mouse mug. She said, "Mia, imagine you were born with the proverbial silver spoon. All your life you've been given everything you wanted. You're lucky enough to be smart, you're very good-looking, both men and women like you, you never have occasion to question why you're at the top of the food chain. Then you and your best buddy from childhood attend Bennington Prep, and you come up with the idea to roofie and rape one of the girls. If she's not willing, who cares? You're bulletproof. You go ahead with your twisted teenage fantasy, and it's great. Nothing happens. You get away with it. No harm, no foul. So you do it again. And again.

"It becomes another amusement you share with Kent, like gaming, but you know you have to keep yourselves safe. You might be worried the first couple of times the girls might remember, but they don't say a thing. You realize even if a girl did say something, she wouldn't have any proof against you. You're the golden boy.

"You hear about the rave at Godwyn University in Pennsylvania. It sounds like another great place to hunt yourself a girl. It's everything you expected. The place is packed with students, there's fountains of booze, and drugs, and dozens of girls. It's Kent who spots Serena, this great girl who's a gamer, and you agree, she'll do just fine. But something goes wrong, very wrong. Suddenly she's dead or dying. You're smart enough to set a fire to cover getting her out of there. You never think of yourself as a murderer, you don't for a minute blame yourself, it was an accident. You're lucky there's plenty of open land and wilderness nearby. Where to bury her where she won't be found? Not in a field or a forest owned by someone you don't know.

"I remember Valley Forge National Park is fairly close to Godwyn, maybe a thirty-minute drive. The park's closed for the night, and no one's around, easy enough to drive in. You carry her body far off the road, bury her, go on your merry way. And you know that was smart, too, because her body has never been found, not in seven years. Maybe you're shook up for a while, but again, it wasn't your fault, maybe it was even that stupid girl's fault for wondering what you put in her drink. The years pass, and you enjoy your life, and both of you move up in the world, as you knew you would. Enough time you even take up your sport again.

"Amazing you end up roofieing even Juliet, your fiancée, for your and Kent's pleasure. Why would you do that? Did she enrage you by not supporting your decision to enter politics, so you decide she's no more use to you, that you're not going to marry her? Did she deny you sex? Whatever your reasons, it seems like madness, but not to you. Sure, it would have blown up on you, but a little risk is part of the sport, and once again, you're lucky. I wonder if Harrington discussed it with Kent Harper or just told him they were going to have some fine sport?" Sherlock paused, shook her head. "It's still hard for me to understand why Alex Harrington would roofie and rape his own fiancée, much less invite his friend to rape her as well. But I guess to do this to her, he obviously doesn't respect her or value her, even care all that much about her." She shook her head. "I'm being dense. The guy's a psychopath; he has no empathy, no conscience, and his reasons for doing anything wouldn't make sense to you or me. I wonder if Kent Harper was appalled at the idea of raping Juliet, but he was used to falling in with Alex's plans? It certainly could have blown up on them, but once again, they're lucky."

Sherlock gave Mia a big smile. "Lucky until a pretty young reporter is assigned to cover your campaign for mayor of New York City. You're happy to hear it, you believe she'll write good things about you because, after all, you're tall, good-looking, charming, who could resist you? You're pleased when the reporter tells you she's going to Boston to interview friends and family for the article she's writing. Then you get a call from one of the people the reporter interviews, maybe the lacrosse coach at Bennington like you said, who tells you about some strange questions the reporter asked about an old photo she showed him. Coach describes it, a profile, couldn't really tell who it was, but the boy had an ear injury, like yours. You're a bit alarmed. You google her, find out she went to Godwyn University. Now there's a nibble of panic. Was she at the rave? Did she know the girl who disappeared? You don't remember her name, but Kent does when you meet with him. You call your fiancée. You don't tell her the truth, of course, you tell her you think Juliet might have made up a story about you and you're concerned. Whatever Pamela says, it's enough. You decide you have to act before the reporter goes public. But with what? No proof of anything, you're safe, but a hint of this getting out and your campaign is done before it gets off the ground. You want this. Pamela wants this. You arrange for your staffer to have drinks with the reporter at a specific time and place, pump her, find out what she thinks she knows, what her purpose is."

Mia stared at Sherlock. "That's amazing, it's like you see it."

Sherlock only shook her head, continued. "But as we've agreed, it's doubtful it was either Alex Harrington or Kent Harper who tried to run you down. Much too great a risk. So that means we have to find someone close enough to Harrington to have done it, most likely for a price.

"Which brings us back to our problem. We have only circumstantial evidence, not enough to even make it worthwhile to interview them."

Sherlock sat back in her chair and regarded Mia. "You know the easiest way to keep you safe is for me to go to Alex Harrington, tell him someone tried to kill you last night, tell him you've gathered information about him and Kent, and that information is now in FBI hands. That would keep you safer. Unless they're insane."

Mia was shaking her head before Sherlock finished. "He'd demand to know exactly what you're talking about, he'd take the high road, demand you tell him exactly what I believe he did. And what would you lay out for him exactly? You'd have to admit there isn't any proof, not yet. He'd laugh at you, at me, and threaten to sue us both and the *Guardian* if these ridiculous accusations came out.

"I can't see Alex Harrington folding his tent. He'd play the aggrieved party, the victim of an ambitious reporter willing to do anything to get herself publicity, willing to trash an innocent man's name, ruin his life.

"Sherlock, nothing good could come out of facing him down. I'd instantly be persona non grata, worthless in helping find the proof to put him and Kent away."

Mia saw Sherlock was about to disagree, and she added quickly, "Don't forget Juliet. If you faced him down, told him what we know he did, wouldn't it put her in danger? He'd have to suspect she told me what happened." Mia sat forward, grabbed Sherlock's hand. "You've got to agree to let me continue to investigate. I could pretend I think it was an accident last night, a drunk driver or some idiot on drugs."

Sherlock eyed her, drank the rest of her coffee. "That was very persuasive, Mia, and all right, logical. I'll even say this for you—without more proof he'd try to get you blackballed. He'd certainly hound you, smear your name." She sighed. "What you really want is to be bait, right?"

"Yes, if that's what you want to call it."

Sherlock took a deep breath, drummed her fingertips on the table, studied Mia Briscoe's very serious face. "All right. We'll see what Tommy has to say."

"Thank you."

"Don't act guileless, Mia, you can't pull it off. I'll be your bodyguard until Tommy ties up his case in Washington—he hopes to be here tomorrow. Then he can be your second skin."

Mia would have shot a victory fist in the air, but she wasn't a dolt. She said, "As you've noticed, my apartment is on the small side. Do you mind sharing a queen-size bed with me?"

Sherlock smiled. "Not a problem." Then she took a deep breath, drummed her fingertips on the table, studied Mia

Briscoe's face. "You know after what could have happened to you last night, I hope Juliet will be willing to step up, show what kind of woman she is. I have an idea how she can help us and we can still keep her safe. Would you call her, then let me speak to her?"

When Sherlock ended the call, she slowly nodded. "We'll see."

36

MIA AND SHERLOCK

Cheesehead Coffee Shop
Houston Street

THURSDAY MORNING

A taxi dropped Mia and Sherlock off in front of Cheesehead Coffee Shop with its signature bright green-and-gold-striped awning, the only place downtown with nonfat cheddar cheese Danish, at least according to the owner, Quillie Rodgers, a longtime fan of the Green Bay Packers and a Cheesehead every Sunday during football season.

Milo Burns was already pacing outside the coffee shop when Mia and Sherlock spilled out of the taxi. He looked from Mia to Sherlock. "Good to see you again, Agent Sherlock. Let me say again, you gave us a great interview. It'll appear in the Sunday Life section. Millie Jones is still dancing around the newsroom. Pain in the butt. Now, what are you doing with Agent Sherlock, Briscoe? I didn't even know you knew each other. Let's get inside before we freeze our parts off."

There were only a few customers midmorning. Quillie herself showed them to a back booth and Sherlock eased Mia out of her coat. When the three of them were seated, coffee and tea ordered, Milo said, "Agent Sherlock, why are you with Briscoe here?" He gave Mia the stink eye. "She never said a word about knowing you."

"We've only just met. It's a friends-of-a-friend deal."

Milo tapped his big blunt fingers on the tabletop. "All right, Briscoe, I'm here. You didn't tell me a thing, insisted on talking here at Cheesehead's. Since you're with my reporter and you're here with an FBI bigwig, I'd have to be an idiot not to figure something big is going on. That, and sorry, Briscoe, but you look like crap on a pancake."

Mia sighed. "Disgusting visual even if true."

Sherlock said, "It's true. I did meet Mia through a friend. We're here because Mia says she trusts you implicitly, Mr. Burns."

"Just Milo," he said. He looked at Mia, said slowly, "Talk to me, Briscoe, and don't leave anything out." He cocked a dark eyebrow at Mia. "Implicitly?"

"Saying it's big doesn't start to cover it, Milo. I asked you here to Cheesehead's because there's no way I could simply waltz into the newsroom with Agent Sherlock and pretend to everyone nothing's happened. Look at me, I'm a walking bruise. Yes, Milo, I trust you, or it would be time to hang it up. I'm your reporter, and you should know what I've been doing. You're expecting five thousand words from me on Harrington's campaign for this weekend, but I'm working on something else, maybe the *Guardian*'s biggest exclusive since you started there."

Milo sat back against the cushioned booth seat, looked from Sherlock to Mia and back again. "Still waiting, Briscoe."

After two more cups of coffee from Roxy, a waitress who'd known Milo for years, Mia had told him everything. He asked her questions, made her backtrack, filled in more details until he was satisfied she'd spilled it all. Milo gave snorts and grunts, an occasional hmm, and a "You've got to be kidding me." When she was finished, Mia felt limp.

Milo studied Mia's face. "I saw those photos you gave Dirk, saw the meatloaf you gave him, too, so I knew the photos were important to you. It was making me crazy not knowing what you were up to. Alex Harrington, huh?" He took another sip of coffee, tapped his blunt fingertips on the vinyl tabletop. "All right. If you're right about Mr. Alexander Harrington and Mr. Kent Harper, Mia, if you get ironclad proof, and I mean bulletproof proof, beyond-a-reasonable-doubt proof, we'll publish it. Otherwise, you'd be setting up the paper in the middle of a huge scandal, with an X marked on our chests for all those big-money lawyers to shoot at, and they'll come running faster than roaches out of the woodwork. Harrington's supporters will denounce us in any case, call you a vindictive opportunist, maybe even a jilted lover. There's so much wealth and power involved, it's scary. And if there's a trial, you'll be front and center. You as well, Agent Sherlock." Tap, tap, tapping his fingertips, he paused, assessed. "You, Agent Sherlock, have a big rep and you're standing with Briscoe. That'll mean something. You think one or both of these men has already tried to kill you and yet you don't want to face them down, tell them what you know. I can understand that. But if I let you go forward with this and something goes wrong, people will think we were both barking mad." He fell silent, picked up his coffee spoon, and began wiping it on his napkin so hard he could see his face. Sherlock and Mia said nothing, waited. He met their eyes. "But here's the thing—if you bring down these men, prove they're serial rapists, prove they murdered your friend Serena, maybe find her body—it could mean a Pulitzer for you, Briscoe, and a whole mountain of new advertisers and subscriptions for the *Guardian*. Some butt-kissing morons might proclaim me King of All Media." Vintage Milo, but Mia saw a twinkle in his eyes. "All right, Briscoe, knowing all the problems, the risks, the possible payoffs, do you still wish to move forward?"

"Yes," Mia said immediately.

He turned to Sherlock. "How are you going to be involved in all this?"

"I'll be staying with Mia to keep her safe until our mutual friend, an FBI agent, gets here tomorrow."

Milo slid out of the booth, stared down at the two women, and rubbed his hands together. "I'm picking up the tab. Talk about a justified business expense. Tell me what I can do and I'll do it. But that doesn't include any killing."

"Thank you, Milo," Mia said. "I promise, no killing."

He started to pat her shoulder, stopped, and touched his fingers to her cheek instead. "You've looked better, Briscoe, but I gotta say, you've made my day." He shrugged into his coat, paused to speak to their waitress, Roxy, and was fast out the door, coat flapping.

Mia was easing her arms carefully into her own coat when Sherlock's cell sang out Shinedown's "Monsters." When she punched off, she smiled. "My FBI contact touched base with the NYPD detective running the investigation into your attack last night. She was allowed to look at all the CCTVs. She said the sedan that tried to hit you is a black 2020 Audi S8. The CSI team verified. They found a shard of headlight next to one of the overturned garbage cans, and yes, it was from a 2020 Audi S8." She called up the car on her cell. "Look familiar?"

Mia said, "Maybe, but Sherlock, to me it only looked huge and black. I was scared out of my mind."

Sherlock added, "If you hadn't been scared, I'd worry about you. Neither Harrington nor Harper owns an Audi, which means there's another person involved."

"Was your FBI contact able to follow the Audi on the traffic cams?"

"Three blocks, then they lost him. They're casting a wider net. There wasn't much traffic at that hour last night what with the frigid weather so they're hoping to pick him up again and see where he goes. Kelly will call me if they spot him." She shook Mia's hand. "We'll get him. He's the key. Mia, you're going to the *Guardian*, right? And you'll stay there until you take a taxi home this evening?"

Mia nodded. "Believe me, I don't want to do any more dances with garbage cans. I remember you said you hoped to close the case about the murdering psychopath who's a real estate agent. You're going to do that now?"

Sherlock stared at her. "Your memory is formidable." She looked down at her watch. "Yep, I'm off. After today, I'm hoping there'll be one less psychopath on the streets. Be careful, Mia. I'll see you later."

37

26 Federal Plaza
FBI New York Field Office
New York City

THURSDAY

Sherlock locked her eyes on Angela Storin when she walked into the conference room. She saw what she'd expected to see, a plain, proper woman of a certain age who looked faded, disapproving, ultimately forgettable. She wore a baize suit, baize low-heeled pumps, no jewelry. Her eyes were a flat light brown, hard to get a read on her with the oversized black-framed glasses. She wore her hair pulled back into a tight bun, and no makeup. Sherlock stared at her for a long moment, hoping to see a flash of nerves, a hint of some anxiety, but there was no outward sign the woman felt anything at all other than boredom. Storin looked back at her, placid and disinterested as a cow.

Special Agent Kelly Giusti slowly rose. "Mr. Clooney, Ms.

Storin, this is Special Agent Sherlock, who has kindly come up from Washington for our meeting." Abel Clooney rose, shook her hand. "Agent."

Sherlock gave him her sunny smile. "Counselor." He looked like Matlock in the old TV series, with his silver hair and his comfortable paunch, artfully minimized in a dark pin-striped thousand-dollar Hugo Boss suit. He looked pleased with himself, quite happy to be who he was, confident he'd close down whatever this latest summons of his client would bring. He was giving Sherlock an appraising look, doubtless deciding how to deal with her. Clooney knew who she was, of course, but why ask her in particular?

Sherlock nodded to Benjamin Varno, the federal prosecutor. He was younger than Clooney, tall and fit with hair as black as sin, with only a few silver flecks at his temples. He was endowed with an evangelist's deep voice that would resonate in the courtroom. He knew what was coming, of course, and looked hungry for blood.

Clooney sat down again, leaned back, and tapped his Mont Blanc pen on the tabletop. He said to Sherlock, "I do not understand why you are here. There are no terrorists for you to take down."

Sherlock said, "Believe me, Mr. Clooney, if I never see another terrorist in my lifetime, I will consider myself blessed. It was all a case of being in a certain place at a certain time."

"Then why are you here?"

"I was asked to provide a new eye." And she said nothing more.

Clooney said, "New eye? Not that it matters. Agent Giusti, I agreed to this meeting because I'm hopeful we can clear up any remaining concerns you have about Ms. Storin's involvement in this tragic incident in Brickson and finish this witch hunt. Then you can all turn your attention to finding the real murderer. We have offered plausible alternatives: a patient or one of their family members who might have blamed Dr. Madison for an injury or a loved one's death seems the most logical. You have focused on my client for long enough, wasted valuable time. It must stop. When we've answered your questions, when my client and I leave today, I expect your assurance she's been cleared of all suspicion and this harassment will stop."

Varno said, "That will depend on your client's answers, Mr. Clooney. We have a lot to cover, so let's proceed."

"Ms. Storin," Sherlock said and she smiled at her. Storin started, blinked behind the glasses, and remained silent, still the continued picture of disinterest. Sherlock said, "Ms. Storin, even though I'm new to this case, they've told me a lot about you."

Say something, I want to hear your voice.

"I'm sure they have, Agent Sherlock, and yes, I've heard of you as well. Some people think you're important," Storin added with a touch of impatience in her voice and a dismissive shrug.

Storin's voice was low, sort of husky, really quite lovely.

Kelly rose. "Ms. Storin, you have stated on record that your Walther PPK was stolen two weeks prior to the three murders at the Madison house, is that correct?"

"Yes, it is."

"You further stated that your first husband, Mr. Martin Orloff, purchased the gun for you and showed you how to use it, but you rarely touched it. Is that correct?"

"I told you he showed me how to fire the gun, so I knew how it worked. I never used it again, as I've told you several times already. I've also told you I don't approve of guns, the reason I never wanted it in the first place."

"You found the gun missing and reported it stolen to the Brickson police. Is that correct?"

Storin merely nodded and studied a fingernail.

Clooney began tapping his Mont Blanc pen on the conference tabletop. "What is the point of going over all this again, Agent Giusti? Move along. Let's get this done."

Kelly nodded. "Let me remind you, Ms. Storin, that lying to a federal agent is a felony."

Storin gave her a flat-eyed stare. "I have no reason to lie to anyone."

Sherlock saw Mr. Clooney's hand close over Storin's—to keep her from saying more? Probably.

Kelly said easily, "Moving along then. Agent Sherlock visited the Madison house on Tuesday. Do you know what she noticed?"

"Get on with it, Agent," Clooney said. "Cut the cute drama."

Sherlock said, her voice matter-of-fact, "I noticed one of the kitchen chairs was pulled out from the table and faced out, toward the kitchen doorway. After you shot Mrs. Madison in the face, Ms. Storin, you sat in that chair with Mrs. Madison's body nearly at your feet and waited for your ex-lover to return. When Dr. Madison came in he wasn't alone, and I imagine you were surprised, but it didn't deter you, probably didn't even particularly concern you. You stood up from that chair and shot both men between the eyes. After you shot them, you did your best to make the murders look like a robbery, but of course no one bought that scenario for very long." Sherlock paused a second, hardened her voice. "In short, Ms. Storin, you shot both men from at least twelve feet away, which means you're an excellent shot."

Storin stared at Sherlock with her cold flat eyes, raised her chin an arrogant fraction, and said in a voice as smooth as glass, "What you're saying is impossible. I couldn't do that. I barely know how to fire a gun."

Clooney again pressed his hand on Storin's and said, his voice dismissive, "I don't know what you're trying for, Agent Sherlock, with this tedious tale about the placement of a kitchen chair. It's wild supposition, a not-very-clever spin on what might have happened."

Storin shook off Clooney's hand, sat forward, and now there was anger in her voice. "I understand what you're doing. Your superiors sent you up here to close this case however you can, so you don't continue to blunder around like incompetent clowns. Really? Me? Firing a gun from twelve feet away? That's longer than this table. Impossible.

"You will listen to me now. After the FBI got involved, I was hopeful, all of Brickson was hopeful, this horrible situation would be resolved, the Madison murderer would be identified, but instead of doing your jobs and finding the murderer, you decided I was your best shot to save face, so you've continued to browbeat me." Her voice dripped contempt. "So much for my prayers that there might finally be justice, that a man I cared about would be avenged." She splayed her hands in front of her, small hands, buffed nails, no rings. "I am more than disappointed with the lot of you."

Clooney nodded, looked pleased. "My client could not have

summed up the situation better. Now, I expect you to make clear why you asked my client to appear here today or we are going to leave."

It was hard not to applaud Storin's brilliant performance, but Kelly kept her voice calm and steady. "We've asked you before about your frequent trips to Washington, D.C. Have you now remembered where you've stayed when you visited?"

Storin shrugged, pursed her lips. "As I've told you before, I've stayed at various B&Bs around the city, to sample the different neighborhood flavors, you could say."

Clooney said, "Again, Agent Giusti, Ms. Storin told you this. Do you have anything more to say?"

"And there were times you and Dr. Madison traveled to Washington, D.C., together."

Impatience simmered. Clooney said, "Is that supposed to be a question, Agent?"

Kelly ignored Clooney. "Ms. Storin?"

"As I have told you, Agent, Dr. Madison and I were adults and since he was married, we were discreet. I am very fond of Washington, and we traveled there to enjoy ourselves as often as we could."

Clooney said, "If you have a new point to make, Agent, spit it out or move along. My client doesn't remember or simply doesn't choose to discuss where they stayed. It doesn't matter."

Kelly said, "You're on the record stating you always paid cash."

"I prefer cash," Storin said. "Some people do."

Sherlock picked it up. "Ms. Storin, it appears you neglected to inform your attorney about a lovely property in Washington, D.C., more a picturesque cottage, really, at 743 Black Street NW."

Sherlock saw it, a flash of fear in Storin's flat eyes, then calculation. *You never thought we'd find that cottage, did you?* She waited, but Storin merely shrugged, said nothing.

Sherlock continued. "We ran a computer search of real estate deeds of private homes in your name or either of your ex-husbands' and of course didn't find it. However, when we searched further afield, we found a property at 743 Black Street NW, owned by a Mrs. Mary Gilbert. As you very well know, she's the mother of your first husband, Martin Orloff. The name isn't the same because she remarried. This first husband, Martin Orloff, was murdered, too, his killer never identified, but that's not what we're addressing here today. You no doubt visited that lovely little cottage in Washington with your first husband, and it appears you wanted it.

"After Mr. Orloff was dead and buried, you renewed your relationship with his mother. Mrs. Mary Gilbert was living in a nursing home in Albany, New York, suffering from Alzheimer's. We know from the facility's records you spent a lot of time with her before her death last year. You consoled her for the tragic death of her son, long enough for you to manipulate her into turning control of the cottage over to you, or rather to an LLC we traced back to you. The LLC has been making quite a nice profit over these years from the cottage, as a short-term rental, without sharing any of that profit with Mrs. Gilbert, the real owner. That is, when you weren't there yourself or with a lover, most recently, Dr. Madison.

"Our agents visited your cottage with a search warrant and found your caretaker, Mrs. Jernigan, very helpful. Our agents came away with personal items that belonged to Dr. Madison as well as photos of the two of you."

Sherlock lined up the three photos side by side in front of

Storin. "It appears you have a very different look when you're in Washington, Ms. Storin. Look at that red spiky hair, the flamboyant makeup, the black stiletto boots, the short leather skirt."

Storin stared down at the photos, said nothing.

Clooney shoved the photos back toward Sherlock. "You have no proof that woman in the photos is Ms. Storin, and if it is, what of it?"

Angela Storin interrupted him. "No, she's right, it's me in the photos." She shrugged. "Who cares? I enjoy changing my look. I'm certainly not causing harm to anyone. A different wardrobe, a fun wig, and using Mrs. Gilbert's house doesn't make me guilty of murder."

"True, but it helped us realize why none of the gun ranges we contacted to find out where you honed your shooting skills recognized our photos of you."

Sherlock turned to Clooney. "Your client practices at Curly Johnson's Bivouac, a gun range outside of Plankton, Connecticut, about a half hour from the New York border. Curly looked at these photos and grinned from ear to ear. He said, 'That's our girl, Misty Lee, the biker chick, a little long in the tooth, sure, but you should see her shoot. She roars up on her Harley and usually takes some of the guys' money, but they don't mind too much because she buys them all beers afterward.'

"So, hi, Misty. I really like your look, it's an amazing transformation. I imagine it must be very liberating for you to travel to Washington or Connecticut and shed your dowdy professional image, become Misty Lee, and sling your leg over the seat of your Harley. It must have been fun for Dr. Madison, too, I imagine, to see the proper Ms. Angela Storin transform into wild-as-the-wind Misty Lee.

"You keep that Harley in a storage locker somewhere, but we'll find it, along with Misty Lee's clothes and that cute red wig."

Sherlock leaned toward Storin. "Tell us, Ms. Storin—or Ms. Lee—is there a reason you play at being two vastly different people, or is it really simply for the fun of it?"

"I don't have to say anything."

Kelly continued before Clooney could object. "After Curly Johnson identified you, we presented him with a search warrant. It turns out you keep a locker there, Ms. Storin."

Kelly leaned down and opened a small box on the floor beside her. She pulled out a labeled clear plastic bag with a Walther PPK inside it and held it up. "You really shouldn't have kept the murder weapon in your locker at Curly's gun range, Ms. Storin. I know you never imagined we'd find out about your identity in Washington, and even if we did, we'd have no reason to think you were an expert markswoman." Kelly leaned toward Storin, and smiled. "It appears we're not as incompetent as you seem to think."

"Agent Giusti—" Clooney began.

Kelly shook her head at Clooney, continued in a rapid-fire voice. "It was your arrogance in keeping it there that brought you down. You should have tossed the gun in the river, where you doubtless tossed the jewelry and the wallets you took from the Madison house."

After a beat of dead silence, Sherlock said, "Tell us, were

you Angela Storin or Misty Lee when you killed your two ex-husbands?"

Storin stared at Sherlock, slowly shook her head. "I have nothing more to say." She paused, a rictus of a smile on her pale mouth. "You are all so common."

Kelly rose, looked down at her. "I'm arresting you for the murders of Mrs. Ellen Madison, Dr. Douglas Madison, and Mr. Stanley La Shea." And Kelly read Storin her rights.

Clooney slowly rose, placed his hand on Storin's shoulder. "I wish to speak to my client."

As she was leaving the conference room, Sherlock looked back to see Angela Storin staring after her. Sherlock was relieved the Walther wasn't loaded, or Storin might have tried for it.

38

Alex Harrington Campaign Headquarters
Forty-Ninth at Sixth Avenue

THURSDAY AFTERNOON

Mia walked through the controlled chaos of Alex Harrington's campaign headquarters for the second time in three days, but it seemed much longer. So many people's voices clashing, sending the noise level to record levels. And everyone was moving, carrying pizza boxes, piles of bumper stickers, laptops, posters of Alex Harrington's face.

She gave little waves to people she'd seen on her first visit, and they smiled, nodded to her. Evidently she belonged or, more likely, everyone had been told she was a reporter and to be nice. She spotted Miles Lombardy in what seemed very serious conversation with Cory Hughes, Harrington's campaign manager. She wondered briefly if Miles had been part of the ambush last night, if he'd known what would happen when she left the bar. She prayed he'd been Alex's dupe for the

261

simple reason she liked him. He didn't come over or acknowledge anything might be wrong.

Mia hurried past them, nodded and smiled to Mrs. Millicent seated at her post, guarding the candidate.

"Hello, Ms. Briscoe. We weren't expecting to see you today." Mia saw through the glass-fronted office Alex was on his cell, his back to her. Mia nodded toward him. "I know he's terribly busy, but I was hoping Alex could give me five minutes?"

"I don't see why not. He should be off the phone in a minute. Why don't you go on in."

As she quietly opened the door, she looked back to see Miles and Cory looking at her. She gave them a wave.

Mia listened for all she was worth, but she could only make out his voice, not his words. Alex ended his call, turned back, and froze. Then he was on his feet, coming around his desk, smiling at her. "Mia! What a nice surprise on an insane Thursday afternoon. It's good to see you. Wait, what happened to you?"

He was good; the surprise on his face would have convinced the pope. Mia smiled back at him. "Oh, the bruises—they're not so bad, I'd forgotten about them. I guess I still look pretty scary."

He took her hand gently in his. "What happened?"

"Probably something that happens all too often, I imagine. I was walking to the subway last night after meeting with Miles for drinks, and out of nowhere some drunk or drugged-up idiot nearly hit me. I'm okay, really, I just look a bit on the edge, but nothing's broken, only some bruises. Don't worry, I'm fine." She waited a beat, added smoothly, "When the police asked me if I had any enemies, someone mad enough to try to run me down, I told them I was a political reporter, and they laughed. But then I told them I couldn't think of anyone."

"Did they get the guy?"

"He freaked out at what he'd done and screeched out of there, fast. It's too bad I couldn't identify the car or the driver, but the police held out hope they'd spot him on the CCTV cams."

Alex lightly touched her arms. "We can hope. Thank heaven you're all right. Can I get you some water? Coffee? Help you off with your coat?"

She smiled. "No, thank you, I'm fine. I think I'd just as soon leave my coat on. I won't take up much of your time, Mr. Harrington—"

He raised an eyebrow.

She laughed. "All right, Alex."

"That's better." He gently guided her into a seat, walked around his desk, and sat down to face her, his hands clasped in front of him on the desktop. "What can I do for you, Mia?"

"You remember I flew to Boston and Bennington Prep yesterday for interviews. I hoped you'd have a spare five minutes for some follow-up questions."

"I understand you were very thorough, and I appreciate it. We'll take all the time you want. What can I clarify for you?"

Mia opened her tablet, called up a page, pretended to read, then looked up, forcing a smile when in truth she wanted to smash her fist into his handsome face. Of course he wanted to know everything she'd done in Boston, what everyone had said to her. She said, "I also spoke to your former fiancée, Juliet Ash Calley. Reading over my notes, I realized I have some questions."

He cocked his head to one side, clearly puzzled. "Juliet? Whyever did you see her?"

"You said you appreciated my thoroughness. Of course I saw her, she was a big part of your life. She's a lovely woman, and so very talented."

Mia saw alarm, fleeting, but she saw it. Then it was gone, and she could have imagined it. Only she hadn't. He said nothing, merely kept his head cocked, with that faint look of puzzlement.

"She—Juliet—told me a bit about how you met, eventually got engaged, but she didn't want to talk about why your engagement broke off. Was that her decision, or yours, or was it mutual?"

Alex blinked at her. "What?"

"Your fiancée at the moment, Ms. Barrett, believed you had called it off, but you decided to say it was mutual so as not to embarrass Ms. Calley."

His smile slipped, he stiffened, and for a moment he looked like he wanted to throw her through the office window.

Then, the snap of the fingers, and Mr. Candidate was back. A dark eyebrow up in charming question, the practiced smile now firmly in place. He shook his head. "I can't imagine why the electorate would care about a former engagement. It isn't like it happened last month. It was more than two years ago."

"Alex. I've told you this before, your personal life will be endlessly fascinating to voters, and as you know, it all goes much smoother if you're willing to be an open book and leave no unanswered questions. Believe me, people scent when you're not being completely honest and open, and they'll talk and wonder. Now, if voters read a former fiancée broke your heart, they will feel sorry for the pain you must have felt, empathize with you, admire your brave face. Hasn't Cory mentioned to you it's usually best to feed the beast?"

"Yes, of course, it's Cory's mantra. It's simply disappointing the electorate don't dig into the issues, and leave the distant past buried."

Mia burst out laughing. "Sorry, but I can't believe you—a politician—just said that. Alex, of course you know people are endlessly curious about a candidate's past, transgressions and experiences, whatever."

"Yes, of course, particularly if there's a meaty scandal, but, Mia, I can't imagine there'd be much interest in an old engagement if Juliet weren't so beautiful and talented, and more famous now than two years ago."

"That sounds a bit cynical, if you don't mind my saying. I think people would have seen you and Juliet as the ideal couple, both picture-perfect. And when you didn't marry, they would have been disappointed and wondered what happened. So let's get it out of the way. Tell me, did you call it off? Or did she?"

He tapped his beautiful pen on the cheap desktop, and Mia knew he was playing for time to think. Then he smiled, shrugged. "Feeding voters' curiosity is one thing, but in this political climate, I can't afford any hint of personal indiscretion out there, present or past. It could be the end of my campaign, if the wrong people disapproved. Very well, I'll go out on a limb and tell you, but you have to promise me it will be off the record. You have to agree it doesn't leave this room."

"If that's what you want, sure. Off the record then."

He managed to look both ashamed and embarrassed, actually hung his head. She couldn't wait to hear what he'd come up with.

Alex tapped his pen on the desk again, dropped it, then shook his head, as if reaching a decision. "The oldest reason in the world, I imagine. I feel stupid about even saying it. I cheated on her. I know this will sound like I'm making excuses, but the fact was she was completely focused on her music, on her next concert, and not much else in the world. And that included me, her fiancé. I was annoyed because she'd broken another of our dates. I met someone, I got drunk, but it was only the one time. I felt like scum about it the next day. I couldn't lie to her, not Juliet. She's amazing, but she's also terribly serious, something of a prude, like her mother, as a matter of fact, but the one thing I didn't realize was how unforgiving she'd be. I swore to Juliet I'd never see the woman again—and I haven't—but as I said, Juliet decided she needed only music in her life. If she said anything about all this, well, let me add I wouldn't expect Juliet to cut me any slack. To her I'd gone beyond the pale, and there was no regaining her trust. When she broke us up, we agreed we would tell everyone it was a mutual decision."

"It surprises me she agreed to make it seem mutual if she's unforgiving. I don't suppose you told your current fiancée, Ms. Barrett, the truth about your breakup?"

"Of course. We are completely honest with each other. I'm

older and wiser now, Mia. To be honest, Pamela is everything to me Juliet wasn't." He shrugged. "What I mean is Pamela's a realist, sees the world for what it is, warts and all, and faces things head-on. That's exactly what a mayor's wife needs to be, why she's perfect for me."

"According to Ms. Barrett, Juliet couldn't deal with your political ambitions, she was too sensitive and avoided confrontation at all costs; in other words, she runs from anything unpleasant. That made her unsuitable for you, and Juliet finally realized it, so you being unfaithful to her wasn't the real crux of the problem."

He said evenly, "Pamela is right about that. Juliet usually shrank back from anything unpleasant. She was, and still is, from what I hear, much more comfortable with her piano than with the rancor of politics. Would we have married if I hadn't cheated on her?" He gave a charming Gaelic shrug. "Two years ago—it's a long time."

"So you're saying Juliet wouldn't stand up for herself if something bad happened to her? She wouldn't say anything to cause comment, worry her parents, create a scandal?"

"I hope Juliet didn't hint anything bad had happened to her. I can't imagine what it would be."

"No, certainly not. I just wondered. Thank you for clearing that up for me. I suppose you know your fiancée is very jealous of Juliet."

He threw back his head and laughed. "I expect ninety-nine percent of women on the planet would be jealous of Juliet. You saw her face. Helen of Troy wouldn't stand a chance next to her."

Mia knew he wanted to know what it was Juliet had said to her, but she wasn't about to oblige him. "Thank you for your honesty, Alex. Next, I spoke briefly to the professors at Harvard, and as I expected, they were quite laudatory since you gave me their names."

It was time to dig in the spurs. Mia made a show of looking down at her iPad a moment, before saying, "I spoke with some of the departmental secretaries there as well, and they remembered you had quite a reputation with the girls. You partied with Kent quite a bit, even went to other universities, some even out of state. Do you remember any of the girls you dated? I'd love to get an idea of what you were like in your twenties."

Impossible for him not to realize she was baiting him. He waved a dismissive hand. "You have to remember it was a different time, young men and women behaved differently, partied differently. Sure, I sowed some wild oats—most everyone did in my social circle—but I never went overboard."

"So you didn't inhale," Mia said and gave him a big grin.

He pulled up a smile. "That's right. I kept up with my studies and even excelled at them, well, most of them, as I think you found out.

"I certainly hope these topics we spoke of today won't be the focus of your piece. It wouldn't be fair to me or to the people of New York. Don't you want what's best for New York, Mia?"

She had to hand it to him, he'd batted the ball back at her quite well. She consulted her notes again, looked up. "Yes, of course, but let me finish giving you a rundown of my interviews.

I also stopped in at Bennington Prep, met Coach Wiliker. I showed him a photo of you I'd happened upon that showed you with a torn earlobe. He remembered clearly when you were injured playing lacrosse. He made you out to be the wounded hero, quite a story. And you won the championship for Bennington, two years in a row."

"Yes, we did. But the ear was no big deal. One of my teammates hit me by accident with his lacrosse stick. It hurt like blazes, ripped my earlobe, and I ended up with a notch in my ear. I got it repaired three years ago. Ah, did the coach say anything else?"

"He said you were an excellent leader"—she paused, looked again at her tablet—"that you always drove the bus, even with Kent, your best friend. Of course I'd heard that before. It's appropriate the leader do the driving, isn't it?" Mia rose. "I'm sorry if Coach Wiliker thought I was snooping. Lots of people do when all I ever want is to get something interesting. I imagine he called to tell you what a pest I was?"

"No, of course not."

You said that too fast, Alex.

He came around his desk, shook her hand. "I hope you're feeling better after last night."

"Yes, I am."

"You never told me what you thought of Pamela."

Mia said honestly, "I found her very impressive, Alex. She's smart, committed to your future and hers with you. I'd say she could be relentless in getting what she wants. I agree with you, the two of you fit hand in glove. You'll make an impressive team. Let me add she looks excellent in black Armani. Thank you for giving me some of your precious time. I'm sure we'll speak again. Soon."

She walked to the office door, turned, and smiled at him. "It was a pleasure speaking with some of the people who influenced your life, Alex. You can look for my first article sometime next week."

"Of course. I'll look forward to it, Mia."

When she closed the door behind her, she saw he was standing tall behind his desk, the committed leader in rolled-up sleeves, looking every bit the workingman's champion.

Sherlock was waiting for her in a small café near the campaign headquarters. Mia slid into the booth across from her, gave her a fist bump. "He's first-rate at cat and mouse, Sherlock, played the game like a pro. Hardly any tells, but I saw them."

Sherlock fist-bumped her back. "It sounds like you hit exactly the right note." She pointed down at a steaming mug. "Tea, Dillon's favorite, plain. Drink it, Mia, it'll warm you up."

Mia poured in milk and added two fake sugars, clicked her mug to Sherlock's.

Sherlock said, "Tommy called a few minutes ago. I told you he'd tracked down the cars registered to Alex Harrington and Kent Harper seven years ago—a red Jaguar XJ12 and a BMW 330i, and their license plates. He called Creighton's police chief, asked him to look again at the photos they'd collected from students' cell phones at the rave. Great piece of luck—turns out we've got a red Jaguar with a visible out-of-state license plate. It belonged to Harrington. A big nail, Mia, a very big nail."

"That's amazing—but, it's not enough, is it?"

Sherlock took Mia's hand in hers and squeezed. "No, but it is the first big nail. It puts them at the rave. It means we're on our way. Everything's going to move fast now." Sherlock's cell belted out Post Malone's "Into the Spider-Verse." She listened, tapped off, gave Mia a big smile. "Good timing, she's on her way. We'll meet her there."

39

Harper Building at 320 Madison Avenue
Harper Strategic Services
New York

THURSDAY, LATE AFTERNOON

When the express elevator door opened directly onto the executive offices on the forty-fifth floor, they saw Mrs. Wallaby, Kent Harper's administrative assistant, pulling a brocade handbag out of a drawer. Mia walked forward. "Thank you so much for waiting for us, Mrs. Wallaby."

Mrs. Wallaby smiled at Mia, looked beyond her. "Three of you? Well, I did tell Mr. Harper you, Ms. Briscoe, would be coming by. Poor young man, he's up to his neck in contract negotiations. I hope you have some pleasant news to make him smile."

"I don't know about that, but I'll certainly try to make him forget the contracts."

Mrs. Wallaby's eyes locked on Sherlock. "Goodness me,

272

you're Agent Sherlock." And she hurried around her desk, thrust out her hand. Sherlock obligingly shook it.

"Such a pleasure to meet you. Kent will be so pleased to meet you as well, and to see you again, Ms. Briscoe. He never says much, but he was smiling the rest of the day after you left. I have to say, though, he hasn't quite been himself today. I suppose it's the stress of work. I'm sure the three of you will make him feel better."

Mia said, "Isn't business good?"

Mrs. Wallaby gave a discreet cough. "No, of course business is splendid. I shouldn't have said anything. But I think he could use a pleasant surprise. Would you like me to tell him you've brought Agent Sherlock?"

"Please don't bother. We'll surprise him."

Mrs. Wallaby nodded, pulled her coat from the rack behind her desk. "Well, three pretty young women, he'll think he's in one of his video games." The phone on her desk beeped and she picked it up, listened. She winked at Mia as she said, "Yes, sir, I'm on my way. I'll see you tomorrow."

Once the elevator door closed on Mrs. Wallaby, Sherlock sat down in a visitor's chair. "That worked out well. Good luck, Juliet, and thank you for coming. What you're about to do, it takes guts. Don't think we don't know that."

Juliet sucked in a deep breath. "I won't lie, this is scary, seeing Kent again—but it will be worth it. And it's time I stepped up to the plate."

Mia and Juliet walked the short gray-carpeted hallway with the old photos of New York City on the walls. "You okay?"

Juliet's beautiful face looked fierce. "Yes." She paused. "Like

I told you and Sherlock in the lobby, I might not have come, hard to say now, but Sherlock's call talked me into it. I'll admit, Mia, I wanted to shoot you for telling her, an FBI agent. But you know what she said to me? 'Imagine lying in an unmarked grave, no one knows where you are or what happened to you. Imagine what your parents feel, their child, gone with no idea where or why, think about what they'd live with the rest of their lives.'" Juliet paused, swallowed. "I thought of my mom and dad, and I knew if I simply disappeared, no word, no trace, it would kill them."

Mia laid her hand on Juliet's arm. "What Sherlock said is true. You can't know how much I admire you. You ready?"

Juliet took a deep breath, nodded. "Let's do it."

Mia tapped on Kent's door as she opened it. He was standing in the middle of the office, holding a gilded medieval sword over his head, ready to bring it down. He jerked when he saw Mia in the doorway. He slowly lowered the sword, gave her an embarrassed smile. "It's been a hard day. I've found exercising with this sword de-stresses me. What a great surprise."

But it was anything but great. So he'd spoken to Alex, and now she was the enemy. Then Kent saw Juliet and froze, a look of horror on his face until he smoothed it out. He said, "Juliet, ah, I don't understand. Why are you here in New York? Do you have a performance at Carnegie I didn't hear about? Why are you with Mia?"

"Hello, Kent," Juliet said. "No, I'm not here to perform. It's been a long time. You're looking well." She waved her hand at the walls. "You're still playing with your sword. And I see you're still surrounded by your gaming toys."

"They're bloody collectibles, worth a mint!"

Mia shook her head at him and said, her voice filled with censure and disappointment, just like Mrs. Marvin, one of her third-grade teachers, "Sure they are, Kent. The sword, every-thing in here—in a grown man's power office—is make-believe, a teenage boy's fantasy. Aren't you a little old to be slashing around that ridiculous sword?"

Kent slowly laid the sword against his desk, to give himself time to think. When he finally looked at Juliet, he said, "Why are you here?"

"I'm here, Kent, to right past wrongs."

"What past wrongs? What is going on here? Mia?"

Mia gave him a blazing smile. "I'm Juliet's backup."

"Backup for what?"

But he knew, Mia saw it in his eyes. He was afraid.

Juliet said in a clear, steady voice, "Mia knows you and Alex roofied and raped me two years ago, both of you. I believe I know why Alex raped me. He was furious when I told him I wouldn't be a politician's wife, that I didn't want to spend my life being in a fishbowl with him, the brunt of the daily com-ments and conjecture.

"But you, Kent—why did you rape me? I thought you liked me, maybe even respected me. And here I was your best friend's fiancée. But I guess I was wrong. To be honest, I always wondered why you were always hanging around, like you were tethered to Alex's side. Did Alex invite you to have at it, to hu-miliate me, and you simply did as he told you, like always? Did you enjoy it, Kent? Did you enjoy raping me?"

Kent stood still, tall and stiff, then sat down at his desk, clasped his hands in front of him on the desktop. When he looked up at them, he looked bewildered, hurt, and confused. It was well done. He said in a stern patriarchal voice, exactly like his father's, if he'd only known, "Juliet, I don't understand what you're talking about. That's all nonsense, and you know it. The breakup with Alex . . . well, you know the two of you were like oil and water, not meant for each other. Everyone knew it.

"Of course I liked you, admired you. Alex used to tell me he pictured the children he'd sire with you, all of them smart, talented, but with his backbone, his guts. He said he knew he'd have to toughen them up because you were so sensitive and, well, unwilling to disagree with anyone. He insisted he didn't care you weren't interested in politics, he told me you were so beautiful he'd be content to simply sit and look at you. He loved you, Juliet, and you broke his heart."

Juliet spurted out a laugh. "Now that's rich, Kent. As far as I can tell, Alex has only ever loved one person—himself. Well, maybe you think he loves you, too, so long as you keep to your place and be a good dog. But you know what? It's easy for me to see him kicking you to the curb if he doesn't need you anymore. Have you ever thought about that? Have you ever wondered what Alex really thinks of you? If you're really nothing more than a doorknob to him? His little shadow who does whatever he tells you to?"

Kent sighed, a reasonable man striving to be patient, difficult with a gamer's sword propped against his impressive desk. "Are you saying these things because Mia wants to write an exposé, make a name for herself? And she picked Alex's career to destroy?

"Juliet, listen to me. You know none of this is true. Alex and I are best friends, have been since we were kids. There's no big man and his shadow, that's absurd. Yes, Alex did tell me you actually accused him of raping you and he was floored, deeply hurt. He didn't understand why you would make such a horrible accusation. I wanted to talk to you myself, try to find out where all that was coming from, but Alex told me to stay away. He didn't think there was any way of talking you out of this crazy idea we'd both raped you.

"I did not rape you, Juliet. If Alex did rape you, which I don't believe for a minute, then he did it alone. I don't know why you've brought me into this." He looked at Mia. "You did this, didn't you? It's true, isn't it, you want to ruin Alex and me, as well. Juliet, you can't believe a word she says. Believe me, I know nothing about what happened two years ago."

Juliet didn't answer him. "Mia, he hasn't even asked us to sit down, hasn't offered to hang up our coats." She turned and helped Mia off with her coat, laid it and her own on the backs of the two chairs in front of his desk.

"I hope you don't mind," Mia said as they seated themselves, made themselves comfortable.

"I do mind. I've had enough of this. I want you both to leave."

Juliet looked at him and slowly began to applaud.

"Stop it!"

She did, nodded, and said in approval, "What you said, Kent, it was well done. A lawyer couldn't have been more fluent, more convincing. If I didn't have my own personal firsthand experience with what a pervert you are, I might have been fooled. Being in charge of the New York office has toughened you up. Has it made you tough enough to maybe even disagree with Alex once in a while?"

Kent turned on Mia. "You're responsible for this, aren't you? You talked Juliet into saying these ridiculous things to me, to make all these vile accusations. None of it is true. It's obvious Juliet has suffered a breakdown, and I'm sorry for it, but it has nothing to do with me. Or with Alex. Why are you doing this?"

Mia said quietly, "Because seven years ago you and Alex drove from Boston to a fraternity rave at Godwyn University in Pennsylvania. You wanted new prey, and you wanted anonymity. You picked out the girl and Alex roofied her drink, but something went very wrong. You had to set fire to the frat house to get her out of there."

His expression of shocked disbelief turned to angry insult. He kicked back in his chair, folded his arms over his chest. "Godwyn University? I've hardly even heard of it. Drive to Pennsylvania for a stupid college rave? That's crazy, and it's fiction. I don't know what you're talking about."

Mia continued, "Do you remember her name, Kent? It was Serena. You and she spent time talking about gaming. Maybe she only told you her handle—Aolith. She told me all about you when we were in the bathroom. She was having fun with you, another gamer. You and Alex murdered her, Kent, and you buried her. And we have proof."

"I will say it again. I don't know what you're talking about. I've never known a girl named Serena or Aolith, and I've never been to Godwyn University. Juliet, I suggest you consider getting some help for your issues. As for you, Mia, you're a disgrace to your profession. I'd like both of you to leave."

Mia said, "I'm sure Alex told you about the two photographs I showed around of the two of you at that rave seven years ago. One photo clearly shows Alex's silver link bracelet and his notched ear from his accident playing lacrosse. It shows him next to Serena's drink, about to put the roofie in it. And there you are, Kent, wielding your imaginary sword, and Serena's laughing. All in good fun, until she took a drink."

He slammed his palms on the desktop. "That's enough! None of this is true. Show me these ridiculous photographs. It can't be Alex or me. We weren't there.

"Both of you, listen to me. You misunderstood Alex, that's all. Yes, Alex mentioned a couple of photos to me. He said Coach Wiliker called him about your showing them to him. They were blurry and who knew who the men were? I wasn't there. Alex wasn't there, at least not that I know of. He had other friends. Ask him. I don't know." He rose, his hands clenched at his sides. "I will say it one last time. I wasn't ever at Godwyn University. I wasn't at this stupid rave. I know nothing about this girl. Now, leave, both of you."

Already throwing your lifelong friend under the bus, Kent?

Mia heard the panic in his voice, kept pushing. "Serena described you to me that night, Kent, when she met you. She was so excited, full of your praises for knowing as much about gaming as she did. Imagine my surprise when I saw those photos and then saw a silver link bracelet on Alex's wrist when I interviewed him at his campaign headquarters on Tuesday, only two days ago. People who knew you then, like Juliet, can testify that it was Alex and you in those photos at the rave. It's only a thirty-minute drive north from there to Valley Forge National Park. That's where you buried Serena, isn't it?"

279

"I've never been to that park, either. I didn't even know it's a national park. Stop this now!"

Juliet said, "You're forgetting the Revolutionary War belt buckle and two buttons Alex found there. He was stupid to have kept them because I saw them, Kent, many people have, displayed in his living room trophy case. I asked him about them, and he told me he'd visited Valley Forge National Park with you a couple of times. Did he find them in the dirt while you were digging Serena's grave? Or nearby?" Juliet leaned forward, raised her finger at him. "Ring up one lie."

Mia said, "And before you say all of that is supposition again, let me tell you exactly what I believe happened. Alex drove the two of you in his precious red Jaguar to Godwyn that night seven years ago. And guess what? We have a photo of the Jag parked outside the fraternity, the license plate nice and clear. Alex gave the Jag to Pamela's younger sister four years ago. No supposition there, she's posted photos of Alex with her and the Jag. The Jag's being impounded as we speak by the Boston FBI, and their CSI team will be going over it. You'd better hope Alex did a good job cleaning up that car. A single hair root, a tiny drop from blood splatter, and they'll identify Serena's DNA. The technology is that good now.

"Don't forget your cell phones. There'll be records. Did you know wireless carriers keep billing and cell tower records for seven years? Did Alex make a call that night? Maybe from the rave? Or from where you buried Serena at Valley Forge? I can't imagine after all that excitement, all that work burying Serena, the two of you wanted to drive all the way back to Boston. They'll find out where you stayed, count on it."

Kent went as pale as his white walls.

Mia said, "You're remembering, aren't you? Remembering Alex made a call? It was Alex who would have, because he was always in charge, not you. He was the one with the big-shot friends, not you. You were always the hanger-on. I don't think you were the one who killed her, Kent, Alex did. He was the one to put the roofie in her drink.

"Were you upset when she died? You were unless you were faking all your gaming fun with Serena that night. And I don't believe that. I saw the two of you, laughing, carrying on. Are you going to let Alex dominate you forever, until you're both in prison for life? Don't you think it's time you start protecting yourself?"

His eyes locked on Mia. His expression hardened, and when he spoke, he was once again the big boss, the man in charge, his voice low and vicious. "If you dare to print a word of this, Harper and Harrington lawyers will bury you, bury your whole muckraking newspaper. They'll hound you until you can't even find a job writing about snowfall in North Dakota. And you, Juliet, if you accuse us of anything at all, we'll show you're the bitter, vindictive bitch you are. Your parents will be ostracized, and your precious concert career will be over."

Mia smiled at him. "That's a meaty threat, Kent, but you know what? It sounds pretty lame to me after you tried to kill me last night. Or was it Alex who tried to run me down? He knew exactly where I'd be since he had Miles Lombardy buy me a drink."

Kent stared at her. "Run you down? You believe I tried to kill you? Don't be ridiculous. Yes, I see some bruises on your face, but I have no idea where you got them. With your mouth, I wouldn't be surprised if someone you insulted went after you."

"As I said, either you or Alex was driving that car. Believe me, Kent, I really don't have any other enemies who would like to do away with me."

"I did not try to run you down!"

Juliet rose. "The police are tracking the car on the CCTV cams. And they just might see the driver. They might see you, Kent. Listen, Kent, your threats won't work anymore, it really is over. I'm not paralyzed any longer by what you and Alex did to me. I know now how really vile both of you are. I will do my best to see you both pay." She paused, cocked her head. "Listen to Mia, Kent. Alex is a monster, and in the end, I suppose you're his victim, too. It could go much easier for you if you go on record and tell us the truth. Special Agent Sherlock is in the waiting room now. She can help you."

"I've put up with more than enough of this. Get out. You'll be hearing from my lawyers."

They left Kent standing in front of his desk when Mia quietly closed the door behind them. She said low, "Pretty much what we expected. Now he'll be calling Alex."

40

Safe House

THURSDAY AFTERNOON

Agent Gaylin sat forward, his hands fisted on his knees. "Look, Savich, I think your plan is good; it even has a more-than-even chance of succeeding. But you and Olivia know as well as I do it's dangerous, lots of chance involved, and unknowns, moving parts, people acting and reacting a certain way to make it work. No, I'm not shooting it down, but it should be me, Savich, not you."

Olivia said, "Gay, you know why it has to be Dillon. Not only is it his idea, his people from his Criminal Apprehension Unit are a part of it. Believe me, I've met some of them, they're a well-oiled machine, they know what they're doing. You know we can't take a chance of involving the CIA, too many questions and talk about unknowns.

"Give it up, Gay. You know it's our best chance to find out what's going on here." She lightly touched her hand to his shoulder. "It will be all right." She gave him a crooked grin. "I thrive on unknowns and the unexpected, you know that.

"Now suck it up, Gay. We have to get a move on. Dillon, do you have anything to add before you winter up, and we'll see if you pass muster. Gay's gear is in the front closet."

Savich said, "Gay, I know exactly how you feel, but trust me, this is the best way to proceed. Think of it as a chess game; we're good, we've thought it all out, prepared. All our pieces are in play and the odds are excellent the opponent will make the moves we're predicting."

Gay sighed. "Yeah, yeah, you two should be lawyers. I understand, but I don't like it. Both of you, be careful, all right?"

As Savich donned Gay's coat and scarf, Olivia went down on her knees and hugged Helmut close. "I know you want to come with me, but I'm not about to put you in danger. You and Gay will guard the house. I've left you water and food in the kitchen, you know the drill. Sorry, Gay, but I didn't leave you any food or water." She gave Helmut a last big hug, felt his tongue lap over her face. She kissed his forehead, straightened, and turned to study the winterized Dillon. "Not bad. Wrap the scarf more around the lower part of your face. With the sunglasses and the knit cap, you look enough like Gay to me. For at least two minutes."

Savich turned to Gay. "Do I look like your brother, at least?"

"No." Gay sighed. "You're taller than I am and I have twenty pounds on you. As for my brother, he's short, too heavy, and bald. Okay, like Olivia said, you could fool people for maybe two minutes, from a distance."

"Good enough. We're lucky it's so cold." Savich's cell sang

out "Whatever It Takes" by Imagine Dragons. He listened, disconnected. "Agent Noble says it's time. The car's still out there, tucked away near a driveway, half a block away." He looked at Olivia, who'd slipped on her coat, scarf, and knit cap. "You ready?"

Olivia nodded. "It'll be all right. Helmut, stay. Gay, you stay, too."

It was thirty-three degrees, the sky a gray bowl overhead, bare tree branches were being whipped about by gusts of a bitter wind. Olivia and Savich ran to Gay's Honda, jumped in, fastened seat belts. Savich shot her a look, saw she was hugging herself, and switched the heat on high; right away warm air blasted into their faces. She met his eyes and nodded. "Never thought I'd be grateful to be freezing my butt off in mid-March."

He laughed. "We couldn't have ordered up better weather."

"I can feel them watching. Do you see them in the rearview?"

"No, but they'll follow." Savich slowly backed out of the driveway. "I'll pretend I'm trying to evade, but not enough to lose them."

Olivia's last view of the house was of Helmut sitting on his haunches watching her from the living room window.

A dazzling slice of sun burst through the gray. Savich nodded. "Now even our sunglasses make sense. Keep an eye out, Olivia, but try not to be obvious."

"Yeah, yeah, you're saying this to a CIA agent? You were

right; they'd know right away where the new safe house is. And I didn't tell anyone." She fretted with her leather gloves. "So it has to be someone at Langley, someone with access. Gay knows it, too, and it really pisses him off." She paused, turned to face him. "I hate it's someone I've trusted with my life, Dillon. And I hate it even more that some of them still believe Mike is a traitor. Even Gay, though he didn't come right out and say it because he felt sorry for me."

Savich shot her a grin. "No, if he kept it to himself, it's because he didn't want you to deck him."

He took another left turn, then another. Not much traffic on a Thursday afternoon, most people not out of work yet, heading home or to their favorite watering holes. "You know some of the questions about Mike's loyalty were disinformation, Olivia, purposefully planted, and watered with great care. But it's no longer a problem. Ah, there they are, the big dark blue passenger van, the Chrysler Voyager. Ruth said the license plate is muddied over, a pity."

Olivia pulled out a makeup mirror and angled it so she could see the trailing cars. "I can't make out the license plate, either, and CIA agents are trained to see through mud."

Savich laughed, took another left, then right. "That should be enough. They're good. If I didn't know they'd be following, I might not have seen them yet."

He turned on Wilton and drove straight toward High Point Mall, three miles ahead.

Olivia turned in the seat to face him. "I can't believe I'm about to run an operation out of the ladies underwear department at Macy's."

"Makes sense. You couldn't go back to your house for more clothes, so you talked Gay into taking you there to pick up a few necessities."

Olivia drummed her fingertips on the dashboard. "I wonder how many there are? There was that man at my house on Monday, he could be one. And the Frenchman from yesterday. So at least two of them."

"If I were running their side, I'd want to keep it small and tight, maybe three, four max. We'll see soon enough." Savich drove for three blocks, then slowed to turn onto Southby, which fronted the High Point Mall. Savich said, "He's there, still hanging back."

As Savich drove the Honda toward the Macy's, the anchor store at the north end of the mall, Olivia felt her heart begin to thud. She was both excited and terrified. Today it would all end. And she prayed.

Savich parked the Honda halfway down a lane in the open parking lot, thirty yards from the Macy's entrance. He said, "Olivia, we both know this is dangerous since we don't even know all the players. No, let me finish. I know you're a pro, you understand the risks. If the worst happens and we lose you, the tracker you're wearing will at least let us know where you are. It's good for another twenty-six hours." He lightly touched his hand to hers. "Know I'd come for you. Are you ready?"

"More than ready, Dillon, let's go. I want this over with."

They walked together, heads down against the wind, and stood in front of a window a moment, Olivia pointing to a pair of running shoes. Savich paused and looked again, just as Gay would. He saw nothing, made a big deal of gesturing her into the store. Once inside, Savich's cell played Jimi Hendrix's "All Along the Watchtower." He listened, then ended the call. "Davis has the Chrysler van four cars away from the Honda. Two men, one driving, the other in the back seat. Both men are looking at us, not moving."

They rode the escalator to the second floor, to the lingerie department, a place no man would go unless he had a gun to his head. Savich took a seat in one of the two chairs thoughtfully placed nearby for waiting men and looked long-suffering. He saw women carrying shopping bags, heard their voices, some laughter. One woman paused, sent him a little wave. He answered his cell twice. Ten minutes later, Olivia walked out with a Macy's bag. "Underwear and flannel pajamas, in case they want to look," she said, patted the bag.

They took the escalator back down, walked through a cloud of perfume spritzed on a customer by a saleswoman in towering heels and bright red lipstick. They stepped out into the frigid cold and walked quickly toward Gay's Honda. Nearly there, and Savich stopped cold, felt around his neck, looked chagrined. He raised his voice. "Olivia, I left my scarf in the store. Get in the car and lock it, turn on the heater, I'll be right back." He looked around the parking lot again, nodded, saw the two men in the Chrysler had slid down so the van looked empty. He whispered to Olivia, "Showtime," turned, and headed back toward Macy's at a fast trot.

41

East Sixty-Seventh Street
New York City

THURSDAY EVENING

Alex opened his front door, frowned at Kent, looked down at his Piaget watch. "What's going on with you? Why did you call? You know I'm busy with the campaign. What is it?"

Kent stepped in, forcing Alex back. "We need to talk. Now. I wasn't about to do it over the phone."

Alex had never seen Kent look so upset. "All right, I can guess what this is about. It's that bitch reporter, isn't it? What did she do now?"

Kent followed Alex numbly into his newly redecorated black-and-white living room. It was signature Pamela, the walls stark white to match the carpet, the furniture all black, the only splashes of color a single blood-red pillow on the black leather sofa and the orange flames shooting up in the hearth. Even the paintings on the walls were lined up like soldiers, all of them white with a single black streak across the middle that lined up perfectly with the next canvas. Kent couldn't look at them, they made him mildly nauseated. Alex claimed he liked the new look, but Kent didn't believe him. Standing in this room Kent felt like the life was being leached out of him. He took off his coat, tossed it over the back of the sofa, and sat down. He picked up the red pillow, began fretting with the fringe. He managed to say calmly enough, "Not only the reporter. I couldn't believe it, Alex. She brought Juliet to my office. Juliet!"

Alex eyed him. Kent looked pale, shaky. "Juliet? You've got to be kidding me. What did she want?"

Kent sat forward, squeezed the pillow between his hands. "They know, Alex, they know everything. They even claimed there was an FBI agent waiting outside."

Alex felt a punch to the gut, but he wasn't about to let Kent see it. He shrugged, looked dismissive. "Get a grip on yourself, that's impossible. So Briscoe got Juliet to come to New York. Now, that does surprise me. Pleasant, shy, nonconfrontational Juliet. Wonders never cease. So what did she say to you, Kent? Wait up a minute, you need a drink first. You look like you've been shot." Alex turned and walked to the glossy black sideboard, splashed whiskey into two glasses. He handed one to Kent, tapped his glass.

Kent downed the two fingers of whiskey in one gulp, savored the jolt of heat in his gut, and leaned back against the leather sofa. He hated he was afraid, hated it. He closed his eyes and saw Aolith—her face blurry from passing time—but there she was, excited, laughing up at him. Then he saw Mia Briscoe's bruised face. His eyes flew open and he jerked forward. He saw Alex had moved to stand behind a winged chair, his whiskey in his left hand, looking impatient. With him? Of course with him.

Kent said, "Mia had bruises on her face, Alex; it was obvious she'd been hurt. I couldn't believe it when she asked me which of us tried to run her over last night, you or me."

Alex jerked back. "What? Run her down? That's ridiculous. Sure, I saw the bruises. She told me it was an accident, most likely some drunk. Now she's accusing one of us of trying to kill her? Why would either of us do that? That's beyond stupid, it's crazy. Kent, I'm running for mayor of New York City!"

He looked both insulted and disbelieving. Was Alex that good an actor? Kent could never be sure if Alex was telling the truth since they were three years old. He remembered the first girl Alex had roofied as a lark at Bennington. She was sixteen years old and her nickname was Perky. She'd been unconscious for eighteen hours, and it scared the crap out of everyone. But not Alex. Not that he let on anyway. When she surfaced, she didn't remember a thing. Alex had calmly told Kent what he'd done then, that now he knew to use a smaller dose. The two of them could have at it, a banquet lay spread out in front of them. And Kent had gone along. No, Kent could never be sure if Alex was telling the truth. But to try to kill Mia Briscoe? Could he be that reckless?

Alex said finally, "So somehow Briscoe got Juliet to come to New York, got her to come see you. Tell me exactly what happened. And don't tell me Juliet threatened to go public, accuse us."

"She's not the Juliet we knew two years ago, Alex."

"What do you mean by that?"

"She was calm, angry at me, at you, for what we did to her. She seemed strong, more determined."

"So she put on a good show, what with the reporter there propping her up." Alex smirked. "It doesn't matter; at her core Juliet is the same. Who she is will never change. I know she couldn't handle going public, no way could she stand up to what would happen next. Her pleasant little world would crumble around her. Her career would go down the toilet. You know she'd never subject her parents to that kind of scandal."

"You didn't see her, Alex, you didn't hear her speak."

Alex actually laughed. "Juliet knows very well what I'd do if she went public. I'd tell the world she's a bitter, vengeful woman and this is her revenge for my dumping her. I'd bury her, Kent, blow up her world. Don't doubt it. I know she doesn't." He paused a moment, searched Kent's face. "All right, tell me exactly what Juliet said to you."

Was that worry Kent finally heard lurking under the bravado? "She accused me to my face of raping her, Alex, and she asked me why I did it. She said she knew why you'd raped her, for revenge, to humiliate her. Did you want her to remember, Alex? Did you lighten the roofie so you'd be able to look at her and smile later, knowing she wouldn't say a word?"

Alex saluted him with his glass. "You have me there. Juliet was always about herself—just listen to me play, listen to all the people applaud me and worship me." He took another sip of whiskey, shook his head. "You want the truth about Juliet?

I thought she was a beautiful cow, exquisite to look at, like a beautiful painting to be admired, nothing more, but boring to be with, and as uptight as her mother. She and that ridiculous piano she polished herself every frigging day. What we did to her—it served its purpose. Don't try to tell me now you didn't want her, that you didn't enjoy that gorgeous body. You had her two times."

Kent said nothing.

Alex stepped away from the fireplace, looked off in the distance. He wondered again how Briscoe had gotten Juliet to New York. He'd have sworn Juliet would take what he and Kent did to her to the grave. He'd never underestimate Briscoe again. Briscoe had taken Juliet to see Kent first because she'd read him, seen what he was, and she'd used Juliet to frighten the spit out of him, hoping he'd break. And there he was, sitting in Alex's living room, a scared little boy. Alex raised his glass and toasted it toward Kent, a smile playing on his mouth. He remembered taking Juliet, seeing how pliable she'd been. He remembered kissing her hard, biting her lip, not caring if he hurt her.

Kent said, "If she did go public, it would end your campaign. You'd be blackballed at the slightest hint from her of what we did."

Alex said, "True enough. And yes, my parents would hate that, but they'd believe what I tell them, Kent. They'd back me to the hilt, particularly my father, and he's the one who counts. Of course there wouldn't be a trial, there'd only be speculation, and sooner or later it would all die down. You know as well as I do my family has the power and the money to spin anything Juliet accused me of. So stop your worrying, I don't think she'll say a word publicly. Not the Juliet then, not the Juliet now."

He watched Kent worry the pillow fringe some more. How could he be so weak, like a hysterical woman? Alex took another small drink of his whiskey. "Kent, think about it. Even if Juliet did accuse us, Briscoe's paper couldn't print anything she said except as an allegation, without proof. And there is no proof and there never will be." Still, he had to give Briscoe credit, figuring out what happened to Juliet, but he knew the only reason she'd been able to was those damned photos. She'd somehow put it together.

He said, "Briscoe somehow managed to get Juliet down here hoping to frighten you, to manipulate you into panicking, maybe even confessing."

"I didn't. I told her I didn't know what she was talking about."

Could he believe him? Alex said, his voice very quiet now, "Good. Because they went to you hoping to turn you against me, to put us at odds. Don't you understand? If they had any evidence, they wouldn't have approached you. Why would they?"

Kent sat forward. "You still don't understand; what I've told you isn't the half of it. Alex, listen to me, the Boston FBI has impounded the Jag you gave Pamela's sister, Belinda, the one you drove to Godwyn seven years ago. They're going to look for her DNA—Aolith's. Her name was really Serena, and she was Briscoe's best friend. She said they'll find traces of blood in the trunk or maybe a hair and they'll have her DNA."

Alex felt a punch of gut-cramping fear, shook it off. Why hadn't Kent told him this already? Because he was an idiot, always confusing pythons with garden snakes. Who cared about Briscoe's accident, or about that pathetic Juliet? It always amazed him Kent was so successful in business. Patience, he had to have patience. But there was no way he would let Kent be a loose cannon. He went into what he thought of as his "Kent mode." He kept his voice deep and soothing. "Calm down, Kent. I haven't heard a word from Belinda, and believe me, she'd have called me if someone took her car, or she'd have called Pamela."

"They must have ordered her not to tell you. Or maybe she doesn't know. You know Pam and her little sister don't get along all that well, given how Belinda is always eyeing you, so I'll bet she didn't tell her."

"Look, I had the Jag detailed after we got back from Pennsylvania seven years ago and a few times since then, and once again when I gave it to Belinda. There won't be any DNA, they won't find anything in that car. It's a bluff. How did they even know about the Jag?"

"Briscoe said they found a photo taken that night outside at the rave. Your Jag was in it, with the license plate."

Alex laughed again, and Kent saw the hint of contempt, for him. He wanted to put his fist in that arrogant face.

"Kent, you're not thinking logically. There's a big difference between being at a rave and killing someone. So they know we were there. That's not a crime."

"I told them I'd never been to Godwyn, so they know I lied."

Alex shrugged. "So you forgot. Who'd remember a dippy

rave after seven years? Even if they say you lied, that's not a crime, either. You weren't under oath. Out of the blue, these two women were attacking you, you were understandably flustered. Don't forget it was seven years ago. You went to a freaking party. And that's all. You should have told them to call your lawyer and ordered them out of your office."

Kent stared at him, listened to his smooth dismissive tone, and for the first time, the curtains parted. It hurt to say the words, but he did. "What you're saying is that Briscoe brought Juliet to me because they think I'm the weak link."

Of course you are, you idiot. You're only now realizing it? Alex shook his head. "You're a good businessman, Kent. Think of this as a business crisis. You examine the facts, weigh the risks, the pros and cons, the possible fallout. Use your skills, like always, Kent."

Kent studied his friend's face, so arrogant, so certain he was smarter than anyone else. Was he even capable of seeing what could happen? They could both be destroyed, even end up in prison, despite all their money and influence. Kent shook his head. "No, Alex, it's not the same thing at all. This isn't a freaking business problem. If my father finds out about Juliet, and there's any publicity, an official investigation, and there could be, he'll have me removed from my position. It's not just your bloody campaign, it's my career, my life. And that's not all. They'll be looking at charging us with murder."

"Murder? Tell me all of it, Kent."

"Briscoe said they're getting a warrant for our cell phone records. I remember you called Alan and we drove to

Philadelphia—after—and we stayed with him that night. What if they interview him? What if he tells them we arrived with dirt all over us? Did you tell him what we'd done? Did you?"

"Of course not." Alex gave an elegant shrug. "Don't worry about Alan. Sure they keep cell phone records. We live in a big brother world now. So if we must, we admit that yes, we were in the area. But there's no way they could pinpoint where we were seven years ago closely enough to help them find her body. It's another bluff." He rose from his chair and poured Kent more whiskey. "Drink up and relax, okay?" He remained quiet until Kent had downed his second glass, gave another little shudder. "You shouldn't have let that bitch get to you, Kent. Sounds like she played you like a violin. Murder, that's ludicrous. There was no murder. It was an unfortunate accident, that's all it was."

Kent clearly saw the moment Alex hit Serena's head with his fist, remembered her falling down, remembered carrying her between them out to the Jag. He remembered the moment he realized she was dead and Alex had calmly tossed her into the trunk. If only Aolith hadn't seen Alex put the roofie in her glass. If only— Kent shut it down, he couldn't bear to hear her voice, see her face, her lifeless body. He took another drink, let himself relax into the whiskey's pulsing warmth. Could Alex be right? Could it all be a bluff? He said nothing, leaned his head back against the sofa again, closed his eyes. It felt cold and expensive, smelled almost alive. He heard Alex get up, heard more whiskey splashing into his glass. Kent started to drink, realized he had to stop or he wouldn't be able to think clearly.

When he opened his eyes, he saw Alex was leaning against the mantelpiece, stark white Italian marble that cost a small fortune.

Kent got slowly to his feet. He eyed his lifelong friend. "I told you, they said an FBI agent was waiting outside. To make a deal with me. They wanted me to throw you under the bus."

Alex's heart skipped a beat. "Which, of course, you'd never do, right?"

"Of course not, but you're making light of everything. The FBI is involved, Alex. Briscoe is relentless, and now they've got Juliet." He looked around the living room. "And why did you let Pamela turn your living room into this soulless pit of hell?"

"What?" Alex took a step forward. "What did you say?"

Kent only shook his head. "Nothing, not important, it's the whiskey, I guess. They said I've lived my life under your thumb, that I've done pretty much everything you've told me to do. That I've always been second to you."

Of course you have, you pathetic piece of crap. Alex put humor in his voice. "Not a bad strategy, trying to set us against each other. They probably flipped a coin, and that's why they came to you. But we've always been too close for that, nearly brothers."

Kent said more to himself than to Alex, "I'm a successful, respected businessman in New York City. Our profits are up, and that's because of me, no one else. I'm not second to anyone."

Alex kept his voice soothing. "Of course not. Everyone knows what an excellent job you've done. And you're my best friend. We've been together, done everything together, all our lives, two halves of a whole.

"Go home, Kent, get some rest. There's nothing for you to do now but hunker down, make sure there's nothing incriminating on your cell phone or your computer. Get yourself your own lawyers, don't ever speak to the reporter or Juliet again. We'll get through this together, Kent. We always have."

Kent said slowly, "I never asked you, never had the nerve. I remember you were so angry when Jordan Jeffers ripped your ear with his lacrosse stick at Bennington, tore it in two. I always wondered, did you run him down? Did you try to kill him, Alex?"

Alex looked directly into Kent's eyes. "I cannot believe you'd ask me that. Do you think I'm a monster? I had nothing to do with his accident."

Kent didn't believe him, not for an instant. He felt sober as a judge, and the sober judge saw a cliff coming up fast. He said slowly, "For the first time in our lives, Alex, I really see you. You never really cared about me, you can't care about anyone. You needed me to play your wingman, you needed someone to lord over.

"I saw seven years ago exactly what you were, but I refused to accept it. I felt horrible about what happened to Aolith, how we dumped her into that grave, how you killed her. You didn't care, you had no remorse. All you felt was irritation she'd had the nerve to die and you didn't get a chance to have sex with her. And we never talked about her, once she was under all that dirt. She no longer existed for you. I've never forgotten her."

Kent grabbed his coat, walked to the arched doorway, and turned. "I'm going to be looking after myself now, Alex, doing what's best for me. I won't be voting for you, by the way. If you make it that far."

Alex stood motionless, the blazing fire behind him hot on his back. He heard the front door open and close.

42

THURSDAY NIGHT

Tommy Maitland was coming out of Mia's kitchen when the doorbell rang.

He called out, "I'll get it, Mia. Hope it's our pizza."

He opened the door, eyed the bundled-up woman standing there. "You didn't bring the pizza? I don't see the box."

Juliet blinked at the big man standing in front of her in jeans, boots, and a thick light blue sweatshirt. He had dark hair and striking light gray eyes, rough chiseled features. Tommy Maitland, she assumed, here earlier than Mia expected. She said, "Not unless the concierge at my hotel gave me a lovely surprise and put a pizza in my overnight bag. Shall I check?" She leaned over, sniffed. "Sorry."

Tommy grinned at her, shook her hand. "You're Juliet Calley, right? I'm Thomas Maitland though Mia still insists on calling me Tommy." He paused a moment, grinned. "Actually, all my friends and family do too."

Mia walked over, poked him in the side. "He tells me no self-respecting FBI agent is called Tommy so he insists crooks call him Thomas. Juliet, come in. I'm so glad you decided to come stay with me."

Juliet said to the big man, "Mia didn't expect you until tomorrow."

"One of my snitches gave us the break we really needed, so we closed the case faster than expected."

"Where's Sherlock?"

Mia said, "She'll be back later. She volunteered, well, really, she insisted she be the one to follow Kent since she's certain he'll hightail it right to Alex Harrington. She'll call us later with an update.

"As for the big guy here, Tommy pulled some strings and arrived an hour ago. Come in, Juliet. Tommy, please put Juliet's carry-on in the bedroom and I'll hang up all her winter gear." Mia leaned forward, hugged Juliet, whispered in her ear, "Everything will work out, you'll see." She leaned back. "You got checked out of your hotel all right? You left your forwarding address for curious minds?"

"Yes, just as Sherlock told me to. You think someone might come here?"

Mia said as she hung Juliet's coat and scarf in the small entrance hall coat closet, "Sherlock believes it's possible. But we'll have Tommy now and both of them later, and they're as tough as his hiking boots, so Tommy says. Come in, come in."

Like everyone else who visited Mia, Juliet walked directly to the wide picture window and stared down at Central Park. "It's beautiful even though you know you'd freeze in a Boston minute if you were out there."

Tommy said, "Boston minute? That's not right, it's stealing. Even in Washington, we call it a New York minute. There's the doorbell again, that's got to be the pizza."

While Tommy was at the door, Juliet said, "It's very kind of you to let me stay here." She huffed out a breath. Even at the hotel I felt antsy, jumped at every noise."

"Not a problem. Do you know what Sherlock said about you? She said she wasn't surprised you're so brave, that after listening to you play Beethoven's Sonata Pathétique, someone with your passion could face down the devil."

"Me? Brave? Passionate?" Juliet looked surprised and delighted. "That's the nicest thing anyone could say to me. But the truth? If it weren't for you and Sherlock, I might have never confessed to anyone what they did to me."

Mia said, "I agree with her, so shut up. I've told Tommy about our interview with Kent Harper and Sherlock keeping an eye on him tonight." Mia shrugged. "Now we wait."

Tommy carried two big pizza boxes into the living room. "No, don't move, Mia. Only girls need napkins and paper plates for pizza. It's like pouring beer into a glass. Dive in, ladies."

Tommy watched Juliet pick up a slice of pepperoni pizza, take a bite, sigh. "Better than the concierge offered me."

Tommy waited until she swallowed, then asked her, "Do you think Kent Harper will go running to Harrington like Sherlock believes? And what do you think Alex Harrington will say? Do?"

Juliet said thoughtfully, "If you'd asked me that question two years ago, my stomach would have gone queasy. I'm sure Mia told you what they did to me. I'll be frank. I nearly fell apart, but at least I had the sense to go on sabbatical, to try to get my life back together. And I did. I took back control. I learned self-defense, and after two years, I'm pretty proficient at tae kwon do. And today? Seeing Kent? I was scared going in, but it turned out to be a revelation. Kent was—just a man." She took a ferocious bite of pizza. "I scared him. Mia and I scared him. You wonder what Alex will do. He won't scare, he'll examine everything in detail, and he'll make his plans. He's as cold as ice."

She patted her stomach. "Look at me—not queasy. Another slice of pepperoni, I think," and she grabbed another slice, bit in, and a string of cheese clung to her chin.

Tommy stared at her. He knew what she'd been through, could imagine the helplessness and impotence she'd felt. He reached over and flicked the cheese off her chin, said easily, "Mia tells me you play the piano for a living."

"I try."

Mia leaned over, punched her lightly on the arm. "She's having you on, Tommy. This woman has performed at Carnegie Hall."

"Yeah, I knew that," he said, grinned at her. "Looked you up on my way here."

Juliet shook her head at him. "Do you have the warrant for Alex's cell phone records yet?"

"The warrant will come in sometime soon. I know you're scared, Juliet, I don't blame you. What you did today—it was a huge step, you faced down Kent Harper. The FBI has impounded the Jag. Like Sherlock said, if there's a single hair—" Tommy swallowed, then forced her name out as he went on. "If there's a single strand of Serena's hair, the CSI team will find it." He sat perfectly still, frozen, the pain of her loss clear on his face.

Juliet lightly laid her hand on his arm. "I'm so sorry, Tommy. I can only imagine what you went through seven years ago, what those memories and feelings coming back now must be like."

Tommy felt his voice shaking and hated it. "At least now there's a good chance Serena's folks will get some justice. It's not enough, nothing could be." He paused, then said, his voice harsh, "Even if we get them both in prison for what they did, it won't mean a bloody thing until we find her."

Mia said quietly, "We will find her, Tommy. It will mean a lot to her folks and to us."

The FBI agent was suddenly back, his voice strong and controlled. "Harrington and Harper will have a dozen lawyers speaking for them. Everyone in law enforcement has seen it often enough. Sometimes, whatever you have, it isn't enough. But this time, it will be. This time I'm not about to stop."

Mia said, "And your dad, Tommy, he's not going to sit on the sidelines. He'll be leading the charge with us."

Juliet cocked her head.

Tommy said, "My dad's a big kahuna in the FBI, assistant director." He looked over at Juliet, really looked. "I'm very sorry about what those bastards put you through."

"Thank you. Do you know, I've fantasized about visiting them in Sing Sing, and crowing. Taking a big photo of the two of them and posting it in Times Square, with a caption like, *Aren't You Glad He's Not Your Mayor?*"

Tommy raised his beer, clicked it to hers. "We'll make it happen."

Mia's cell phone rang. She looked down, frowned. "Hello, Mia Briscoe here." They both watched her face freeze.

Then Mia pushed the end call button and stared blankly at them. "That was Sherlock. Kent Harper's been shot. She was there. She's riding in the ambulance with him to Bellevue. She'll give us all the details when we get there."

43

Macy's
High Point Mall

THURSDAY

Olivia looked back to see Savich jogging through Macy's front doors to find his supposedly forgotten scarf. She waited a moment, took a big breath, kept her head down even though she'd spotted them when she and Dillon had come out of the store, waiting, waiting. Of course they were watching him, too. *Come on, boys, he's out of the way, let's get this show on the road.* Her hand closed on the Honda door handle. In a matter of seconds, the van started up, reversed, and screeched to a halt behind the Honda. A man jumped out, pinned her arms to her sides, threw her into the back of the van, one fast practiced series of moves. He slammed the door shut. Olivia kicked up at him, heard a hiss of pain, but the driver grabbed her by the neck, jerked her head back, and pulled a pillowcase over her head. Still she lashed out with her feet. A fist slammed against her head and she saw white and fell back, stunned. She heard him yell, *"Allez!"* It was the Frenchman. He threw Olivia on her stomach against the rough carpet, came back over to her, and dug his knee into the small of her back. The van hurtled through the parking lot, tires shrieking, people yelling after them.

He shouted to the driver, "Slow down, you fool! The *flics* will come!"

The van slowed. Was the driver the man who'd shot at her at her Monday night?

Olivia tried to push herself up, but he pressed the muzzle of his gun into her back. "You do not want to ever walk again? Answer me!"

"I want to walk again."

"Smart girl." The pressure from the gun eased. He called to the driver, "Go carefully, turn left out of the mall, then straight ahead." She felt his attention on her again. "You think the agent will follow us? *Non*, I broke the car. I see *le bouffon*—he yells on his mobile, calling for help. But it will not matter, we will be long away. And the license plate it has *la boue*—the mud on it. And this Chrysler van, it is everywhere." He looked back down at her. "Now I take your guns. *Non*, you will not fight me again." He drew her Glock from its clip at her waist, reached down and pulled out her ankle pistol. He patted her down, found the knife strapped at her waist, and pulled her cell from her jeans pocket. Olivia felt a gust of frigid air when he opened a window. She heard her cell phone clatter to the pavement.

She had to keep her wits, but it was hard to even breathe. "Please, take off the pillowcase, I can't breathe."

"You will be a good girl, *oui?*"

"Yes."

He pulled the pillowcase off her head, shoved her onto her back. Olivia stared up at his swarthy face, and its two days of beard scruff. His eyes were covered with opaque sunglasses, his hair dark and curling, a few flecks of silver at the temples, so maybe in his early forties. Even with his heavy coat, she could see he was well built and very strong. He called out, "Turn left here, Claude, keep straight. They will not know where to send the *flics.*"

He leaned back, grinned down at her. "We were ready to take both of you, but that stupid agent made it easy. He forgot his scarf, right? And the fool left you alone to go get it." He laughed, looked pleased with himself.

Olivia ran her tongue over her dry lips, swallowed. At least she could breathe again. "Why don't you tell me your name?"

He grinned at her, nice teeth, but a bit yellow from smoking Gauloises. "You will call me René."

His real name? If so, it meant he planned to kill her. "How did you find me? How did you know where the safe house was?"

René stroked his pistol over her earlobe, light as a lover's fingers. Olivia didn't move. He laughed quietly. "It is good for a woman to be in her place, quiet, obedient. And now you will tell our driver exactly where Mike Kingman is hiding. I know for sure you have the knowledge. You also know what I want. This time do not think to tell me the lie." He leaned close. "I have won, accept it. The brain, the patience, I have them both. Fortune now shines on my head, that is something you say, *oui?*"

Olivia nodded, let acceptance and defeat bleed into her voice. "Yes, you have it exactly right."

He patted her cheek with the muzzle of his gun. "Good girl. Now give Claude directions—*oui*, that is the name we give him—tell him how to get to Kingman or I shoot your kneecaps, like your old American gangsters. Do you comprehend?"

She drew in a deep breath. "If I take you to him, you'll kill us."

He moved the pistol to her breast, leaned close, his hot breath on her cheek. "If I get the flash drive, why waste bullets?"

She slowly nodded. "You must know he hasn't been able to access that flash drive, it's encrypted. He can't even copy it without the key and you can't either. Only certain people at the CIA have the key."

"That is not your concern. Tell Claude the directions. *Maintenant*—now." He pressed the muzzle hard against her left knee and started humming. It was scarier than anything he'd said.

"Why don't you call Mike? Negotiate a trade?"

"So he can run again?" He laughed. "Give Claude the directions."

Olivia looked through the windshield. "Go straight until you see Brewer Avenue, turn left."

It was the slower way to Galesburg. After Claude turned left, she called out, "Turn right at the next street, Culver, and stay straight. We're going to Maryland, to the Potomac."

"How long?"

"Forty minutes."

René forced her onto her side away from him. She heard him speaking French on his cell. Reporting in to his boss in France?

He tapped off, then said to her in English, "No one follows us. Claude, do not drive beyond their limit."

"Who are you working with in the CIA?"

"Maybe someday you will know this." He paused a moment, grimaced, slowly flexed his shoulder. "Maybe I hurt you to pay back for your lucky shot. *Mon épaule*, my shoulder, Claude took care of me or it could be very bad." The van hit a bump and René hissed out a breath. He shoved the pistol against her side, hard enough to make her suck in her breath.

"I wish I'd shot you in the head, ended you."

"*Salope!* Bitch. *Ferme ta gueule*, I want no more from you or I strike you again."

René didn't speak again. The minutes passed slowly, like coarse sand sliding through the neck of an hourglass. The driver, Claude, hadn't said a word yet. Again Olivia wondered, Was he the man who'd shot at her Monday night?

When they'd left the red lights and stop signs behind, René poked her with his pistol again. "Sit up now and look out the window. Forty minutes have passed. How close are we to Mike Kingman?"

Olivia struggled to sit up, felt a moment of dizziness, and looked out the window. "In about a mile, turn right on the unpaved road. There isn't a sign."

Claude slowed, turned the van onto an unpaved old potholed

road that led down to the Potomac some fifty yards ahead. There were no houses nearby, only bushes, tangled vines, short stretches of broken-down fencing, groves of hemlocks and oaks crowded together. Through the trees, Olivia saw the derelict boat ramp sinking into the steel-gray water, the bitter wind whipping waves over the rotting boards.

René said, "Claude, no closer, we take no chance Kingman sees us. Stop behind these trees."

Claude gently turned the van off the narrow road to the right and drove slowly over low-lying shrubs to stop behind a copse of hemlocks. Twenty yards ahead was a battered old wooden boathouse, weathered to a sullen gray, its windows long broken, covered with cardboard. It was like a still life painting, no sign of life.

Claude came around to the back of the van and opened the door. He held a gun on her as René pushed her out, jumped out behind her. Olivia stumbled, went down on her knees, slowly got to her feet.

"Claude, wait with her, I will see what goes on. She is trained, so keep away from her and do not let down your guard. Keep your Beretta pointed at her."

"Believe me, René, I saw what she could do Monday night. I will not let her close to me. She won't do anything. Don't worry."

Olivia said slowly, "So you were the one I heard speaking English. You were with the Iranian. But you don't have a French accent."

Claude took a step back, grinned at her. "Actually, I grew up in Indiana."

René frowned at him, leaned close to Olivia, murmured in her ear, "Now we find out what this Mike Kingman thinks of you. If he does not give me the flash drive, I will make both of you dead. If he does, well then, we'll see, won't we? Claude, shoot her in the leg if she tries anything." He patted her cheek with his pistol and disappeared into the hemlocks.

44

Bellevue Hospital

THURSDAY

Kent couldn't move, couldn't feel his body, couldn't see. Was he blind? Where was he? Were those voices he heard? Yes, a woman's voice, and two men's, calm, ordinary voices, workaday voices, like a team, calling out numbers, saying words he didn't understand. There was something in his throat, a machine hissing in and out, like a bellows. He realized his brain was working even though his body was elsewhere. Should he be afraid? Before he could decide, his thoughts turned fluid, flowed in no particular direction, gently, slowly. He saw his grandmother, Kiki, smiling at him, her gold molar on display. He hoped she was all right, but no, she'd died, hadn't she? Some time ago? He couldn't remember how long, not that it mattered. He heard the machine huffing, in and out, in and out, and he let himself fall into the steady rhythm. Everything seemed to soften, as if he were floating on a cloud, content as he drifted. He knew nothing could hurt him here, wherever here was. He wondered if he was Snake, wondered if he'd sink into the cloud or draw his sword. No, he wasn't Snake, he really wasn't. He was himself. He heard a man's urgent voice, "Blood pressure's dropping!"

He saw Kiki again, on her knees in front of him, pulling his arms through the sleeves of his winter jacket. She smelled like strawberries. She always smelled like strawberries. She kissed him, laughed, kissed him again. He felt the sweetness on his cheek.

MIA

Mia heard a man nearly snarling as she, Tommy, and Juliet approached the surgery waiting room and stopped to listen.

"You're telling me, Special Agent Sherlock, you were really there, as in right on the spot, and you watched Mr. Kent Harper get shot? The FBI ordered you to be there, watching him?"

Sherlock's voice was lower, controlled, but Tommy heard the frustration boiling below the surface. He bet she wanted to punch the guy's lights out. "Detective Hoolihan, as I've told you, Mr. Harper is a person of interest in a rape and murder investigation from seven years ago involving the FBI. As I told you, it wasn't a formal op, I was doing a favor, all right? Keeping an eye on him, ready to follow him if he ran."

Out came a snarl, fast and sarcastic. "Didn't do such a good job, did you, Agent Sherlock? Yeah, I know who you are, but you didn't shine very bright tonight, did you? I'm thinking you being there was probably what got him shot in the first place.

The guy takes two bullets in the back with you sucking your thumb fifty feet away?"

They didn't hear what Sherlock said because his voice was louder and overrode hers. "And you're actually telling me Alex Harrington is involved? In rape and murder? Kent Harper's in the papers now and then, but Harrington is running for mayor of New York City. Lady—smack my disrespectful mouth, I mean Special Agent Sherlock—cool your heels, try not to get anyone else shot. I've got to make some calls, get this going up to the big brass, see where they want to steer this boat. Then you're going to give me every single detail. You and those people you say you're working with, as soon as they arrive."

"That's our cue," Tommy said, and the three of them walked into the waiting room to see a tall, stick-thin man in a rumpled suit, cruising close to sixty, his head bald as an egg, shining bright beneath the fluorescent light. He was standing maybe a foot in front of Sherlock, in her face, dismissive and impatient, a sneer on his thin lips, trying to intimidate her. Good luck with that. Tommy saw Sherlock was holding on to her patience and realized she was blaming herself for allowing Kent Harper to be shot, and that was why she hadn't taken the detective apart. She felt guilty.

Tommy said in a deep, authoritative voice, "Detective Hoolihan? We're the three who can tell you everything you like. I'm Special Agent Thomas Maitland, FBI." He introduced Mia and Juliet.

Hoolihan turned to them slowly, nodded toward Mia and Juliet, eyed Tommy. "You freaking feds always travel in packs, don't you? This one"—he shook his head in Sherlock's direction—"tells me the New York City mayoral candidate Alex Harrington is not only a suspect, along with the guy who's in surgery with two bullets in his back, but that candidate Harrington himself might have even been the one who shot him, afraid the guy would roll on him? Let's give the poor schmuck a name—Kent Harper. As to her"—he gave Sherlock a dismissive glance—"I hope you're going to tell me you've never seen her before and she's barking nuts. Yeah, sure, I know who she is, who cares?" He ran his hand over his bald head, a longtime habit, back from when he had hair.

Tommy said calmly, stepping closer to look Hoolihan in the eye, "If you know about Agent Sherlock, you know she's brave as a lion, which should make you realize there had to be circumstances outside her control. I also overheard you'll be calling your lieutenant, who will of course contact his captain, and up it goes to police commissioner—"

Hoolihan looked pained as he said, "Up to the freaking current mayor." He glanced at Sherlock. "Circumstances? She admitted she screwed up."

Tommy continued, "You probably would have, too, if you'd been on her watch and in her shoes."

"She shouldn't have been alone!"

Sherlock said, "Detective Hoolihan is right. I should have known it was possible, Tommy, but I didn't think it through. If Harper dies, it's on my head."

Mia wasn't about to remind her that both she and Juliet had wanted to go with Sherlock and she'd been appalled to think of taking two civilians on a stakeout. Would there have been a different outcome? Very likely not.

Tommy said simply, "Then it's on our heads as well; none of us gave a thought to there being a real threat, just Harper running. What's done is done. Stop wallowing or I'll call Savich and he'll read you the riot act."

"I already did," Sherlock said, frowning. "I got his voice mail and that's never happened before."

Tommy turned back to Hoolihan. "There's going to be a huge ruckus and the mayor will decide how to deal with it. He needs as much warning as he can get." Tommy looked down at his watch.

Hoolihan wanted to punch this good-looking kid who looked to be younger than his own son. "When I get back, the four of you better be here." He wagged a finger at all of them, turned on his heel, and marched out of the room, cursing under his breath, his cell phone in his hand.

Tommy said, "Sherlock, tell us what happened before our charming Detective Hoolihan comes back."

Juliet was looking after him, clearly bewildered. "I don't understand. He's a cop. Just like you guys are cops. Why is he being a jerk?"

Sherlock said on a short laugh, "Territorial rights, and to be honest, I wouldn't be happy either since, as I said, it's my fault Harper got shot. This is a local matter now, as he sees it, no reason for the federales to stick their big noses in. Come, sit down and I'll tell you what happened."

Juliet thought Sherlock looked both exhausted and angry, with blood splattered all over her white shirt, black and stiff. She ran her fingers through her beautiful curly hair, making a clump stick up. Like Sherlock, Juliet still couldn't believe

shots, center back. I was afraid he would bleed out on me before the ambulance arrived."

She looked down at the stiff blood covering her white blouse. "You forget how much blood there is in the human body."

An older man with white hair in tufts spiked up around his head appeared in the doorway. He studied them briefly. "I'm Dr. Morgan, one of the surgeons. I was asked to give you an update. Kent Harper is still in surgery, will be for at least another two to three hours. We're having trouble keeping up with the rate of his blood loss. I suggest if you haven't contacted his family, you do it quickly."

They were silent after the surgeon left. Mia didn't say it out loud, but she knew if Kent Harper died, there might very well be no case, and that was why Alex had his lifelong friend shot.

Juliet said, "I don't want him to die. I want him in prison. Sherlock, shouldn't we go see Alex, see what he has to say about this?"

Sherlock shook her head. "I'm sorry, but the FBI can't be involved."

Juliet cursed under her breath, and only Tommy heard her. He smiled.

45

Abandoned Boathouse on the Potomac
Near Galesburg, Maryland

Olivia studied Claude, considered trying to take him. He was a man you'd pass on the street and never notice—medium height, slender, brown hair and eyes, unremarkable in every way, except for his eyes. She saw a dark pit behind his eyes, and oddly, a look of pleasure. Was it at the thought of killing her? And he wasn't stupid. He kept his distance, his Beretta aimed at her chest, not her legs. She said, "Are your parents French?"

He eyed her a moment, as if wondering if she had a hidden meaning. Finally, he nodded. "My father, yes."

"You were raised in Indiana. I doubt your parents wanted you to be a criminal. Do you kill people?"

He smiled. Like René, his teeth were yellowed from smoking. He shrugged, said only, "My parents are dead, past caring what I am or what I am not. Yes, I kill when necessary. As do you. You killed Razhan, a man at the top of his profession. Rock-hard, deadly. If I had a beer, I'd toast you."

She raised her chin. "Well, he's not deadly any longer, is he? He's just dead. Who hired you to come to my house?"

"You tempt me to shoot you in the mouth, just to shut you up. I wonder if René has killed Mike Kingman yet? He will, you know, he wants to, hates the guy's guts."

"Why? He doesn't even know Mike."

"René hates to be thwarted. He hates to think anyone is smarter than he is, even if only for a little while, even if, in the end, he wins. He told me once he liked killing a worthy opponent more than he liked having sex. I imagine he's facing this Kingman down right this minute, getting that flash drive."

MIKE

But René was still walking the perimeter of the derelict boathouse, looking up into the trees, searching the bushes for shadows, for movement. He heard nothing and saw no one. He walked around to the front of the boathouse, marveled it was still standing, and finally he knocked once on the decaying wooden door, called out, "If you shoot me, my partner will kill Olivia Hildebrandt. She is nearby. I am here to trade her life for the flash drive. I want only what is mine, the flash drive, not your lives. Will you agree to a trade?"

René heard boot steps, then, "Come in."

René heard no surprise in Kingman's deep flat voice. Had he tried to call her again with no luck? Impossible when her cell phone was smashed in the parking lot at the American mall. Of course Kingman had known he'd come.

René pushed the sagging door inward, his pistol held against his leg, and stepped in, blinked to adjust to the dim light. He saw Mike Kingman standing silent and still in the middle of the room, a Glock in his left hand pointed at René's head. He'd seen photos of Kingman—at least ten years younger than he, tall with blue eyes, shaggy dark hair, a hard, handsome face. He was wearing only a flannel shirt, scruffy jeans, and scarred boots. There was no fear in his eyes, only calm determination, like the rhino René had barely escaped in the Serengeti. Well, the rhino had died as easily as anything else with a bullet between his eyes. René hated him on sight. He said, "Lower your gun, Mr. Kingman. There is no reason for you to shoot me, and I have no reason to shoot you. A gentleman's trade, that is all I want."

Mike lowered his Glock to his side. "What's your name?"

"You may call me René. Are you alone?"

Mike waved a hand around him. "Do you see anyone else?"

René looked about the long, narrow room, perfect for a large boat, he supposed, three windows on each side covered with cardboard. Boat hooks and chains hung down overhead, like ancient torture devices. The floor was a dirty green linoleum, cracked and chipped, the wooden floor beneath it rotting. A fortune-teller's beaded curtain closed off a bed, he supposed, another a toilet at the back of the room. There wasn't a kitchen, only a rough wooden plank laid over drawers. On top stood a small refrigerator and a microwave. There was an ancient sagging blue sofa, the material ripped and worn, stuffing poking out. There was a small folding table, two chairs. A small generator rested beside the table.

"Pull back the beads, show me no one hides there."

Mike kept his eyes on René as he lifted the beads, showed him a narrow cot with two blankets stacked on top, two boxes on the floor, clothes flopping over the sides.

"Now the other. Show me."

Mike pulled back the beads to show a narrow shower and a toilet. He dropped the beads and they chittered together.

Mike studied the Frenchman. He was in his early forties and well built, his face lean, carved in stone, his eyes onyx, filled with a killer's knowledge, a killer's lack of empathy for his fellow man. He looked watchful. He looked relentless. Mike wouldn't underestimate him.

He said, "Prove to me you have Olivia. I want to speak to her before we make the trade."

René said, "Very well. I pull out my cell phone now, I do not reach for another weapon."

"Two fingers."

Slowly, René pulled out his cell, dialed a number. "Claude, tell Olivia to say hello to Mike."

"Mike? Be careful, don't believe him, he's a killer, he's—"

René tapped off, slipped his cell back into his coat pocket. "How is it you say? Proof of life? Now you have it." He shook his head. "It always amazes me how a man will do anything for a woman he believes he loves. You went to grand trouble to hide the flash drive, to keep it out of my hands, yet all I have to do is take your woman, and you have the willingness to hand it over gladly. You are a common fool, like most men. It is time for you to show me the flash drive."

Mike said, "You must know it cannot be decrypted without the key."

"I have no wish to decrypt it. I wish only to make certain it is the flash drive given to you by your CIA agent in Iran."

"I know your boss is French, just as you are. Is he afraid Hashem names him on the drive?"

René said, "Do not waste my time with your stupid questions. Show me the flash drive, prove to me it is legitimate."

Mike stepped to the ancient blue sofa, pulled the flash drive out from under a tear in the fabric.

"Show me."

Mike plugged the flash drive into an adaptor, pushed it into his cell phone, punched the screen. He held up the cell for René to see. "Satisfied? Nothing more than a prompt for the encryption key. That's as far as anyone can get without the key. I will give you the drive when you give me Olivia."

René said, "Did you try to decrypt it?"

"Of course I tried, but since I don't have the key, it was impossible. You won't decrypt it either."

René smiled. "Me? I would smash it under my foot but I am asked to take it back instead."

"To whom?"

René smiled. "As we agreed, I will bring Olivia and we do our business."

46

OLIVIA

Boathouse on the Potomac

René came loping out of the copse of hemlocks, looking pleased with himself. He said in French to Claude, "I searched the boathouse and there is no one, only Mike Kingman. I have seen the flash drive. It is legitimate." He looked at Olivia. "Kingman is a fool; he trades for something more important than you could ever be. You are only one woman of many."

He turned again to Claude. "Kingman is no problem. I looked all around the boathouse. There is no one." Still, he paused, looked around yet again, saw nothing. "You have looked as well?"

Claude said, his voice impatient, "Of course. No sign of anyone. We are the only ones here."

Suddenly, René whirled around, searched the trees, his gun at the ready. "I heard something."

Claude said, "You're hearing the tree branches rustling in the wind. You have looked, I have looked. Time to finish it,

René, time to get this over with and get out. I don't like this place." He turned to Olivia. "At last you are silent. If you are planning something, believe me, it will not succeed. And I will be forced to kill you."

Olivia laughed in his face. "Yeah, sure, that'd be smart. If you do kill me, you'll never get your precious flash drive. Mike will make certain of that."

Claude said, "No, no one's going to try anything because Kingman is your lover. He won't take a chance of our killing you. He will do as he's told." He turned to René. "I spoke to your brother. He is pleased, but impatient for you to call him with news of the drive."

René said slowly, with hint of contempt, "Henri always has the impatience. Very well, but Claude, *faîtes attention*, nothing must go wrong." He gave Claude a vicious grin. "Timothy told me Henri kills you if you return to France without it—he laughed, called it Henri's mortal discipline." René looked around again, past the stripped oak branches whipping around in the bitter wind, shuddered. "I hate American winters. They are too cold."

Olivia's heart beat a mad tattoo. So René was the boss's brother? So Henri was another Frenchman. He wouldn't have let her hear his name unless they'd planned to kill her and Mike all along.

"Claude, I walk behind her. Then you. Do not forget, *faîtes attention*." René shoved his Sig into Olivia's back. "Walk, girl." Claude took his place behind them, scanning the trees, his Beretta moving, ever moving.

They walked into a small open space at the front of the boathouse, René still behind her. There'd once been a stone path to the boat ramp, but there were only chunks of rock left, dead winter weeds nearly covering them. René stopped, and now he pressed his Sig against Olivia's temple. He called out, "Mike Kingman, open the door. We are here with Olivia. She is dead if you do not obey."

The sagging door was slowly pulled inward. Mike stood in the doorway, the flash drive in his right hand, his Glock in his left, again trained on René. He saw Claude, frowned, but stepped back. "Come inside. If this man tries anything, you will be the first one I shoot."

Mike quickly closed the door against the frigid wind. He met Olivia's eyes and smiled. "Hello, beautiful."

René laughed. "Keep the close eye on her, Claude." René walked to one of the beaded curtains, pulled it back. It was the same as before, a narrow wooden cot, several blankets piled on top. He walked to the other beaded curtain, pulled it back, saw only the toilet and a small shower. Satisfied, he turned to Mike. "You are still alone so you are not entirely stupid. Now you will again show me the flash drive on your mobile, prove to me you did not switch it."

Mike did as he asked, difficult with one hand, but he managed, his Glock still pointed at René's chest. Again, René looked at the cell phone display, saw only the prompt asking for the encryption key. He grunted. "That is wise of you. Here is the woman, unharmed. Give me the flash drive."

Mike said nothing, pulled the drive from his cell phone, but he didn't give it to René, he waited.

René nodded. "Claude, release her and Kingman will give me the drive."

Claude didn't release Olivia. He calmly pulled her back

against him and pressed the muzzle of his Beretta against her left ear.

René grinned. "And now we have the impasse, do we not? You shoot me and she is dead. You try to shoot Claude, and you are dead. So give me the flash drive, it is easier."

Olivia said, "Don't give it to him, Mike. He's planned all along to kill us. He told me he's working for his brother, Henri is his name, in France."

Claude dug the Beretta into her ear and she sucked in her breath. "Shut up, woman, or you are dead where you stand."

Olivia believed him. She watched Mike toss René the flash drive, saw René slip it into his coat pocket. "And now what, Kingman? Will you shoot me and watch her die, or will you throw your Glock to the floor?"

Mike saw the look of surprise on René's face when he laid his Glock on the floor, straightened. "Let her go now. Send her over to me."

René was enjoying himself. He loved the feeling when he'd beaten an enemy, when he'd won it all. It was as he'd always believed. The Americans were easily duped, a fine term Claude had taught him. Kingman was willing to do anything to save a woman, the fool. He said, "Claude, send her to her lover. It warms the heart, does it not, that they want to be together?"

Claude pushed Olivia toward Mike. Mike shoved her behind him. René laughed. "You play hero to the end, eh?" And he raised his Sig, a look of anticipation on his face.

Savich stepped from behind the beaded bedroom curtain. "René, Claude, drop your weapons. Do it immediately or my agents at the windows will fire."

René froze, but only for an instant. He kept his Sig pointed at Mike's chest. "You cannot shoot me. I will kill him if you try. Where were you hiding? I looked."

"The wall beside the bed, behind the boards."

"Who are you?"

"You don't know? I thought you saw me in my red Porsche. Not a good lie, was it? Ollie, unless he lowers his weapon, shoot him in the arm."

"*Batard!*" René whirled about to fire, not at Mike but at Savich.

A shot rang out and René's Sig fell from his fingers. He gasped, grabbed his arm, felt blood ooze out between his fingers. He stared blankly toward the window, no longer covered with cardboard, at the face of a man with a rifle pointed at him.

Savich said, "Claude, gently place your Beretta on the floor or the next bullet will be for you. If Ruth's aim is good, she might hit your shoulder, or maybe it will be your neck. It's not that important to me."

Claude slowly bent down and laid his Beretta on the floor.

Savich said, "Olivia, pick up the guns."

As she bent down to pick up his Beretta, Claude lashed out his leg.

Olivia jerked away, but his foot clipped her thigh. She felt nothing but joy as she whirled about and sent her foot into his groin and smashed her fist into his throat. Claude fell to his knees, gagging, trying to suck in air. Then he moaned, fell on his side, and hugged himself. Olivia stood over him. "Thank you for that, Claude. Don't worry, you'll be breathing again, in a minute or so." She turned to Savich, said with a huge grin,

"Do you know Claude is from Indiana?" She kicked him with her toe. "And would you look what he chose to do with his life."

Mike said, "That's my girl. Excellent timing, Savich. I guess we'll need an ambulance for the French idiot. They actually believed they could walk in, take the flash drive, and kill us."

Claude had his breath back. He yelled at René, "You arrogant moron! You swore there was no one hiding in this god-forsaken shack! You swore no one was outside, hiding in the trees. I told you before we took her it had to be a trap, the flash drive was too important to the CIA for them to just hand it over to you, but you laughed at me, said no one would beat you, the incomparable René Delos! You're more of a fool than your sadistic brother." He broke off and began coughing, as he frantically rubbed his throat.

René's face was white with pain, but he was so furious he managed to pull himself into a sitting position. He waved his fist at Claude and yelled in French, "You were the one waiting outside? It was you to see, not me."

Savich said, "I imagine both of you gentlemen will have countless years to discuss who's more at fault here. As you've learned from firsthand experience, my agents are very good. Now, Claude, if you are unwilling to tell us your last name, I suspect you will be in Interpol's facial recognition database." He looked dispassionately down at René. "So you are René Delos, and your brother is Henri. I strongly doubt he will be pleased with you when the French police arrive at his house."

Olivia pulled René's cell phone from the inside of his coat pocket, waved it at him. "Dillon, look what I have. A magic phone. Because René believed he would walk away with the flash drive in his pocket, leaving us dead, he had no hesitation about calling his bro to brag how easy it was to drag me into the van. I'm sure everything we need is right here on his cell. Let me see." She scrolled to the most recent call. "Ah, here it is. A French number. Your brother's number, René?"

René raised furious eyes to Savich's face. "You are a dead man. I will enjoy killing you, after I slit her throat."

Savich went down on his haunches, studied René's white face. He said, his voice matter-of-fact, "Seems to me, *monsieur*, given your current condition, you should admire my guile, tell me what a worthy adversary I am. And then you will want to make other plans." He smiled over at Olivia. "She fooled you, you never had a doubt, did you?"

The boathouse door pushed open and four CAU agents—Ruth, Ollie, Davis, and Lucy—filed in, bundled to their ears in winter gear, the dull brown shades blending in nicely with the surroundings outside. Ruth said, "Hello, everyone. Olivia, good to see you again. I saw what you did to our boy here from Indiana. I like your moves. Well done."

Olivia said, "Hello to all of you, and thank you. I looked for you as well as these two morons, didn't see even a shadow. Ollie, that was an excellent shot."

Lucy laughed. "I hate to admit I didn't want to be a big bush as a disguise, but it worked."

Mike shook hands with each of them. "Good job staying hidden. Thank you all." He looked down at René. "You're not looking so good, mate. All your plans, kidnapping Olivia, murdering without a bit of remorse, didn't work out for you."

René felt a raging mix of fury and pain. He wanted to smash that face above him. But he couldn't raise his arm. He fell back, moaning.

Mike pulled a handkerchief out of his pocket, handed it to René. "Press this against your shoulder, hard, to slow the bleeding. I don't want you to bleed to death. I want you to spend the rest of your life in a French prison."

Ruth said cheerfully, "Our only problem was the cold. I swear my fingers are still numb. Ollie suggested that all the bushes move closer together for warmth."

Ollie said to Ruth, "Suck your fingers, that's what I did. It works." He knelt down beside René, looked at his wound, shook his head at him. "The bullet passed through. No reason to whine."

Olivia didn't know a laugh was lurking, but out it came. She wanted to kiss all of them. She walked to Mike and hugged him tight. He rubbed his cheek against her hair.

Davis said to Savich, "I called an ambulance for this French bozo."

Lucy walked to Claude, went down on her haunches, jerked him onto his stomach, put her cuffs on him. She leaned down, whispered in his ear, "Didn't work out well for you, either, did it, kidnapping Olivia?" She grinned up at Savich. "I think he called me a bitch."

Savich looked at Olivia still standing close to Mike. "You know it isn't over."

She nodded slowly. "Yes, I know. I know."

"I'm sorry, Olivia, very sorry."

47

One Police Plaza
New York City

FRIDAY MORNING

It was cold, a stiff wind blowing, but the plaza was packed with reporters and camera crews, and vans lined the street. Mia watched Alex Harrington, flanked by Pamela Barrett, his campaign manager, Cory Hughes, and his senior staffer, Miles Lombardy, and other staffers form a phalanx around him. He strode tall onto the makeshift stage set in front of the fourteen-story New York City Police Department headquarters, his shoulders back, his handsome face set in austere lines.

He stood at the front of the stage, a dozen microphones in front of him, a sea of media faces staring up at him. He stood a moment, a middle-class winter coat flapping around his legs, a sharp wind blowing his hair, stoic and silent, as dozens of photos were snapped. If Mia didn't know exactly who and what he really was, she'd have thought he looked heroic.

When at last he spoke, his deep voice resonated to the far reaches of the plaza. "I thank you all for coming. It is with profound regret I stand here in front of this impressive building to announce I'm stepping out of the mayoral race of this great city."

He turned and nodded to the line of people behind him. "I want to thank you, my tireless campaign staff, and tell you how sorry I am to let you down so unexpectedly. Thank you for all your hours of work, for the resources you provided, and for believing in us. What you did was humbling and inspiring. I feel lucky that for a while I was a part of it. I will be forever grateful.

"I especially want to thank you, Cory Hughes, and you, Miles Lombardy, for your dedication and hard work. With people like all of you leading our dedicated campaign, we might well have won this race.

"I also want to thank Pamela, my fiancée, for her unwavering belief in me, and, of course, my family, my parents, especially, for helping us make this campaign possible.

"I so wish I could continue this effort to address so many pressing issues, from health care to quality education for those of us less fortunate." He paused a moment, studied the faces looking up at him. "I've always believed each of us has infinite value, no one individual more than any other. I believe New York should be the vibrant proud soul of our uniquely American spirit.

"I am proud of this city, and I see what it's capable of becoming. I firmly believe our way forward is to work toward crossing the chasms that divide us, racial and political. We share so much more in what we value than we sometimes realize.

"It is with a heavy heart I must now give up my hope to pursue that vision as your mayor, at least today, in this election. All of us have obligations, our families being our touchstones. Both personal and family matters have arisen unexpectedly, and now require my full attention."

He paused, looked over the sea of faces. "Thank you very much."

Questions roared at him like a tsunami, so many voices it was a chaos of sounds. Alex stood tall, held himself straight, his expression somber, and waited for the voices to die down. He pointed to Cynthia Pederson of FOX. She called out, full volume, "Is there a connection between your quitting the race and your lifelong friend, Kent Harper, being shot last night at his home? Do you have any comments on that shooting, Mr. Harrington?"

Alex's jaw turned to granite, but when he spoke, he seemed suddenly to be hanging on by a thread, pain clear in his voice. "Yes, my friend was shot last night outside his home, and that is part of why I am suspending my campaign. Mr. Harper is not only a fine man and one of our civic leaders, he's been one of my best friends since childhood. I and all his friends and family are praying for him. We trust that our police force"—he turned toward the building behind him—"will discover those responsible for that heinous act."

He pointed to Jana Zugoni, CNN. She called out, "There are rumors you are leaving the race because of allegations Mr. Harper was involved in sexual improprieties, even sexual crimes, and that you are, in fact, involved. Would you please comment, Mr. Harrington?"

Mia smiled. She'd known Alex wouldn't ever acknowledge her, so she'd given Jana that question. She'd nailed it.

His hands clutched the edges of the podium, his look both startled and bewildered. "I don't know where you heard such a ridiculous rumor, Ms. Zugoni, but since you think it responsible to ask, the idea of harming a woman in such a way is abhorrent to me, and to Mr. Harper." He let anger show. "That is all I will say, more than such a vicious allegation is worth."

Before Alex could point to another reporter, Jana shouted out again, "But isn't that why you're dropping out, Mr. Harrington? You're afraid women will come forward?"

He leaned in, his anger banked again, his voice stern and cold as a Puritan preacher's. "I do not know where you've heard this nonsense, Ms. Zugoni. I will say it again, I am dropping out of the campaign because of personal family issues. Those involved deserve privacy. There is nothing more to it than that."

Jana shouted back, "I'm told the allegations stem back to the years you and Mr. Harper attended Bennington Prep together. Would you care to comment?"

Mia saw no trace of guilt in Alex's expression, only honest puzzlement and insult, and the controlled anger of the righteous man. He really was very good. He glanced back toward Pamela, whose expression was not as controlled, fury clear on her face. Alex gave a slight shake of his head but she ignored him, strode forward like a force of nature, and placed her gloved hand on his sleeve, ready to leap into the fray. She stared out over the sea of faces in front of her, and slowly, the voices died until there was only the sound of the traffic. When she spoke, Pamela's voice was filled with pain mixed with fury, a potent combination and very effective. "Kent Harper is also one of my own lifelong friends. He is at this moment fighting for his life, so I will answer for him. He would be as appalled as Mr. Harrington by these slanderous rumors. They are unconscionable and malicious. My fiancé, all of us who love Kent, are suffering along with him from this brutal assault. I think it's time for you to show some compassion, and some restraint." Pamela swiped her hand over a tear.

Alex gently eased her away and stepped back to the microphones. "As you can see, we are all upset. I thank you for coming, and I ask all of you to pray for my friend. We are on our way to Bellevue to be with his family." He managed a stiff smile toward Pamela, whose tears sparkled on her cheeks.

And Mia wondered. Tears of pain or tears of rage?

More questions rang out, but Alex shook his head, took Pamela's hand in his, and stepped down from the dais, followed by his silent entourage.

Mia stepped out from behind big Jumbo Hardy of *The New Yorker*, willed Pamela to see her. Their eyes met and the look Pamela sent her way could have burned asphalt. But only for an instant. Her sad, brave smile returned. She walked with Alex to a long black limousine that idled at the curb. He and Pamela disappeared inside.

48

MIA

Mia watched Kent's family trail to the elevator headed down to the cafeteria for lunch. She'd just gotten back from One Police Plaza for Alex Harrington's news conference. It was her chance and she had to hurry. The doctors had told the press his condition was critical, but he was still alive, even breathing on his own, and that was amazing enough. The surgeons refused to speculate whether he'd survive, and the Harper lawyers and family wouldn't let the police near him. If he died, Alex Harrington would win. Everything Kent knew would be buried with him.

Would he even be able to talk to her, understand her? She had no idea, only that she had to try. When a nurse walked out of the automatic SICU doors, Mia slipped in. She walked purposefully, as if it was natural for her to be there, as if she belonged, directly to his cubicle and pulled the curtains closed behind her. The small space was dim, utterly still and quiet except for the faint hiss of his oxygen.

He lay on his back on the bed, white as the sheet pulled up to his neck, a clear plastic half-shell oxygen mask over the bottom half his face, loose enough for him to speak.

He looked diminished, a shell of himself, insubstantial as a ghost. He looked like a man who was dying. His arms lay exposed on top of the sheet, intravenous lines running to his wrists and to his neck. Vital sign monitors and infusion sets on aluminum poles surrounded his bed.

Please be awake. Please hear me, please be able to talk to me.

Mia leaned over him, whispered close to his cheek, "Kent?"

She waited, whispered again, "Kent, wake up. It's important you speak to me."

Slowly, as if with great effort, his eyelids fluttered. She held her breath, waited, willing him to answer her. He slowly opened his eyes and stared up at her blindly. He looked disoriented, uncertain, but he'd heard her voice, so at least on some level he was aware of her.

"Kent," she whispered again. "Can you hear me? Understand me?"

His eyes stared at her, through her. He whispered, "Aolith?"

She froze. Aolith? He thought she was Serena?

Mia drew a slow breath and gently took his hand in hers. His flesh felt slack, his skin clammy. She squeezed lightly, to reassure him, and said quietly next to his cheek, "Yes, Kent, it's me, Aolith."

His voice was only a whisper of sound, his words slurred. "You came because I'm dying? Did you come to tell me you forgive me? I'm so sorry, Aolith, I never wanted you to die. I can feel your hand. How is that possible?"

Mia leaned in close, lightly touched her fingertips to his forehead. "I know, Kent, I know. Perhaps you can feel my hand because soon we'll be together again. That night, Kent, my last memories. We had so much fun. You were Snake, dazzling me with your swordplay."

He fell silent, the soft hissing of the oxygen again the only sound.

"Kent?"

He forced his eyes open, but they seemed empty, still blind. He breathed out her name. "Aolith, the mystical one, perfect for you. I'm so sorry."

She squeezed his fingers again, leaned in closer. "I was in a void, floating, just floating, no one to talk to, then suddenly I was here with you and I knew why. I need you to tell me where you and Alex buried me."

"Am I dying?"

"I don't know, Kent, but maybe that's why I'm here. I know you didn't kill me, Alex did."

"You saw Alex put a roofie in your drink and he was really mad so he hit you, hit you with his fist against your head, too hard, and you were just—dead." He jerked at the memory. Mia kept stroking his fingers, prayed for all she was worth.

"I know you didn't want me to die. Please, Kent, tell me where I'm buried. I can't bear this not-knowing. I'll be trapped in this void until I know."

Tears slipped out of his eyes, trailed over his cheeks.

Mia wiped his tears away with her fingertip. "It's all right,

Kent. I forgive you. It was Alex, not you. Why did Alex start the fire?"

"So we could get you out. Aolith, I hated that you died, I hated burying you, leaving you alone. I never forgot you."

"I know you didn't. You're not like Alex. He forgot me, as if I'd never existed, as if he'd never killed me. But Kent, I know you're different. Please help me."

He blinked, his eyes still sheened with tears. She wiped away another tear before it slipped under the oxygen mask. She said in a soft voice, "Remember that night at the rave, how we were laughing? I enjoyed that so much, I thought we were so much alike, but then I saw what Alex did, and then I was afraid, and felt this great pain, then nothing at all. Kent, please tell me where I am. No one knows what happened to me, where I'm buried. My parents grieve for me. Please tell me, Kent, tell me where I am."

"You're in a beautiful place, Aolith, in Valley Forge National Park. Near Pauley's Farm."

He was fading again, his eyelashes fluttering, his breathing slowing.

"Where near Pauley's Farm?"

His voice was dreamy, as if he was seeing the place again. "Not far off the dirt road, by that huge old oak tree that stands alone. In the summer I knew its leaves would cover your grave, shade it. It would be nice."

"Where, Kent?"

She was losing him. She leaned close, her warm breath on his cheek, willing him to speak, and he whispered, his voice insubstantial, "A rough path off a narrow road that leads to the

Schuylkill River Trail and that old oak tree. I'm sorry, Aolith, I'm sorry."

She leaned down, kissed him on the cheek, whispered, "Thank you, Kent. I hope you won't die."

One of his monitors began to beep. The curtain flew back and a nurse stepped in. "Who are you? Why are you here?"

Mia jumped out of her way. "I'm his sister. He was awake and we were talking. Please, help him."

49

Wild Oaks Motel
Fort Lee, New Jersey

FRIDAY

Only his mom and his sister called him Oliver, his father didn't call him anything. He liked what everyone called him now better—Whistler. With that name, he enjoyed being both feared and admired by those in the profession. He even called himself Whistler when he finished a job and always smiled into a mirror and whispered, "Well done, Whistler."

But he couldn't say that this time. He sat on the side of the crappy bed, his hands clasped between his knees, an empty pizza box beside him. For the first time in his professional life, he'd failed. Not once, but twice. It burned, burned deep.

He hadn't wanted to run down that damned woman reporter, it was too uncertain, like shoving rich Aunt Mildred down the stairs, no broken neck guaranteed. It was his agent who'd told Whistler the person he worked for wanted it done that way.

He could have finished it if not for that idiot kid shouting at him, even with the reporter scooting behind those overstuffed garbage cans. How was he to know garbage was picked up the next morning in that neighborhood?

And the second job, the second failure. Two clean shots center mass that should have dumped the target right into his grave. How was he to know an FBI agent was right there on the street to call an ambulance? Obviously the principal hiring him hadn't known that either.

His agent had told him the principal had called, screamed at him for incompetence. Well, it was true it was his fault, and Whistler had acknowledged it, what could he say? There were always circumstances, but he was fast on his feet, and he'd never failed before. Now he'd have to make it right. Not the reporter—the principal took her off the table for the moment—but Harper had to die. There was still a good possibility he would, everyone said so. If he did live, Whistler would have to find a way into the hospital and pull his plug once and for all. Without getting caught. Well, he'd managed harder jobs.

He looked over at the crappy TV sitting on top of an equally crappy dresser, the picture wavering enough to give him a headache. He saw a news report with that Harrington dude up on a dais, looking like a regular tragic hero, giving his withdrawal speech. He listened with half an ear to the garbage flowing like smooth honey out of Harrington's mouth when he heard Harrington say the target's name—Kent Harper—and he straightened like a shot. What was going on here? What was that all about? His agent had told him Harper had to die because he knew some things that couldn't get out, but that was all. A reporter shouted out something about Harper and sexual improprieties. What a stupid way of saying he liked to screw around. He wouldn't be much of a man if he didn't, would he? And it was Harper and Harrington together? Was Harper blackmailing Harrington? Or maybe Harper had screwed the wrong man's wife?

Whistler decided he didn't really care what it was all about. In his experience, everyone was always screwing around on everyone else, trying to gain an advantage, no matter what it took. He'd get his one hundred thousand dollars. If it looked like Harper would live, he'd just have to kill him before the doctors let the cops question him.

He took a deep breath, upended his Coors can, swallowed the warm beer. He tossed the can into the stingy wastebasket, got up, and began to pace. He was proud of his record. No way would he allow anyone to ruin it, not some schmuck in a freaking hospital.

Whistler paced the skinny room back and forth, and each time he did, he walked by the bed with its cheap faded chenille bedspread. He wished there'd been a room at the Holiday Inn down the road. At least he'd get good breakfasts and the maids wouldn't have cigarettes hanging out of their mouths, looking at him like he was some sort of rodent.

But he always kept to his deals, and this low-end piece of crap motel was close to I-95 and a quick exit, or an easy drive back to Bellevue Hospital.

A spear of light splashed across one of the dingy walls and he automatically started his shadow play his mother had taught him when he was a kid. Now it was a lifelong habit that eased his mind and relaxed him. He stretched his fingers, turned them this way and that until he saw Brutus, a huge mongrel from his neighborhood, a mean bugger who used to chase the kids. He wiggled Brutus's nose, his ears, then gracefully segued into a rooster that had no name, twisting his fingers just so to form a rooster's comb. He finished off with an alligator he'd named Lou, who always made him smile.

Whistler had nothing more to do now but wait and hope Harper died nice and easy in Bellevue. Then his agent would deposit the rest of his money, minus his own 20 percent, and he could go home.

But why was a fricking FBI agent surveilling Harper?

The door crashed inward, and a man shouted, "Down, now! On your belly, hands behind your head. Now!"

He dove for his gun on the table beside the bed, but a bullet caught him behind his left knee, and his leg gave way. They were all over him before he could crawl to the table.

He heard a woman say, "Hey. And what have we here?"

Whistler raised pain-filled eyes to a red-haired woman holding his burner cell phone.

50

CIA Director's Office
Langley, Virginia

FRIDAY

The CIA headquarters at Langley wasn't in the middle of Washington like the Hoover Building. It sat near the Potomac off the George Washington Memorial Highway, a huge campus that housed Fort Peary and the Farm, surrounded with acres thick with oaks and maples and parking lots. Savich had visited the CIA headquarters before, but never the seat of power.

Director Marlan Hendricks rose to stand at the head of the conference table in his large corner office when Savich, Mike, and Olivia walked in. It wasn't unlike the FBI director's, a large square corner office with a large mahogany desk, a seating arrangement in dark burgundy leather, and a cabinet holding awards, photos with the great and famous, souvenirs from his operational days. Hendricks shook their hands, stepped back, and smiled. "Thank you for coming, agents, and Agent Savich.

Ah, here are Mr. Lodner and Mr. Grace. Gentlemen, please sit down." Rose Jefferson Lee, a tough, grizzled thirty-year veteran, walked in behind them carrying a fresh pot of coffee. She set it down, raised a gray eyebrow at the director. "Everyone can serve himself, Rose. Thank you."

Olivia hadn't said a word. Savich saw her face was set and pale, Mike's hand on her shoulder.

Director of Intelligence Fulton Lodner stared at Savich. "What is the FBI doing here? Agent Savich only came into this situation on Tuesday. I thought this was an operational meeting."

Hendricks said, "Calm yourself, Fulton. All will be revealed. Have a cup of coffee."

Agent Carlton Grace smiled at Mike and Olivia, nodded toward Savich. "Fulton and I have already heard about the French nationals attacking Olivia in the High Point Mall parking lot. Is it true we have the flash drive?"

Director Hendricks laughed, said to Savich, "I'm sure the halls of the Hoover are ringing with that story as well."

Savich nodded. "Anything happens at the Hoover and the taco people in the cafeteria know about it before ten A.M."

There were a couple of laughs, but a stone face from Lodner. The director smiled, said to Grace, "Yes, we have the flash drive and it's been decrypted. Let me add, Agent Savich was integral to its retrieval, as were his team of FBI agents and, of course, our agents Hildebrandt and Kingman."

Lodner rose halfway from his chair, waved his hand toward Mike. "Sir, why weren't Carlton and I informed of this plan? Why were we excluded?"

Hendricks said easily, "We'll get to that, Fulton. Please sit down, take deep breaths. Your wife would be upset with me if you stroked out on my office floor."

But Lodner wasn't done. "Sir, how could the FBI be involved in what should have been a CIA op? And what proof do we have that Kingman was not a part of this? As our field agent, he should have turned the flash drive over to Carlton or to me the day he arrived in Washington! What he did was disappear. That callous disregard for accepted procedure is totally unacceptable."

Savich saw both anger and insult on Lodner's aesthete's face. He couldn't blame him. He wondered what he'd think if a CIA agent waltzed into his unit, took over, and used his own people. A tough pill to swallow.

"Enough, Fulton." There was a bite to the director's voice, a touch of the spurs. "Drink your coffee." Hendricks waited until Lodner took an unwilling drink of his coffee, not that it appeared to calm him, before he nodded to Mike. "Agent, explain to Mr. Lodner and Mr. Grace why you did not follow protocol. Tell them what happened when you landed in Washington."

Mike sat forward, his hands clasped in front of him. "I spotted two men following me in the airport terminal. I've had enough experience to recognize they were foreign operatives. I know the airport very well and managed to elude them. Since they knew exactly when and how I'd be arriving in Washington, I realized they wanted the flash drive." He glanced toward Grace and Lodner, then at the director. "Sir, I also realized only someone here at Langley could have told them, someone I'd trusted, and that included—and I'm very sorry to have to say this—you gentlemen, so I stayed out of sight in an old abandoned boathouse that belongs to my uncle, who occasionally hangs out there to escape his wife." Mike cleared his throat, studied Lodner's set face, then looked at Carlton Grace. Was that a faint smile he saw? Carlton kept things so close to his vest, you never knew what he was thinking. "I knew the information on the flash drive had to be critical, but of course, I couldn't access it." There was no need to mention his computer friend at the NSA. "I hadn't contacted any of my team yet because I was afraid whoever was compromised at Langley would find out and I didn't want to risk involving them. But after the attack on Olivia Monday night, and then again on Wednesday evening, I was afraid for her and called her.

"Olivia told me about meeting an FBI special agent she trusted. It was Agent Savich and he was in charge of the shooting at Olivia's house." Mike paused a moment. "I called him. He convinced me we had to contact Director Hendricks."

Savich continued, "Olivia's kidnapping at the High Point Mall—yes, what you heard is true. It was part of a plan we agreed on to lure the men who'd already attacked her into believing she knew where Mike was hiding and giving us proof of who'd hired them."

Hendricks added formally, "And that joint FBI/CIA operation led by these three led to the retrieval of the flash drive intact and the capture of two internationally known criminals who work for Henri Delos, the CEO of Armament Météore, a leading French weapons manufacturer headquartered in Lyon, France. Both men are in FBI custody."

Savich picked it up. "One of the men is René Delos, the

younger brother of the CEO of Armament Météore and a known assassin, and the other is Claude Dumont, an American with a French father who moved his family back to France when he was a teenager. Both men were 'problem solvers' for Henri Delos. Claude Dumont was one of the two men who attacked Agent Hildebrandt at her house Monday night.

"Let me add, it was my privilege to work with Mike and Olivia. Both of them put their lives on the line." He grinned at Hendricks. "I asked them if they'd come into the light—to the FBI—but they told me they're CIA to the core.

"It's no surprise Claude and René aren't cooperating, but it's hardly necessary. We've found all the information we need on René Delos's cell phone and the flash drive. French authorities and Interpol have already arrested Henri Delos on charges of crimes against the state, and a lifetime's worth of others—theft, bank and wire fraud, money laundering, and tax evasion, for a start, tax evasion probably the offense to carry the most prison time."

Carlton Grace smiled. "As it doubtless would be here as well. There is still, however, the big question. Who betrayed my agents' mission in Iran? Who led Delos to Olivia?"

Olivia closed her eyes a moment, placed the cell phone on the table. "I'm very sorry, sir." She punched up the recorder, hit play. Andi's voice filled the room.

"I am so sorry, Olivia, for everything that's happened. I ended up betraying you, my dearest friend, and everyone else I've loved and admired. I never meant for you and Mike to be in danger of losing your lives. They told me they would never contact me again if I helped them get the flash drive, swore no would else would be

hurt. Yes, I was a fool to believe them. I suppose I didn't, really, but it was easier to pretend. There were reasons, of course, there are always reasons, but the fact remains I betrayed you.

"On our mission to rescue Hashem, we weren't supposed to be attacked. The Iranian captain was under strict orders to apprehend Hashem and retrieve the flash drive and not to engage us, but he arrived late, panicked and disobeyed. As I said, his orders were meant to keep all of us out of harm's way, at least that's what I was told his instructions were. A lie? I don't know. As it was, we could all have been killed. We were all very lucky to escape, except for poor Hashem. I tried to get the flash drive from him, but we were under heavy fire and I couldn't move. I saw him give it to Mike, saw you, Olivia, close by, trying to help Hashem. Then it was mayhem and you were wounded by the RPG and unconscious. Mike picked you up and Higgs grabbed Hashem, and we ran for it. We got to the helicopter and were flown to Balad. The three of us stayed with you until we made it to the hospital. I was so worried about you, Olivia, please don't ever doubt that. But I also tried my best to steal the flash drive from Mike, and I failed.

"I informed Henri Delos when Mike was due to arrive in Washington. My only demand was that Mike not be killed and Delos agreed. I was an idiot. Of course René Delos would kill any of us without a qualm.

"But you were too smart for him, Mike. I congratulate you.

"I met René Delos in Cannes two years ago while on R&R. I realize now he'd arranged to meet me, knew exactly who I was, though he pretended to be surprised when I told him. The long and short of it is he handed me five hundred thousand dollars in cash and assured me it was only to provide him with any information

I chanced to come across that might affect his brother's company. I justified my taking the money by telling myself no one could be hurt, no information I would give him would be critical to national security. And I wanted the money, wanted the freedom it provided me and my family. And for a while he asked me for very little, only enough, I soon realized, to incriminate me. Then Henri Delos himself suddenly contacted me as we were preparing for our mission, surprised me by knowing exactly what team I was on and where I was assigned. I realized later, of course, my cell phone had been compromised. Delos wanted to know whether I knew anything about where Hashem was headed, where he could find him. When I refused to tell him anything, he said he would release the information I'd already given him to the CIA, ruin my career, and I would be sent to jail, disgraced. Still, I balked. He threatened my family, said he would send his brother, René, to visit them, that all of them would die if I refused. Of course, as I told you, Delos assured me none of my team would be hurt, that the retrieval of the flash drive was his only aim.

"Olivia, I know you're thinking I'm great at making excuses, at justifying what I did, and you're right. I know you can't forgive me, but you and I, we've known each other from the beginning. You have to know I've very pleased you and Mike survived and that Delos and his vicious brother will end their lives in prison. I do know French prisons will be worse than anything we can imagine. As for René, rather than prison, I would prefer he be shot like a rabid dog.

"I will have to live the rest of my life with what I've done, with what could have happened to you and Mike. I have severed ties with my family, but at least they will be safe. By the time you listen *to this recording, I will have left the United States. You will not find me. If nothing else, I know how to disappear.*

"Good-bye, Olivia. I wish you and Mike great happiness."

Savich heard a sharp intake of breath from Lodner, saw his expression was cold, hard, his hand fisted around his coffee mug. He saw tears pool in Carlton Grace's eyes, and he looked away.

Hendricks said quietly, "I'd say we're all very sorry, Olivia. At least Agent Creamer's recording clears the air for us. There need be no more suspicions. Carlton, Fulton, I'm charging you with finding Agent Creamer, though I doubt it will be easy." He paused a moment. "No, it won't be easy at all, very probably impossible."

The director studied Fulton Lodner's face. "I need hardly say there will be no reprimands for either Agent Kingman or Agent Hildebrandt. In fact, I will see to it they both receive commendations for their valor. Mike, Olivia, don't underestimate the importance of what you accomplished. I thank you. The CIA thanks you."

Hendricks paused a moment, smiled. "Agent Savich, it's been a pleasure to work with you and your team. Perhaps you should consider coming over to the CIA?"

Savich smiled as he slowly shook his head.

51

Valley Forge National Park
Near Pauley's Farm

SATURDAY MORNING

Dooley, the three-year-old beagle cadaver dog from the Philadelphia Field Office, whined softly, his body quivering, as he slinked over a low mound of bare winter earth. The sound was heartrending. His person, Special Agent Gil Payne, knelt down and hugged Dooley against him. "You did good, Dooley, you did really good. Come away now, come away."

A disparate group of people surrounded the grave of Serena Winters as the forensics team began carefully digging.

"Agent Payne tells me Dooley's never wrong," Creighton's police chief, Moseley, said.

NYPD Detective Hoolihan, a born doubter, said, "Well, he must have smelled something. There are a bunch of old graves around here from the Revolution."

Mia stood beside Tommy, squeezing his hand tightly. "This

357

is where Kent Harper said Serena was buried, so we'll find her. He wouldn't lie with death sitting on his shoulder. He was heavily drugged, but still it was obvious he regretted what happened to Serena." She paused a moment, swallowed. "He cried."

Tommy said calmly, "Doesn't matter. Both he and Harrington deserve to rot in hell for what they did to Serena. I want them in a cell where they'll have years to think about it every single day. And we'll know they'll never have the chance to hurt another woman in their miserable lives." He swallowed, stopped talking. Mia squeezed his hand tighter.

Detective Hoolihan said, "Amazing Kent Harper's still alive. His surgeon is even hopeful now he'll make it. The D.A. actually smiled, I'm told." He looked at Mia. "But what really surprises me is Harper believed he was talking to Serena, who called herself a gaming character, Aolith, and gave himself and his puppet master away. You must be some actress, Ms. Briscoe."

Sherlock said, "Puppet master. That sounds right, Detective. Harrington was Kent's Svengali, a man born without a moral compass, a classic psychopath. And he made sure he damaged Kent Harper's compass enough to manipulate him."

Juliet pointed. "Look!"

The circle around the grave tightened. They saw a swatch of black hair spilling out of a rotten, molding tarp. One of the forensics team looked directly at Sherlock and nodded. "I think we found her."

Sherlock said, "Tommy, Mia, Juliet, all of you, walk away now."

Mia choked on a sob, but she didn't move. "I'm not going anywhere." She turned to Tommy, saw tears shining in his eyes, and pulled him to her. Juliet gathered them both in her arms, squeezed tight. "You found her, Tommy, Mia. You guys did it, you did it."

Mia whispered, her voice liquid with tears, "It wasn't a week ago Gail Ricci sent me those photos. Less than a week when it all started."

Sherlock said quietly, "And now, because of you, it's over, Mia."

Mia, Tommy, and Juliet stood silent, holding one another's hands as the tarp was lifted carefully out of the ground. Mia felt so many things at once, relief they'd found Serena, fury at the men who'd put her here, and relentless grief. Beside her, Tommy seemed frozen, no expression on his face, barely breathing. How could she comfort him when she wanted to curl up and sob? Juliet leaned into Mia and pulled her closer. Mia was grateful Juliet had asked to come, said it was important to her to see it through.

The wind had died down but the air was cold and damp. Detective Hoolihan had stood beside too many graves in his thirty-two-year career. None of them had ever been easy, some, like this one, a punch to the heart. He looked over at Mia Briscoe and Thomas Maitland, at Agent Sherlock, their anchor, their support. He had to admit he'd been lucky she'd asked to be included in his investigation.

Life, Hoolihan had found, happened in ways that always surprised you. At least for Serena Winters, there would finally be justice, even if it was seven long years in coming. He looked over at the amazing young woman, Mia Briscoe. She'd never forgotten and once she had the photos, she hadn't stopped. He looked again at Serena Winters's grave and wondered if there was ever any real peace at the end of a road like this.

Police Chief Moseley thought of the fat file that had sat on his desk for so long the pages were yellowed. Seven years, but he'd never had the heart to file it away. And in that thick file had been the blessed photo of Harrington's Jaguar that would bring justice. Quietly, he said the Lord's Prayer.

52

Alex Harrington's Brownstone
Upper East Side
New York City

SATURDAY EVENING

Good evening, Mr. Harrington."

Alex stared at the cop he'd met yesterday, near Kent's cubicle in the ICU, bundled to his ears against the frigid weather. "It's Detective Hoolihan, isn't it? You came to tell me you've found out who shot my friend?"

Hoolihan said, "We'd like to speak with both you and Ms. Barrett."

"But we've told you everything we know, Detective, yesterday. Have you at least learned anything new?"

Hoolihan said nothing, nodded behind him. "I believe you know Ms. Briscoe, and these are FBI agents Sherlock and Maitland."

Sherlock gave Alex her sunny smile, held out her creds. Tommy did the same. Harrington waved them away.

Pamela appeared behind him. "Alex? What's going on? Who are these people? Oh, good evening, Detective, I'm sorry, I don't remember your name."

Alex said, "Pam, it's Detective Hoolihan. We spoke to him yesterday, about Kent."

"Yes, of course, Detective Hoolihan. Forgive me, I'm so worried about Kent, and of course, Mr. Harrington had to end his mayoral race—" She abruptly stopped, shook her head, but then she spotted Mia, and her eyes fired. "You! Why are you here? Don't think we don't know who was behind those ridiculous sex questions at Alex's press conference yesterday. I'm going to see to it you're fired. I already called your boss." She paused, frowned. "You're a disgrace."

Mia knew what Milo had said to Pamela, and he hadn't been all that pleasant. She said, "Actually, Pammie, you have no idea what I am, but I promise you, you're going to find out."

"How dare you call me that! And just what does that mean, you unethical—"

Detective Hoolihan smoothly interrupted. "Actually we're here to speak to you about the murder of a student, Serena Winters, seven years ago at Godwyn University."

Pamela snapped out, "Who? What are you talking about? What does a murdered student have to do with Alex? Where in the world is Godwyn University?"

Even though Pamela had tried to hide it, Mia heard alarm in her voice. *So Alex told you something about it, did he, Pam? A nice believable lie? Bet he didn't tell you about Juliet.* Mia didn't look at her; she kept her eyes on Alex, almost applauded him when he smoothly morphed a brief flash of shock into bewilderment.

Mia smiled at him, watched him start, then frown at her. *The tsunami's here at your front door, Alex, no escape for you. And you're wondering how to play it.* She'd bet he was weighing whether to cry lawyer. She prayed he was too arrogant to let any lesser human being speak for him, at least not yet. *Yes, Alex, deal with this yourself. You don't need a lawyer. You're so much smarter than they are, aren't you?*

She wanted to cheer when she saw his ego win out. He said calmly, with only a civilized hint of annoyance, "I don't recall that name, Detective."

"Serena Winters," Hoolihan said, stolid as a judge. "She was a twenty-year-old student at Godwyn University seven years ago. Godwyn University is in Pennsylvania, thirty or so miles west of Philadelphia."

Alex merely looked at him, ignored the sarcasm. "Thank you for the location. As I said, I don't recall her name. Is that all you wanted to ask me?"

Hoolihan said, a bit of steel in his voice, "No, Mr. Harrington, we're far from through. We can either speak about this here or we can go down to the station. Your choice. But make it snappy, the wind out here is frigid."

Alex stepped back, waved them in, and closed the door. "Very well. Ms. Barrett and I are quite busy. It isn't easy to close down a campaign. I hope we can clear up any misunderstanding quickly."

He took Pamela's hand and they turned together to lead them down a wide hallway, its white walls covered with incredible Dutch pastoral paintings, not, thank heavens, with Pamela's signature minimalist style. An elegant antique table was centered beneath them, a tall clear vase on top filled with red roses so abundant they overflowed the surface.

They walked into a living room with twelve-foot ceilings and ornate plaster moldings that took you back in time. What looked to be the original wooden shutters covered the oversized windows that faced a line of brownstones across the street, dark gold draperies pulled tight against the frigid night. *Ah, but this room had enjoyed Pamela's stark hand, all black-and-white pictures, stark and flat. No soul,* Mia thought. She felt Pamela's barely banked rage from six feet away, violent and hot. Mia gave her a fat smile, watched her blink in surprise.

Tommy was staring steadily at Harrington with a look as violent as Pamela's. *Keep it together, Tommy, we're at the finish line.*

The room felt warm and cozy, with the fire burning sluggishly in the Carrera marble fireplace. Alex walked to the fireplace, turned to face them, his arms crossed, calm, poised. Pam walked to stand behind a stark black chair, her eyes once again on Mia.

No one sat down.

Alex's clipped Boston accent slipped out. "Detective, let me say I am perfectly willing to cooperate with you, whatever it is you wish to know about this student at Godwyn University. I would ask you to understand, though, that my fiancée and I are not only busy, we're grieving. My best friend, Kent Harper, is fighting for his life. This is hardly the time to discuss another investigation."

Mia said, "Isn't it lucky for us we found both of you at home, and not at Bellevue at your best friend's bedside?"

Alex ignored her, said to Hoolihan, his eyes tortured, pain-filled, "We would be happy to give you more information about Kent, but I doubt it will help catch who shot him. We are still at a loss as to why anyone would shoot a man who was well-liked and respected. I think it must have been a drive-by, some kind of mistake. Nothing else makes sense."

He paused, as if waiting for the supplicant cop to offer to polish his Ferragamos, and looked discreetly at his watch, like an important man being harried unjustly. "Very well, Detective, I will say it for you. You are here to question me about some supposed sexual misconduct on Kent's part, something you believe relates to this student—Winters, you said her name was? Let me state categorically I don't believe Kent Harper has ever harmed a woman in his life. He focuses his aggression on his competitors. The rumors some of those reporters asked about yesterday at my press conference are both preposterous and untrue, probably planted by one of my opponents, even accusing me of complicity to drive me out of the race." He stared at Mia. "With the help of a reporter who decided she'd use me as a springboard to launch her career, such as Ms. Briscoe here."

He looked down at the stark white carpet beneath his feet, his expression infinitely sad, but stoic. "That vicious ploy succeeded enough to destroy my campaign, and now I am left to pick up the pieces of my life. I am the victim here, Detective, as is Kent, who can't even defend himself. So if you're here about those absurd rumors, to try to dig up dirt, then I want you to leave. I will give you my lawyers' number. I will say it again, this has been a very difficult time for both Pamela and me. We want to be left in peace."

Mia said, "We found Serena."

Alex cocked his head at her. "What are you talking about? If you found this girl, then why are you here?"

Mia wanted to punch him in the face, she wanted to obliterate him. She felt Tommy's big hand tighten around her arm, and she took a deep breath. "We found Serena this morning, exactly where Kent told me the two of you buried her after you murdered her at the Godwyn frat rave."

Stone silence. Mia added, "If you've forgotten, you buried her near Pauley's Farm in Valley Forge National Park."

Pamela lunged toward Mia, her fists raised. "That's a lie, you vicious bitch! A hateful, ridiculous lie!"

Tommy quickly stepped in front of her. He said, "You don't want to touch her, Ms. Barrett, or I will arrest you. Try me."

Mia wanted to pull away from Tommy, break Pamela's perfect nose, maybe loosen some perfect capped teeth. Tommy said softly, "You, too, Mia. Get hold of yourself."

Alex caught Pamela's arm, pulled her back against him. She whispered to him, "Why is she saying these things, Alex?"

Mia said, "Because they're true, Pam. You got something out of him about Serena, didn't you? But not the truth, not what really happened that night."

"No, that isn't what happened!"

Hoolihan took back control, said in his calm way, "Mr. Harrington, this morning, as Ms. Briscoe said, we recovered the remains of Serena Winters in a grave in Valley Forge National Park."

Sherlock said, "We'd never have found her if Kent Harper hadn't told us exactly where you'd buried her."

Alex stood straight, shaking his head back and forth.

Tommy stared at the monster who had killed the girl he'd thought he'd marry. The rage he felt for what he'd done, for the grief he'd brought to everyone else, was a violent brew, but he held himself in check. He said in his deep, calm FBI voice, "The Jaguar you drove seven years ago? We matched it to a photo taken by a student outside the fraternity house the night of the fire, the night Serena disappeared, with your old license plate. It appears you know quite a bit about Godwyn University."

Alex said nothing, looked mildly bored, but Mia knew he wasn't, he couldn't be.

Tommy continued, "The autopsy showed Serena was struck hard at the base of her skull, hard enough to kill her. The odds are good we'll find traces of your DNA on her clothes and on the tarp you wrapped her in."

Mia sent a questioning look to Detective Hoolihan, who nodded. She said, "You and Kent drove from Boston to Godwyn to find a girl to roofie and rape. But you ended up killing her because she saw what you were doing—namely, sprinkling a roofie into her drink." She felt rage building, burning her throat. "You murdered my best friend, and neither of you even knew her name. Did you know Kent knew her only as Aolith, the gaming character?

"You hit her, Alex, killed her, set the fire so you could get her out without being noticed. You and Kent wrapped her in a tarp and threw her into a hole." Mia felt herself beginning to spin out of control, but she managed to dial it back, there was too much at stake. "You killed her and forgot her, didn't you,

Alex, once she was in the ground, once you dumped dirt on top of her? She no longer existed. If you felt anything, it was impatience because she'd ruined your evening. Was Serena the only girl you killed?"

Alex Harrington stood silent and stoic, the innocent man in the dock. Mia wondered if the others could see the calculation in his eyes. She saw the instant he decided what to do. He began shaking his head back and forth and whispered, his voice steeped in pain and regret, "All right, if you must know the truth. It wasn't my fault, her death. I hate to say this, hate it, but it was Kent who struck her. I was talking to some guys, drinking too much, I'll admit, and when I happened to look over, they were dancing in place, talking over each other to be heard, when Kent suddenly hit her. I don't know what happened, maybe she said something, but it all happened so fast—her dying, but it was an accident, he really didn't mean to hurt her."

He swallowed, managed to make his voice shake. "He was my best friend, I had to help him or he'd go to prison. Yes, I've told Pam about what happened and she understood. We were discussing whether to tell you, Detective Hoolihan, because of those rumors at the press conference, but it's so difficult. Kent could be dying, maybe shot by someone taking revenge, I don't know. You must believe this, the girl's death was an accident, Kent didn't mean to kill her."

Mia pulled her cell phone out of her coat pocket and touched play. Kent Harper's whispery voice sounded in the silent room.

"You saw Alex put a roofie in your drink and he was really mad so he hit you, hit you with his fist against your head, too hard, and you were just—dead."

The only sound in the room was Alex Harrington's harsh breathing and the pop of an ember exploding in the fireplace.

Pamela said, "What Kent said, he was obviously out of his mind, you can hear it. He was so drugged, he'd have said anything. What does he mean 'you' saw anything? None of it makes sense. That was pitiful."

Sherlock said, "Kent Harper believed he was talking to Serena, but it makes no difference. He knew exactly where she was buried and what he said makes sense in every way." She looked from Alex to Pamela. "I imagine the two of you have been sitting here hand-clasping, praying Kent Harper will die. The newest word? Your very best friend in the whole world, Mr. Kent Harper, is going to live. Do you think he won't testify against you, Mr. Harrington?"

Alex drew himself up, smoothed out his breathing. "I want to call my lawyer."

Detective Hoolihan said smoothly, "That's your right, sir, but you will make your call from the station. I am arresting you for the murder of Serena Winters, human being," and Hoolihan read him his rights. "Do you understand these rights?"

"Of course I do." His face turned cold. "I will tell you again. It was an accident. Kent said I was responsible because he was trying to protect himself. You can't prove otherwise." He crossed his arms, gave them a full-bodied sneer. "The whole lot of you are vultures, each with your own agenda. Quite a thing to bring down a man only trying to serve this city, destroy a man who could buy and sell all of you, make or break your reputations. And you . . ." He stared at Mia. "You started this. Your whole purpose was to create some tacky rumors, turn them into a front-page investigation, and you picked me to go after." He shook his head at her. "Pamela's right. You're a disgrace. You're despicable."

Alex paused, looked at each of them, as if memorizing faces. "When this is over, I will personally destroy all of you."

He stepped away from the fireplace. "Let's get this over with, Detective. I imagine the New York Police chief will have something to say." He turned to Pamela. "Wait here. I'll be back."

Hoolihan said smoothly, "Actually, Ms. Barrett will be coming with us."

Alex took a step back toward him. "There is no reason to force my fiancée into such an unpleasant situation. I don't want her exposed to the violent scum you deal with."

Hoolihan said, "Actually, there is every reason."

53

MIA

Detective Hoolihan continued to Pamela, "And you, ma'am, you'll be wanting to call your lawyer as well."

Alex stepped forward, stopped when Hoolihan frowned at him. "What are you talking about? Why would Pamela need a lawyer?"

Hoolihan locked eyes with Pamela. "Because you, Ms. Barrett, hired a broker by the name of Reily Flint, of Boston, Massachusetts. We don't know as yet how you knew to contact him, but the Boston PD is working with us. We will find out, never doubt that. The broker, Mr. Flint, in turn hired one of his best operators, known as Whistler. Whistler was instructed to run down Mia Briscoe last Wednesday night. He failed because a bystander stopped him.

"You hired Whistler again, through Mr. Flint, to murder Kent Harper this past Thursday night. He failed again because Agent Sherlock was there surveilling Mr. Harper's house. After Whistler shot him two times in the back, she was able to get him help immediately.

"Of course, Whistler didn't know who you are, knew you

371

only as the principal, Ms. Barrett, for his protection and for yours, so he couldn't roll on you." He nodded to Sherlock.

She said, "A very committed FBI agent spent hours tracking the sedan Whistler drove the night he tried to run down Mia Briscoe. When she finally spotted Whistler's sedan on a camera feed, she was able to follow it to the Wild Oaks Motel in Fort Lee.

"Unfortunately for you, Ms. Barrett, Whistler made two mistakes. He should have ditched the sedan he used to try to run down Mia Briscoe Wednesday night, but he didn't. His second mistake was he neglected to change out his burner cell phone in time. That's how we found Mr. Flint, and records of your four calls to him, both before and after the attempted murders, including, I imagine, your screaming matches when Whistler failed to kill Ms. Briscoe—and Kent Harper?

"We also know about your two-hundred-thousand-dollar withdrawal from your private accounts. We are confident that with the right incentive, Mr. Flint will give us full details, including evidence of the two-hundred-thousand-dollar deposit into his own account."

Hoolihan shook his head at Pamela. "What I don't understand, Ms. Barrett, is why you got so involved. For what? To save your fiancé from his own misdeeds? You were willing to commit murder?"

Alex Harrington stood white and shaken, staring at Hoolihan and then at Pamela. His voice was barely above a whisper. "Pammie, that can't be true? You didn't hire some fricking professional assassin? That's crazy, all of it's crazy. Why would you do that?"

Pamela shouted, "I didn't! It's absurd. For heaven's sake, I'm Pamela Raines Barrett of the Boston Barretts!" She whirled on Mia. "All these lies are your fault, you'd do whatever you had to do for your precious career, ruin Alex, ruin me!" She took a step toward Mia, paused when Mia smiled and beckoned with her fingers. "Come on ahead, Pammie, just try it, you murdering bitch."

Hoolihan said, "That's enough from both of you."

Pamela whirled about. "Alex, don't believe them. I wouldn't do anything like that, I wouldn't. You've known me all your life."

Alex said slowly, "Kent knew you, too, all your life. He never did anything to you."

"I didn't try to kill Kent! All of you go away, I have nothing more to say to any of you."

"We're not going anywhere, Pam," Mia said. "You tried to kill me because Alex told you I'd write about Serena's murder. I was the obstacle to what you've wanted your whole life, climbing aboard the political power train. With me out of the way, no one would be digging into Alex's past. But you were wrong. Agent Maitland would never have given up.

"And Kent? I'll bet Kent came here to see Alex after Juliet and I left his office on Thursday. I'll bet he was scared, angry—"

Pamela yelled, "Wait! You're saying Juliet was here? In New York? Why?"

Alex held himself stiff and silent, all expression wiped from his face. Mia said, "So you didn't tell her about Juliet, Alex? You could confess your young man's mistakes, and I suppose she might buy it, but no way could you explain away you and Kent roofieing Juliet and raping her."

"They were going to marry! It makes no sense! Alex, tell her it's crazy!"

Mia said to Pamela, "It's true, Pam. Alex roofied her and both he and Kent raped her, two years ago. That was why Juliet broke off the engagement. She remembered what happened, Pam, but Alex didn't care because he was sure she would never accuse them publicly, never blow up her family with so devastating a scandal. But once she found out Alex is not only a rapist, but a murderer, she was perfectly willing to help us."

Pamela whirled on Alex, openmouthed. "Juliet? She's not lying? You and Kent really raped Juliet?" She started shaking her head. "No, of course that can't be true. They're making this all up. You'd never do such a thing. Yes, yes, when you were young, you told me Kent talked you into some foolish mistakes, but Juliet? Kent couldn't have talked you into raping Juliet. Alex, tell them you didn't do that."

Alex said between clenched teeth, "Of course it's not true. Juliet made it up, as revenge because I dumped her two years ago. And now she wanted to ruin my career, and she helped them do it."

He fell silent. Another ember popped in the fireplace. No one moved. Alex whispered to Pamela, "I knew how badly you wanted to be the New York mayor's wife, and that's why I trusted you, told you as much as I did." He stared at her with new eyes. "So you tried to kill Mia? To keep her away from me? But why Kent? Damn you, why Kent?"

Pamela drew herself up. Even though Hoolihan still towered over her, she managed to look down her nose at him. "I am innocent. You, Detective, I will see you hounded out of the police force, I will sue this wretched city. I want to speak to my lawyer."

Hoolihan nodded, said, "Pamela Raines Barrett, I'm arresting you for the attempted murder of Mia Briscoe and Kent Harper." He read her her rights, his deep professional voice the only sound in the living room.

Epilogue

The Savich Home, Georgetown
Washington, D.C.

SUNDAY

Mama smelled like roses. Sean snuggled against her, felt her heart beat steadily against his cheek. She was home, here with him and Papa. She'd called him every single day, told him how much she missed him, and loved him, but it just wasn't the same thing. He burrowed closer, felt her arm tighten around him. He was full of popcorn, worn out because he'd thrown a zillion pieces of popcorn to Astro until he told Papa his arm was going to fall off. Astro was already asleep, on his back, all four paws in the air, in front of the fireplace.

Sean heard an ember pop, felt his mama jump at the unexpected sound, give a quiet laugh. He heard her talk about someone named Serena, and she sounded sad. Then she said in her mad voice that even getting justice would never be enough, and he heard his papa agree. They were whispering now and Sean wondered if Papa was going to kiss her again. Sometimes he'd kiss her, then pick him up and kiss him, too, and Astro would jump around barking his head off, wanting a kiss, too.

Sean heard Papa say something about Olivia, and he recognized her name. He'd heard his papa speaking to her on his cell phone. At least he sounded pleased, and not so sad like Mama. And he said she was getting married to Mike on Aruba, wherever that was, and laughed.

Astro snored, Sean heard him, and smiled. "Mama?"

"Yes, sweetheart?"

"I'm glad you're home. Papa really missed you."

"Did you miss me, too, Sean?"

Sean squeezed her as tight as he could. "Maybe I missed you more than Papa did. He said nothing felt right when you weren't here. Do you know he gave Astro Cheerios?"

Sherlock laughed, whispered against his cheek, "Nothing ever feels right to me either when I'm away from you and your papa."

Sean felt her kiss his forehead as he slipped into sleep.

Epilogue

Bainbridge, Maryland
Fairlawn Cemetery

ONE AND A HALF WEEKS LATER

So many people were here to honor Serena, finally home now after seven long years. Classmates from Godwyn, Tommy Maitland and Juliet Ash Calley, law enforcement officers from Creighton and from New York City, FBI agents from the New York City Field Office, and FBI agents Sherlock and Dillon Savich from Washington, as well as most of the staff from the *Guardian*. Of course the media was out in force, not unexpected given the high profile of Serena's accused murderers. Mia and Milo had made calls requesting the Winters family not be approached, and were pleasantly surprised by other news outlets' agreement. Everyone else was free game.

Father Chillworth remembered Serena's baptism in his

eulogy, spoke to how beautiful she'd been when he'd first held her in his arms, so small, so precious, never crying. He would never forget how she'd stared up at him, smiling, he'd said so later to her parents. He'd watched her play basketball, heard her sing in the choir in her lovely soprano, and he'd heard her confessions when she'd come home from college, usually about her boyfriend and all the temptations, but saying Tommy had never pushed her. He saw Tommy Maitland standing next to her parents, beside him the most beautiful woman Father Chillworth had ever seen. She was supporting him, Father Chillworth thought, squeezing his hand. Or maybe they were supporting each other.

Both Serena's parents, Livvie and Gray Winters, stood tall, leaning into each other, their hands tightly clasped, their two surviving daughters hugged close. Father Chillworth talked of their devastating grief, their not knowing what had happened to their daughter for seven long years. He knew they would now find some peace, peace of a sort, though Serena's death would always be a rent in the fabric of their lives.

The Winterses hadn't wished to celebrate a mass, asked for only a graveside service. He hadn't approved, but now that he saw the large, mixed crowd and the media, he knew it was the right thing to do. He met Mia Briscoe's eyes, knew the role she'd played in finding Serena. Beside her stood a tall young man, obviously very close to her, his dark hair ruffled in the wind, and he was holding her hand. Good, she had someone there for her. He raised his hands and prayed. "—let your perpetual light shine upon her, and through your mercy rest with you in peace." He looked directly at Mia Briscoe again as he ended with the ageless words that said so little yet meant so much. Simple words, both heartbreaking and comforting. "Earth to earth, ashes to ashes, dust to dust."

Tommy was grateful so many people were here for Serena, to celebrate her short life, grateful its violent end would finally land squarely on Alex Harrington and Kent Harper. He smiled at Gail Ricci, who'd flown from Rome to New York two days before, and now stood beside Mia, Travis Gilbert, Mia's fiancé, on her other side, all staring straight ahead at Serena's coffin covered with a blanket of white petunias, Serena's favorite flower.

It was a cool early spring day, the sun bright overhead. Livvie Winters's pale hand trembled as she gently laid a red rose atop the petunias. She whispered words no one heard before she turned into her husband's arms. Serena's two sisters hugged both of their parents.

Tommy stood over her coffin, said his good-byes with tears sheening his eyes, and laid his red rose beside the Winterses'. His father, mother, and three brothers formed a phalanx behind him, and Juliet stood beside him, holding her own red rose.

The line slowly moved until it was Mia's turn. She looked down at the blanket of red roses that now covered the white petunias. She gently laid hers atop all the others and whispered through the tears streaking down her face, "I'm so sorry, Serena. You'll be in my heart forever." She turned slowly and was enfolded in Milo's arms, then Travis's. Most of the *Guardian* newsroom stood silent, ranging behind Milo.

When the service ended, Mia waited beside Gail and Sherlock for Travis and Dillon to get the car to take them back to the Winterses' house. Sherlock lightly stroked her fingers over

Mia's face, wiping away tears, taking Mia's gloved hands in hers. "You're a formidable woman, Mia. It is my pleasure to have met you, to have worked with you. I only wish I had known Serena. She'd be so proud of you."

Would she? What Mia knew for certain was that Serena would be her touchstone. She'd be forever the laughing girl walking with Tommy Maitland on Godwyn's campus, their hands clasped as they swung their arms. She spotted Miles Lombardy, Alex Harrington's senior staffer, standing alone beneath an ancient oak tree. She walked to him and took his hand. "Thank you for coming, Miles."

He said quietly, "I am so sorry for what he did, what he might have continued doing if you hadn't stopped him. Thank you." He leaned down, lightly kissed her cheek, turned, and walked away through the rows of gravestones. Now, after seven years, Serena would have one of her own.

Beneath the brilliant blue sky, atop a hill close by, as Serena's coffin was lowered into the ground, a lone bagpipe played "Amazing Grace."

ABOUT THE AUTHOR

Catherine Coulter is the #1 *New York Times* bestselling author of eighty-seven novels, including the FBI Thriller series and the Brit in the FBI international thriller series, cowritten with J.T. Ellison. Coulter lives in Sausalito, California, with her Über-mensch husband and their two noble cats, Peyton and Eli. You can reach her at ReadMoi@gmail.com.